REBELS OF SANDLAND

RENEGADE
Hearts

NIKKI J SUMMERS

NIKKI J SUMMERS

Cover Image: Michelle Lancaster
Cover Design: Lori Jackson
Editing: Lindsey Powell & Book Nook Nuts Proofreading
Interior designed and formatted by: LJ Designs

OTHER BOOKS BY NIKKI J SUMMERS

Rebels of Sandland
Renegade Hearts
Fractured Minds

Soldiers of Anarchy
The Psycho
The Reaper
The Joker

Standalone
Luca
This Cruel Love
Hurt to Love

Joe & Ella Duet
Obsessively Yours
Forever Mine

All available on Amazon Kindle Unlimited.
Only suitable for 18+ due to adult content.

PLAYLIST
Available to download on Spotify

Just A Girl – No Doubt

Ill Manors – Plan B

Die Trying – New Medicine

Stay Awake – Example

Good As Hell – Lizzo

Jungle – Professor Green, Feat. Maverick Sabre

She Hates Me – Puddle of Mudd

I think I'm OKAY – Machine Gun Kelly, Feat. YUNGBLUD

Firestarter – The Prodigy

(All Along The) Watchtower – Devlin

Big For Your Boots – Stormzy

That's Not Me – Skepta, Jme

Uprising – Muse

White Rabbit – Egypt Central

Cruel Summer – Taylor Swift

Omen – The Prodigy

Bedshaped – Keane

Get Through This – Art of Dying

Human – Rag 'n' Bone Man

Last Resort – Papa Roach

End Game – Taylor Swift

Nightmare – The Veer Union

Invincible – Adelitas Way

* Trigger warnings *
A message from the author

This story is for readers 18 years and upwards due to sexually explicit content. It also deals with issues that some may find difficult to read and may cause distress.

There is also bad language throughout.

That being said, I hope you enjoy this enemies-to-lovers, New Adult Romance.

ONE
Emily

I don't know why I expected anything would be different. Why would my parents change the habit of a lifetime and put me first? I mean, it's only my eighteenth birthday. No big deal, right? And yet, when they told me they wanted to throw me a party, that little girl I usually kept hidden from the world, the one who'd lived in the shadows for all these years, craving any scraps of attention they'd throw her way, she became excited that maybe they'd do something selfless.

But no.

Their idea of celebrating their only daughter coming of age

turned out to be a pretentious, black-tie garden party, full of people of influence that they wanted to schmooze, but secretly despised behind closed doors. Men and women I'd never even met before, who didn't have the first clue what this day meant to me. To them, it was a golden ticket to grace the social pages of some brainless magazine. A peak behind the curtain that was the picture perfect Winters' family homestead.

To me, it was as fake as their pumped up lips and Botox frozen smiles.

Why did I expect anything to change?

I had to hand it to them, my parents had done a stellar job of making our garden look magical; otherworldly. A simulated smokescreen of perfection that'd make even David Blaine marvel. There were fairy lights in the trees, waiters and waitresses milling about with trays of champagne and canapes. Even the custom-made flower arrangements were a feat of artistic engineering, twisting around archways my mother had had specially constructed just for today.

If you didn't know better, you'd think this was a wedding.

Who brought flower arrangements into a garden already full of flowers?

My mother, that's who.

My father had done his part too, overseeing the set-up of an extravagant stage inside the stifling, expertly orchestrated marquee, but there was no D.J. set, no band playing. This stage was for him to address his devoted audience. To let them know what an upstanding father, husband, and pillar of the community their Member of Parliament was.

Our whole lives were a photo opportunity. A press call.

We were his ticket to winning the next election, and that

was what came first and foremost, always.

I still hadn't forgotten how he used my brother's death to increase his popularity in the polls. I'm sure he didn't mean to do it, not directly, anyway. But the grief I felt everyday seemed to have drifted over him pretty quickly. There was no room for emotion in politics… and families, apparently. My father had taken the stiff upper lip to a whole new level.

Standing at the doorway, leading out onto our terrace, I prayed I'd blend into the background, camouflaged from the heat of their stares and pseudo friendliness. It usually worked. I was a shadow in my world. A bystander to my own life. The after-thought of the day.

I smoothed my hands down the boring white shift dress my mother had insisted I wear. The heavy wool blend of the material clung to every curve, but not in a sexy, seductive way. No, I felt like I was being smothered by a snake, suffocating my body and bleeding me dry. Beads of sweat trickled down my back as I tried to look like I was comfortable and at ease with everything around me. I wasn't. I'd rather have stayed in my room watching a Netflix box set, eating the Doritos I had stashed under my bed, hidden from my mother. God forbid I should ever eat such filth and gain a few extra pounds. I looked and felt like I was heading into an interview, not a party. The skirt of my restrictive dress reached safely below the knee and my dark brown curls were pinned up into a twist that mirrored my mother's.

The perfect package for the tabloids.

Smoke and mirrors had nothing on my family. We were a goddamn fire of contradictions and falsities. My eighteenth birthday, and yet this was the last place I wanted to be.

"Emily, stop slouching. Remember your posture and smile, for Christ's sake. A Winters is always on show. The last thing we need is a picture of you scowling splashed all over the internet. You know what vultures they are out there."

My mother breezed past me and glided down the steps, leading to the garden. Her floral perfume swirled in the air around us, making my already heavy chest feel like it was drowning. I glared at the back of her head but stopped myself from rolling my eyes. Instead, I gave a sigh.

"Thanks for the party. It's lovely to see so many of my friends here. Oh, wait. You didn't invite any of them. Was this party meant for me at all?"

She stopped in her tracks and gracefully spun around to face me, painting on that well-rehearsed smile of hers.

"Your father went to a lot of trouble to organise this for you. There are some very influential people here today. You could show some gratitude, young lady." Her face remained calm and serene, but her tone was as sharp as a knife. If we didn't have guests, she'd be a completely different version of my mother. This was the 2.0 version. I think I preferred the other one. At least that one was real.

"Grateful? Why should I be grateful about spending my birthday with people I don't know? I'm the only one here under thirty. This party is shit."

"Watch your language, Emily." She marched back up the steps and grabbed my arm, leading me down onto the lawn and towards the marquee, like a child.

"It is though. It's a chance for you and Dad to put on another show. Fool the press into thinking we're the poster family for modern Britain. Too bad we're so fucked up behind closed doors, *Mother*." I tried to free myself from her grasp, but she wasn't having any of it.

"Enough with the language. Not everything is about you, Emily."

And there it was in a nutshell. No, nothing ever was about me.

Was I a spoilt brat, seeking out her parents' attention? Maybe. But then, I'd never had it. Not even as a young child. I was a loner in my own family. I preferred to think of myself as a closet rebel. Doing the right thing in public, but secretly I fantasised about doing something to break free from these stifling chains of duty. I hadn't chosen this life. Why should I conform to the restraints put upon me because of it?

"You weren't complaining this morning when you saw the Tiffany necklace, were you?" my mother spat out. "Now, you need to earn that gift by toeing the line. Don't let your father down."

She plastered on her award-winning smile, dazzling the men and making the women clench their jaws and hold their partners a little tighter. That was my mother. The quintessential English rose. A beauty who knew her worth and wasn't afraid to flaunt it.

We made our way into the marquee, where my father was holding court with a group of men, smoking cigars and laughing. I played my role of the perfect daughter and followed my mother, then when Dad saw us, he stopped and introduced us to the group, putting an arm around each of us and smiling. He kissed Mum and then kissed me on the top of my head. I smiled up at him, because despite everything, I did love him. They had their faults, but I loved them both. They were my mum and dad, after all, but deep down, I wished they'd realise that I needed them too.

"I can't believe our little Em is eighteen today," Dad said with pride in his eyes.

"Alec, Anthea, you don't look old enough to have a grown-up daughter," one of the men replied, holding up his glass in a toast to my parents. Not me. Oh, no. A toast to them for having me and continuing to look so youthful.

Welcome to my perfect life.

"It's wonderful what a good plastic surgeon can do these days, isn't it?" another suit guffawed, but my mother didn't join in. Her face froze. Humour wasn't her strong point.

Me? I couldn't help but stifle a laugh. I doubt he'd be invited to one of their parties again.

"She's a natural beauty, my Anthea." Dad beamed down at her and she smiled back. I just stood there feeling numb, like an accessory in their perfect world.

"Isn't it time for your speech, Alec?" Mum nodded over to the stage and guided Dad and me away from the red-faced truth-teller. I think he was glad of the reprieve too.

We made our way onto the stage as the crowds began to gather and a gentle hush ascended over the marquee. My father stood centre-stage, with my mother to his right and me to the left.

"Ladies and gentlemen, thank you so much for coming here today to help us celebrate something so wonderful and so important to our little family." He looked down at me and smiled. "Not only is my daughter turning eighteen, but today we made a landmark victory in our campaign. Our war on the drug culture that's plagued our younger generation for far too long is finally reaping its rewards. The gang mentality that's desperately trying to infiltrate its way into our little town is dying. That's all thanks to the support you've given me during my current term in office. But we aren't finished yet."

I felt the lump in my throat harden and I dug my nails into my palms to stop myself from tearing up.

"As you all know, my son, Daniel, was tragically killed in a car accident this past December. We still have many unanswered questions about the events leading up to his death. What happened that night still remains a mystery to us. Don't get me wrong, the police have gone above and beyond, but there are people out there; young men and women, who know more than they are letting on. So, to them I say this… We will get justice for Daniel. We will find out the truth. And when we do, know that we are coming after those with blood on their hands.

"Not a day goes by when he isn't at the forefront of our minds. We wish that life could be different and we never want another family to go through what we have. That's why my wife and I have campaigned tirelessly to bring the issues of drugs and alcohol in the youth of today to the forefront. There's a virus in our society; an evil that needs to be cut out. The statistics on the flyers being handed out explain a little more about…"

I zoned out. I couldn't hear this speech again. I knew the statistics off by heart. I knew the message he was sending through his work, because I'd lived and breathed it for months. I loved my brother with every inch of my soul, but I couldn't stand here and listen to another minute of his death being picked apart. I applauded my father, but on my birthday, the last thing I wanted was to remember why my brother wasn't here to celebrate it with me.

"You need to ditch this lame-ass excuse for a party," he'd probably say if he was here. *"Get out there and have some real fun, Ems."*

I smiled, imagining him throwing some rude gesture Dad's way, like he always used to, and while I drowned my father out, I got lost in thoughts of the Danny I remembered. Cheeky, insolent as mum called him, and a lover of life.

"So today, I would invite you all to make a donation to our cause and join us in this crusade in any way you can. We've made great headway in tackling the drink and drug culture and stamping out the criminal element that plagues our streets. Let's do the same on our roads too. Take back this town and use our power; grow with it. Make this a safer place for all our children. I'm sure I don't need to remind you, with the up and coming election, we need all the support we can get. Remember... Winters for the win. Thank you."

The marquee erupted into a sea of applause and my dad held our hands and lifted them up, like he was championing himself at some political rally. My mother gave him the look of adoration that would secure the front page of the papers for them tomorrow. And I focused on breathing; wishing I could sink into the floor to escape the pitiful looks the room was giving me.

I heard raised voices in the distance and glanced over the heads of the guests, noticing some kind of commotion going on at the doorway into the house. The security staff were talking into their earpieces and marching towards it. When I saw my two best friends emerge from the house, I knew why. They didn't want any uninvited guests, and my friends weren't welcome at my eighteenth birthday party. Go figure.

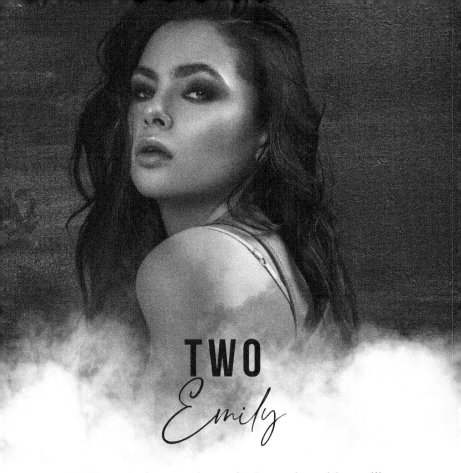

TWO
Emily

I marched across the perfectly manicured lawn, like a woman on a mission, and made it to the doorway just as one of the security guards was manhandling Liv, getting ready to throw her out. She was giving as good as she got though, telling him in no uncertain terms what an asshole he was.

I couldn't believe they'd shown up here. Word must've got to them that I was stuck in the parental twilight zone of hell. I smiled at their ripped skinny jeans and tight tops. They mustn't have got the memo about the shitty dress code for my little shindig either. Hell, they hadn't got any memo. They weren't invited. They were my personal superheroes swooping in to save the day.

"You couldn't have come at a better time." I sighed and then turned to glare at the security guy still holding Liv in a death-like grip.

"You can let her go now. She's not a gate-crasher."

Liv sniggered and Effy just looked mortified by it all.

"Their names aren't on our guest list, Ma'am." The security guy made the effort to look contrite in the knowledge that he was speaking to the boss's daughter. Not that that made any difference. He probably had more say over this event than I did.

"You're looking at the wrong guest list. Try the one entitled non-arse-lickers." I elbowed him out of the way as his nostrils flared at my insolence. I didn't care. He was rude to my friends, so that gave me free rein.

"Please tell me you haven't come to spend the rest of Friday evening here in this Stepford wives' tribute? As much as I love you girls, I really need a get out of jail free card." I led us through the lounge to the hallway and away from the pomp and ceremony. Another minute in the company of my parents' fake friends and I'd have self-combusted.

"Do you really think we'd be here to sip mocktails and suck ass with those oldies?" Liv laughed, turning her nose up. "We came here to get you and take you to where the real party is happening tonight, and it's about as far away from shitty drinks and ass kissing as it gets."

That's what I loved about Liv. She was a no-nonsense, straight-talking kind of girl. If there was ever a feisty female you'd want in your corner, it was her.

"Thank God. You guys are awesome. Do I have time to

change? I look like a freak in this dress." I glanced down at the white monstrosity and grimaced.

"Sorry, no can do. We're on a deadline. Time is ticking away, and your carriage awaits, Cinders," Liv said, sprinting for the door.

"Do you have a curfew tonight?" I laughed at Effy's attempt to stay within the lines of acceptable teenage behaviour. Where I had the devil, Liv, sitting on one shoulder; Effy was my angel, perched on the other side.

"Doubtful. I think the parentals will be too engrossed in sucking up to the press to notice where I am. Let's do this. My eighteenth birthday sucks balls so far, but I've a feeling you girls are gonna change that for me."

I could feel the ripple of excitement running through me already. I was down for anything tonight. After eighteen years of this bullshit, it was time to set myself free.

I headed out to the driveway, where Effy was parked in amongst all the performance cars and four-by-fours. The two of them jogged down the steps and across the gravel, but I could only totter in my ridiculous heels and curse under my breath about the constraints of my dress.

"Are you sure there isn't time for me to change?"

"Quit whining," Liv said as she jumped into the front seat next to Effy. "I think you look cute. Besides, we won't lose you tonight. You'll stand out like a sore thumb."

"Thanks. Now I feel so much better." I gave her the eye roll I'd been holding in all day and jumped in the back seat.

"Pull your hair out of that roll and let it loose, that'll help soften the look," Effy said, trying to make me feel better. I just sighed and pulled out the pins holding my curls in place, then fluffed them out and groaned at how good it felt to finally let my hair down.

"So, where are we off to? I might be eighteen, but I'm not sure I'll get into any of the clubs in town. I haven't got any I.D. on me." I hadn't got anything on me. My purse was empty. All I had was my lipstick and phone.

"Relax, Em. We've got you covered." Liv winked from the front seat and my heart flipped and sank at the same time.

I knew what that phrase meant. We weren't heading to a club or bar. Oh, no. My friends must've got the details for the latest illegal warehouse party this weekend. Parties that Sandland was becoming notorious for, and all the work of the Renaissance men.

I Googled what a Renaissance man was once. I had to laugh when it told me there were six attributes to being one.

First, you had to be intelligent. A deep thinker. Smarter than your average guy. Yeah, right. The four guys who called themselves the Renaissance men in our town wouldn't be blowing up Mensa any time soon. Not by my reckoning, anyway. It took four of them to coordinate an illegal party, and even then, word around town was they got shut down more often than not.

Next, they had to be knowledgeable, voracious readers; using what they'd learned to give them an advantage in life. From what I knew, Ryan Hardy, Renaissance caveman number one, was still working at his father's garage for minimum wage. I was no snob, but don't paint yourself to be something you so obviously are not. I knew Ryan Hardy from school. He'd been in the same year as Danny, and they'd been good friends for a few years before he died. Not that Danny would ever let Ryan anywhere near me or our house. My brother's friendships with the Renaissance boys was kept strictly on the down-low. He said he wanted to keep Dad in the dark, but I'm guessing he was protecting me too.

Quality number three, they had to be artistic. Singing, painting, sculpting, music; that was the forte of a pure Renaissance man. Finn Knowles had spread his art all over this town, tagging his graffiti onto every railway bridge and abandoned building he could find. Don't get me wrong, he was good, like Banksy good, but he wasn't a pioneer or a trailblazer. He was a follower, just like Zak Atwood. Zak might be able to D.J. his way into most girls' beds, but he was no Mozart. He played the music, he didn't make it. I guess you're starting to get the picture. These boys held themselves in very high esteem, regardless of what the world around them was trying to say.

Fourth up was physical strength. I couldn't fault them on that one. They did look like Sandland's very own Magic Mike troupe, but they knew it. There was no humility where these guys were concerned. Not from what I'd seen growing up. Brandon Mathers loved nothing more than to use his fists whenever he could. The illegal fights and betting scams they ran at their 'parties' were the stuff of legends, or nightmares depending on which way you looked at it. I'd overheard my brother and a few of his friends talking about how dirty Brandon fought. He had no compassion. He was like a British bulldog in a china shop. Artistry and sportsmanship didn't exist in his repertoire, apparently.

Fifth on the list was being socially confident and having strong personal relationships. I knew without a doubt that half the female population would probably agree with this one. They had no shortage of women fawning all over them. Liv, Effy, and myself were probably the few remaining girls in Sandland who didn't have a story to tell about those four. Plus, they were as thick as thieves. Friends from childhood who always had each other's backs. I was surprised my brother spoke to them. They were a pretty exclusive group, to put it mildly, and they didn't trust outsiders.

Finally, the modern Renaissance man could pull off all of these attributes with ease, style, and sophistication. Organising illegal warehouse parties and bare-knuckle fights, setting up betting scams and God knows what else was far from sophisticated. I'd never been to one of their gatherings before, but I'd heard the gossip. There was no style involved in fighting, underage drinking, drug taking, and whatever else they got up to. They were the reason my father stayed up late at night, trying to find new ways to shut down their outfit, and that fact alone made me curious. Ryan Hardy, Brandon Mathers, Zak Atwood and Finn Knowles were the devil incarnate as far as my father was concerned.

"Do I even want to know how you found out about this party?" I asked, looking between the girls. They both grinned back at me as if they'd landed the jackpot.

"One of the girls at my gym got the message. I overheard her in the locker room telling her friends they'd posted in the 'we've got you covered' group and she announced to everyone where it was. There's no harm in us checking it out, is there? It is your special day, Em." Liv shrugged as she spoke, then started rifling through her bag until she found what she was looking for.

"Now, let's get this party started," she said, holding up a bottle of vodka.

I made a grab for the bottle as Effy explained that she'd

bought cans of Coke, seeing as she was our designated driver. I took a swig and winced from the burn it left down my throat. Then I stared out of the window, wondering how those boys had managed to fly under the radar so successfully for so long, and why none of my friends had ever been invited to join the 'we've got you covered' group.

THREE
Emily

Effy's car started to jolt about as we drove off-road and across a dirt track that lead us into the unknown. It was so dark out, I felt sure that Liv had either misheard the directions or gym girl had sent us on a mad goose chase to some long since forgotten shithole.

We bumped and jostled around as she bounced us over the rough terrain, vodka splashing everywhere as Liv complained about the state of her jeans and waste of good alcohol. Then she swerved around some trees and we saw the sea of cars parked anywhere and everywhere. Ahead of us stood a sinister looking building with barbed wire fencing running around the perimeter.

A single floodlight shone from one corner of the warehouse and we could just about make out a lone figure sat, hunched over.

"Well, this isn't creepy at all," Effy said, swerving the car into a space and cutting the engine.

Liv turned in her seat and smirked at me. "You do realise you'll be the first one to die, right? The cute girl in the ridiculous outfit always gets mutilated first in the movies."

"Happy fucking birthday to me." I leaned forward and grabbed the vodka out of her hand to take another swig. I was gonna need all the liquid courage I could get tonight. "Anyway, isn't it the blonde who cops it first? In which case, you're screwed my friend."

Liv scoffed and flicked her long blonde hair dramatically, then snatched her vodka back. "I'd need to give a fuck first. Don't think you'll find me screaming and running away any time soon. I'm all up for this shit."

We each opened our doors and stepped out. The thick oozing mud under our feet made us groan. My stilettoes were well and truly stuck and I had to grab onto Effy to pull my feet clear and walk to the little gravel path that lead to the eerie looking building.

"I don't think anyone will be running anywhere in this field," Effy said, scraping her feet free of the caked-on mud when she got to the path. "So much for making a grand entrance."

"Quit whining, will you? There's no need to get your knickers in a twist. Nothing gets solved and it only makes you walk funny. Em is struggling enough in those heels as it is." Liv laughed at herself. "Anyway, this is Em's birthday blow out. Let's keep the drama to a minimum, you know, less diva more party fever." She shimmied her hips to state her point and led the march forward.

The thump of the steady bass from the warehouse filled the air, and the shouts and chants coming from inside made my stomach clench with a mixture of fear and excitement. I had no idea what to expect, but I liked it. I liked the feeling of the unknown. I'd never done anything like this before and it felt good to be a teenager. A normal teenager. Not one who wears designer clothes and poses for the cameras; just a girl. Me.

"Come on then, Houdini. How are we supposed to get into this place?" Effy asked as she scrunched up her little pixie face and rattled the security fence in front of us. "Looks like this place is on lockdown."

"There's got to be a way in somewhere." Liv started to pace up and down frantically, bending to find a hole or some magical tunnel that the rest of us couldn't see. "I could probably scale it. What about you?" She looked up at the barbed wire above and grimaced. "No pain no gain, right?"

"What the fuck are you on, Liv?" I folded my arms defensively. "I'm not scaling any fences tonight. You might be okay with your jeans, but in this dress, I'd struggle to climb a step let alone a bloody fence."

"Chill your boots, princess. If we get in, we can always find someone inside to come back out and get you."

"And leave me here on my own? Great fucking plan. Not."

"No one is scaling any fences or being left on their own," Effy piped up in an effort to halt the impending argument. "Let's walk to the end there where that floodlight is. Maybe there's a gate we can use?" Effy was always so positive; eternally hopeful. That's why she was always the designated driver. She didn't take risks. If it was left to Liv, we'd be starring in our own version of *Prison Break.*

We stumbled along the path, checking the fencing as we went, looking for some hint of a way in. When we reached the edge of the area, a deep voice bellowed over to us.

"Bottom right-hand side. Fence is cut. You can climb through."

"Thanks," Liv shouted back and began to wrestle with the metal fencing, lifting it up and gesturing for us to shimmy our way under. Easy for those two in their jeans, for me, I had to pray that my skirt wouldn't split open with the effort.

"Who is that?" Effy asked absent-mindedly, walking towards the light where the lone figure that we saw from the car sat on a tarpaulin surrounded by cans, stencils, and other tools. He was lost in his own world; oblivious to the noise of the party within. Instead, he was gazing at the wall like it held the key to another world, one hand cupping his chin in thought.

"Looks like Finn Knowles is having a party for one," Liv huffed and we all followed to see what had caught his attention.

When we reached the side of the building and saw what he was looking at, we all gasped. Finn had painted what appeared to be a blasted hole in the wall. The effect of the brickwork crumbling looked so real it was as if you could climb through it. But it was what was pictured inside the hole that was heart-stopping, jaw-dropping, utterly amazing and disturbing at the same time. He'd painted a field like nothing I'd ever seen before. An urban futuristic landscape where trees were mechanical monstrosities, flowers looked like spiked weapons ready to cut you if you went near, and grass as grey and desolate as any wasteland. A beautifully broken barren land; a hostile hell. Was this how he saw the world around him? A reflection of his warped mind?

Liv was the first to break the silence.

"So, what do you call this then? A cruel world or Alice in doomsday land?"

Finn huffed and shook his head, not looking our way as he spoke. "Come on an urban safari, have you?"

"What's that supposed to mean?" I said, cocking my head and narrowing my eyes at him. I knew he was mocking us, and I wasn't gonna let him get away with it.

"You know damn well what it means. You're slumming it for the night. Keep your eyes peeled, you might spot some hoodies, a few low-lives maybe, and if you're really lucky, someone who even works for a living."

"You know nothing about us," Effy said in our defence, beating me to it.

"And I don't want to know. If I throw a stick will you go away? You're messing with my creative flow." He carried on gazing at his masterpiece like he was waiting for the damn thing to tell him the meaning of life.

"Jesus, sorry we disturbed you. You're clearly disturbed enough already." Liv scoffed. "Come on, girls. Let's leave Banksy's little brother, Wanksy, to his painting. Wanksy? You need to calm down. Take a breath and maybe hold it for ten or twenty minutes." Liv strutted away, not listening to the sarcastic retort that Finn was no doubt aiming her way.

I hoped we'd get a better reception when we finally made it into the party, but something told me that Finn Knowles was just the warm-up act. There was a reason me and my friends were never invited to these things. We were the town exiles. The good girls. Well tonight, good girls were going bad.

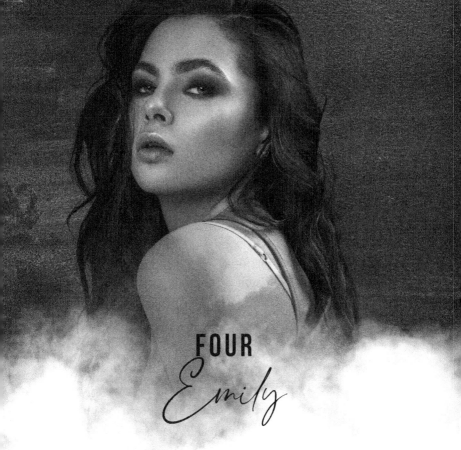

FOUR
Emily

We reached the beaten-up metal doors that led into the venue, if you could call a discarded warehouse that, and waited for the bouncer on the door to let us through.

"Got your phone message to show me, ladies?" he said, looking between the three of us suspiciously. I was rubbish at hiding my guilt, so I shuffled my feet and prayed one of the others had a good explanation.

"Oh, shit. I knew I forgot something. I'm such an airhead. Could you let us through anyway? Just this once?" Liv batted her eyelids and he shrugged, not really giving a fuck that we didn't have the right means to get in. Good save, Liv.

"Suppose. Don't do it again though."

We paid him the entrance fee and he grabbed our hands, one after the other, and stamped us with an ugly black mark to show we'd gone through his rigorous checks. I would say it showed we belonged here, but I felt as far out of my comfort zone as I'd ever been.

As we stepped past him and into the main area, the sound of the music was deafening. All three of us stood still just to take it all in. The place was packed. There were people everywhere, dancing, drinking, letting go and not giving a damn. Sure, the floors were sticky with spilt drinks and goodness knows what else. The smell of sweat and stale beer hung in the air like a thick fog and took some time to get used to. The walls were grey, and the windows mostly broken or boarded up, but if you looked carefully, you could see artwork Finn had created, dotted around. There were strobe lights cutting through the dusty air, making the whole atmosphere come alive. From dirt and ashes they had created something magical. It was electric. Soul-lifting even. I'd never expected it to feel like this.

I glanced around and spotted Zak Atwood in the far corner of the warehouse with his headphones on. His dark floppy hair fell into his eyes as he nodded along to the beat. I'd expected to see a sea of girls swarming around him, but a few guys stood close by to where he was working, keeping the girls at bay. Zak was in the zone; his face a picture of concentration as he mixed U.K. grime with old school hits seamlessly. I was mesmerised by him. The sounds he was playing were calling out to everyone here. When he switched up the beat the crowd cheered. He was their messiah, this was his church, and everyone here was his faithful congregation.

"He's good, isn't he?" Effy smiled. "Do you think he ever comes out from behind there to mingle?"

"If he does, I'll make sure you're the first one he talks to." Liv shoved Effy forward and we pushed our way further into the party. I could tell Liv was itching to get going, dance, and really let go. Effy was more like me, a little more guarded and still taking it all in.

A few people turned and stared for a moment as I walked past. I wasn't dressed like them, but they were polite enough to turn away after a second take. I smoothed my sweaty palms down my skirt and tried not to let my anxious thoughts and self-conscious mind get to me.

"You look cute, Ems. Head high, girl. There's a guy over there wearing a Chris de Burgh T-shirt. I really think you've got nothing to worry about. Obviously, anything goes here if his choice of music and fashion is anything to go by," Liv said, grinning at me.

I glanced over to where she was looking, and sure enough, some guy was throwing some very random shapes and wearing his throwback eighties statement with pride. His long curly hair was flying in all directions as he let go like it was nineteen-ninety-nine and he was at a *Prince* concert. I must've been staring for way longer than was socially acceptable, as I suddenly noticed him wink at me and thrust his hips suggestively.

Not tonight, pal. Tonight is not your lucky night.

We started to make our way around the event, pushing through the throngs of revellers. I was sure Liv and Effy felt like they blended in, but I didn't. I felt like a round peg trying to fit into a square hole. I didn't like feeling this way, and I decided that after tonight I needed to make some changes. I had to take back control. I wanted my life to be mine. Maybe this party wouldn't end up being as lame as I thought it would be. Maybe it'd be the kick up the backside that I needed to sort my shit out?

The music changed, becoming darker, eerie almost, and the slow steady beats penetrated through me like it was trying to shock my body into life. I looked around, watching people dancing and swaying, oblivious to everything and lost in their world, but for me it felt like a wake-up call. I was on high-alert and I couldn't relax.

My mouth went dry and I tried to swallow, but it felt like sandpaper scraping down my throat. Something felt off. I was nervous, but at the same time, I wasn't about to let this place get the better of me. I wanted to experience this, and I needed to find out more. Find out what it was about these parties and the four men behind them that had everyone in Sandland so transfixed.

"Do you have anything to drink?" I shouted to Liv and Effy over the music, but they both shook their heads.

"I left mine in the car, sorry." Effy gave me a remorseful smile and a shrug then carried on dancing.

I glanced around, looking for a bar or drinks station, anything that could help to ease my scratchy sore throat.

"I'm gonna head over there," I said, pointing behind me towards a large set of doors that a lot of people had congregated around. "I need to find a bar. I'm thirsty."

Liv gave me a thumbs up and Effy just grinned and carried on staring up at Zak Atwood as he worked his magic. Girl was obsessed already.

I pushed through the crowds and made my way to the doors. I couldn't see a bar, but there were concrete stairs leading to the basement area of the warehouse. Maybe there'd be a bar down there? It was worth checking out. There didn't seem to be anything else other than drunken dancers on the main floor.

I started to climb down the steps, grabbing onto the railings to stop myself from falling arse-over-tit in my heels, and people parted for me as I did. No doubt they knew who I was. My face had been plastered on enough newspapers alongside my father's over the years. Anything to further the career of the perfect family man. But here, in this building, I was the fly in the ointment, the cat amongst the pigeons as far as these people were concerned. I may as well have sounded a claxon and told them the party was over, judging from the looks of distain they threw my way.

Who invited the MP's daughter to piss on our bonfire?

I got to the bottom of the stairs and had to climb over a couple making out on the floor. I would've told them to get a room, but I think they liked the audience they were attracting. Strange thing was, I couldn't drag my eyes away from them either. Kind of made me a hypocrite, I suppose.

I shook that thought out of my mind and glanced down the narrow and dimly lit hallway. Cheers and chants echoed in the dark passage and an even bigger crowd gathered around a doorway a few feet away. People were jostling to get inside and see past each other to witness what was going on. I made my way down there, intrigued to find out what had got so many people all fired up. When I made it to the doorway, I slid through a gap in the crowd and managed to push my way into the room.

If I thought upstairs was stuffy, it was nothing compared to this room. It was stiflingly hot and the stench of sweat, tinged with a metallic odour that clung to your skin like filth, hung heavy around us. A few men in front of me turned around and then parted a little to give me a better view. There were hay bales set up as a makeshift ring, and two men, shirtless and dripping in sweat and blood were fighting. Bare-knuckle fighting. One guy was wiping blood off his face and panting, trying to catch his breath. But no matter how much he wiped, the blood just kept on pouring. He had a nasty gash on his forehead and he needed stitches. Hell, he looked punch drunk. I think he needed an ambulance. But that wasn't gonna stop his opponent. The other guy stalked towards him and smacked his fist into the guy's face, making him fall backwards and causing the whole crowd to cheer or jeer, I couldn't tell the difference. Then he leaned over and said something, before spitting in his face and kicking him in the ribs, making the guy curl up into a ball. I felt sick watching this. It was barbaric. How could this be called entertainment? Watching someone beat the crap out of someone else. He could've killed that guy.

The guy left standing turned around and glowered at the crowds with a smirk straight from hell and my stomach rolled.

Brandon Mathers.

I should've known.

His dark hair was dripping with sweat and sticking to his forehead. Blood was splattered over his bare tattooed chest and soaking through his jeans. But the guy was full-on grinning, looking truly psychotic, as if he hadn't felt a thing. This was all part of the show for him. Forget the poor dude lying on the ground who needed to go to the hospital. Brandon Mathers was a whole new species of feral and he loved it.

He scanned the crowd, winking at a few people and fist-bumping others. Then his eyes landed on me and I froze. That grin on his nasty face grew wider and he pointed right at me.

Chills broke out all over my previously sweaty skin and then…
I felt him before I heard him.

"You're not welcome here, little Winters." I'd recognise
that voice anywhere. Ryan Hardy was standing behind me. I
could feel the heat from his body penetrating through to mine,
but he wasn't touching me. He didn't need to, to get a reaction
from me. He leaned down to whisper in my ear and the feel of
his breath feathering over my skin made me shudder.

"Why are you here? Come to spy on us, have you? Gonna
report us to Daddy?" I didn't move, I couldn't. I stared ahead
at Brandon Mathers, smirking at me like the lunatic he was, as
Ryan whispered his threats, hoping to scare me.

"Big mistake, Winters. You're on our turf now. Daddy can't
help you here and you're pretty fucking stupid to jump into the
lions' den tonight. We're not pussy cats. We fight dirty." He
probably thought his words scared me, but they didn't. What
scared me was how fast my heart was beating right now, and
how much I wanted to turn around and face him.

"I can see that." I kept my eyes on Brandon as I spoke, fully
engaging in his battle to stare me down. These boys were tag-
teaming, trying to frighten me. I wouldn't let them.

"Then why the hell are you still standing here? Run, little
Winters. Run away like the weak little girl you are."

I couldn't deny his voice, his words, damn, just his presence
did something to me.

"I'm not weak and I'm not scared of you, *Ryan*." He laughed,
and I felt his hand brush against my elbow, making me flinch at
the shock it sent through my body.

"Oh? You should be." His voice was deeper now, and it
felt like we were trapped inside a bubble; Ryan, Brandon and

me. One was trying to intimidate me with words, the other with his mind. "We don't take kindly to rats. Is that what you are, Winters? A rat? Are you trying to set us up?" I took a deep breath. His nearness made me feel like I was drowning. Each breath I took was too shallow, not enough to gain oxygen, and I was beginning to feel dizzy.

"I'm not a rat and I don't set people up," I said through gritted teeth.

"And why should I believe you? You come from a long line of rats. Your daddy is the king of them. What would he say if he could see his little princess now?" I knew they hated my father, that was no secret, but they knew fuck all about me.

"He'd probably tell me to knee you in the fucking balls." I lifted my chin, trying to look like I had my shit together.

"I'd have you on your back before your knee got anywhere near my balls, sweetheart. Is that what you want? To fight me?" Why did that statement, coming from him, make my heart skip a beat? What was happening here? Ryan Hardy and Brandon Mathers had barely looked at me growing up. And now, here I was, starring in their fucked-up battle of wits, and thoughts of being put on my back were making me all sorts of flustered and confused.

"I don't want anything to do with you," was all I could think of to say with my brain in its current state of meltdown.

"Then I'll ask again. Why are you here? I think it's time you left. Nothing good can come from you being here… in our world." He stepped a little closer into me, but I couldn't move away. I had to see how this played out.

"I don't want any part of your world. If you have a problem with me, then why don't you cry me a fucking river and drown yourself in it." There it was, my sass was still there, buried deep inside me under all the confusion and… Was that lust?

"There she is, the little Winters drama queen. Just because you're daddy's little princess, doesn't mean we're gonna treat you like royalty, sweetheart. Maybe we need to show you what we do to rats in our world?" Again with the threats. I wasn't scared of him. Brandon Mathers looked like a scary motherfucker, but I wasn't gonna let these guys spook me.

"Careful you don't choke on all that shit you talk."

"What makes you think it's all talk?"

In that instance, I couldn't hold back, and I turned around to face him, ready to go toe-to-toe with Ryan bloody Hardy, but when I did, he'd disappeared into the crowd. I stood on my tiptoes and tried to see around the people behind me, but I couldn't see him anywhere. I shook my head at his cowardice and turned back around, but Brandon Mathers had gone too, and I was left standing in a room that felt like a pressure cooker and I was the one about to explode.

Ryan Hardy had made my blood boil and turned my body inside out and I hadn't even looked at him. Brandon Mathers had psyched me out with nothing but the evil behind his eyes. And now, I needed to get out of that room, away from these boys, and digest whatever had gone down here tonight. To them, me and my father were one and the same, and they hated my father with a passion.

I shoved my way past the people in that room, elbowing and shouldering my way towards the door, but when I got there I couldn't get down the corridor to go back the way I came. Crowds of people were blocking my way and I suddenly felt vulnerable and alone. A perfect target. A sitting duck.

I turned and headed in the opposite direction. The passageway was quieter, and I didn't stop to think about where it would lead. More concerned about getting myself as far away from the boys as I could. I say boys, but they were three years older than me. The same age as Danny, who would've been twenty-one next month. I started off speed-walking, but as I wound my way through the corridors underneath this forgotten, shithole dump of a warehouse, I started to feel the nerves and fear settle in. So I picked up the pace, jogging through the maze of identical corridors and getting nowhere. I could hear the thumping bass above me, but why wasn't I getting any nearer to the exit? Where were the damn stairs?

I heard a bang in the distance that made me jump. It sounded like a door crashing against a wall, and on instinct I turned my head, but no one was there. Then I heard another louder bang, like someone was hitting something off the walls. Maybe a bat slamming over and over again, only this sound was getting closer and closer. Another bang and then another. Jesus, I was stuck in a bad nineties' horror movie, just like I'd joked about earlier. Only, I wasn't laughing this time. This felt all too real. The banging got louder, a regular beat, like someone was heading towards me, stalking me. Then I heard a man's laughter. Low, wicked cackles reverberating off the walls and into my very soul. I wasn't sticking around to see how this movie ended. I ran like my life depended on it, heading towards a set of doors at the end of the corridor. When I reached them, I threw the doors open to escape. All the time, I could feel the weight of someone following me. Chasing me down like a hunter toying with it's prey. But I wasn't anyone's prey. Not today. Not ever.

I fell out into the night air and panted as I ran across the grass towards the metal fence. I stopped and turned around, expecting to see someone, anyone come out after me, but I didn't. It was just me, back outside. Alone. I bent forward, trying to catch my breath, gasping like I'd run a marathon.

"Are you okay?"

I jumped up at the sound of a voice. It was Finn Knowles, walking hesitantly towards me with his hands outstretched like that'd show me how friendly and non-threatening he was.

"I'm fine," I panted back. "No thanks to your loser asshole friends."

"I've no idea what's gone on, but you shouldn't be on your own out here."

No shit, Sherlock.

"Do you want me to go inside and get your friends?" What was this guy's deal? He actually seemed human compared to the other two I'd encountered tonight.

"I'll be fine." I shrugged, feeling anything but.

"No, you're not." He took a tentative step towards me. "You're Danny's sister, aren't you? Emily? I saw you came here with Effy. I'll go and get her." He didn't wait for my response, just stalked off and left me, mouth wide open, wondering what the fuck the deal was with these guys.

Ryan and Brandon had tried to floor me with their fucked-up games, and yet it was the kindness of Finn Knowles that totally knocked me off my feet. I didn't know which way was up and which was down, but I was sure of one thing, I was relieved that he was going to get Effy and Liv for me. I didn't want to stay here a minute longer than I had to. The Renaissance assholes had played with me enough for one night.

Their time would come though.

I hadn't finished with them either.

FIVE
Ryan

"What the fuck was that?" Brandon said, wiping his sweaty blood-soaked towel over his face and grimacing at me. It wasn't the pain of the punches he'd received tonight that'd made him wince. No, that was all my doing. He wasn't happy, and he was about to make damn sure I knew about it. I couldn't give a fuck. He didn't run this show.

"Fuck you. I don't know what you think you saw, but you know fuck all," I spat back. I wasn't about to take shit from anyone, least of all my best mate who knew how to piss me off better than anyone.

"You and her. The little whispers," he said, screwing his face up. "You had your face buried so far into her neck you looked like you were on a fucking date, making out."

"Jealous?" I grinned back at him.

He threw his towel down onto a plastic chair in the corner and folded his arms over his chest.

"Maybe. Maybe I don't want to miss out on all the fun. If we're gonna fuck with her, I'd like to do some of the fucking too."

The minute he said that my blood started to boil and my muscles clenched in anger. I wanted to knock him the fuck out. She wasn't his to play around with. She wasn't his to even talk about or think about.

"No one is going to fuck with that girl... Except me. I swear to God, Brandon, stay the fuck away." I pointed at him, my teeth gritted so tightly I felt like I could've broken my jaw. He held his hands up and laughed like what I'd said was fucking funny. It wasn't. He knew the score. The Winters were fair game. But Emily? She was mine.

"Dude, you need to chill the fuck out." He flicked his towel off the chair and onto the floor then sat down. "It's one thing to chase her down a corridor and scare the shit out of her, but that's high school crap, man. We need to step it up. If you want to fuck with Daddy Winters, really fuck him over, she's your best bet. She is the key to all this. And he owes us big time."

Zak chose that exact moment to walk in. I could still hear the music playing above us and I glanced up and over to where he stood by the door.

"Did you stick a mixtape on?" I joked.

"Kian's covering the decks for me. He knows his stuff." Zak shrugged and closed the door behind him, leaning against the wall with his arms crossed. "So, what's the deal? What's going on?"

"Little Winters, that's what's going on," Brandon said, smirking right at me as he answered Zak.

"Yeah, I spotted her and her friends earlier. How the fuck did they get in here? I thought we'd shut that shit down a long time ago. Do you think we've got a mole?"

"What, a mole giving away our coordinates? Nah, I think they got lucky. It's her birthday today. She probably got the deets from someone else," I said, and Brandon's eyes bugged out of his head.

"And you know this how?" Brandon said, narrowing his eyes at me in an accusatory glare.

"Danny. He told me. It's just a date I remembered. It's the same as my grandma's birthday." It wasn't, but I wasn't gonna tell him that. The less he knew, the better.

"Get her a card, did you?" Brandon laughed.

"Fuck you."

"Are you pussy-whipped for this chick, Ry?" Brandon was really trying to push my buttons. He loved getting a rise out of me. Dude always had my back, but he'd fuck around with the best of them to get me riled up.

"Am I fuck. I wanna destroy her and her fucked-up family, probably more than any one of you. It's about time the Winters house of shitty cards came tumbling the fuck down. He's got away with it for far too long."

"So, what do you suggest?" Zak looked between the two of us. I knew he'd be down with anything we decided to do. He always was. "Should I go get Finn, you know, group meeting and all?"

"We don't need Finn to make this official. You wanna fuck shit up, Ry? She's the key. Get in with the daughter and get the answers we need. We know what's gone down, but we gotta get the evidence if we really wanna destroy him. Zak's hacking has only gotten us so far. We need more. That's where she comes in. Or are you too smitten to break her delicate, fragile little heart?" He fake pouted at me and sensing the change in the mood of the room, Zak pushed away from the wall and stood in-between us. He knew when shit was about to go off, and like a pro, he knew how to diffuse the bomb we were capable of setting off.

"Do I look like a pussy to you, Brandon? Do you think I can't do this?"

Come at me, fucker. I dare ya.

"I think I'd do a better job than you." He looked me up and down, but I shook my head and laughed. I wasn't taking his bait. Not yet.

"Like fuck you will. I'm running this show. You'll get your chance, mate. But not with Emily. Stay away from her and let me do my thing."

"That's a shame. I was looking forward to breaking in little Winters." He grabbed his crotch and groaned, and that was my cue. I couldn't stop myself. I flew across the room and grabbed Brandon up out of his chair. Zak stood to the side of us, ready to intervene, but he didn't need to worry. I still had my shit together. Just.

"That pleasure will be all mine, *mate*." I gave his cheek a playful, but not so friendly slap. "You just need to sit tight and wait for me to deliver the goods. I'll leave the mother for you if you're that desperate to tap some Winters' ass though. Or maybe you can *really* fuck with Daddy Winters? If that's your thing." I shrugged, knowing my comment would get to him.

Brandon pushed me off, flaring his nostrils at my insinuating that he'd go anywhere near her fucked-up father. He was a depraved sod at times, but even he had a line he'd never cross.

Hoping to steer the conversation down a less confrontational path to stop us butting horns, Zak piped up, "Do you really think she'd go for you?"

We both turned to face him, giving him a '*What the fuck, dude,*' expression.

"Of course she'll go for him," Brandon answered for me. "Girl could barely breathe when he was whispering to her earlier. She's a woman, isn't she?"

"Barely. She's only just turned eighteen and she's Danny's sister. Don't you think that's kind of fucked-up?" I knew where Zak was coming from. Danny had been a friend to all of us. There was a time when I'd have called him one of my best friends. But he was part of the reason we were doing this. There was no room for sentiment or second guessing, not now. A job needed doing, and I was the best, damn it, the only man to do it.

"She's collateral damage. She'll get over it." Brandon was good at staying focused. I knew I'd have to use some of his steadfast determination to keep my head in the game though. I had to bring Winters down. Whether that meant father and daughter remained to be seen, but I couldn't lose sight of the end goal.

I couldn't deny Emily Winters had always held a fascination for me. She was the ultimate forbidden fruit. The M.P's daughter, friend's little sister, always perfectly turned out and so fucking pretty you couldn't help but stare if she came into a room. Worse thing was, she didn't even know it. She was like bloody kryptonite to me, and sometimes, when no one was watching, I saw her. I mean, really saw her. The girl who hated the restrictions put upon her by her family. The rebel who wanted to break free. The little hellcat that I knew she could be. Nobody had ever intrigued me like she did. Nobody held my attention like Emily Winters, and that's what made her dangerous.

"She might get over it, but will he?" Zak said, nodding to me. Guy could read me like a book sometimes.

"Oh, I'll be fine. Don't worry about me." I gave Zak a reassuring pat on the back. "I'll worm my way in, get what I need and get out. No harm done. Not for me, anyway."

"I hope you're right about that," Zak said, then shook his head at us both before walking out of the room.

Brandon and I looked at each other.

"Game on, motherfucker," I said, and left him to clean up his bloody, beaten-up face.

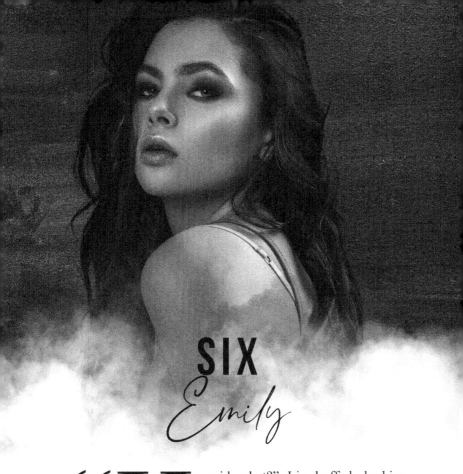

SIX
Emily

"He said what?" Liv huffed, looking ready to tear all those Renaissance losers a new one.

"He said I was a rat and that he'd have me on my back before I'd get anywhere near his balls." I laughed at the last part, I couldn't help it.

It was the day after the warehouse party and we were all sat in Liv's bedroom, picking over the bones of the evening and discussing what a shit-show it'd turned out to be. After Finn fetched Effy and Liv for me, we'd gotten ourselves out of that place quick smart. Neither one of us felt up to the challenge of going against those boys on the night. Now, we'd had time to think it all through and we were fuming.

"He's got a death wish, Em. I swear to God, if that fucker ever touches you, I'll-"

"You'll what, Liv? Do you really think we could do anything to hurt those guys? Emily needs to stay away from them. Especially Ryan and Brandon," Effy said, shaking her head and looking concerned. I think she'd have put me on house arrest if she could. She was our little peacemaker after all.

"I know those boys don't like us all that much, but I never thought they'd be such complete and utter knobheads. I wouldn't have taken you there for your birthday, Em, if I thought they'd threaten you and chase you. What kind of asshole does that?" Liv was seething.

"A Renaissance asshole," I answered, raising my eyebrow at her to show her I wasn't surprised by their games at all.

"Renaissance my ass. Even their name is ridiculous. They're all twisted fuckers," Liv said, making me laugh.

"Not all of them," Effy replied defensively, and then bit her lip, knowing she'd said too much.

"Which brings me to my next point..." Liv turned to face Effy and I gave her a reassuring smile. I knew exactly what was coming. "What was up with the whole Finn Knowles thing? He came up to you like he knew you already. How? And why did he want to help out Em?"

"I've no idea. I've probably spoken two words to Finn Knowles in my whole entire life." Effy spoke, but she couldn't look us in the eye.

"Well, it didn't look like that from where I was standing. Dude was looking at you like you were a straight-up snack and he was fucking hungry."

Effy's cheeks went bright red.

"Leave her alone, Liv. If Finn hadn't gone inside to get you two, I don't know what I'd have done."

"Oh, he didn't come in to get me. Just Effy here."

I gave Liv a pointed stare and watched as Effy swallowed and looked nervously at her hands twisted up in her lap. Why was she nervous?

"Don't worry, Eff. Finn didn't come across as an evil twat like the others. Liv, back off."

"Fine," she huffed, looking put out. "But I won't hold back if they come for us. I'll be ready."

"So will I," I shot back. I was more than ready to stand my ground. I'd had a lifetime of being pushed around. That shit wasn't happening anymore.

***

I left Liv's house and made my way down the driveway towards my car. In the distance, I heard the screech of brakes and looked up to see an old black Ford speeding off down the road. I didn't give it a second thought though, just got into my car and started the engine. My little Audi purred like a dream and I pulled off, ready to head back home and start looking into universities and courses that I liked. My parents wanted me to go to Oxford or Cambridge, but it wasn't about them. I wanted to make the decision for myself. Do what was right for me. I had no idea what that was yet, but it would come, in time. School was over for the summer; finished. I knew I was later than most to sort my options out, but I figured I'd take a gap year, a bit of breathing space after the stress of the last few months dealing with Danny's death. My careers guidance could wait, and that way, I'd make the right choice in the end. At least that's what I'd hoped.

I indicated to turn right, heading towards town. I'd decided to take the scenic route, seeing as the sun was shining. Nothing better than an open road where you could put your foot down and blow out the cobwebs. I was driving without thinking, and daydreaming about my future, when I felt the car shudder. I turned my music off and at that precise moment the power died, and I rolled to a stop at the side of the road.

Fucking brilliant.

There wasn't a house or building in sight. No other cars had passed me since I'd turned into this lane, and when I got out, all I could hear were birds chirping and the bloody breeze blowing through the trees. I slammed the car door shut and leaned against it, then grabbed my mobile out of my pocket and dialled the breakdown service my dad had set up when he got me this car.

Two minutes later, and I was even more pissed off than before. Over an hour until someone can get to you, they said. We'll try to get someone out sooner, seeing as you're a woman on your own, they promised. But I knew I was probably gonna spend the rest of my day sat in a layby, waiting to be rescued. I tried calling Liv or Effy, but all I got was their voicemail. So, I swallowed my pride and rang my home phone. Surely one of my parents would be concerned enough to come and help me?

"Emily, did you run out of petrol?" my mother scolded, after picking up the phone and letting out a disappointed sigh when she found out it was me.

"No. I'm not stupid. There's something wrong with the car. Give me some credit, Mum."

"Have you rung the breakdown service? That's what they're

there for." She really wasn't getting why I'd rung her.

"Yes, and the waiting time is over an hour. Mum, can't you come and pick me up?" I knew what the answer was going to be. I didn't even know why I'd asked.

"No, darling. I have errands to run myself. I can't drop everything just because you can't manage your affairs."

"I can manage myself just fine. You know what, just forget it. I'll wait here. I'll probably get murdered by some psycho and you can live with that on your conscience for the rest of your life, but that's your *affair* to deal with."

"Stop being so melodramatic, Emily. It's your problem, solve it. Oh, and don't bother your father with this. He's in Westminster for the week. He doesn't need to know about your dramas."

They really broke the mould when they made my mother. I knew she was still pissed that I'd bailed on their "kick-ass" garden party, but she didn't have to put my life at risk to hammer home her point.

"This isn't a drama, it's…" Typical, she hung up. I really was a blot on their landscape of perfection.

I threw my mobile onto the front seat and sat in the car with the door open and my legs on the road, contemplating walking back in the direction of Liv's house, just to give me something to do.

Twenty minutes later, and I was lying back in my car, the driver's seat reclined as far back as it'd go, and my eyes closed, trying to make sense of everything and everyone in my life. There was no sense. That was my conclusion and I was sticking to it.

I heard the hum of a motor in the distance and sat up, looking in my rear-view mirror to see a recovery truck making its way down the lane. I got out of the car and painted a huge smile on my face, ready to greet the breakdown guy. He was early, and I felt like doing a happy dance right there in the middle of the road. When the red truck pulled up behind me though, my stomach dropped out. Hardy and Sons was emblazoned along the side.

Great.

Just my fucking luck.

I folded my arms and braced myself. This wasn't going to be pretty. The driver's door swung open and Ryan Hardy stepped down from inside. I half expected him to be grinning at me, but he wasn't. It looked more like a scowl, but it did nothing to stop the butterflies from attacking my system. My hands were shaking, and I couldn't quite look him in the eye. Ryan Hardy had always done this to me. Turned me into a blithering wreak. I'd hated that Danny had been friends with him, but thankfully, he'd never been invited to our house. So my contact with him growing up had been minimal.

He was wearing grubby blue overalls, but even I could appreciate how hot he looked. He'd always had muscles. He'd always been *that* guy. The one that takes care of himself, likes to look good and knows he does. His dark blond hair had a wave to it and did that thing where it fell into his eyes all the time, so he was always running his fingers through it or dipping his head whenever he looked at you, giving him that sexy vibe that most girls drooled over.

Who was I kidding? We all lost our shit over Ryan Hardy whenever he was around. But I wasn't dumb enough to fall for his bad boy charm. Not that he ever sent any of that charm my way. I don't even think he knew who I was until last night.

He stalked over to where I was, running his eyes over my car and then onto me. He ran his hand across his tanned, stubbled jaw and gave a low chuckle.

"Well, what do we have here? Got into a bit of trouble, Winters?"

I was grateful my voice didn't come out as a squeak when I answered him.

"I've broken down, but then you can't be that dumb, surely? Why else would I need *you*?" I said the last part on a sneer. I needed him to know he was a blip on my radar.

A nothing.

A nobody.

"I think you need me more than you realise. But I can always go… Leave you to sort this shit out yourself." He turned and went to walk away. Asshole.

"Fine, wait!" I called out after him and he stopped, looking back at me under that damn curtain of hair. "Can you get it started again?"

"That depends?" He smirked, coming back towards me.

"On what?" I put my hands on my hips and stood my ground.

"On whether it's fixable? Pop the bonnet open and I'll take a look." He swerved past me, brushing against my side as he did and then stood in front of my car. He motioned to the bonnet, nodding his head down as he did, and bit his lip to stop another smirk escaping. He was loving this.

I grabbed the door handle a little too hard and flung it open, then pulled the lever to free the bonnet. The hood clicked open and he rolled his sleeves up, showcasing his forearms, veins, and muscles that he'd been hiding. Damn, what was it about a guy's forearm that was so sexy? He lifted the bonnet and fixed the arm to hold it in place, then he started fiddling about with things, unscrewing caps and pulling things off, blowing on them and putting them back. He did a really good job of making it look like he was an expert, but when he sauntered to the side of the car and bent down to rest in a squat, leaning his arm on my car window, I wanted to push him off, expert be damned.

"Looks like your head gasket." He brushed down the front of his overalls, ridding himself of some imaginary lint in an effort to look nonchalant.

"Can it be fixed now?" I gripped my useless steering wheel to stop myself from shoving him and making him fall and roll backwards like a fucking beetle. I smirked at the image, but he soon wiped that off my face.

"Those parts will probably take a couple of days to order. Another couple of days to fix. This," he gestured to my car, "is gonna need towing."

I smacked my hands on my steering wheel in anger.

"Mother fucker."

"Does daddy know you have such a dirty mouth?" He grinned and then stood up and opened my door.

"What are you doing?" I made a grab for the handle to close it again, but he put his body in the way, forcing me to pull back.

"You need to get out. I'll get your car onto the back of the truck and then you can ride with me back to the garage."

"I'm not getting into that thing with you. I'll stay in here and you can tow me with it."

He laughed and shook his head, crossing his insanely muscular arms over his broad chest.

"Sorry, sweetheart. No can do. It's against health and safety.

The car goes on the back," he said, pointing to his truck and talking to me like I was a five year old. "And you go in the front… With me. Or you can stay here and enjoy the view a little longer."

I was so done. This day sucked balls, big time. Every day of being eighteen sucked ass. In fact, things had been pretty shitty ever since Danny had gone, but I pushed that thought to the back of my mind. Instead, I took a steadying breath, braced myself, and got out of the car. I could do this. It couldn't be more than five or ten minutes tops until we made it into town, where his father's garage was.

Seeing me acquiesce he gave a smug, satisfied smile and started getting things ready to hitch my car up onto his truck.

I made a point to give him a wide berth as I headed towards the front of his pick-up and then I noticed a car heading towards us. A red sporty number that slowed down as it got closer, and once it was parallel with my own, the tinted windows came down and a familiar head poked out. A friendly face beamed back at me, and the relief it gave me made some of my butterflies disappear.

"Emily, are you okay?"

Chase Lockwood had been in our year at school. He was a good guy, worked hard, and always had time for everyone. Effy had had the biggest crush on him a year ago, but I didn't see it myself. That goofy, nerdy, but secretly hot librarian thing he had going on did nothing for me. He made us all laugh though, and he was super kind.

"Chase, hey." I went to walk over to his car, but Ryan blocked my way, giving me a warning glare as he did. What was his problem?

"Have you broken down?" Chase asked.

"Observant, isn't he?" Ryan said under his breath.

"Do you need a lift anywhere?" I felt Ryan tense up as Chase said this. He obviously wasn't a fan of the nice guys.

I went to speak, but it wasn't my voice that answered.

"No, she doesn't." I frowned at Ryan and gave him a warning glare.

"I can speak for myself," I snapped, but Ryan turned his back to me and muttered something I couldn't hear to Chase.

Instantly, Chase sunk back in his seat and looked at the road straight ahead. "I'll see you around," he said, not even daring to look at me, and sped off down the road, leaving me at the mercy of the psycho mechanic.

"What the fuck was that?" I marched over to Ryan, feeling braver than I had all day. "What did you say to him?"

"I told him to mind his own fucking business. Now, get in the truck."

"Mind his own business? Are you crazy? Chase is my friend. I wanted to go with him. I'd rather get a lift off him than take my chances in this shit heap with you."

"Stay here then, princess. No skin off my nose."

"You'd like that, wouldn't you? To leave me here on my own. You're making a habit of fucking with my life just lately, aren't you?"

"You've got no idea," he said, coming closer towards me and penetrating me with his stare.

"I wouldn't give you the satisfaction of leaving me here. I'm gonna get in this bloody truck, and not because you've ordered me to. You're the last person I'd take orders from, but because I want to get out of here. I want my car fixed and I'm getting really good at blocking your crap out."

He laughed at me, full-on threw his head back and laughed.

"Whatever you say, sweetheart. But just know this…" He came right up to me, forcing me to back up against the truck. "You have no idea how bad I can make things for you. Keep trying to block me out, Winters, but you won't succeed. If I wanna be heard, I will. And you will fucking listen."

SEVEN
Ryan

This was not going how I'd planned it in my head. It certainly wasn't going the way we'd discussed back at my place. It'd been all Brandon's idea to mess with her car. Cut some wires, loosen up a few things. I wanted to wait a few days, bide my time, but Brandon was all for striking while the iron was hot. He thought we had her spooked after last night, thought now was the perfect time to chip away a little more. Get her while she was weak. Only thing was, this girl was anything but weak. She might've been spooked at the time, when we cornered her in those hallways, but she wasn't scared now. Just one look at her standing there in the middle of the road, with her hands on her hips and that pissed look on her face when she saw me, told me she was ready to fight back, and I liked it.

It wasn't supposed to go down like this though. This was supposed to be my chance to get a bit closer to her. Show her what she was missing. I think Zak's exact words were, "Woo the shit out of her."

Brandon's had been the complete opposite. Something about bending her over the bonnet and fucking her into submission. But that was his M.O., not mine. I knew I had to tread carefully where Emily was concerned. She was no pushover. So, I opted for a happy medium. A bit of wooing maybe, but I wasn't smooth like Zak. Throw in some charm, but not force myself on her at the first chance I got like Brandon would've. I needed this girl to trust me, so I could fuck her over and use that trust to get us what we needed.

Answers.

Answers to all the fucking questions and some goddamn evidence to back us up when the shit really hit the fan.

We had it all planned out. Brandon would drive down to her friend's house, tamper with her car whilst no one was looking, and make it so she could still drive away, but she'd have literally minutes before the engine cut out. I knew she'd ring the breakdown company. I also knew their waiting times were ridiculously long. I wanted to go to her after ten minutes, but both Brandon and Zak thought twenty was better. We didn't want to make it look too suspicious with me turning up too early, but twenty minutes was enough time to make her feel desperate and truly grateful to see me. Yeah right. Her face dropped faster than a fat kid falling on his ass when I rocked up. And damn, if her feistiness didn't do something to me. Wooing I couldn't do, I was clueless. But banter? Going toe-to-toe with her? Now that was my fucking forte. It was what got me going, and every roll of her eyes and huff from her pretty little mouth spurred me on even more. I knew this wasn't the result the lads had wanted, but I couldn't help myself.

Emily Winters was my nemesis. A perfect opponent in this little battle of wits we'd started playing. She was my muse.

Watching her squirm as I got out of the truck made my heart race. The little yellow sundress she had on, with the thin straps over her tanned shoulders made me want to run my fingers under each strap and watch them fall down her arms, so I could see the perfection she had hiding underneath. But her scowl was what turned me on the most. The way she flicked her curly hair back when she got annoyed made me hard. Her hair was thick and long, just right for wrapping around my fist as I yanked her head back and took her from behind. But fuck me, when she spoke, that anger and venom she had for me shot an arrow straight through my heart and my dick.

This girl would be the death of me.

The fact that she'd probably have preferred Freddy Kruger to come out of my truck instead of me made me want to conquer her even more. I loved a challenge. But what I didn't love, was a fucking pissing contest.

Chase fucking Lockwood.

The guy was an idiot. A loser. And he had the hots for Emily Winters, that much was clear. Dude was probably heading home to rub one out right now after seeing her today. When he pulled up, I wanted to drag him out of his flashy red extension of his dick and show him what I really thought of him. Dude was a puppet for his father, and we all knew what they got up to in their spare time. If he thought he was getting near Emily, he had another thing coming. The thought of her getting into his car made me show my cards sooner than I would've liked where he was concerned. I didn't like being forced into a corner, but he needed to back the fuck off.

There was no way I was gonna let him swoop in and play the hero, even if I was doing a shit job of being one myself. Hell, the joker always was my favourite kind of hero anyway. Sure, I could be a good guy if I needed to be. Not Chase Lockwood's kind of fake-ass good though. That guy set my teeth on edge.

I got busy hitching her car up to the truck, trying to ignore how pissed off I felt about Lockwood storming in and fucking up my shit.

"What the fuck was that?" she snapped, stomping over to me and making my breath catch in my throat.

Another step, sweetheart, I dare you. Just one more step and I'll have you up against this truck so fast you won't know what's hit you. I'll enjoy sticking my tongue down your pretty throat to shut you up.

"What did you say to him?"

Enough to save your ass. Jesus, thinking of her ass had me all messed up.

"I told him to mind his own fucking business. Now, get in the truck," was what came out of my mouth. In my head I was screaming, *fight me, baby. I love it when you make me work for it.*

She started spouting some bullshit about Lockwood being her friend and I zoned out. Picturing what it'd feel like when I did get her where I wanted her, on her knees sucking my dick. I was more than done with *him* being the topic of our conversation. And then I heard her say how I loved fucking with her life right now, and that was like a red rag to a bull.

"You've got no idea," I spat back, and those walls that I liked to keep firmly in place were locked, bolted and fortified to the motherfucking hilt. I needed to remember to have my wits about me with this girl; keep my guard up. Sure, she played the role of the good girl really well, but was she really that clueless about how far down the rabbit hole her family went? She was smart. She had to know something.

She argued with me some more, telling me she was getting in the truck, but not because I'd asked her, but that she needed a ride and she was getting good at blocking me out. Again, another challenge. So much for wooing her, I was about to break this girl's defences with a fucking sledgehammer.

I wasn't gonna be blocked out.

Nobody ignored me.

Ever.

I threw my head back and laughed, trying to make it look like I didn't care. I couldn't let her see that she was capable of pushing every one of my fucking buttons. She held enough power over me as it was, I couldn't give her anymore.

"Whatever you say, sweetheart. But just know this…" I walked right up to her, forcing her up against the truck, and hoping to God she couldn't feel how hard she was making me. "You have no idea how bad I can make things for you. Keep trying to block me out, Winters, but you won't succeed. If I wanna be heard, I will. And you will fucking listen."

She blinked up at me with those big blue eyes of hers and I willed myself not to react. Not to swallow or flinch. I couldn't do anything that'd show her that she affected me. Deep breaths were all I was capable of. That and some pretty fucked-up thoughts about where I could take this to next. She put both her hands on my chest, and for a split second I thought she was gonna lean up to kiss me, but her second of faltering was just that; a moment. A moment where she could take a breath and push me back away from her.

She muttered something under her breath and stalked off to the front of the truck. Then she threw me a glare that was probably meant to kill me dead on the spot and pulled herself up into the cab, slamming the door as she got in. This was going to be a ride I was going to enjoy, for every God damn second that it lasted.

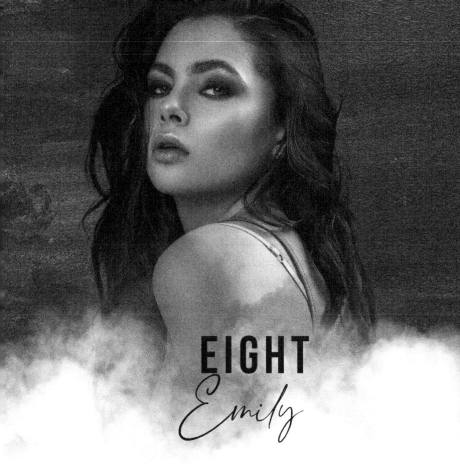

EIGHT
Emily

Deep breaths, Em. Deep breaths and focus. Do not let him get to you. Never let him see how he affects you. You can do this. You have the power here. Don't lose it.

Who was I kidding? I was a fucking mess and barely hanging onto my sanity by a thread. Having him so close to me just now did things to my body that I wasn't sure I liked. Or maybe I liked it a little too much. Whichever way I looked at it, I was screwed.

When he'd pushed himself against me, I felt something stir inside me, something so strong I didn't think I had the willpower to fight it. I wanted to kiss him. I wanted to lift up on my tiptoes and feel what it was like to have those plump lips of his pressing against mine.

Without a second thought, I'd put my hands on his chest and almost lost it when I felt his heart beating ten to the dozen under his overalls. Sure, he was cool, calm and collected on the outside, but touching his chest, I could feel the turmoil he felt deep inside. Angst that mirrored my own. Did I affect him as much as he affected me?

I used the last ounce of self-control I had in me and pushed him away. When I did, I saw something flicker in his eyes. Regret? Disappointment? I don't know. This guy was good at masking his feelings. Not that I thought for a minute he had any kind of feelings for me. I was probably a conquest he hadn't made yet. An easy target. If Danny was still alive, he'd have kicked Ryan's ass for even looking at me. But he wasn't here. And now, I had to do the ass kicking myself. I always had really. But it'd been nice to have a big brother around to back me up.

So, here I was, sitting in the truck waiting for him to drown me with his presence. Being near Ryan Hardy felt like being smothered by a shroud or choked by a dark fog. You didn't know it was coming until it was too late, and then all you could focus on was him and how to survive. I needed to channel some soul-stifling vibes of my own. Assert my position in his fucked-up little mind games.

I felt the truck rocking as my car was secured on the back, and then the driver's door opened and he jumped in next to me. He didn't look at me though. Oh no. He was guarded and ready to go. As always.

I kept my head to the side and looked out of the passenger window as we pulled off and drove towards town. The atmosphere was tense, but I knew he wouldn't stay quiet for long. He couldn't help himself. He loved goading me.

"Doesn't Daddy have his own mechanics on the payroll? I'm surprised you'd stoop so low as to need our help," he said, keeping his eyes on the road ahead. I huffed and shook my head. Always with the daddy's little girl bullshit. He knew nothing.

"First of all, what makes you think my dad even gives a shit about my car breaking down?"

"Doesn't he?" He turned to face me, giving me a confused look, then he frowned and turned back to concentrate on driving.

"I rang my parents. They told me to deal with it. I'm not a pampered princess, despite what you and your little gang might think." I folded my arms but kept going. "Secondly, yes, my dad has people on staff, but I don't get involved in all that. Why? Are you pissed that you didn't get the contract to maintain his collection?"

"Collection?" That'd sparked his interest.

"Yes. My dad collects classic cars. He has a guy who does all the maintenance. He's never looked after my car though. Why would he?"

"Doesn't daddy want to check you're okay? Keep tabs on his prize little P.R. princess? Great spread in the *Daily Mail* the other day, by the way." He was trying to mock me. It wouldn't work.

"I didn't take you for a *Daily Mail* reader." I scoffed, hitting the ball right back into his court.

"I'm not. We sent screenshots to each other to take the piss out of how orange your mum and dad looked."

I laughed at that one. I'd thought the same too. They loved their spray tans a little too much.

"So, how many does he have?"

"What, spray tans?"

"No, cars." He gave a genuine laugh this time. "But I can imagine the spray tan bills are through the fucking roof."

I stifled a laugh. I hadn't expected to bond with Ryan Hardy, of all people, over my parents' tanorexia.

"About fifteen the last time I checked."

"Fuck. That's impressive." He nodded to himself. "What models?"

"Like I'd know that. One's green, two are blue, he likes red the most, so he's got about five of those…"

Ryan shook his head and laughed.

"Okay, I get the picture. You're not a petrol-head. So, who's the guy? The mechanic? Would I know him?"

"Why the sudden interest in my father's affairs?" I turned in my seat to face him. My version of an interrogation.

"I've got no interest in your father whatsoever. I just like cars. I'm in the business. Thought I'd know him, that's all."

I narrowed my gaze at him, but it sounded legit, so I let it go. But for him, the subject of my father was still very much open for discussion.

"Must cost him a bit, to collect all those and keep them running. I didn't think a politician's wages were at that level. Got some dirty dealings you're hiding there, Winters?" He was digging for dirt and doing a shit job at hiding it.

"Like I'd discuss my father's income with you. I don't even know myself." I shouldn't have added the last part, but he was starting to piss me off again. "I'm the last person my parents would ever confide in."

"Is that so? You make it sound like they've got something

to hide?"

"Haven't we all?"

He turned to stare straight at me. "I don't know, have we?" The intensity of his gaze made me feel uncomfortable and I shuffled nervously in my seat.

"I'm an open book," I said, relaxing back into the seat. "No secrets here. But you? I think you've got a lot of things going on that you wouldn't want my dad finding out about. It's kind of fucked-up that you use the Renaissance as a label for your shady shit. Doesn't Renaissance mean rebirth? I don't see how beating people up or ripping them off with your betting scams could be called a rebirth."

"And that's where you're wrong, Winters. You know fuck all about us. The Renaissance was a time of discovery, taking us from a darker period to a more modern way of life."

"And that's why you hide away in the shadows, sending out cryptic messages to stay off the police radar? Because you're all about the light, aren't you, *Ryan*."

"We're staying off the system's radar. Those at the top of the food chain who think they have a God given right to fuck the rest of us over." I was pissing him off, I could tell. His jaw was clenched and he looked ready to bite back.

"Power to the people, hey? Are you the modern day Marx?"

"We make money. We're not communists. But we don't shit on the little people like your father does. We want to make life better, not bleed it fucking dry." Yep, he was pissed.

"I agree." I must've floored him with that retort, if the bulging of his eyes was any indication.

"Careful, don't let Daddy hear you talk like that. He might cut your allowance."

"Enough with the Daddy bullshit. I already told you, I'm no pampered princess. My parents couldn't give a shit about me. They tolerated me when Danny was alive, and now... Now, I'm just biding my time until I can get out. Not that I need to explain myself to you."

"Boo fucking hoo. So, you've got Daddy issues."

I was getting bored with this game of verbal tennis and I didn't feel the need to explain myself when it came to my family.

"Do you know your problem?" I said, hoping to bring him down a peg or two.

"Enlighten me."

"Your problem is, you don't know you're the problem. It's actually pretty easy not to be a shitty human being. You should try it sometime."

"Sweetheart, if you're waiting for me to give a fuck, you'd better pack a lunch. It's gonna be a while."

If I could've jumped out of the truck in that moment, I would've. Ryan Hardy was getting under my skin, big time. I hated that he judged me, labelling me the weak little girl like everyone else. His derision only made me more determined to fight back; show him that I had strength. I was tough. Anyone who'd had to live the past eighteen years in my family had to have some backbone. They wouldn't survive otherwise. Life for a Winters could be cutthroat. I was used to fighting my own corner.

He could chip away all he wanted, but he wouldn't break me.

***

We pulled onto the forecourt of his father's garage and I could see his dad and another guy standing by a car, looking under the bonnet with confused expressions. Ryan brought the truck to a stop at the side of the building and got out. Such a gentleman. He couldn't even tell me, "We're here," he just slammed his door and sauntered off to the rear of the truck to start unloading my car.

I opened my door and stepped down. As I looked up, I spotted Brandon Mathers, leaning up against a black Ford and grinning at me. I saw Ryan shake his head at him out of the corner of my eye. What was that all about?

"When will I get it back?" I asked, pulling my phone out of my bag and scrolling to look for the number of a local taxi firm.

"You'll get it back when it's ready," he replied in a bored, monotone voice.

"Well, well, well, my boy works fast. You giving him your number already, little Winters?" Brandon Mathers was walking towards us looking as smug as shit. "Do I get it too?"

Ryan threw him a dirty look, then carried on working on getting my car off the truck.

"Hell and freezing over spring to mind." I glared back at him. Where sparring with Ryan was fun and kind of a thrill, I hated Brandon with a passion. He was crass, rude, and a bully. He didn't care about anyone, not even himself. Even Ryan had some redeeming qualities. Like the way he blushed sometimes when he smiled. The way his smiles were crooked when he found something amusing, but he always threw his head back when he found anything hilarious. The way he…

"You're blushing, Winters. What's going on in that pretty little head of yours?" Brandon waggled his eyebrows at me, yanking me out of my warped daydreams by the scruff of my neck. "Are you thinking about me?"

"God, no," I bit back as Ryan banged something really loudly behind me, making me jump.

"Don't scare the girl, Ry." He smirked, then came to stand over me, trying to intimidate me no doubt. "Do you like being scared?" he whispered low into my ear and I pulled away, feeling disgusted by his closeness. "Because if you do, I think we could have a lot of fun together."

"I'd rather stick pins in my eyes whilst listening to *Aqua's "Barbie Girl"* on repeat than spend a second in your company. Isn't there a fist somewhere that you could be jumping in front of?"

Ryan laughed and came to stand next to me.

"I guess that's my cue. I'll leave you lovebirds to it." Brandon winked and turned his back on us, sauntering back over to his car. Then he shouted over his shoulder, "I'm starting to like you, Winters. If he fucks it up, I'm right here waiting to pick up the slack."

I had no idea what this guy was on. He was certifiably crazy. As if I would go anywhere near him. Dude scared the shit out of me in a bad way. He made my skin crawl. And what the hell was he on about, *"If he fucks up?"* He obviously didn't know me at all. Everyone in this town knew I was single.

"I need your number," Ryan said, breaking my trance. I turned to face him and gasped. He wanted my number? Why?

"So I can call you when the car is ready," he said, rolling his eyes. I hadn't realised I'd spoken out loud. I must've sounded like a complete idiot.

"Oh, right. Yeah. Hold on." I scrolled through my phone to find my number and heard a friendly voice behind me.

"Hey there. You're Alec Winters' daughter, aren't you?"

Ryan's dad was coming towards me. He wiped his hands down his overalls then held one out for me to shake.

"Yeah, Emily." I took his hand and he smiled, a really genuine, heart-warming smile.

"I hope my boy is looking after you," he said, giving Ryan a questioning look.

"He towed me here. My car broke down." Nothing like stating the obvious.

Ryan's dad slapped him proudly on the back. "He's a good kid. I'm glad he was there to help you. Do you want to come into the office and we can get some paperwork filled out?"

"I'm sorting it, Dad. It's okay."

"You haven't even offered the girl a drink. She's been stood here for five minutes," his dad chastised him.

"Two, actually, and she was just calling a cab. I'm getting her number."

"I bet you are." His dad grinned, and Ryan actually blushed. "You don't need to call a cab. Ryan will take you home."

"Oh, no. That's okay, Mr Hardy. I can find my own ride."

"It's Sean, and we're more than happy to see you home safely. Aren't we, son?"

"She's sorting her own ride, Dad. Chill out."

Mr Hardy, Sean, shrugged. "Suit yourself." He shook his head and laughed. "I'll never understand your generation." Then he walked back towards the office, leaving Ryan and I to our awkward stand-off.

"Your dad seems nice."

"He is, but I'm not. Write your number on here and I'll get one of the guys to call you when it's ready." He thrust a piece of paper and a pen at me, and I grabbed it, leaning against the wall to write my number and then I slapped it back into his chest.

"Can't wait," I said sarcastically and strode away, heading towards a coffee house to grab a much needed caffeine fix to calm my shredded nerves.

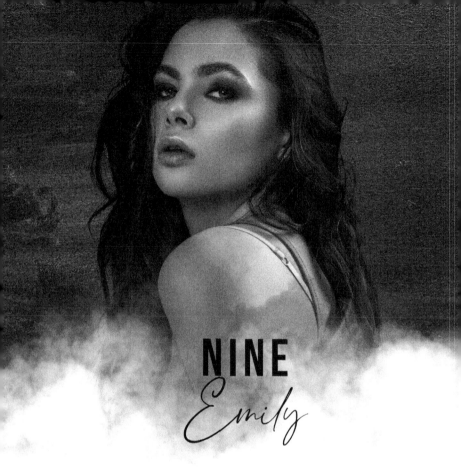

NINE

Emily

I t'd been four days and I still hadn't gotten my car back. I don't know why I was surprised. I doubt my little Audi was a top priority to them. It was a pain in the arse to have to keep relying on others for a lift though. To be honest, I was quite happy with walking or catching a bus, but to everyone around me that was like committing a heinous crime.

My mother hated public transport; thought it was unsanitary. Although she'd never admit that publically. That'd be political suicide. And my friends? They felt sorry for me, I guess. So, they messaged me daily to check that I was okay and asked me whether I needed anything. Hence the reason why I was riding shotgun with Effy to the hairdressers, while Liv sat in the back. I say sat, she spent more time leaning forward in-between the headrests than actually sitting down. I think she was scared she'd miss something if she chilled out.

"Have you ever thought of dying your hair, Em? I think you'd really suit blonde. Or maybe you could spark some more fire in you and become a redhead?" Liv said, popping her gum as she spoke.

"I'm happy with a trim. I like the brown. I know it's boring, but it's me."

"I like the brown too," Effy said in solidarity. "Chocolate curls. That's your look, Em. Stick with it."

I pulled the sun visor down and looked in the mirror, fluffing my hair as I did. Maybe a little something extra to brighten it up might work?

"I could add in a few highlights, I suppose."

"Oh my God, yes. That'd catch the sun and make it pop. Do it." Liv urged me, nudging her shoulder into me. "It doesn't have to be a permanent colour, just try something out and see if you like it."

I glanced across to Effy to gauge her reaction.

"Go for it, Em." She smiled and pulled into the car park in front of my hairdressers.

***

Three hours later, and I was waltzing back out into the sunshine, sporting a new, shinier look. Steph, my hairdresser, had teased my curls until they fell in spirals down my back, and the chocolate was now complemented by honey and caramels to soften the look. I'd never dyed my hair before. Okay, so I hadn't gone drastic and dyed it blue, but for me, this felt edgier. The first step to a new, bolder me.

I spotted Effy's car across the car park. Bless her for coming back to pick me up, she really was the sweetest. I told her she didn't have to, but she'd insisted. I was lucky to have such good friends. I got into the car to a chorus of "Ooo's" and "Ahh's." Liv was sitting in the back still and reached forward to stroke my hair in appreciation. I pushed her off, laughing at her playfulness.

"You look amazing, chick. We need to…" Effy didn't get to finish her sentence. The simultaneous ping coming from all three of our mobile phones stopped us in our tracks and had us all reaching for them. I tapped my unlock code onto the screen and saw the message waiting to be opened.

We've got you covered.

What the hell?

"The fuck is this?" Liv said, mirroring my own thoughts.

I opened the message and saw the coordinates for what I assumed was their next party. Question was, why were we getting this all of a sudden? They'd already said we didn't belong there. Now they were sending us invites? It didn't add up.

"I was about to suggest that we needed to take you out and show off that new hair, Em. Looks like we have the perfect excuse now," Effy said, waving her phone at me to show she'd got the same message and grinning like she'd won the lottery.

"Fuck that. We aren't going," Liv spat back, throwing her mobile back into her handbag in anger.

"Aren't we?" Effy frowned and glanced back at Liv. It was written all over her face, Eff wanted to go, and I found myself wondering what'd happened to change her mind. Days ago, she'd told me I needed to avoid those boys like the plague. Now, she was buzzing from getting an invite.

In all honesty, I was as curious as fuck to find out what the hell these boys were playing at. One minute we didn't exist, didn't even register on their radar; we were pariahs. The next, we were threatened, mocked and chased because we didn't belong there, apparently. And now? Now, it was all weird mixed signals, mind fucks and secret messages. I had to know what the deal was here. These boys were starting to play with my head. Ryan Hardy was getting under my skin and I knew something wasn't right about all of this.

"No, we're not." Liv wasn't going to be easily swayed on this one. "They scared the fuck out of Em the last time. Didn't make us feel all that welcome either. The music was good, but the company? I think it's a hard pass, girls." Liv folded her arms and sat back, looking out of the side window. She didn't look chilled out though, she looked pissed as fuck.

"I'm okay, Liv," I said, trying to calm her down. "And to be completely honest with you both, I'm kind of wondering why they've invited us in the first place." Liv turned to me and shrugged, but I could tell she still wasn't convinced. "We've never had these messages before. So, why now? I think we should go, even if it's to find out what their game is." Liv rolled her eyes and huffed. "I mean, why do they want us there? Is this some kind of trick or trap?"

"If it is, why do we want to fall into it?" she argued back.

"But we wouldn't. We're smart." I gave her a wink. I knew she loved a challenge.

"Maybe we should think of a dumbass name for ourselves.

We'd think of something a hell of a lot cooler than Renaissance girls." Liv laughed and rolled her eyes again. She was starting to warm to the idea.

"Renegade girls," Effy said smiling.

"Eff, I like your thinking. We're the rebels." Liv snorted at me, but I kept going. "The new rebels. We'll defy anyone who fucks with us or tries to control us. Renegade warriors. Warrior queens."

"Jeez, you girls are really getting ahead of yourselves. It's a fucking party invitation, not a declaration of war," Liv said.

"Isn't it?" I lifted my phone as I spoke. "This right here is them throwing down the gauntlet. They think we're weak little princesses who'll crumble under the first sign of trouble. We need to show them that's not true. We're going." I gave Liv a pointed stare. "We're all going, and we'll play them at their own game. Come on. It'll be fun. I've never known you to stand down from a challenge, Liv."

Liv huffed and gave me one last eye roll before saying, "Fine. We'll go. Eff, you can be designated driver again. I'll need all the alcohol to get through this."

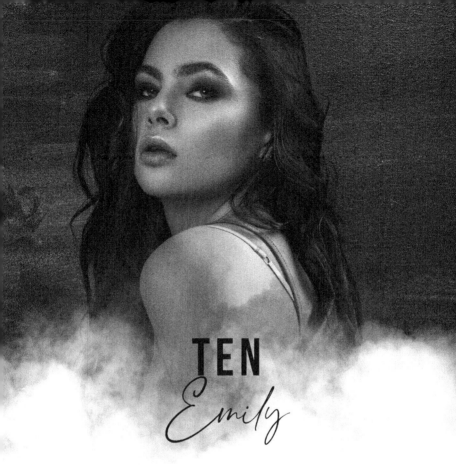

TEN
Emily

"This can't be it, surely?" Effy said as we made our way down the dirt track, following her Sat Nav's directions.

It was dark out, and the trees that hung over the path we were driving down enclosed all around us, like eerie death-eaters. Everything about this journey so far screamed set-up. Shit, in all our confusion about whether we would go or not, we hadn't countered in the fact that we might be the only ones to get that message. What the hell were we driving into? Maybe we weren't as clued up as we thought?

I needed to sharpen my brain if I was going to engage with

these four boys. They always did their homework and then some. I was barely showing up to class. Had I just dropped a major ball putting us out here like this? Jesus, I'd probably painted a massive red bullseye on the three of us.

"And we have a winner," Liv said, pointing ahead where we could just about make out a bonfire in a clearing up ahead. There were a few parked cars and trucks, but nowhere near the number of vehicles that'd been on that field by the disused warehouse last week.

"I'm not sure about this. It doesn't look like the same type of party we went to on Em's birthday," Effy said, peering into the darkness ahead of her. "It looks… Exclusive. There's not that many people here."

"More chance for Finn to notice you then. Or is it Zak, still? I can't keep up," Liv joked, and I shot her a warning glare.

"The three of us should stick together. Safety in numbers. Let's let them show their hand first. There's a reason they invited us here tonight and I want to know what it is." Effy blew out a low breath and Liv nodded along in agreement.

"Let's do this, bitches," Liv said, and opened her door as we rolled to a halt.

We picked our way over the uneven ground. I thanked my lucky stars I was wearing my ripped skinny jeans tonight paired with my trusty converse. I'd brought a pair of heels along too, just in case, but I didn't think I'd be needing those. They could stay in the car.

There were about a dozen or so people sat around the fire. A few more were up and dancing close to where a truck was blasting out music. I guessed Zak had turned mobile D.J. tonight. He was sitting on the back of a pick-up truck, next to a set of huge speakers, and nodding his head in time with the beat. A girl with long dark hair walked over to him, swaying her hips like crazy to catch his attention, and handed him a beer. He grabbed it and took a long swig, then wiped the back of his hand over his mouth and grinned at her.

I had no idea who she was, but it looked like she'd caught Zak in her net already, hook, line and sinker. I peered across at Effy, but she didn't seem to care. I don't think she'd even noticed Zak. She was too busy staring at a particular guy sat huddled on the floor, next to a tree trunk. Finn was carving something into the tree, and the look of concentration he was giving it told me he was oblivious to the party going on around him. All his focus was on the masterpiece he was creating. Effy would need all the luck in the world to crack that one.

I was hoping to make a quiet entrance. Sneak across to the bonfire, grab a beer on the way from the cooler that was sat close by. But subtle entrances, exits, or any kind of grace seemed to elude me just lately. I wasn't looking where I was going, too busy taking it all in and wondering where the last two demons in the devil's foursome were, when I got my foot caught in the root of a tree and I stumbled forward onto my hands and knees.

Oh the shame.

I peered up to find every single person here looking straight at me. The girls were grimacing at how uncool and totally unwelcome I was. A few of the guys actually looked concerned, Finn included. But nothing could overshadow the smirks I was getting from Ryan and Brandon as they stood by the bonfire.

"Shit, chick. Are you okay?" Liv whispered, as she pulled me up from the floor. Effy went to grab my other side, but I shooed her away. I already felt like a complete idiot. I didn't want to prolong the misery. I dusted myself down and winced as I felt the twinge of pain on my left knee. Great. I'd have a scab like a kid for the next few days. That'd be attractive.

"I'm fine, but I need a beer to numb the pain," I hissed back.

"Are you really hurt?" Effy asked.

"Yeah, my pride is fucking crushed." I tried not to limp too badly as we headed in the direction of the alcohol.

"Took a nice little trip there, Winters," Brandon shouted over the bonfire at me. "Always knew you'd fall hard for me."

"In your dreams, *Mathers*," I shouted back as I grabbed a beer and then passed one to Effy and Liv.

"Always in my dreams, Winters. Me and you get up to all sorts of crazy shit in my dreams." He took a sip of his beer then grabbed his crotch and leered at me like a sicko. Brandon was a shady motherfucker and the thought of being in his dreams, let alone near him now, made me shudder.

"I'd rather suck a rhino's balls than go anywhere near you."

He laughed at me and then winked.

"You like balls, don't you, Winters. First you wanna get near my boy Ryan's here, and now you're getting me all hot under the collar thinking about you sucking mine."

I sneered at him, having absolutely no clue what the fuck he was on about. Was this some sort of fucked-up mating ritual for him?

I glanced at Ryan and couldn't help but notice how tense he looked. His eyes were boring into Brandon, but Brandon didn't care. He was on a roll.

"Why don't you come and sit over by me, Winters? I've got a really nice… Big… Lap for you to sit on. And maybe later, you can sit on something else?"

"Fuck off," Ryan said to him in a low voice.

What the hell was that?

Was Hardy trying to step in for me?

That was fucking rich. The demon overstepping the devil. I didn't need him doing his knight in shining armour shit. Even if it was a crap effort.

"Is the big guy bothering you?" Zak was standing behind us, smirking over at his boys.

"No, he's not bothering me. I stopped paying attention about five minutes ago. Is he still talking?" I shrugged trying to look unfazed.

"Sit down, ladies. Where are your boyfriends tonight? Don't tell me three beautiful girls came all the way out here on their own?" Zak shook his head with mock sadness. "Now, that's a travesty. I think we'll have to do something about that. What do you say, Ryan?"

I made the mistake of looking over at Ryan, to find his eyes were on me. Piercing me with a stare, and I couldn't work out if it was threatening, goading, or just plain nasty. I guessed all three, seeing as every encounter I'd had with Ryan Hardy so far was more hostile than a wasp in a jam jar.

"We're single," Liv sang back, sounding pleased to have Zak's attention. "Em's never had a boyfriend."

I almost choked on my beer and whipped my head around to tell her exactly what I thought about her little group sharing effort.

"What the fuck, dude?" I hissed and waited for the impending laughter to begin. It didn't.

"No boyfriend? I find that very hard to believe," Zak said, sitting down next to us and giving me a kind smile. I wasn't fooled.

"She's been saving herself for me," Brandon chipped in. Not the reaction I was expecting from him. I'd have thought some put-down about me being a prissy virgin might've been more his style, or something about how he'd break me in later tonight. But no, he gave me a pretty tame response by his standards, and I'd take it. I would have told him, "In his dreams," but I didn't really want to go there again.

And Ryan? He sat down on the opposite side of the bonfire to us and didn't say a word. More interested in his beer bottle than the conversation we were having. Zak was looking straight at him though, as if he was waiting to see what his contribution would be. When he didn't get one, Zak turned his attention back to me.

"Why haven't you dated, Emily? Are you holding out for the one? Has Brandon hit the nail on the head?" He said that last part in a whisper and brushed his shoulder against mine.

I scoffed at his suggestion. "No. It was my brother, Danny. He warned the guys off. He was protective."

Zak glanced back over to Ryan and said, "Is that so? Danny, huh?" He kept his gaze on Ryan as he sipped his beer and Ryan stared straight back.

"What the fuck, man? Seriously?" Brandon snapped. "Tell me you were getting your fucking ducks in a row and not playing the pussy all this time." He stared down at Ryan like he was ready to go at it with him. Ryan stood up and faced Brandon, the two of them almost nose to nose.

"You know fuck all. Back off, or I'll-"

"Or you'll what, huh? Make me?"

I had no idea what was going on. It looked like Ryan and

Brandon were seconds away from a fight.

"Cool it, ladies," Zak said to the two lads. "Not in front of the guests, please."

"I don't fucking believe you," Brandon said, throwing his bottle of beer onto the ground right by Ryan's feet. Then he marched away, grabbing two beers in each hand as he did and storming off into the woods. Just as he reached the thick set of trees, he spun back around and shouted over to a girl who was dancing by the speakers.

"Sarah, get your ass over here. I have tension I need to work out, and you're the lucky girl who gets to sort that for me."

Like a bloody lap dog, Sarah trotted over to him, looking like she'd been picked for *The Price is Right*. There was no price in the world that'd make that shit right for me. But who was I to judge?

Brandon strutted off into the woods without a second glance, and Sarah followed close behind, giggling and skipping as she went.

"That dude has issues." There went Liv, stating the obvious again.

"He'll have crabs by the morning too, if he hasn't already," Zak replied and we all laughed.

"Who the fuck invited him?" Ryan suddenly snapped, standing up and giving whoever was behind us an evil glare.

We all turned to see who he meant, and saw Chase Lockwood sauntering over with two friends either side of him. He had a cocky grin on his face and was staring straight back at Ryan.

"Fucking Lockwood," Zak said, turning back around. "You need to sit down." He pointed his beer bottle at Ryan as he spoke, and I was totally floored when Ryan did exactly as he was told. He didn't like it though. That jaw of his was clenched so tightly he could've cracked a walnut.

"Do you not like Chase Lockwood?" Liv leaned into Zak as she spoke.

"Guy's a total douche canoe."

"No, he's not," I answered, trying to stick up for him.

"Maybe he is?" Liv said, leaning around Zak to address me. "I heard he wasn't quite the gentleman we all thought he was last Christmas with Lyla Thomas."

"Don't believe everything you hear on the grapevine." I wasn't sure whether what she said was true, but I'd trust Chase over these four guys any day of the week. We'd known him for years. Lyla Thomas wasn't the most trustworthy either. But I knew to keep my wits around all of them. You didn't grow up in my house without learning how to stand your guard. Everyone had an ulterior motive. Or so my father said.

"I swear to God, he'd better stay the fuck away from me," Ryan announced, and as if he'd heard him clear as day, Chase walked right over to us and sat down next to Effy.

"Effy, Liv." Chase nodded at my two friends. "Emily, hey. Are you okay? Did you manage to get home all right the other day?" His eyes were kind, but I felt like he was directing his concern to the group more than to me. Making some kind of statement.

"Yeah, it's all good. Ryan's dad is sorting my car out."

"Good job he was there." Chase took a swig of his beer and looked at Ryan as he spoke. "Funny how he managed to find you. Out of all the mechanics in Sandland, he was the one to save you."

"The fuck you saying, Lockwood? You trying to cause shit

again, you little fucker?" Ryan looked ready to launch himself at Chase at the first opportunity he got.

"Where's your guard dog, Hardy? Did Mathers run away with his tail between his legs?"

"You're right about the chasing tail part," Zak piped up, earning a chuckle from Chase at his effort at humour.

"Probably saw you coming and decided he'd seen enough shit for one day." Ryan flung his empty bottle onto the bonfire, making the flames crackle and sizzle higher.

"What, no fight tonight? Not gonna use that mathematical genius of yours to rob us blind with your betting odds?"

"You want a fight, Lockwood? It can be arranged." Ryan stood up as if he was gearing up for a showdown, but Zak stood too and put his hands up, trying to show some peace needed restoring at this piss-poor excuse for a party.

"Come on, guys, seriously? Are we gonna do this here? And in front of these beautiful women? I don't think so." Jeez, Zak was a smooth talker.

"I would fight you, Hardy, but I don't want to be accused of animal abuse." Chase smirked to himself smugly, but Ryan just laughed and grabbed a beer off a guy walking past him, before sitting back down. That mist of fury had evaporated, and he was back to being his usual guarded self.

"Anytime, mate," Ryan said on a low growl. "I'll go against you anytime."

"Okay, let's try and pretend we're here for a good time," Liv said a little too chirpily and stood up, grabbing mine and Effy's hands as she did. "Girls, let's go and dance, or do something other than sit here watching these boys compare dicks."

We headed to another part of the clearing and it didn't take long for Zak to join us.

"Listen, I'm sorry if we scared you away," he said looking regretful.

"Oh, we know. That's not how you scare girls away. You chase them down dark hallways in deserted warehouses, banging on the walls and laughing like a bunch of fucking freaks." Liv was back into her bitch mode and obviously ready to fight my corner.

"That was nothing to do with me, and for the record, I don't think they really wanted to scare you, Em. I think they wanted to make sure they got noticed."

"There's better ways to get into a girl's knickers. Making her run for her life isn't one of them," Liv spat back before I could even form a sentence.

Zak gave a low chuckle and ran his hand over his face.

"Why were we invited tonight? We've never been welcome before," I asked, hoping that of all the boys, Zak would be the one to give us a bit of honesty.

"Who said you weren't welcome? Okay, yes, Danny didn't want you, well, any of you at our parties, but it was nothing personal. Now, we just wanna make amends."

"No, I don't buy it." I waited to see a flinch or something in his expression that'd give him away, but there was nothing.

"What's not to buy?" He shrugged. "Fine. I'll level with you. My man, Ryan, he might have a little crush on you. He's shit at doing something about it though." I almost choked on my beer. That was the biggest crock of shit I'd ever heard. I told him as much too.

"Bullshit! He told me I didn't belong in *this* world. Told me to run away and never come back. What the fuck? That's the furthest from a come-on that you could get."

"That's his version of foreplay. Sweet talk. I told you he was shit at it." Zak shrugged again. He obviously bought that idea and he was sticking to it.

"I don't believe you. Something is going on. I'll find out what it is, and when I do, I'll-"

"You'll what? Piss all over our business? Run to Daddy and tell on us?"

"Careful, you're starting to sound like them. Worried I'm the rat you all accused me of being before?" I said, nodding over to where Ryan and Brandon had been by the fire. Ryan wasn't there anymore, and I did feel a jolt of something inside me, wondering where he was. I looked around the clearing, but I couldn't see him. Had he left already? Did *I* still want to be here? This party wasn't what I'd thought it'd be, especially since Chase showed up.

"I'm just trying to be a friend. We could all use one of those, right?" Zak gave me a sympathetic smile and I shrugged back.

"I've got enough friends."

"Then keep your friends close and your enemies closer," he said, then bowed down and walked away, leaving us to mull over that little nugget of wisdom.

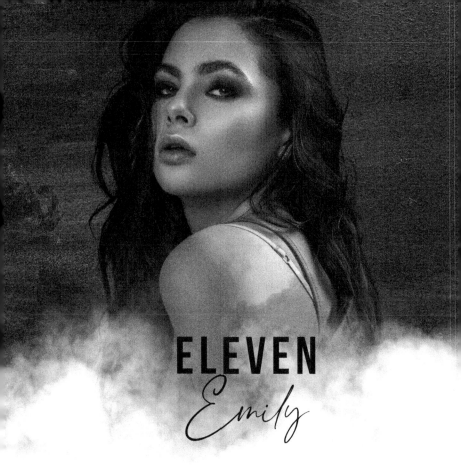

ELEVEN

Emily

I'd drunk way too much, and the party was starting to blur into a hot mess of people dancing, falling about, and making out. I hadn't seen Brandon or Ryan since we left the bonfire area. Chase had kept a pretty respectful distance too, just giving me the occasional nod or smile from where he stood. I glanced over to where Effy had been chatting to Finn, asking him about his carvings and trying to get blood from a stone in response. Funnily enough, they weren't there. I looked around, but I couldn't see them anywhere. Interesting.

I could see Liv as clear as day though, glued to the front of

Zak Atwood with her tongue stuck down his throat. Seems like both of my girls had gotten lucky tonight. I suddenly felt self-conscious and lonely and didn't know what to do with myself. I was drunk and not thinking straight, clearly, since I decided that a walk around the woods to straighten my head out was a good idea.

Why did alcohol force you to make the most ridiculous choices in the heat of the moment? And yet, I didn't question myself once when I thought a breath of fresh air, away from the rest of them, was just what I needed. Just tattoo *dumbass* on my forehead now.

I wandered to the left of me, into the thick darkness of the trees, taking small steady steps so I wouldn't fall. I felt that awkwardness slide off me the further into the woods I went. My shoulders eased back slightly, and I felt less tense. There was no one here, in amongst the trees, to witness how awful I was at fitting in. That group back there wasn't my group of people. I think I preferred my own company, really. Apart from a few select friends growing up, I'd always kept myself to myself.

I took a few deep breaths, enjoying the cold bite of the air as it entered my lungs. The laughter and music had died down to a distant hum. Then realisation hit me like a smack in the face. I hadn't realised I'd come out this far. Shit.

Did I know the way back?

I spun around, looking at the trees surrounding me, suddenly feeling dizzy and unsure of which way I'd actually come. I started to walk ahead, using my ears to try and find the direction of the party. That's when I heard the snap of a twig not far behind me.

There was someone else here.

Someone was following me.

My heart started to beat out of my chest, but I slowed my breathing right down, so I could focus on listening. I put one foot slowly forward, trying not to draw attention to myself.

Maybe it was an animal? I was in the middle of a forest at night, there were bound to be all sorts of sounds I wasn't familiar with.

I heard another crack behind me and suddenly my whole world spun on its axis.

I was yanked backwards into a hard chest. One strong arm wrapped tightly around my waist and another jammed in front of my face, the hand clamping over my mouth so I couldn't scream. Then, as quick as a flash, before I could even register what was happening, I was pulled down to the ground and dragged behind a bush, well-hidden from sight. I tried to wriggle, tried to free myself from his grasp, but it was pointless. I was powerless in this man's arms.

"Shush!" A familiar deep voice tried to soothe me. "I'm not gonna hurt you. Just stay quiet."

Ryan Hardy had me pinned to his front and was shushing me like this was all for my own good. He kept his hand over my mouth and didn't loosen his grip in the slightest when I made every effort to escape.

What the fuck was his deal?

I clawed at his arm, using my nails to scratch him and possibly get some kind of upper-hand so I could escape. My legs kicked out, but they didn't connect with anything other than the woodland floor. My heart was beating like a bass drum in my ears and the adrenaline pumping through my veins was electric.

"Quit wriggling and wait. Trust me," Ryan whispered into

my ear, and at that moment, I noticed movement in amongst the trees where I'd just been standing.

I panted hard through my nose and tried to shake my head free, but when I saw Chase Lockwood walk out in front of us, I stopped. We both lay behind the bush, me being constrained, and him barely breathing, but tense as hell. His face was right next to my ear and the warmth of his breath as he hushed me one last time made my skin prickle. My drunken brain was now as sharp as a tack.

Chase stood still and looked around him. Had he come to find me? Make sure I was okay? I was about to give him a muffled cry from behind Ryan's hand, when Chase's mobile phone lit up without making a sound and he answered it.

"Mate, I lost her," he said sounding disappointed and then he laughed. The guy actually laughed. "Looks like I'm gonna have to get my dick wet somewhere else tonight."

My stomach turned over, hearing him talk like that, and I stopped fighting against Ryan's hold on me, and felt him tighten his grip, pulling me further into him.

"Yeah, I swear her tight little pussy better be worth it. I've waited long enough." He chuckled at something being said to him and smirked. "Oh, I know, mate. Virgin pussy is always the sweetest and Emily's will be the ultimate."

I felt sick.

I watched as Chase started walking back the way he came, muttering disgusting filth down his phone and laughing. So, nerdy boy was a prick just like the rest of them.

I hadn't noticed Ryan had moved his hand away from my mouth until he whispered into my ear, "You're welcome."

I scrambled up from the floor and moved myself away from

him as quickly as I could. I brushed the leaves and dirt off me and scowled at him.

"What the fuck is it with you? Are you stalking me now? Jesus, make your mind up. One day you're scaring me away, the next you're following me in the woods like a creeper."

"Aren't you glad that I did? Otherwise, your man Lockwood over there would've had you right where he wanted you." The way he glared at me made me go cold.

"Chase is not *my man*. He never will be," I spat back.

"Good." He folded his arms over his chest and I faltered in my argument. I wasn't expecting that answer.

"Second," I said, still frowning from his last response. "You've already told me to fuck off. So, why did we get invited here, today? Why the one-eighty?"

"I meant every word I said last Saturday. You didn't belong in that room, watching men kick the shit out of each other, with all the blood and filth. That's not you." His face had softened slightly, and he took a few steps towards me.

"How do you know what's me? We've barely ever spoken. You might've been Danny's friend, but you know fuck all about me."

"I know enough," he said, staring straight into my eyes like he needed me to understand him, to believe what he was saying.

"You know what you want to know; see what you want to see. Don't fool yourself into thinking I'm the weak little girl you accused me of being last Saturday."

"Did I say that?" He scrunched his face up in confusion.

Yes, asshat. Yes, you did.

"I've never seen weakness in you, Emily. But I know what I do see. I see you better than anyone."

I didn't know what to say to that. He saw me? What did that even mean? The guy was full of bullshit. Did he think I couldn't smell it from a mile off?

"If you see me better than anyone, then tell me, what do you see?"

I couldn't wait to hear his response. I was calling his bluff.

"I see a girl who hates who she is… To other people. I also see a girl desperate to be herself. To live her life the way she wants to. To have just a fraction of the freedom that we have. Me, Brandon, Finn, Zak; we have a life you can only dream of, but you want it. You want in so badly you'll do anything to get it. At least, I think you will. Question is… How far are you willing to go, Emily? How far would you go to have it all?"

"You're really good at talking in riddles, aren't you, Ryan? What makes you think I want to be like you?" I shook my head and turned to walk away.

"You *are* like us." He spoke with such conviction I could almost believe him. Almost.

"No. I'm not." I spun back around and stood my ground.

"I think you are. In fact, I know you are." He was so sure of himself. And me? I was getting more confused by the minute, but I wouldn't ever show him that.

"I've had enough of this. I need to get out of here."

I turned my back on him and started climbing a steeper incline at the edge of the woods.

"Don't do that," Ryan shouted after me. "Don't go up there."

"Why not? Why should I ever listen to you?"

"Because that's where the quarry is. Shit, you really don't know your way around these woods, do you?" He was marching over to me now and looked pissed off. "Get your fucking ass back down here."

I didn't like giving him the upper-hand, but I was fucked. I had no clue where I was or how to get back to Liv and Effy. So, reluctantly, I shuffled my way back down the incline.

"Come on. Take my hand and I'll get you back to your friends," he said, climbing up the incline to get to me.

"I can follow you just fine, I don't need to take…" I missed my footing and skidded down the slope, doing the splits as my legs slid all over the wet leaves. Ryan reached out and grabbed my arm, stopping me from falling flat on my ass.

"You were saying?" He gave a cocky grin then reached up and threaded his fingers through one of my curls. "I meant to say earlier, I like your hair like this. All the browns and golds. It suits you."

I jerked away from his grasp. "Don't touch me," I said, but his comment sparked something inside me. My own parents hadn't even noticed my new haircut, or if they did, they didn't say anything.

Ryan noticed.

Ryan seemed to notice an awful lot more than I realised.

He huffed a smile and took my hand in his, pulling me along with him. To anyone else, we'd probably look like two young lovers, out for a romantic stroll in the woods. But look closer and you'd see how tense we both were. We might've been touching, but our body language was screaming at each of us to be on our guard. At least, mine was.

"We should have your car back to you in a few days." He spoke with a quieter, more gentle tone. I wasn't buying into his tricks though. I don't know why he was even attempting to make small talk. All I could focus on was what it felt like to hold his large, warm hand. It sent a shockwave right up my arm and into my whole body. It was all I wanted to focus on, not pointless chatter. I was at war with myself, erecting my own damn walls, and yet, questioning everything. Was he feeling as mixed up as I was?

"Great. I'll call your dad to sort it out."

We walked together in a relatively comfortable silence. The crunch of the woodland under our feet and our gentle breaths was the only sound that could be heard. That, and the thumping of my heart as it threatened to break free from my chest and attach itself to Ryan Hardy.

Shit, why was I thinking like that?

If my heart went anywhere near him, he'd chuck it on the floor and probably stamp all over it.

When we finally came to the clearing, the party was dying down. People had paired off and were together, entwined in dark corners. The fire was starting to burn itself out, but nobody cared. That wasn't what they'd come here for.

"I'm going home," I announced as I scanned the area for Effy or Liv.

"I'll drive you," Ryan said from behind me.

I scoffed at his weak and frankly shitty attempt at chivalry. The last thing I felt like doing was getting into his car. I needed space. He was scrambling my well-established wavelength and making my brain short-circuit.

"I'm not leaving my friends. I came with them. I'll leave with them." I stepped slowly around the edge of the clearing to see if either one of them was here. Effy was still MIA, but I spotted Liv pulling Zak into the woods by his hand and turning to give him a seductive look.

"I don't think your friends have the same values as you, Winters. Looks like Liv's more interested in the contents of Zak's underwear than getting you home safely. As for Effy, Finn's probably taken her to show her his etchings." He laughed at himself. Good job someone found him funny.

I folded my arms over my chest and looked around, weighing up my options. That's when I noticed Chase and his friends on the other side of the bonfire. He was staring straight at me, and the way he licked his lips made my skin crawl.

"Fine. I'll get a ride home with you. But don't speak to me." I spun round to catch Ryan rolling his eyes.

"Such a shame I'll miss out on all the witty banter we could be having. But I guess I'll live," he said sarcastically and strolled away.

I followed, taking my phone out of my jeans and sending a group text to the girls to let them know I'd gotten a ride home and trusted they'd keep themselves safe too. I knew Finn was a good guy, he'd look after Effy, wherever they were. But Zak? The jury was still out on that one.

Ryan stopped next to a beat-up old van and smiled. "Your chariot awaits." He bowed down, making himself look like a dickhead, and I laughed, then tried to open the passenger door. "Not that door. Locks broken. You'll have to use this one and climb over."

"Call yourself a mechanic and your own van doesn't have a working passenger door?" I stalked over to the driver's side and got in, probably giving him a great view of my ass as I climbed across the middle console.

"Never got round to fixing it." He shrugged, getting in and slamming his door shut. "Why would I? It's not like I ever have any passengers, anyway."

"Right, you use this for your little night-time adventures and save the smarter ride for your dates. God forbid anyone should think this was an extension of your dick. What a disappointment."

He threw his head back and laughed at me.

"This is my only ride, Winters. And I don't need anything to help extend my dick. I've had no complaints so far."

I swallowed as I felt his stare on me. I wouldn't give him the satisfaction of looking at him or responding. I wasn't interested in what he got up to, or maybe I just didn't want to know. His mentioning no complaints made my stomach twist. I didn't like that.

The van bumped us around as he drove away and headed back onto a proper road. I held onto the handle above my head to stop myself from falling into him. My seatbelt was tight, but I was still sliding all over the place.

"You okay over there?" He glanced across at me and smirked.

"I'm fine."

He swerved onto the road and put his foot down, making me tense in my seat.

"You sure about that?"

I wasn't about to admit to him that ever since Danny's car accident I'd felt nervous riding with people I didn't know. I didn't want to admit to a weakness.

"Is this what Zak was talking about earlier? Keep your friends close and your enemies closer?" I asked, steering the conversation away from my fears. Hopefully a bit more sparring with him would also occupy my mind away from other things too.

"Is that what he told you?" He wasn't giving anything away with his answer.

"I'm the rat, aren't I? The one you think goes running back to Daddy every chance she gets."

"Don't you?"

"No. I've barely spoken to my father in the last few years. I doubt he even knows or cares where I am half the time."

"And that bothers you?" He was doing a rubbish job at hiding his contempt for my father. The anger coming off him was palpable.

"No. I couldn't give a rat's ass. I'm interested to know why it bothers you though."

"Why do you think I'm bothered?" He was clenching his jaw tight and tapping his hand on the steering wheel, all tell-tale signs that he was mad.

"If you wanna know something, just ask. I'm not fluent in bullshit."

He flared his nostrils and huffed. "Be careful what you wish for, Winters. That perfect little life you lead might come crashing down around your ears one day."

"Perfect little life? Fuck off, Ryan. If you have something to say, say it."

"Fine. Ask your Dad about the Rotherham account." I screwed my face up. I had absolutely no clue what he was on about.

"Ask him." He turned to face me now, his expression deadly serious.

"Fine. I'll do that."

He pulled into my road and stopped a few houses down

from mine.

"I'll park here. Wouldn't want Daddy getting pissed about the battered-up old van bringing down the neighbourhood."

I went to open my door then remembered it was broken. He didn't move though. Instead, he gripped his steering wheel and blew out a low breath.

"Danny was a good friend to me." His comment came from left-field. "I respected him." He turned to look at me. "I don't respect your father though. And right now, I'm still not sure which one you take after."

"Not everything is black and white, Ryan." I batted that ball straight back at him. "Danny was a good guy, the best brother any girl could wish for, but maybe I don't take after either of them. Ever think of that?"

He smiled to himself and shook his head. "That's exactly what I thought." Then he pushed his door open and got out.

I stretched my legs across to climb out and clung to the driver's door to pull myself up.

"I'll walk you to your door," he said, but I shut him down.

"No need. I can find my own way home. I don't need your help."

He folded his arms over his chest and gave me a stare. "Rotherham account," was all he said back to me.

"I haven't forgotten."

I marched towards my house and stopped when I got to the foot of my driveway. I turned to find him still standing there, arms folded and watching every step I took.

"Why me?" I mirrored his stance, waiting for the impending put-down. "Why are you targeting me?"

"It's always been you, Winters. Always."

I was fed up with his riddles, so I headed for my house and didn't give him another backwards glance. I knew he was still there though. I didn't hear his engine start up until I'd closed my front door.

TWELVE
Ryan

Isat down in the only spare armchair in Zak's living room. I had to brush off the papers and other shit he had covering it, but apart from being ridiculously untidy, the dude's apartment was relatively clean. I couldn't complain. I still lived at home with my dad. I was saving up to get my own place and the money we made from the events kept that topped up nicely. That, and the commission I made off my cars. The only problem was, Dad needed my help. It wasn't easy running the garage, keeping the house going, and bailing out my brothers when they fucked up. I hated to see him struggle, so more often than not, I paid him extra rent to help.

One step forward, two steps back. That's what life was like for us Hardys though. I was used to it.

"Talk," Brandon said, side-eyeing me.

I took a sip of the scolding hot coffee Zak had handed to me the minute I'd walked through the door. I needed to word this right. I had to have my head straight.

"I made headway." I put the mug on the floor next to my foot and sat back in the chair.

"Made headway how? Last I saw, you were sloping off into the woods, following her." Zak smirked as he spoke. I know we'd organised that whole charade to get her there, but it hadn't stopped either one of them from getting their kicks.

"I'm surprised you noticed. You had your tongue so far down Liv Cooper's throat, I didn't think you could see further than your dick."

He chuckled and grinned to himself. "She's a firecracker that one."

"Are you seeing her again?" Finn asked looking genuinely interested in his answer.

"Fuck, no. She was a bit of fun. She knew the score. She got what she wanted and so did I. The question is, did you, Ryan?"

All three pairs of eyes turned to look at me.

"Emily's not like that."

"Fuck me." Brandon ran his hands through his hair in exasperation. "Do you need tips on how to get into her knickers, Ry? 'Cos I can help you. I could show you, if you like. Maybe she's into that?" Brandon wiggled his eyebrows and Zak laughed. Finn just shook his head.

"And scare the girl away before I've hit the jackpot?" I leaned forward. "I don't need to fuck the truth out of her. I do things differently."

"That's not what I've heard." Brandon was seriously starting to piss me off.

"I told her to ask him about the Rotherham account," I said, thinking that'd wipe the smug smile off his face. Considering he was one of my best friends, had been for years, he could really grate on me.

"You did what?" He stood up, coming to stand over me. That smug smile had definitely gone, but it'd been replaced with a grimace. "Are you fucking suicidal, mate? He'll know it's us that got to her. Shit, all this will have been for fucking nothing."

"No, it won't."

"How do you know? Jesus, mate, you're really ballsing this up. I knew I should've taken the reins." He was pacing the living room now, wearing a hole in Zak's carpet.

"Like I said, I'm doing things my way. She doesn't take any bullshit." Zak nodded along as I spoke. "She'll come to me when she gets what I need. I know she will."

"I hope for your sake she does, 'cos if Daddy Winters gets wind of this, he'll fucking crucify us."

Brandon sank back down onto the sofa and glared over at Zak. "Have you found anything else online?"

"I can see deposits were made into the account, but the bloody firewalls are ridiculous. I can't catch a break. I've got no idea where it's all coming from. Let's hope Em comes up trumps for us."

"And the accident? This shit has gotta be connected in some way," Brandon said, and we all felt ourselves tense up. I hoped to God we were wrong. I hoped for Emily's sake we were, but I doubted it.

"Listen, I'm telling you now, the softer approach is working with Emily."

Zak laughed. "Softer? You treated her like shit at the party. If that's softer to you, I'd hate to see you go hard on her."

"I think hard is what she needs," Brandon piped up again.

"My way." I gritted my teeth as I spoke. "This is going my way. If any one of you wants to question me on this again, I won't be as understanding. Do you hear? This is not up for discussion."

"I agree with Ryan." Finn spoke out in my defence. "Emily's more like Effy than Liv. You won't get anywhere if you bulldoze her. She's a good girl."

I knew there was a reason I liked Finn so much. He might be quieter, but when he spoke, he made sense. A lot more sense than any of us sometimes.

"Well, you can't deny the ball is rolling now. Let's just hope it doesn't become a fucking boulder and crush us all in its path," Zak said, standing up to collect our mugs.

"The only thing getting crushed around here is that corrupt fucker." Brandon looked at me and smirked. "And Ryan's heart, when Emily fucking Winters shits all over him."

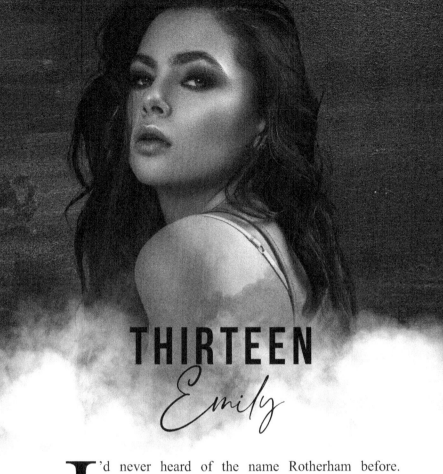

THIRTEEN

Emily

I'd never heard of the name Rotherham before. It'd never been mentioned in our house, not to my knowledge, anyway. I googled it, but nothing jumped out at me. Was Ryan playing more mind games? Or was there more to it? My dad was away at Westminster for a few more days, so I couldn't ask him yet. I would though. When I needed to know something I was like a dog with a bone.

Two days after our bonfire fiasco, I got a call from Ryan's dad to tell me my car was ready to be collected. He offered to send Ryan round with it and drop it off, but I refused, telling him I'd be over later. I took a cab into town, and when we pulled up on their forecourt, I couldn't see Ryan's van. I paid the cab driver and headed into the office. Sean, Ryan's dad, was sitting behind the desk and his face beamed when he saw me.

"Emily, it's so lovely to see you again," he said, holding out his hand to shake mine. "Ryan will be disappointed he missed you. He's at an auction this afternoon with our other mechanic, Kieron. They won't be back for hours."

I grinned back, feeling some of the tension ebb away, knowing I wasn't going to be facing another stand-off. I also felt kind of disappointed. As much as he wound me up, I liked the way he put fire in my belly. He always made me challenge myself; stand up for myself.

"That's okay. I'm sure we'll catch up another time. Do you have paperwork for me to sign?"

He busied himself looking through papers on his desk. His filing systems looked like they were straight out of the nineteen-eighties. I noticed another young guy walk in from the back and when he saw me, he smiled.

"Hey, anything I can help you with?" The guy came over then leaned against the desk, giving me the once over.

"Back off, son," Sean said forcefully. "This is Ryan's girl. The last thing I want is another one of my sons missing from around my table because of your wandering eyes."

I just stood there with my mouth hanging open, probably looking like a demented fish.

Ryan's girl?

I was so taken aback by his comment I couldn't even speak.

"I'm Connor," the guy said with a sparkle in his eyes and he held his hand out to shake mine. "Ryan's older brother, but then you probably already knew that."

No. I knew nothing about Ryan's family. I'd only met his dad days ago. Had I stepped into some freaky Hardy twilight zone?

"I'm Emily," I said feeling stunned.

Sean looked between us both as Connor held my hand for slightly longer than was necessary. "You can let go of her now." He tutted at his elder son and then thrust some papers in front of me and gave me a genuine, heart-warming smile. "Sign there, my love."

I took the pen and signed, then got my credit card out ready to pay.

"No charge," Sean stated abruptly.

"What? But I want to pay my way."

He chuckled. "No. No charge. Just keep my son happy." Then he winked and shoved the paperwork into an overstuffed drawer.

I frowned. I had no idea what was going on. I didn't like accepting freebies, not when they came under dubious circumstances like this, and to be honest, I had no clue what to say back, so I nodded and kept quiet. I didn't think screwing up my face and telling him, "As if. Your son's a bloody psycho," was the right response.

Sean sighed then looked up at me again. He had my car keys in his hand, but he held onto them a little longer and said, "Can I show you something?"

"Err, yeah, sure."

He stood up and opened the hatch that separated the office from where I stood. "He'll probably bite my head off for showing you this, but then again, maybe not, seeing as it's you."

These Hardy men sure liked their cryptic conversations.

I followed Sean as he beckoned me into the office, then led me out the back and across their outdoor workspace towards an outhouse at the bottom of their premises. He pulled the metal door open and nodded his head inside.

"This is Ryan's workshop. For his cars."

We stepped inside, and Sean clicked the lights on.

"Wow!" The car sat in the middle of his workshop wasn't fully assembled, but it already looked like something that was out of this world.

"He made that. Designed it and built it from scratch. Even welded the chassis himself. It's amazing, isn't it? Kieron and Connor help him with the donkey work, but he does all the main stuff. He's a prodigy, my son."

Sean stood to the side with his arms folded, looking on proudly as I circled the silver piece of art in front of me. That's the only way I could describe it; art.

"He gets commissioned to make them. He's making quite a name for himself." Sean rubbed his chin in thought. "He's too good for this place, but then you already know that."

I nodded, stunned once again into silence.

"I've told him he needs to go into engineering or be out there designing cars for the big companies. Not stuck in here with me day in, day out. He's got talent, my lad. Real talent."

He pointed to the back wall and I wandered over to find polaroids of other cars he'd made, pinned up on a corkboard.

"These are amazing, Sean. You're right, more people need to know about this."

I glanced down at his notes and drawings scattered across his makeshift desk; numbers and mathematical calculations that looked like hieroglyphics to me were written all over them. That's when I noticed another polaroid sticking out from underneath the pile of papers. I slid it out and my breath caught in my chest. It was a picture of me, taken at the warehouse party a couple of weeks ago. That damn white dress stood out like a sore thumb amongst all the darkness. In the photo I was standing by the doors leading downstairs, where I'd run into Ryan and Brandon in the fight room. I'd had no idea Ryan had spotted me before then. In fact, I had no idea why he was taking pictures of me at all.

I slid it back where I got it from and turned to face Sean, hoping he hadn't seen it too. Suddenly, I felt uncomfortable being here, like I was intruding on something that I shouldn't. Secrets I hadn't earned. Lies I had yet to uncover.

"He's a good kid," Sean added as if he'd read my mind and wanted to smooth things over for his wayward son. "I know of all people, he wouldn't mind me sharing this with you, but he's so private. Even I'm not allowed back here normally."

"I'm glad you showed me. I won't say you did." I smiled at him and his shoulders relaxed.

"I'm glad he's found you, Emily. I've noticed a difference in him these past few weeks. It's like he's got his spark back."

I knew I couldn't take credit for that, but I didn't want to burst Sean's bubble. That spark he'd seen in his son came from the revenge he was out to get and the lifestyle he led. Not me.

Sean carried on, oblivious. "He took it harder than any of them when his mum died. He's the youngest of my lads, and yet, he's always been the one to step up, the carer. I don't know what I'd do without him." Sean shook his head as if he was shaking away bad thoughts and smiled at me, holding my keys out to me as he did.

"Thanks, Sean." I took the keys from him and then I don't know why, but I hugged him. He probably thought I was a complete weirdo, but I couldn't help myself. I liked Sean. He was what a real dad should be. He was light years away from my father, and in a way, I was jealous. Ryan might have gone through the heartbreak of losing a parent, and I wouldn't wish that on anyone, but he'd lucked out with Sean.

"Come round for dinner one night," he said, hugging me back and planting a fatherly kiss on the top of my head. "I'll tell Connor to behave. We'd all like to get to know you better."

"Maybe." I pulled away and sighed. I'd have liked to have had a father like Sean, and it made me sad to think I'd never have that. The closeness and ease of being so familiar. Unconditional love. I could've built a thousand cars and my father would never have looked at me with the pride that Sean did.

"Tell Ryan I stopped by," I added, feeling a little guilty. As much as I liked Sean, I knew by leaving that message it'd rile Ryan up, and I didn't care. If anything, I wanted it to. Ruffling his feathers was becoming my new favourite pastime.

***

Friday evening rolled around, and at about eight, my father came through the door. His driver carried his bags through and my dad went straight into the living room, calling out my mother's name. Not mine. He wasn't here to see me.

I wandered over to the doorway and watched them hug and kiss. I don't know why she didn't just go to Westminster with him when he was working. She didn't do that much when she stayed back here. Only shopping, hair appointments, coffee mornings, and getting on my back about sorting out my future.

I gave them another few minutes alone together then

sauntered in to cast my shadow on their idyllic little reunion. Dad came over to hug me, but I didn't feel any warmth there. He was good at playing a part, putting on a show. It was his job.

"Got any further with those university applications, Emily?" No, *how are you?* No, *did you miss me? Because I missed you.* I think he just wanted another soundbite for his campaign. *Look, here's my daughter, the future… Please insert whatever upstanding and highbrow profession you like here.*

"I'm still looking. I haven't decided what I want to do yet. I do have a gap year to finalise things. There's no rush."

"You know, I have ties to Oxford and Cambridge. I don't know why you won't let me use them. It'd make life so much easier."

Not for me it wouldn't. I didn't want to owe my future to one of my father's associates. I'd do this all on my own.

"And another thing, Emily…" He frowned at me like he was getting ready to read me the riot act. "I had a call from the breakdown company the other day. Something about responding to a call out and you not being there. Is that a thing now? Making prank calls about your car breaking down?"

He wasn't happy. His face was bright red, and he looked at me like I'd committed armed robbery or something. Thing was, I was as shocked as he was. Hadn't Ryan done the necessary calls and paperwork or something?

"I have absolutely no idea what you're on about. My car was collected. It's been fixed. No bloody prank calls were made."

"Language, Emily!" my mother scolded. "She's right, though. Emily actually sorted it all out herself." Mum said it like I'd organised some mammoth feat. It was a broken-down car for God's sake.

"Whatever. I'm not a kid. I don't do prank calls. Give me some credit."

"It's probably an oversight on their part," Dad replied, not wanting to give any more time or effort to something which was obviously insignificant in his life. "You can't get good staff these days."

I plonked myself down onto the sofa and let them wander off, caught up in their own little world. I wanted to ask my dad about the account Ryan had questioned me on, but now wasn't the right time. I didn't have to wait too long though. About two hours later, my dad was in his study going over his post and emails, so I let myself in and closed the door quietly behind me.

"Something I can help you with?" he said, looking over his glasses at me. I felt like I was in the headmaster's office. I wasn't comfortable at all, but I was intrigued. I also wasn't afraid to push myself forward and ask questions I wanted answers to.

"I wanted to ask you about something." My dad flicked his hand and motioned for me to sit down in the chair in front of his desk, but he carried on reading something on his computer screen like I wasn't there. "I heard something and I… I thought you could tell me what it is." I didn't even know what I was asking about. So, I decided to jump in at the deep end. "What's the Rotherham account?"

My dad's head jerked towards me and the fear in his eyes burned like flames from hell, and then, as if a switch had been flicked in his brain, he masked the fear with suspicion, throwing daggers of distrust my way.

"Where did you hear that name?"

I stuttered and shook my head. "I heard someone mention it."

"Who? Tell me? Where the fuck did you hear that name?" The fact my whiter-than-white father was swearing told me everything I needed to know. He was pissed.

"Maybe one of your campaign managers or P.R. people mentioned it? I don't know. What is it, Dad?"

"It's nothing. Nothing for you to be delving into." He narrowed his gaze at me in an accusatory manner. "Have you been going through my things? Did you come in here while I was gone? I swear to God, if you've been meddling in things that don't concern you…"

The guilt painted all over his face made me even more curious to find out what the hell was going on.

"I haven't been snooping, if that's what you think." I threw a look of disgust his way and pushed myself up out of the chair. "Forget I said anything."

I wouldn't forget though. That name had got a reaction from him and I needed to know why. As I reached the door and opened it to leave he called out after me.

"Stay out of business you know nothing about, Emily. And don't ever say that name in this house again. Do you hear me?"

I nodded, but inside I was primed and raring to go. There was a story there and I was gonna find out what it was.

***

It was two in the morning, and my house was deadly silent. I creaked the door to my parents' bedroom open and saw them both asleep. Without making a sound, I crept down to his office and when I got to the door I turned the handle, surprised to find it was unlocked. I went over to his desk and tried a few drawers, but they were all bolted shut. I headed over to his filing cabinets, but again they were closed, and I had no idea where the keys were. The only thing left was his computer. I fired it up and when it asked me for the password I typed in a combination of Danny's name, mine and then finally my mother's. Third time lucky. I should've known he'd chose my mother's name for his password. How original.

I opened a few folders, but nothing stood out to me and I had no idea what I was supposed to be looking for. So, I clicked on the search bar and typed in Rotherham. A folder came up straight away and inside were documents, spreadsheets and other information that pertained to some kind of bank account. It appeared to be a foreign account and I didn't recognise any of the names that'd made deposits or withdrawals. But the amounts were big. Huge. The total on the whole account had more digits than I'd ever seen on a bank statement. Eight figures to be exact. How the hell did my father have access to that kind of money? Was it his money? It obviously wasn't something he wanted anyone finding out about, especially me.

I grabbed my phone out of my dressing gown pocket and took a few photos of the statements. I had a feeling this was going to be something I'd want to keep evidence of. Definitely something to look into further. Was this money laundering? Or was it something worse? Whatever it was, even the mention of the name had my father spooked. So I knew that could only be bad news for me and my family.

Whatever this was, I knew it was just the tip of the iceberg.

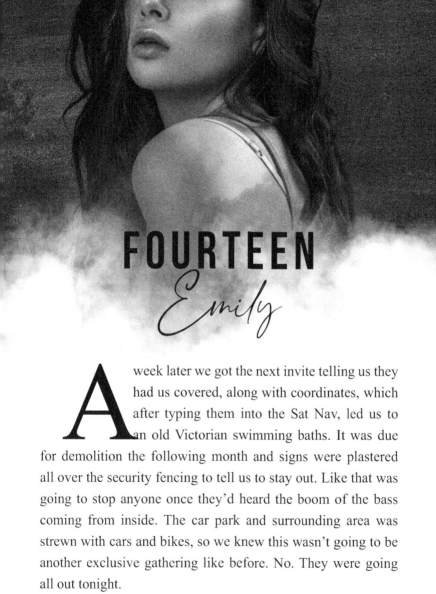

FOURTEEN
Emily

A week later we got the next invite telling us they had us covered, along with coordinates, which after typing them into the Sat Nav, led us to an old Victorian swimming baths. It was due for demolition the following month and signs were plastered all over the security fencing to tell us to stay out. Like that was going to stop anyone once they'd heard the boom of the bass coming from inside. The car park and surrounding area was strewn with cars and bikes, so we knew this wasn't going to be another exclusive gathering like before. No. They were going all out tonight.

There were no floodlights outside signalling Finn's whereabouts like before. But the streetlights in this part of town weren't too bad, so we didn't have to take our lives into our hands picking our way through the debris to get to the building. Well, unless you countered in the fact that multiple signs told us the site was unsafe and displayed hazard warnings wherever we looked.

"Do you think the building itself is safe for this?" Effy asked, looking around her like she expected someone to jump out at any moment.

"It'll be fine. They always put those warnings around disused places like this. They want to keep squatters out." Liv pulled the fencing to the side to let us pass through, then I took over on the other side and held it open for her. Once I let go, the metal pinged back into place.

"Squatters and stoners. How long do you think it'll be before they shut this party down tonight?" I asked.

Liv shrugged. "On a normal day, I'd say give it an hour. But tonight there's a local derby across town. City and United. I think the police will be concentrating their resources that way, don't you? These lads aren't stupid. They know the best time to strike."

I felt that familiar tingle of excitement, hearing the music and shouts coming from inside. I also felt trepidation. My intrigue for these four boys was growing by the day, and yet, the closer I got each time I met them, the more confused I became. It was like trying to hold water in your hands or feel the flicker of the flames. You could see it, feel how it affected you, but you couldn't ever truly understand it, because the minute you thought you had it figured out, it altered, moved, reconfigured, and everything you knew was turned upside down.

I knew they'd be here tonight. It was their party, after all. I also knew they'd want to taunt me, ask me questions I had no answers to. Play with me like a tiger with its prey. If Danny were here, he'd have gone mad at me for engaging in their crazy cat and mouse games. But I liked the adventure. It was like a puzzle I had to unravel.

We saw the same security guy on the door from the warehouse party and showed him our mobile phone messages, which doubled as our ticket to the other side. He stamped our hands and stepped back to let us through, taking our payment as we each passed by. The lobby area was rammed, packed full of people hanging around, singing, dancing, drinking, and smoking. The sweet smell of weed hit me and I grabbed Effy's arm, pulling her closer to the music. Liv followed behind and when we got through the crowds and into the main dance area we all stood to the side to take a moment.

There was a swimming pool, which would've been filled with bathers many years ago. Now, it was drained dry with porcelain tiles hanging off the sides and pot-holes on the floor. Not that it bothered anyone here. The pool was being used as the dance floor. How any of them would get out if there was an emergency was anyone's guess. The deep end came way over their heads, but they didn't seem to mind. The novelty of dancing in a swimming pool with no water was probably highly appealing to them. Quirky. The green algae that'd be staining their shoes and clothes didn't quite do it for me though.

Zak had his D.J. set on the side of the pool at the deep end. Strobe lights danced across the room, giving it a creepy, electric vibe. Zak was in his element, spaced out and focused solely on the tunes he was playing. I glanced around, but I couldn't see any of the other boys. I recognised a few people from school, but no one really stood out.

"Shall we dance?" Liv asked, walking over to the steps and lowering herself into the dance pit.

"You coming, Em?" Effy tapped my elbow in question.

"I wanna explore. This place is amazing and freakishly weird." The gothic ceiling over the pool made it feel like we were in a vault. The black, wrought-iron arches towered over us and hinted at the grandeur or yesteryears. The finest architecture meets urban decay. I bet Finn was in his element tonight.

"You gonna go rogue on us again?" Effy said smiling. "I'm joking. Go and explore. You know where to find us when you're done." She turned round and lowered herself into the pool-dance area next to Liv and gave me a little wave.

I didn't know how safe or stupid an idea it was to wander around here on my own, but I was never one to listen and I was starting to realise I didn't like being told what to do either. Not anymore. Ryan Hardy, all those boys, had awoken something in me that I didn't want to ignore. Curiosity killed the cat. Must be why they have nine lives.

I pushed my way through the crowds and towards the stairs that led to what used to be the changing rooms. The musky damp mildew smell was also laced with sweat. It was so gross it made me miss the sickly sweet smell of the weed from the entrance, but I powered through. I could see a sea of bodies further down the tiled corridor and I knew exactly what they were here for. The adrenaline surged through me as I moved deeper into the throng of people. Zak had his congregation gathered upstairs. Finn was off somewhere creating magic, but here was where

I'd find Brandon and Ryan. This was their domain. The seedy underworld of fighting.

I managed to force my way into a room that was packed full of men and women, all ready to witness something mind-blowing. After what Chase had said about Ryan setting up the betting scams, I expected to find him in here, but I didn't. Three guys I didn't recognise were taking bets and money was being handed over left, right and centre. There were odds being called out, but it meant nothing to me. This room was dingy and musty, dark and depraved. It gave me feels right out of the Victorian England it'd been built in. Where morals were loose, men were corrupt and only the strongest survived.

I noticed a few of the men glance my way, looking me up and down and spending a little too long on my chest. I'd worn tight skinny jeans and a tight cropped vest top, but my boobs weren't that out there. I looked down, ready to adjust myself just in case and I saw a familiar muscular tattooed arm snake its way around my waist.

"I can't believe you came all the way down here to watch me fight. Are you my lucky charm?" Brandon breathed into my ear as he spoke in a low, and what was for him probably seductive manner. He ran his other arm around my middle and pulled me into him, burying his face into my hair and taking a deep breath.

Being held against him like this I could truly appreciate how solid he was. He was like a machine; hard, tense and ready to go. But he didn't give me butterflies like Ryan did. Having Brandon cocoon me like this just made me bristle with irritation. He had no right to put his hands on me and I wasn't here to see him. Not in the way he thought, anyway. Sure, I wanted to see him fight. I was curious. But I wasn't here to catch his attention.

My senses were on red alert, waiting for someone else.

I grabbed his hands to move them off me and he laughed.

"Saving yourself for after? Do I get the prize when I win?"

"What prize?" I snapped back and tried to turn my head to look at him, but he was so close I could barely move.

"You." He chuckled to himself. I don't know why, he wasn't funny. Then he leaned in and planted a kiss on the side of my neck.

"Back off, Brandon. I'm not interested," I said through gritted teeth.

"I like it when you fight me," he whispered. "But you've seen the way I fight, little Winters. You've gotta know by now, I always win."

"Not me," I said, keeping my head high and my body stiff.

"I'll win you round eventually." He loosened his grip on me and then he kissed the top of my head. "Like I said, I always win." He came to stand in front of me and waggled his eyebrows like he expected me to giggle or melt into his arms. I kept my expression neutral and looked straight through him. "Ooo that's cold, Winters." And then he laughed at himself, again. "Cold. Winters. See what I did there?"

I rolled my eyes. He had the bantering skills of a seven-year-old.

"I would laugh at your feeble attempt at humour, but I'm sure you have enough girls around you who fake it. You don't need another one."

He threw his head back and laughed. "No need to fake anything with me, baby. I'm the real deal."

Then he stalked away, high-fiving and patting people on the back as he did. I watched him swagger towards the hay bales that'd been set up to create a makeshift boxing ring. He was like a messiah they all made way for. A God that commanded an audience but gave the clear message that they needed to stay back.

Noticing I was watching him, he winked at me, then took his T-shirt off and stood there in his jeans, taking deep breaths and getting himself into the zone. His chest was ripped and covered in tattoos, and he flexed his muscles and jumped on the spot, limbering up for his fight. He rolled his head and shook his arms out, then nodded to a guy to the left of him, who handed him a bottle of water. There were no boxing gloves or rings for this fight though. This was raw, untamed, bare-knuckle fighting. If you took a hit, you didn't dare go down. Going down meant you'd never get back up. This was dog-eat-dog.

I could feel the ripple of tension in the air as Brandon's opponent entered the room. Then I felt heat at my back again, only this time, my body melted from the iceberg it'd been literally minutes ago, into a pool on the floor, and I felt myself lean into him before he'd even spoken.

"I thought I told you, you don't belong here." Ryan stood behind me, his breath fanning the side of my face as he spoke. I took a deep breath in, inhaling his scent that swirled around me. Like a drug, it calmed my shredded nerves and made me sigh instinctively. "Keep making little noises like that and I'll throw you over my shoulder and get you the hell out of here before you cause any more trouble."

"I'm not the one causing trouble," I said, nodding over to where Brandon was standing, psyching out his opponent. He was wearing a ridiculous grin and his eyes were wide, like he was trying to appear even crazier than he was. He really didn't need to try so hard. Any fool could see he was a bloody psycho. He took two steps forward, forcing himself into the other guy's space and then slammed his forehead against him, saying something threatening to him under his breath. The other guy pushed him off and turned to his crew, laughing. All the while, Brandon stayed focused and didn't flinch.

Ryan put his arm around me and placed his hand over my stomach, pulling me into him like Brandon had done and I gasped. I certainly didn't feel irritated this time. No, I felt hot and bothered and found my concentration had been pulled away from the build-up of the fight, like he'd lassoed me and tethered me to him. He made every nerve in my body spark and all I could focus on was him, his breathing, the beat of his heart that matched my own. I turned my head to the side, not quite sure what to say, but then I noticed what'd made Ryan react the way he did. Chase Lockwood stood at the doorway, staring straight at us, but he didn't look happy. He looked pissed off. I glanced up at Ryan, and sure enough, he was glowering back over at Chase, goading him. Daring him to come over and challenge him in some way. Chase shook his head in disgust and moved his attention to Brandon.

"Are you going to piss on me too?" I pretended to sound unaffected by him, but I didn't make any effort to move his hand or move away. Why would I? I liked feeling like this; a little wild and reckless. Not to mention, I was probably in a position most girls at this party would want to be in. In Ryan Hardy's arms. Damn, my body was a traitor. Shit, my mind was joining forces too. I was becoming way too compliant for my own good.

"Only if you're into that, princess," he said laughing quietly to himself.

"Gross." It was official, my mind was mush and I had no witty comebacks. Great.

"Why are you here?" he asked, nuzzling deeper into my neck as he spoke. I felt the tips of his fingers slowly brush underneath my top and my skin prickled into goose-bumps.

"Because you invited me. I got the text. Or wasn't that meant to go to my phone?" I tried to keep my head clear and not let the gentle strokes he was giving my stomach and hip trick me into falling under his spell.

"I didn't mean in this building. I meant here, in this room. It isn't safe down here." I stilled, feeling a growing warmth inside me from his touch and his words. Hushed, low words meant only for me. He was creating another bubble for us. I liked being in Ryan's bubbles.

"I feel safe." And I meant it. As aloof and cold as Ryan could be sometimes, I felt safe with him by my side. Yes, he'd probably been the one to chase me down that corridor at the warehouse party. But if I was truly honest with myself, I knew he'd never hurt me. He was Danny's friend once and Danny wouldn't befriend someone who was cruel. The fact that Danny had kept a wide berth from Brandon though said it all.

"Well, you shouldn't."

I smiled at his attempt to unnerve me. It'd take a lot more than that. "Shouldn't you be running a scam somewhere, taking bets?"

"I have people to do that for me. I have other *things* on my mind tonight." He rested his chin on my shoulder and the familiarity which he was showing me was breaking down all my defences.

"Like what?" I held my breath waiting for what he'd say

next, willing his fingers to brush further down. God, I was losing my mind here.

"Like, what I'm going to do with you to make you behave." My stomach turned over at the suggestion of him making me behave. Images of the delicious punishments he'd be capable of dishing out flooded my mind and made me blush. Shit, I needed to rein it in. My beating heart was ready to burst free. "Dad told me about your little chat the other day." Ryan moved his hand off my stomach and instantly I missed his warmth. He wound a finger around one of my curls though, keeping that contact between us. I stilled. Had Sean told him about our tour of his workshop too?

"I was collecting my car. I was on my best behaviour." My voice sounded weaker than I'd hoped.

"Oh, I know that. You've been invited to Sunday dinner. You won't be able to make it though." He dropped my curl and in return my heart dropped to the floor.

"Won't I? I do like a nice Sunday roast," I said sounding nonchalant.

"Don't think you'll be sitting at my table any time soon, Winters." And here we were again, with Ryan flipping over to distant and unaffected mode.

"It's your dad's table, not yours. Anyway, what makes you think I'd want to come? I tend to lose my appetite when you're around."

I did, but not for the reasons I was insinuating.

"Nice to know I have an effect on you, *princess*."

"Insects always have an effect on me."

He laughed out loud, earning us a few dirty looks. I tried to drown out the whoosh of my pulse thumping in my ears and focus on the fight that'd started. Brandon was taunting the guy, beckoning him forward and jutting his chin out, begging for a punch. The minute the guy took a swing Brandon dodged it and then threw a punch right into the guy's side, winding him for a few seconds. Brandon was a clever fighter; measured and calculated. He knew how to dance around his opponent, use their weaknesses against them. It was like watching a gladiator teasing a lion or a matador mesmerising the bull. He had that guy right where he wanted him.

"So, did you manage to talk to your dad?" Ryan asked, pulling me back from the action once again.

"I did." If he wanted information, he was going to have to do better than that.

"And?" He wound his arm around me again, as if his body had heard mine and knew exactly what to do to make me talk.

"And what? He didn't tell me anything," I said, keeping my eyes on Brandon the whole time.

"I thought you were a good little spy, Winters. Giving up so soon?"

"I said he didn't tell me. I didn't say I didn't find anything, did I?" I grinned to myself. This game of push and pull was the most fun I'd had in… Well, ever.

"You're sharper than I thought."

Yes. Yes, I am.

I pulled my mobile out of my pocket and tapped my code to unlock the screen. Then I brought up the photos I'd taken of the account transactions. My heart lurched from my chest as Ryan reached for my phone. Both of his arms wrapped around me as he flicked through each image and looked at the photos over my shoulder.

"Fuck," was all he said. I held my breath, feeling like I'd implode at any minute from the intensity of having him in my space like this for so long. "We need to go somewhere quieter. I need to get copies of this."

I went to snatch my phone back, but I wasn't fast enough. Ryan pocketed it and then grabbed my hand and led me out of the room. I didn't need to push my way through this time. People just moved automatically for Ryan. I'd have to start calling these boys Moses soon.

We walked a couple of doors down the corridor and into an old store cupboard that'd been kitted out with bottles of water, towels, and other stuff that Brandon would probably use after his fight. A punch bag was suspended from the ceiling and cigarette butts lay in a dish on a folding table. Ryan closed the door behind us and pointed at a plastic chair and told me to, "Sit," but I stayed standing where I was. Then he took my mobile out of his pocket and proceeded to tap in my security code.

"How the hell do you know my code?"

"I just saw you type it in. I can remember six digits. It's not that hard."

"What are you doing?" I screwed my face up at him as I spoke. As pliable as he'd made me tonight, I didn't like him having control over my phone.

"Sending these photos to my phone so I have a copy." He winked at me then, looking up at me under his floppy fringe. "My number will be in your phone now too, you know, in case you ever need me."

"Why would I need you?"

He huffed and gave me a look that sent sparks flying through my body. Was it a cheeky look? Seductive? I had no idea. My experience with the opposite sex was somewhat limited to say the least, and right now, I felt woefully inadequate.

"Do you have any idea who these people are?" He shook my phone as he spoke, indicating he meant the people from the account.

"I've never heard of them, but I intend to find out." I crossed my arms over my chest defensively. "I'd also like to know why *that* is so important to *you*?"

He shrugged and handed me back my phone.

"Let's just say there are a few wrongs that need to be put right. It's nothing for you to worry your pretty little head about."

"If you want my help, and I will help you if something bad is going down, you need to level with me."

He bit his lip and smirked as he looked at the floor then back up at me. "What would Daddy say if he knew you were being a bad girl?"

"I couldn't give a fuck. My dad is an asshole."

I saw a fire light up behind his eyes and something passed between us. But then, suddenly, the door burst open and Brandon came tumbling through, almost knocking me over, and slumped into the plastic chair. His face was a mess and he had a massive gash over his left eye which was pouring with blood. Even looking at it made me go funny.

"What the fuck happened to you?" Ryan asked.

"Dude had a knuckle duster hidden in his back pocket. Security tonight is shit. How the fuck did he get that past them?"

Brandon was dabbing at the massive gaping wound with a white towel which was rapidly turning crimson. He didn't flinch though. He was so wired from the adrenaline pumping through his veins he couldn't feel a thing; only arrogance and cockiness.

"So, we lost a shit load of money then? You lost the fight, yeah?"

I tutted at Ryan. I couldn't believe I was siding with Brandon, but that was a really shitty reaction to have.

"Like fuck I did. I smashed his head against the wall, broke his nose and knocked the fucker out. He's still lying out there now with half his crew wailing over him. We made a packet tonight." Brandon grinned and the blood coating his teeth made him look demonic.

"Thanks for the concern though. Winters, do I get my prize now?"

Ryan made a grunting noise from across the room and when I looked at him he was doing that whole jaw-clenching fist-pumping thing he seemed so fond of. I think Brandon had had enough fists for one night though.

"You need to go to hospital," I added, trying to break the tense atmosphere.

"Nah. I don't need a doc. You can patch me up just fine, can't you, Winters."

"No! That's not any old cut. That's deep and needs stitches." The thought of touching Brandon Mathers at any time filled me with dread, but even more so when he was gushing with blood and obviously delirious.

"She's right," Ryan said backing me up. "You need to get that seen to."

"I'm not going anywhere. Emily will take care of it." Brandon stated matter-of-fact and threw me a crazy, blood-toothed grin.

"Why me?"

"Because you've got that whole Mother Teresa, Florence

Nightingale vibe going on. Plus, I know your hands will be gentle. You don't want to mess up my pretty face, do you?"

I heard Ryan mutter something about messing it up even more if he didn't pack it in. I shook my head, adamant that Brandon's face was the last thing I'd be tending to. "You're gonna pass out from blood loss in a minute. I'm not touching you."

"I'll do it." Ryan strode forward, grabbing a first aid box from the shelf behind Brandon.

"No, you won't. You can't just put a plaster over that. He'll bleed through any dressings within minutes. He needs to go to a hospital, get stitches, and get a shot too."

"Worried I'll turn rabid?" Brandon said blowing me a kiss.

"You're already rabid, and no, I'm not worried. You know what, if you want an ugly scar for the rest of your life, go ahead. I'm out of here."

I went to leave, but Brandon's voice stopped me.

"Fine. I'll go. But only if you come with me."

I'd really taken leave of my senses, because against my better judgement, I found myself saying, "Okay."

I turned to open the door and heard Brandon say, "Where the fuck are you going?"

I thought he meant me and was just about to roll my eyes at him and give him the fool's answer, accompanied with a question mark over his current sanity, when Ryan piped up.

"Where she goes, I go."

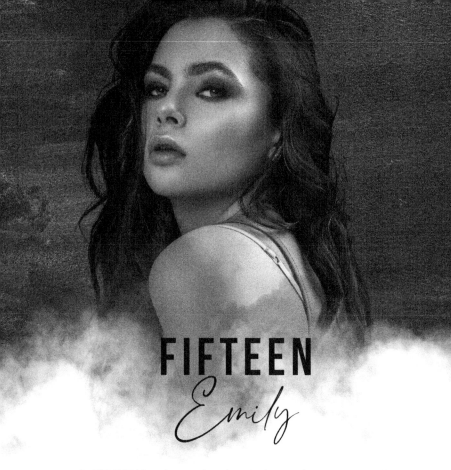

FIFTEEN
Emily

The three of us headed out of the store cupboard and I went to head back up towards the party and out that way.

"Not through there," Ryan said, hooking his hand under my elbow and leading me down the corridor and away from the action. "We don't want everyone seeing. We'll go out the back way."

"Are you driving?" Brandon asked Ryan as he held the blood soaked towel over his eye, but Ryan shook his head and pulled his mobile out of his back pocket.

"I got a lift in with Zak. Maybe Finn could drive us?"

"No chance. Finn's sister dropped us off. Ring Kian. He'll take us."

I didn't know Kian all that well. I'd seen him around school, back when Danny and the others were there, but Kian was a bit of an enigma. Always on the periphery of the group and never quite fitting in. He obviously thought a lot of these guys though, because he answered on the first ring and told Ryan he'd meet him outside without any hesitation.

When we got outside, we saw the car headlights shining right at us and Kian stood leaning against the driver's side door.

"What the fuck happened to you?" Kian's eyes bugged out of his head as he spoke. They obviously weren't used to seeing Brandon take a hit, judging from their reactions tonight.

"Don't worry Ki, the other guy is way worse. I think the fucker is still passed out in there." Brandon gave him a glare and jumped into the front seat, slamming it shut.

"Good to know." Kian nodded at Ryan and me as we both got into the back. I shifted myself along the seat to let Ryan get in after me. I was thankful Brandon chose the front. I didn't fancy riding with him back here. The guy freaked me out on a good day and this was not a good day.

Kian started the car, then glanced back at me. "You're Emily, right?"

I nodded.

"Nice to meet you, Emily. I'm Kian, or Ki. Whatever's fine." He tapped the side of his forehead in salute and then put the car into gear and sped off like he was in training for NASCAR. I went to grab the door handle for support, but Ryan put his arm around my shoulder and pulled me into him.

I didn't like being in other cars, not after what'd happened to Danny, but I guess Ryan sensed that because he whispered, "You're okay. He's a good driver. Nothing bad is gonna happen." I was tense but having him near did help somewhat.

By the time we pulled up outside the hospital my body felt exhausted from being strained and stiff with the tension.

"I should've driven," Ryan said to me. "It's still raw, isn't it?" He must've felt how unnerved I was.

"My brother, my best friend, was killed in a car accident. It's always gonna be raw."

Ryan gave a sad nod and squeezed my knee. I didn't want to wallow in anyone's pity. So I turned and opened the door, getting out and leaving Ryan's hand to drop to the seat.

"Let's get this over with. Get you checked in and sorted out. The less time we spend here the better. I've seen enough hospitals this year." I strode over to the double doors with purpose and the boys followed me. When the staff saw Brandon, they ushered him through to a cubicle and we followed. Kian stayed in the waiting room. He agreed to fill out the paperwork as best he could.

An older nurse in her fifties came bustling into the cubicle and went straight to Brandon, pulling the towel off his wound and clucking her tongue as she did. She looked like the motherly type, all soft curves and sympathy, but when she spoke, she was anything but.

"Jesus wept, what have you done, you stupid boy? Been fighting?" She side-eyed Ryan then tutted back at Brandon.

"The other guy came off worse," Brandon said, trying to give her a cheeky grin and twinkle his eyes. It just made him look like he was having problems focusing.

"I'll look forward to patching him up later then. It's not like

I have anything better to do here, in a hospital, meant for sick people."

Ryan muttered something about Brandon being sick in the head and she whipped her head around.

"If you've got something to say, pretty boy, spit it out. I've got no patience for time wasters. If all you're gonna do is mumble in the corner, you can get out."

I'd never seen Ryan be put in his place so abruptly.

"Sorry, ma'am," he said and sank back into his chair, staring over at me. Did he expect me to dive into this little shit-show and back him up?

"And you?" She turned her attention to me now. "What's a lovely girl like you doing with two reprobates like these on a Saturday night? Haven't you got anything better to do with your life? If you were my daughter, I'd tan your backside and ground you for a month."

"I thought nurses were supposed to be compassionate," Brandon said before I could respond. "I think I want to take a reshuffle."

"This isn't *Wheel of Fortune*, Rocky. You don't get to pick and choose who you see. If you want me to patch this up without leaving a shitty scar behind, you'd better show a bit more respect. They don't call me the queen of stitches for nothing."

"Cool title… If you live in a prison," Brandon replied.

She laughed a full, loud belly laugh at him and then smirked. I could tell she was starting to warm to him. I think she liked Brandon's banter.

"I think I'll move us to a private room for the stitches. The big boys always scream the loudest. Can't have you scaring the kids away." She chuckled and led us out of the cubicle and down corridor.

"I won't scream. I'm no pussy," Brandon said, begrudgingly getting off his chair and following her.

"That remains to be seen, boy. In my book, pussies don't fight and end up in hospital on a Saturday night, dragging their best friend and their girl along for the ride."

"I'm not-"

"She's not his girlfriend," Ryan interrupted me. The nurse, Constance it said on her name tag, turned and gave both Ryan and me a pointed stare.

"Far be it from me to question whatever weird arrangement you youngsters have going on."

I huffed. What the hell was Constance insinuating? I felt Ryan link his hand with mine. He didn't like her jumping to conclusions either, if his hand holding was anything to go by. Brandon looked back at us and then down to our joined hands and huffed his own annoyance.

"What can we say, Constance? We're into some weird, kinky shit."

"Brandon!" I snapped. "Speak for yourself." And I felt the blush rise up from my chest, over my neck and onto my face.

Constance laughed again. "I'm fifty-nine years old, boy. Nothing you say or do can shock me. I've seen it all."

We made our way into the private room and Constance ushered Brandon into a seat. I dropped Ryan's hand and stood to the side. I felt awkward and didn't know what to do with myself. Maybe I should've stayed behind in the waiting area with Kian?

Constance busied herself prepping things for the stitches and cleaning the wound. Brandon hissed a few times, but he wasn't about to show any weakness. Then she held a syringe up, tapping it, ready to numb the area for him, and Brandon's face went ghostly white.

"What the fuck is that for?"

"Anaesthetic," she said without looking at him. "Unless you want me to stitch that with nothing but a piece of wood for you to bite down on."

"I think I'd prefer the wood." We all looked at Brandon as he sat up as straight as a rod, glaring at the syringe like it was an AK-47.

"Great. You're scared of needles." Constance tutted again and forced her way forward regardless, aiming the needle at Brandon's forehead, ready to inject around the cut. Brandon snorted and then slumped in the chair.

He'd passed out.

Big bad Brandon Mathers, bare-knuckle boxer and all-round psycho was scared of needles and had passed out in nurse Constance's chair.

"Oh my God. He's out cold." I gasped, holding my hand over my mouth in shock.

"He does this all the time. He can't do needles." Ryan shrugged.

"And to think I called him Rocky." Constance laughed. "More like Mr T."

"That was planes, not needles." Ryan rolled his eyes.

"Oh, yeah." Constance chuckled and then shrugged her shoulders. "Better get this injected before he wakes up then."

A few seconds later, Brandon came round, but he was groggy and didn't put up a fight. Constance worked her magic, cleaning him up and finishing the stitches neatly. To watch her work was mesmerising. All the while she hummed along to a

Lionel Richie song playing on the radio in the corner.

"Make yourself useful, boy," she said to Ryan, who was leaning against the wall, biting his nails. "Go and ask the front desk to send a porter down here so they can wheel him out."

"I don't need a bloody chair. I can walk just fine." Brandon went to stand up and almost passed out again. Constance pushed him down into the seat by his shoulders and huffed.

"You're not ready to walk yet," she said. "Give it a few more minutes. People are always unsteady on their feet after an episode like yours."

"I didn't have a fucking episode," he growled back. "It was hot in here, that's all."

"Whatever you say, love," Constance said, giving Ryan the nod to do as he was told.

Ryan pushed off the wall and threw me a look, then left. I watched Constance clear away the instruments and then wrap Brandon's head up carefully with her bandages. When she was finished she came over to stand by me, with her back to Brandon.

"He's a handsome boy. They both are." She gave me a knowing smile. "They both love you, don't they?"

I stuttered. "They aren't my boyfriends. They don't... We don't..."

She laughed and then sighed, giving me a stern, motherly look. "Either they'll break your heart, or you'll break both of theirs. If you want my opinion... Choose one and stick to it. You can't keep them both dangling. That shit never works out. Trust me. I'd know. You'll lose them both."

I frowned. "I'm not with Brandon. I don't feel like that about him," I whispered, so he wouldn't overhear.

She nodded. "And the other one?"

"It's… Complicated."

"Uh huh. Complicated and exciting? I was young too once. Be careful. You're heading for a whole heap of heartache if you keep this up. I saw the doe-eyes they were both giving you. For your own sake, pick one and make sure the other knows."

At that moment, Ryan came back into the room, followed by a porter pushing a wheelchair.

"Cubicles are all rammed tonight, Con. Think we'll have to park him in a corridor or the waiting room until he's good to go," the porter said.

Constance patted a grim-faced Brandon on the shoulder and smiled. "He's a tough-nut. He won't need a bed. You could park him in the car park and he'd be all right."

Brandon grunted in agreement.

Ryan and the porter managed to help Brandon into the chair. All the time, Brandon was swatting them out of the way and cursing them, saying he was fine on his own. And me? I was still stunned from Constance's little outburst and looking between the two boys in front of me.

"Made the right choice?" Constance whispered in my ear. "If you go with your heart, you'll never go wrong."

If I went with my heart, would I be hot-footing it out of this hospital and never looking back? I doubted it. For some reason, these boys were pulling me in. But I always knew one was calling to my heart. I just didn't know if he was playing with it in return.

SIXTEEN
Ryan

Another night, another shit-storm in the life of Ryan Jameson Hardy. I felt like my willpower was dying a slow death. Everything around me seemed to be goading me, egging me on. Making me feel like the control I'd craved was just an illusion. I had no control. Not when every little movement, every throwaway comment or look got my back up. I always knew she made me weak, but I'd been good at fooling myself all these years. Making it look like the pretty little liar didn't affect me. Now, I wasn't so sure she was the liar I'd always painted her out to be. In fact, I knew she wasn't. She'd gone above and beyond tonight, for all of us. She was earning her place in this fucked-up little crew we had. Trouble was, I didn't want to share her, even now.

The porter wheeled Brandon out to the waiting room and I glanced over to see Emily talking to *Nurse Ratched*. Emily looked up at me as they spoke, and a blush coloured her cheeks. Usually, seeing her flustered like that would've spurred me on to up the asshole stakes. But something had changed tonight, and I didn't want to be that asshole anymore. Not for her.

I spotted Zak and Finn sitting in the corner next to Kian, and we parked Brandon up close by.

"Who's doing the close tonight?" I asked, feeling irritable and pissed off. Our parties went on for as long as they needed to, and it was still pretty early. With all of us sat here watching Brandon's ass, there was no one to shut shit down. We couldn't afford to lose money, D.J. equipment, or our reputation.

"Cops came and shut us down," Zak said. "We got everything out in time though. Not everybody, but…" He shrugged. "At least we're good."

I knew that meant he'd closed any bets, collected money and got all our stuff out. We were good for another night.

"Were you there when they showed up?" I asked.

"No. Tom texted us with the tip-off. We cleared the place in good time." He looked at Finn and they both nodded in agreement.

We were lucky to have an ally in Tom. He was a local policeman. A good guy. He'd been a few years above us in school, and I think he liked the underdog. That, and living dangerously. Why else would a cop go out of their way to tip four reprobates like us off when a raid was about to happen? If it wasn't for Tom Riley, we'd have failed years ago.

Brandon continued to whine like a bitch in the corner, complaining about anything and everything. I had no filter and no patience for his bullshit tonight. He soon piped down when he spotted Emily coming over. Even he'd mellowed towards her.

"Hey, Winters. You gonna come and mop my fevered brow?

"Fuck off," she snapped back.

He clutched his heart, trying to be dramatic. "She loves me," he joked, and the others chuckled along. Not me. I was getting tired of his sly digs.

"You look fine to me. Let's go." I stalked towards the door, not even waiting to see if any of them would follow me. I didn't care. Well, I did, but I wasn't about to show it.

When we got to the car park, I glanced back and saw them following a few feet behind. Zak was smirking, and he threw his arm around Emily saying, "You're becoming one of us now, Ems. We'll have to find a job for you. Make it official."

She grimaced and pushed his arm off in disgust. "I don't think so. That sounds like everything I don't want to do with my life… Ever." He thought she was joking. She wasn't. That girl was growing bigger balls by the minute.

She whipped her phone out and started scrolling away. I knew what she was doing, looking for her friend's number so she could get a ride home.

Not happening, princess.

I walked over to Kian and held my hand out. "Gimme your keys."

He fished them out of his pocket and gave them to me without question.

"You go with Finn and Zak. Take Brandon home. I'll drop Emily off." I turned to walk away, but Winters had other ideas.

"I don't think so. I'm calling an Uber."

"Like fuck you are. Get into the damn car, Emily." She rolled her eyes at me and I could tell she was about to argue some more, but she thought better of it and stomped over to the passenger door of Kian's car.

"I suppose I should be grateful. At least this car has a working door." She opened it, got in and then slammed the door shut, sitting back with her arms folded and a sour-ass look on her face.

She was pissed, but I liked that she still did as she was told. The perfect combination of challenge, sass and goddamn sexy attitude that sent a message straight to my dick. The others headed over to Finn's car which was parked nearby, and Brandon shouted over to me. "Go easy on her, mate. Leave something for the rest of us."

Suck my dick, Mathers. It'd be a cold day in hell before I let you anywhere near her.

We drove back to her house in silence. She let out the occasional huff, probably to tell me how fucked-off she was, but I liked the little noises she made. They had the opposite effect on me. When I pulled up outside her house, I shut the engine off and she got out of the car without saying a word.

"Aren't you gonna thank me for the ride home?" I asked, getting out to follow her.

She spun round to face me, standing at the bottom of her drive and scowling. "Thanking you would mean I'm grateful, which I'm not. I was only at that hospital because you and your dumbass friends dragged me there. It wasn't the way I'd wanted to spend my night."

I stopped right in front of her, making sure to stand a few steps too close. I liked pushing her outside of her comfort zone. I liked the way her eyes lit up when I got too near. "I'm sorry it was such a disappointment for you. Maybe I can do something to make up for it?"

"Like what? Blow yourself up? Drive off a cliff? Ooo... The possibilities are endless." She tapped her lip in thought and I stared. I couldn't take my eyes off those plump pink lips of hers. The possibilities were indeed endless, sweetheart.

"You did us all a solid tonight. And I'm not just talking about the hospital." I bent down to look her in the eyes, running my fingers through my hair to give my restless hands something to do. "I never thought you'd go against Daddy like you did. Not for us. Those pictures you took... That was above and beyond. I've underestimated you."

I don't know what came over me, but I reached forward to touch her face, cup her cheek and run my thumb across her bottom lip. She felt so soft, so delicate, and it was killing me how much I wanted to have this girl. Wrap her up, make her mine and never let go.

I leaned forward, expecting her to melt into me for our first kiss. Shit, my heart was beating like crazy. I felt like I'd explode if I didn't kiss her now; lock this down and give her what she wanted. What we both wanted. But no sooner had I moved forward than she took a step back and the look of revulsion on her face had me second guessing everything.

She hated me.

"I didn't do it for you," she spat. "If my dad is into some shady shit, I wanna know. I'll do anything to help. But let's get one thing straight... None of it was for you. I'm doing this for me."

I stood there with my mouth hanging open like a fucking freak as she stepped backwards, away from me, then turned and headed towards her front door. She didn't look back, not even when she shut the damn thing. Just waltzed off like I hadn't just put my whole heart on the line, laid myself bare and fucking crashed and burned spectacularly. Thank God the others weren't here to see it. I'd cracked open the doors to my stone-cold heart for her and what had she done? She'd ripped the bloody hinges off, ransacked it and then walked away, tossing the proverbial match behind her to set fire to the ruins. Only thing was, she wasn't about to destroy me.

Her fire only fanned my flames.

Her demons fired up my own.

And I realised in that moment, Emily fucking Winters was all I'd ever want.

She was it for me.

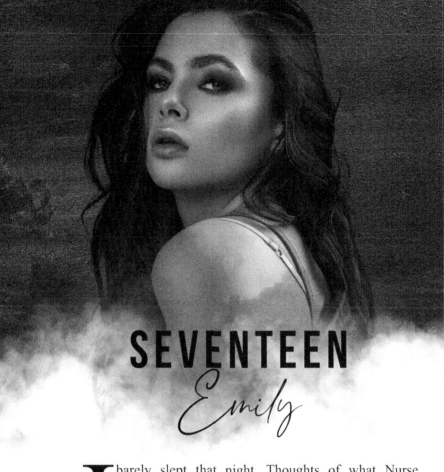

SEVENTEEN
Emily

I barely slept that night. Thoughts of what Nurse Constance had said swirled around in my brain, clouding my judgment and twisting my reasons. Images of Brandon and his wicked intent made my stomach burn with the cloaked insinuations and seedy undertone. But it was Ryan that really consumed me in every way possible.

I never knew where I was with him. Never knew where I stood. One minute, he'd be scaring me or taunting me, the next, I felt sure he was gonna kiss me. I replayed our last conversation over and over again, analysing every look, every word, and don't even get me started on the touches. Ryan touching me had always felt like a shock to the system. But last night, when he put his hand on my cheek and rubbed across my lip, I felt like I was dying and being brought back to life all in one go. It was all too much. Too intense. I couldn't breathe, couldn't focus. It took every last bit of resolve I had to claw myself back and not fall into his trap.

Because it was a trap, right? Why else would a guy like Ryan be teasing a girl like me?

Looking into his eyes and seeing that need, it scared me. I moved away, because it was the only response my lizard brain could conjure up.

Fight or flight.

In a way, I chose both. I walked away from him, but not before giving him a parting shot and putting him in his place. I let him know that I'd made my choice. The choice Constance willed me to make before I left the hospital.

I chose me.

My dad was doing something shady, that wasn't even up for discussion, and I'd find out what it was. But not because Ryan asked me to. I was doing it for me. For my family. I needed to safeguard my own life. When the shit hit the fan, and it would, I wanted to make sure my family weren't in the firing line. I didn't want to put my future on the line, not for anyone. And if my dad was dumb enough to drop the ball and have the likes of the Renaissance men sniffing around his business, then I didn't trust that he'd be able to save me or my mum when push came to shove. I needed to know what was going on.

Where did that money come from?

Knowledge was power, and when the powers in my dad's life came knocking for answers, I wanted to be ready.

***

I was sitting in a local café with my girls, analysing the night before and trying to get my head around what had happened the last few weeks. Things were never dull these days, that was for sure.

"So, you went to the hospital…" Liv sneered as she spoke.

"Yes."

"With Brandon Mathers."

"Yes."

"Why? Don't you hate him?" I wasn't sure how to answer that one. Yes, I did hate him, but I wasn't totally heartless.

"He asked me to and I felt bad. The guy had half his eyebrow hanging off, Liv. What can I say? I had a moment of weakness."

"You're having a lot of those lately where those boys are concerned." She tutted and folded her arms over her chest, letting me know she didn't approve of my actions.

"What's that supposed to mean?" I asked, feeling defensive all of a sudden.

"Nothing. Forget I said anything."

I stirred my latte absent-mindedly and bit my tongue. I knew through Effy that things with Zak hadn't quite gone to plan for Liv. Not to mention, I hadn't been the best friend to either of them recently, but I'd kind of been distracted. It was a weak excuse, but it was the only one I had.

Suddenly, I heard Liv give an "Ooo" sound and I looked up to see Chase Lockwood stroll into the café and wander over to the counter. He gave the waitress a nod and a smile and leaned against the till as he chatted to her. Not a hair was out of place and he had that killer smile painted on just for her. I hadn't told Liv or Effy about my encounter with Chase in the woods at the party. I felt seedy even thinking about it. But I regretted that decision the minute Liv called out his name and beckoned him over to join us.

"What are you doing?" I said, slinking further down into my chair, hoping he'd just wave and move on. I had enough going on in my head without adding Chase Lockwood's bullshit to the mix.

"Ladies. Nice to see you all." Thankfully he didn't pull a chair over to join us, he just stood there grinning.

"How are you, Chase. We haven't seen you since the bonfire. You doing okay?" Liv asked in a flirty manner that made me question what her motives were exactly. After what she'd said about him not being what he'd seemed at the bonfire, I'd assumed she wasn't his biggest fan. But right now, she was acting like she was putty in his hands.

"I'm doing okay, I guess. Things at home are a bit tense. My dad was talking to yours on the phone when I left just now, Em. Sounds like something big is going down."

I shrugged. I didn't know what I was supposed to say to that. My dad had been a small-time investor in some of Chase's dad's businesses, but I didn't think they were that close.

"Sounds like you need a little pick me up, Chase," Liv purred, giving him ridiculous puppy dog eyes.

What was her deal?

He nodded then looked straight at me. "I sure could. Maybe if Em agreed to go out on a date with me that'd give me something to look forward to."

I almost choked on my latte. I gulped it down and looked up at him. I would tell him hell and freezing over had come to my mind, but Chase didn't know I'd heard him that night, and

I didn't feel like airing my dirty laundry in the middle of this coffee shop. Not yet, anyway. He was being so gentlemanly, and it'd just make me look like a bitch.

"I… I can't," I muttered, wiping my hand over the coffee that had splattered over my chin.

"She'd love to go on a date," Liv piped up. Effy gave her the same evil glare as I did.

"Would she? I can speak for myself you know. I'm-"

"Great! You free Friday? Say eight?" He didn't care what I said. He was quite happy to bulldoze his way in via Liv and her couldn't care less attitude.

"No…" I tried to argue.

"Yes. She's free. Pick her up at eight." Liv didn't even look at me and I grabbed her knee under the table to squeeze it and tell her no, but she ignored me.

"I'll see you at eight then, Em."

Chase wandered off with the biggest shit-eating grin on his face, taking his coffee to-go from the waitress and giving her a wink as he went. I'd never realised quite how smarmy he was before. In fact, he took smarmy to a whole new level. I gritted my teeth ready to ask Liv what the fuck she was on.

"What the hell was that for? Why did you do that? I don't want to go on a date with Chase Lockwood. I'm not going."

"Fine, then don't go. If you did go though, it'd give Ryan the kick up the backside that he needs to get his ass into gear."

"What are you talking about?" I didn't like arguing with my friends, but I was ready to go all out on Liv's ass.

"Oh, come on! Ryan is hot for you, Em. And I know you like him too. Maybe, if he gets wind of this date, he might finally do something about it and ask you out himself. Then maybe the rest of us can get a break from hearing about all the dramas between you two."

Oh, hell no.

"What? You need a break from my dramas? Fine. I won't bother you again. But know this, Liv. You're insane. What makes you think-"

I was rudely cut short by Kian, the Renaissance wannabe, who grabbed a chair and plonked himself down at our table. I hadn't even seen him come in. His joining us did nothing to dampen the fire in me that Liv had created by being my un-appointed dating guru though. I wasn't finished with that subject, not by a long shot.

"Wow," he said, looking at each of us in turn. Then he smirked and shook his head. "Chase Lockwood must have a fucking death wish if he thinks he can come in here and ask you out."

"Oh my God. What are you even on about? I'm not going on a date with him. I'm not dating anyone." I was so over this. I felt ready to hunt Chase down and put him in his place. Tell him in no uncertain terms that his dick was never gonna get wet. Not with me, anyway.

"Oh, we know. Ryan shut that shit down years ago."

Say what now?

"Come again?" I sat forward in my chair and screwed my face up.

"Quit talking in riddles, short stack, and tell us what the fuck you're on about," Liv said, getting straight to the point as usual.

"You know… Ryan and the whole 'nobody is allowed to date Emily' thing he kept harping on about at high school. Oh.

Did you three not know about that? Shit. I don't think I was supposed to say anything. On second thoughts, forget I spoke. You didn't see me here."

I threw myself back in my chair, rolled my eyes and let out the biggest sigh of the day. This guy was un-fucking-believable.

Kian went to stand, but Liv grabbed his arm, forcing him back down into his chair. "Not so fast, tiny Tim. We're gonna need you to spill the tea."

"I can't. They're my boys." He grinned like a child that'd been caught stealing cookies and guessed his sweet smile would get him off the hook. Not a chance, dude. Not this time.

"And we are three hormonal teenage girls who can and will make your life hell if you don't tell us exactly what you know," Liv barked back at him. She was immune to his charms. We all were.

"He doesn't have any say over who I date. He never has."

I was so pissed off. I knew they were behind this. They probably sent Kian in on a mind-fuck exercise just to toy with my head a little more. Make gullible Emily think Ryan is a knight in shining armour. Why not? The brother isn't around to deny it. Those boys liked playing me, but I wasn't going to dance to this tune.

"It was my brother, Danny, who warned guys off, not Ryan."

"That's just what he'd want you to believe. Oh shit. I'm gonna go to hell for this. If you ever rat me out, I swear, I will haunt your asses for eternity."

"We have good asses. The pleasure will be all yours. Now spill," Liv said, giving him her best death stare.

"It was never Danny who warned them off. It was Ryan. Ryan's had a thing for you for years, Em. I thought you knew that? When I saw you come out with them yesterday and with you going to the hospital, I figured he'd pulled his head out of his ass and done something about it."

"You're wrong. That makes no sense, at all." Here we go again with the mind games.

"It kind of does. He does look at you like you shit rainbows and unicorns when he thinks you're not looking." Liv spoke like she was jealous, turning her nose up in disgust.

"Liv, that's the shittiest analogy I've ever heard. And he doesn't look at me."

"He does, Em," Effy chipped in. "Even I've noticed it."

"Yep," Kian added like he was one of the girls. "The guy is crazy. Obsessed. Totally and utterly-"

"You can stop now," I said feeling embarrassed, mortified and generally uneasy about all of this.

"If he hears that you're going on a date with Chase Lockwood, of all people, he's going to lose his shit. Like I said, Lockwood must have a death wish."

I wanted this conversation to be over with. I couldn't even think straight.

"No one needs to lose their shit, because I'm not going on any dates. And Kian? I'd prefer it if you didn't tell anyone else about this, especially Ryan."

"Like I'm about to let it slip that I pissed all over his biggest secret."

"For the record, I still don't believe you, but this stays between us. All of it. Understand?"

They all agreed to keep their mouths shut and I sat there, wondering how I was going to avoid Chase Lockwood come Friday night, and how I was ever going to face Ryan again after hearing what Kian had to say.

When Kian finally left with his tail between his legs, probably to report back to his bros, I turned to Liv to let it all out.

"Some friend you are."

"What?" She batted her eyelids like she was the innocent party.

"First, you offer me up to Chase like the sacrificial lamb-"

"Oh, don't be so melodramatic. It's one date. You don't have to marry the guy."

"Jesus, Liv. You sound like my mother. I'll be bloody melodramatic if I want to be. I think I have every right to after you've just pissed all over my life."

"Em, you can just cancel," Effy offered, trying to give a solution that'd avoid an argument.

"I shouldn't have to. I didn't agree to the date in the first place. And second? What the fuck was all that about? The Ryan thing? One minute you're sick of my drama, the next you're causing me a shit load more."

"I didn't cause anything. Oh, boo-fucking-hoo. Emily Winters has such a hard life. She has to live in a massive house, drive a fancy car, get Daddy to pay for everything and if that isn't bad enough, she has two hot guys fighting over her. However will she cope? You know what? I'm done here. You don't like my dose of reality? Then suck it up, buttercup." And with that, Liv sprang up out of her chair and stormed out of the café.

"What the hell crawled up her ass?" I'd sensed she was tense when we'd met up earlier, but I had no idea she'd held that much animosity towards me.

"It's not you." Effy sighed, reaching across the table to rub my arm as I slumped forward feeling despondent. "She didn't mean any of those things she said. They're not true."

"Didn't she?"

"No. She'll regret it in a few hours, but you know Liv, she spcaks before she engages her brain. She's hurting."

"What did I do to hurt her?"

"Not you. Zak. I think she was really into him, and after the bonfire and them hooking up, she thought he might feel the same. He doesn't. We saw him go off with Kelly Hopton last night. He didn't even give Liv a second glance."

Why were guys such dickheads sometimes?

"He didn't spend the night with her, if that helps. I saw him at the hospital later on." I knew it wasn't any consolation. I also knew my original gut-feeling about Zak had been spot on. He was a player. He was not the type of guy you could trust.

"I don't think it would. He's an asshole, Em, but she was heartbroken last night."

"And I wasn't there."

"Even if you had been, you couldn't have done anything to help. I think she's jealous of your friendship with them. They all seem to really like you, even Brandon. I think her stirring up trouble is just a way for her to lash out."

I could understand why Liv felt so pissed off. I just wished she'd told me first, instead of causing waves. None of us knew what these boys were capable of, and now I had to do damage control with Chase and Kian. It was shit I didn't need on top of what my dad was serving up. I needed my friends in my corner, not stabbing me in the back.

"I'll talk to her. She'll probably call you later tonight. You know Liv. She'll be mortified that she's upset you."

I liked Effy's optimism, but I didn't agree. I knew Liv, and it'd take a few days and multiple peace talks for us to smooth this over. It always did when we fought. This time, she felt humiliated by Zak and I was feeling the brunt of her anger. I got it. You hurt those closest to you, and Liv was as close to me as a sister. They both were. I needed to sort my shit out and put an end to all this.

EIGHTEEN
Ryan

"**D**ude, you need your sniper rifle. Mate, he's right there... Fuck..."

Gunshots rang out like we were slap bang in the middle of world war three. I tried my best to fight back, but it was useless. I was getting my ass handed to me on a plate in *Call of Duty*, playing with Brandon over at Zak's place. Fighting in real-life wasn't the only skill Brandon had, he could kick anyone's ass in a game too. I was usually pretty good at holding up my end, but my mind was on other things today. I was distracted by a five-foot-nothing brunette, who was slaying me better than any opponent

I'd ever gone up against.

My feisty little firecracker.

She had me all out of sorts and I liked it. Didn't like it so much last night when she'd burnt my ass, but today I liked the fire she stoked in me. *Call of Duty* just wasn't cutting it.

"Ry, mate. If you're not gonna take this seriously, pass the controller to Finn. You're about as much use as a rice paper condom right now."

I threw the controller to Finn, who caught it mid-air, and I got out of the chair opposite the T.V. to let Finn take my coveted place. Finn wasted no time wading into the game and earning a pat on the back from Brandon. I'd lost interest in it ten minutes ago, so I wandered over to the dining table where Zak had set up his I.T. empire, complete with computers, monitors and God knows what else.

"You found anything?" I asked, flipping through the reams of papers he had spread out on his desk. He rolled his eyes at me and moved the papers out of my way. He didn't like that I was fucking up his well-thought-out filing system.

"Yeah, no. Not yet. I will though. These screenshots and the names, they're a massive help. Em really came up trumps." He tapped his finger on the monitor as if to back up what he was saying, then turned to look at me. "Do you think she'll find anything else?"

"Course she will. She lives with him, doesn't she? If it's there, she'll find it." I had faith in my girl.

"You sure she's not in on this too?" Zak whispered, so Brandon and Finn couldn't hear.

"Not a chance. Whatever all this is…" I gestured around his desk with my hand to make my point, "She has no idea. I trust her."

"I hope for all our sakes she's worth that trust." Zak went back to clicking away, but I didn't like what he said, and I wasn't gonna let him dismiss me that easily.

"She is."

I noticed Brandon look our way and then shake his head. "You still need to keep your wits about you, mate. She might be easy on the eye, but don't let that pretty face fool you. You're not gonna go soft on us are you, Ry?"

Here we go again. Mathers was hooked into our conversation and ready to get in a few digs. He always did where Emily was concerned. She was an Achilles heel for both of us. The thorn in our friendship.

"I know her better than any of you," I argued. "I also know she wants to find out what's going on as much as we do. Why wouldn't she?"

"Because she might lose her allowance and get booted out of that mansion on her ass. You'd be surprised what desperate people are willing to do." Brandon was right. Desperate people did do stupid dumb-ass shit, but not Emily. Her father might be desperate, but not her.

"She's not like that." I folded my arms, squaring my chest to show I wasn't fucking about.

"Damn, you've got it bad, bro." Brandon smirked, then turned back to concentrate on his game and without missing a beat he said, "I think you need to cut her loose. We'll get the answers we need without her."

Zak raised his eyebrow and looked up at me, waiting to see my reaction. I think he expected the fake war from the T.V. to become real at any moment.

"Not gonna happen," I stated. I couldn't make my stance any clearer. I wasn't gonna be told what to do.

"And if she fucks this all up for us? You might need to pick a side, Ryan. When the time comes, make sure you pick the right one." Brandon was deadly serious, but so was I.

"Oh, I will."

I glanced back down to the screen Zak was studying, not having the first clue what I was looking at, but I wanted to move the attention away from Emily. I didn't react well just lately when it came to her. Certainly not as far as these guys were concerned, anyway. They had a habit of riling me up and making me more determined to prove them wrong.

"Do we know what Morgan Rotherham is yet?" I asked Zak, hooking onto a topic I knew would steer us away from my feelings for Emily. "Is it a company? A guy? What?"

The account information Emily had photographed listed the main account holder as a Morgan Rotherham. There was no address. Nothing else that led us any further down that rabbit hole, but the names and numbers we had so far had put us further ahead than we'd ever been.

"No idea. But like I said, I'll find out." Zak carried on tapping away at his keyboard and dismissing me in his roundabout way.

We always knew Winters was a corrupt motherfucker. That's why he'd always tried to take us down and dragged our names through the mud in the press. He hated us. Tried to villainise us in the tabloids. He was the master at deflecting, using us to steer the attention away from his own shit. He painted us as the thieves, but if we were right in our assumptions, he was the bloody king. Scamming the public on a fucking massive scale in comparison to anything we did. I knew his corruption ran further than the financial bullshit we were looking into now, though.

As if he was reading my mind, Finn piped up. "Have you found anything out about Danny's accident?"

"No. And I'm not asking her about it. Not yet." That one was non-negotiable.

"Why the fuck not?" Brandon tossed the controller on the sofa next to him and gave me a stare. One that said he couldn't believe what a weak-ass pussy I was being for not pushing her to talk about it.

Brandon had the empathy of a wet mop, but I could read her like a book. She was still as raw as fuck, and she wasn't ready to hear my little conspiracy theory. I knew what I'd seen though. I also knew what had been reported in the press was complete and utter bullshit. They said Danny had been driving. He hadn't. When I saw him get into the car that crashed just minutes later, he'd been in the passenger seat. They said he was three times over the legal limit of alcohol and had drugs in his system. The guy spent the day with me and didn't drink anything stronger than coffee and Diet Coke. He didn't smoke, never had. And I know for a fact he didn't do drugs. But no one was interested in hearing what I had to say. The last person to see him alive, apart from whoever was driving, and my story had fallen on deaf ears. They didn't want to know. They'd basically pushed me aside during the inquest. My story wasn't worthy, not to Alec Winters' political career, anyway. He liked that he could campaign so honourably for something which had affected his family. His God complex was unstoppable after the accident. He certainly didn't want my alternative narrative fucking things up for him at Westminster.

I wouldn't stay silent though.

I needed answers and Danny deserved them. He'd been one of my best friends and I didn't let my friends down. Ever.

"Ask her if she saw the toxicology report, or better yet, get her to take a photo of it like she did with the account. We can find out who faked it then," Zak suggested.

"Or even better, Hardy can sneak around the house and find it himself after he's fucked her into a coma… Oh… I forgot, you haven't even kissed her yet, let alone tapped that ass." Brandon was back to giving his asshole opinion yet again.

"You haven't kissed her yet? What were you doing last night after you dropped her home, swapping knitting patterns?"

Not helpful Finn. I thought you were on my side.

"Fuck you. You can't talk. You clam up every time one of us so much as mentions Effy Spencer. And you…" I turned on Zak now. "Are you seeing Liv again? Or is it Kelly Hopton now? I can't keep up."

"Don't drag me into this. Liv knew the deal. I don't do dating. I like to keep my options open."

"Great plan. I hope you wrap it up, otherwise the STD clinic will be dedicating a chair in their waiting room just for you," I snapped and turned to face Brandon, but I just couldn't be arsed anymore. "As for you. I have no idea what to say. I don't even want to go there."

In his defence he didn't sugar-coat shit, none of them did really.

"I'm sampling the goods until I get the right girl. She's out there waiting for me somewhere, baking cookies and shit until I come along." Brandon smirked.

"Yeah, you keep telling yourself that. There's someone for

everyone, right? And they do say opposites attract. So hopefully you'll meet that good-looking, intelligent, honest, smart and cultured princess real soon." I chuckled waiting to see what witty comeback he'd give me.

"Maybe I already have."

"What was that?" I'd heard him, I just wanted him to say it again.

"I said, here's a little poem I wrote in my head, especially for you, bro. Roses are red, violets are blue, I've got five fingers, the middle one is for you." He flipped me the bird and picked his controller up, going back into his game and blocking the rest of the world out.

"With sweet words like that you're bound to win her over."

"I take all my relationship tips from you, Ry. I mean, look at you now. You're killing that boyfriend gig."

"Oh, I will be. Just watch and learn my friend. Watch and learn."

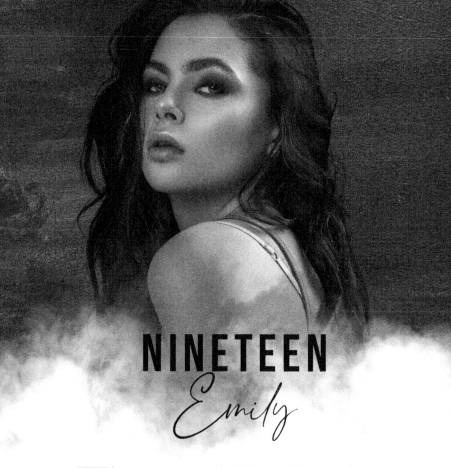

NINETEEN
Emily

I knew I was right that Liv would take a few days to cool off. I'd sent her a text to try and smooth things over, even rang a few times, but all I got was her voicemail. She'd come round eventually. I'd sown the seeds. I just needed to be patient and wait.

As for Chase, he was totally ignoring my calls. Probably because he knew what I was going to say. And my texts? They went unread. That guy was not ready to hear the truth. He was living in cloud cuckoo land as far as dating me was concerned. Between them and all my angst over Ryan, I was slowly going insane.

That's why I'd come into the back garden to do a bit of weeding. Tend to the plants and generally block out my life for a few hours. I had my air pods in and was singing along to Machine Gun Kelly, when something moved out of the corner of my eye and I turned, almost falling backwards onto the grass, ready to scream blue murder at the same time.

"What the hell are you doing here?" I ripped the air pods out of my ears and stuffed them into the pocket of my jeans. Then I stood up, brushing the dirt off my hands and knees and scrunching my nose up at Ryan bloody Hardy, who stood mere feet away from me in my back garden. "How did you get in?" I knew he did some shady shit sometimes, but I hadn't factored breaking and entering into my home to be one of them.

"Your gate was open, and I heard you murdering one of my favourite songs, so I thought I'd better come in and save it."

"Such a hero, aren't you?" I said, my voice dripping with sarcasm.

"I try my best." He was smirking like he had a secret and really wanted me to ask him about it. I wouldn't. I liked making him work for it.

"You've got balls coming in here." I narrowed my eyes at him, but his grin only grew wider.

"Yep, I've got balls. Big ones."

His eyes twinkled as he spoke, and I knew he was trying to make me feel uncomfortable… again. Turns out, he'd succeeded. Discussing Ryan's balls or any other part of his anatomy was not something I was overly keen on doing. Not in front of him, anyway. Now in my room, where no one could see… *Oh shit, Em. You need to stop that train of thought right now. You chose you, remember?* I was starting to think my choices were really fucking lame.

"You'd better leave before-"

He cut me off. "Your dad's not home. I know that for a fact." He took a step towards me, his head resting to one side like he was gauging my reaction. Seeing if what he was doing was okay. "Anyway, I wanted to see you. Is that really such a bad thing?"

"I don't have anything else for you, if that's what you've come for. I looked last night, but there's nothing else on the Rotherham account. Not yet." I spoke way too fast, feeling tense and all out of sorts.

"Who said I came for that? Can't I come round just to see you?"

It was so easy to fool myself into thinking I wasn't into Ryan Hardy when he wasn't stood in front of me, looking deliciously drop-dead gorgeous in black ripped skinny jeans, a tight black T-shirt, and a red and black checked shirt hung casually over the top. It was easy not to get caught up in him when he wasn't looking right at me, with his hair falling into his eyes like it always did. I wondered what it'd be like to brush it out of the way and run my fingers through it. Would it feel as soft as it looked? And those eyes? Don't get me started on his eyes. I must've been daydreaming about what running my fingers through Ryan's hair and getting lost in his green eyes would lead to, because I didn't see my mother until it was too late.

"Who are *you*?" she snapped sharply, looking at Ryan like he was a slug that was invading her perfectly manicured lawn.

"This is Ryan, Mum. He was a friend of Danny's. He's just stopped by to see how we're all coping after, well… You know."

I'd jumped in before Ryan could answer and make things

worse. I was already expecting a mini meltdown from my neurotic 2.0 version of my mother after the morning we'd had. Dad had left without saying goodbye to her, apparently. Which had then resulted in an hour long rant aimed at me and all my failings. Because that was the reason my dad had snuck out at the crack of dawn and headed off to Westminster for another five days of work. I was everything that was wrong in her world.

It did the trick though. As soon as she heard me mention Danny's name she visibly softened and looked at Ryan in a whole new light.

"Ryan?" she said, making it sound more like a question than a statement. "Danny never mentioned you. Mind you, he was pretty private about his personal life in those last few months, wasn't he, Em?"

She'd reverted to calling me Em. She only ever did that when she was in company, trying to make it look like we were close.

"I think Danny had a lot of things going on that we didn't know about, *Mum.*" She scowled at the inflection in my voice when I said her name, then like the seasoned pro she was, she righted herself and gave Ryan the glowing million dollar smile she'd perfected over the years.

"Ryan, would you like to come in for a cold drink? It's awfully hot today."

It was twenty degrees and breezy. A nice day for the U.K., but it wasn't the bloody tropics like she was making out. She obviously wanted an excuse to grill Ryan on all things Danny. I can't say I blamed her though. I'd never asked Ryan about Danny myself. Maybe I should've. Thing was, I felt nervous talking about him to strangers. I was worried I wouldn't be able to hold it all together. Danny was a sensitive subject for me. I missed him every second of every day, and I found blocking it all out was the best coping mechanism. Not great in the long term, but it worked for now.

Mum beckoned Ryan forward, and he grinned back at her.

"I'd love a cold drink, Mrs Winters. Thanks."

She nodded and sauntered off towards the open patio doors. Ryan glanced across at me and raised his eyebrow.

"Should I be worried?" he asked.

"Nope. As much as I love my mum, she's about as self-absorbed as a bag of *Pampers*. As long as you keep talking about Danny, she'll never see through your bullshit."

He threw his head back and laughed. God, I loved it when he did that.

I led Ryan into our house, just as Mum was putting a tray of drinks down onto the coffee table. Most people would've handed out cans or at least asked what drink their guests wanted. Not my mum. She'd loaded up the tray with cut glass tumblers full of Coke with ice, like we were school kids. Oh, and a plate of cookies just to finish off the shitty tea party theme. I shouldn't moan. At least she was trying to be civil.

Ryan sat down on the sofa, man-spreading as he did, and making me feel all hot and bothered again, despite the air-conditioning my mother had cranked up to full effect. I think she was going through the change. Perhaps that was why she was more cranky than usual.

She handed a glass to Ryan and then told him to help himself to the cookies. The way she sat forward, I could tell she was itching for information. Any titbit that Ryan could throw her way about Danny.

"How long were you and Danny friends?" She'd started with the basics.

Ryan chewed the last bit of his chocolate chip cookie and glanced at me before he spoke.

"I knew Danny all through high school, but we became best mates in the last few years. He was a good guy. The best."

Mum nodded and smiled. She actually turned into a human whenever Danny was the topic of conversation, which wasn't that often in our house these days. I missed that about my mum. I missed the softer side that she showed us when we were younger. She hadn't always been the uptight trophy wife she was today. I don't know what'd happened to change things, but she did used to take us to the park and play ball, teach us how to bake muffins and sit playing board games with us, pretending not to notice when we cheated. I don't know why it all went to shit, but it did.

"Tell me some stories about him. I want to know what he was like when he wasn't at home with us." Mum sipped the tea in her china cup and then placed it carefully back on the saucer. She never used mugs for her hot drinks. She thought herself too well-bred for that.

Ryan rubbed his chin and then sat back on the sofa. "Danny was a cool guy. He made us laugh."

Mum smiled and shook her head. "I can only imagine what he got up to behind my back." Fondness clouded her eyes and I could tell any story she heard about him, no matter how gross or cringe-worthy, would've only made her love him more.

"One time, we bubble wrapped Mr. Manderson's whole classroom; chair, desk, computer, the lot. We even did his car too. It was all Danny's idea. Took Manderson hours to cut it all off."

"Oh my God, did you get caught?" Mum gasped, and I raised my eyebrows at her. If I'd told that story she'd have grounded me for the summer and banned my hellraising friends from coming near the house.

"No." Ryan smiled. "The balloons we filled his store cupboard with were the straw that broke the camel's back though. How were we to know he had a fear of balloons? He was traumatised for days."

Mum laughed a proper, full belly laugh and I couldn't help but chuckle too. Danny loved a prank.

"Were the coins glued all over the cafeteria floor your handy work too?" I asked, feeling less on edge with the way this conversation was going. I loved hearing about Danny.

Ryan huffed out a low laugh. "Yep. Me and Danny spent hours gluing those fu… Things down all over the place." He corrected himself, shooting a look my mother's way. "Watching people trying to pick them up kept us amused for ages."

"You like your games, don't you, Ryan?" I said, making sure he knew the meaning behind my statement.

That easy going persona he'd slipped into faded and I felt his guard go up. "The flare set off during the leaver's assembly was nothing to do with us though. That was all on Brandon," Ryan said through gritted teeth, throwing my pointed stare straight back at me.

I'd heard about the legendary flare incident. A hall full of year-elevens and their parents, mine included, listening to the head teacher tell everyone what a stellar year they'd all had, and some dickhead set off a flare, covering everyone and everything in a cloud of purple shit, ruining the whole afternoon. The smoke alarms went off and we all had to evacuate the school. The police were called, but there was no CCTV in that part of the building, so no one was ever held accountable for shitting all over everyone else's day. It wasn't like the Renaissance men would ever rat out one of their own. Typical Brandon, act first think later. He was a bloody liability even back then.

"I remember that. It was awful. Your father never did get the stains out of his suit." Mum scoffed and then her expression mellowed. "Ryan, would you like to see Danny's room?"

I almost choked on my Diet Coke. What the hell was she thinking, inviting someone else into Danny's bedroom? I went in there most days to sit on the windowsill and think about him, but to everyone else that room had always been off limits. Mum wouldn't even let the cleaners in there. We dusted it ourselves. Not that it needed dusting. It was immaculate. We kept it like a shrine to him. Not a thing had changed in that room since the day he left us.

"I'd be honoured," Ryan answered taking me totally by surprise.

Mum stood up and walked out to the hallway and I followed behind Ryan.

"This is really kind of you, Mrs Winters. I've missed seeing him, as a friend. It'd be nice to feel close to him again." Ryan was saying all the right words, but I wasn't sure how honest they were. Did he really want to connect with Danny? Was this all a ruse to get to me? Or was I totally overthinking a nice gesture from my brother's friend? Probably the latter. I wasn't great at reading people at the best of times.

"We haven't changed anything. We've even left the can of Coke on the bedside table that he was drinking before he went out that day." Mum was right. We couldn't even bring ourselves to get rid of a damn can. It was empty of course. A bit like our family home since he'd gone.

"It was his favourite drink," Ryan added, and my heart skipped.

Yes, it was.

Maybe Ryan knew him better than I'd realised? Danny drank Coke like most people drink water, even when he went out for the night. It was why we'd all been so shocked to find out he'd been drunk-driving when he had the accident. Danny didn't usually touch alcohol. It wasn't his style. Well, we thought it wasn't. But what did we know?

Ryan picked up a picture frame from Danny's desk, a photograph of the four of us; Mum and Dad at the back, and Danny and me standing in front of them. Dad had his arms wrapped around my shoulders and Mum was hugging Danny from behind. Ryan smiled and tilted the photo our way and I heard the sob catch in my mother's throat.

"I'm sorry. I can't do this," she cried, covering her mouth and running out of the room. I suppose she'd made progress. Usually, she could only stand at the doorway before she fled. At least today she'd stepped over the threshold.

"I'm sorry." Ryan looked regretful and placed the frame back down with a gentleness I didn't know he possessed. "I didn't mean to upset your mum."

"Don't worry about it. That's the most emotion she's shown in months. It'll do her good to act like a human for a while." I felt guilty the minute those words came out of my mouth, but I couldn't take them back. The woman had lost her son, her eldest child. I didn't have any right to be bitter, and I felt like an asshole, so I sat down on the windowsill and sighed.

"Must be a laugh a minute in your house." Ryan gave me a sympathetic smile.

"It could be worse. I shouldn't complain. I have nothing to complain about. Apart from losing my brother, but then, all families have their sadness. Mine is no different."

I wasn't fishing for sympathy. If anything, I wanted a lifeline out of the sea of despair that me and Mum had drowned ourselves in over the last few months. I wanted to live my life. I knew if Danny was here, he'd be telling me to do just that, but sometimes it was hard. Like trying to wade through treacle every day.

Some days were easier than others, but every day that sinking feeling in the pit of my stomach was what I woke up to. I think that's why I'd been drawn to the whole illegal party scene that Ryan and the others offered. It helped to numb the pain and gave me another focus.

"I know it hurts. I can see it in your eyes. Let me help you," Ryan said, taking small tentative steps towards me.

"I think it's best you leave." I stood up, not able to look him in the eye, and walked over to the door, holding it open to show him his morbid little tour had come to an end.

"When my mum died, there were days when I couldn't even get out of bed. None of us could."

I held my breath. I knew Ryan was sharing something sacred with me now, and as much as I wanted him to leave, I wanted to know more.

"My dad didn't shower or get dressed for weeks. The garage lost customers and we almost went under. It was awful. Three boys and my dad, all left to fend for ourselves. You can imagine what a shit-show that was."

I nodded, but my mouth had gone dry. I couldn't speak.

"But one day, I felt her. Sounds crazy I know, but I felt her at the side of me... And her voice... She told me I needed to be strong for my dad and my brothers. I knew it was her, because that's exactly what she would've said if she'd still been alive. So, I put a notice in the garage window to say we were open, but for carwash and valeting only. I was only a kid. I didn't know how to fix cars then, but I knew how to wash them, and I wanted to do whatever I could to help my dad. Word must've gotten around 'cos a few people showed up and I washed their cars for them. An hour later, I noticed my dad had joined me and was washing right alongside me. My older brother, Liam, he joined us soon after that. The next day, we were open again, business as usual. My dad's worked twenty-four-seven ever since."

He came to stand in front of me and stroked my cheek as a silent tear fell down.

"They never leave us, Emily. Ever. Danny will always be with you."

"I know," I managed to hiccup. "Thank you."

Ryan nodded sadly and then motioned down the hallway.

"Is that your room?"

I turned to look at my bedroom door that still had the unicorn plaque with my name on it.

"How did you guess?" I smirked and then my mouth dropped open when he walked past me and headed down the corridor towards my bedroom. "You can't go in there."

"Why not? I want to see your room." The cocky Ryan was back in full force. I couldn't believe he had the nerve to march over to my door, thinking he could go anywhere he pleased. He had no shame.

He turned the door knob and strode right in, standing in the middle of my room and turning around to take it all in.

Watching him, seeing him standing there, made the hairs on the back of my neck stand on end. Ryan Hardy was in my room and it felt forbidden but enticing at the same time. How could he do that? Have my heart breaking one minute and flipping over the next. He turned to face me, and I felt like he'd sucked all the air out of the space around me. He wasn't just standing in my room, he was dominating it. Making everything else fade into the background.

My mum had kept the décor pretty neutral with cream walls and pale pink curtains and bed linen. There was the usual clutter of girlie memorabilia scattered over my shelves. Photos of Liv, Effy and me at high school, alongside those of my family. I felt embarrassed about the number of soft toys I had sitting on my bed and along the window. I was eighteen, but my bedroom made me look like I was twelve. Ryan didn't seem to mind though. He picked up a beanie baby unicorn from my pillow and squeezed it, then smiled. Not a nasty smile, just a smile. Then he walked over to my dressing table, where my make-up, creams and perfumes were neatly stored. He picked up my perfume bottle, Alien by Thierry Mugler, and he sniffed it, closing his eyes as he did. Was that his way of smelling me? Whatever it was it made my stomach clench.

"You shouldn't be in here," I said with zero conviction. In a twisted way, I kind of liked it.

"I think this is exactly where I should be." He put the perfume bottle down and walked over to where I stood by the door. Then he reached up and brushed a stray hair from my forehead, tucking it behind my ear and making my breath catch in my throat. "I think you've been alone for long enough. We both have."

I was struck dumb. He stepped further into me and I moved backwards. My back was flush against the door jam and my heart was beating so fast I could hear it drumming a steady beat in my ears. He leaned towards me and I froze, then melted into him all at the same time. He smelt divine, intoxicating even. Like freshly washed linen on a summer's day, mixed with a gentle hint of cologne and a scent that was uniquely him. Having him so close did something to me that I'd never felt before in my life. It made me yearn for more. I wanted to be reckless and lose myself in him. In that moment, I wanted everything with him.

He closed the distance between us and his nose grazed the side of mine so delicately it made my heart flutter. Then his lips touched mine in a gentle soft kiss. I didn't push him away. I couldn't, even if I tried. I wanted this as much as he did. His lips were warm and tender, and they made me hungry for more. I groaned, and he pressed his body against me, his hands skimming over my jaw as he held me in place and deepened the kiss.

He glided his tongue along my bottom lip and I opened up to him, letting him taste me and explore with his tongue. He tasted just as good as he looked, like sin and sweetness all wrapped in one wickedly ruthless package that I couldn't help but fall for. This kiss, it was what I'd waited for all these years. He was what I'd waited for.

We stood there at my door, our tongues twisting and stroking, our lips fused together in the most sublime way. I never wanted it to end. Ryan's bubbles were the ultimate, but this? This was unlike anything I'd ever experienced before. I could feel my body sparking to life, wetness like I'd never known pooling in places that'd usually make me blush, but today, I didn't want to hold back. I could feel how turned on he was too, as he ground his hips into me and the thickness in his jeans rubbed against me. The kiss turned heavier, faster, more urgent and then…

"What the bloody hell is going on here."

We jumped apart at the sound of my dad's booming voice breaking through our joint hypnotic lust-filled haze. I gasped, my eyes darting from Ryan, who was touching his lips like he couldn't quite believe where they'd been, and then my dad, who looked like he was about to get out the family shotgun, if we actually owned one that is.

"Dad. I thought you were at work," I said in a breathy voice. The ground opening up to swallow me right about now would've been awesome.

"I can see that," he said, his voice dripping venom. "I came back home because I felt guilty for leaving without saying goodbye to your mother. But that's beside the point. What the fuck is he doing in your room?" He glared daggers at Ryan and then took a step towards him. "You're not welcome here. I thought I'd made that clear a long time ago. Stay away from my daughter."

Ryan smirked and then looked right at me. "Never gonna happen, *sir*." He turned to face my dad, looking like he was squaring up for a fight and I knew I had to intervene.

"Ryan's just leaving. Please, Dad. Don't make this a big deal."

Ryan muttered something about it being a big deal, but I grabbed his hand, stalked past my dad and headed for the stairs.

"If I ever see you in my house again I'll call the police," Dad bellowed over the bannister.

Ryan just looked back up at him and grinned. "I'd expect nothing less from a man who has half the police force in his back pocket."

Dad's face turned a worrying shade of scarlet, but I didn't want to stay around for the impending fireworks, so I dragged Ryan to the front door and out onto the porch.

"I'm sorry. He's-"

"An asshole," Ryan finished for me.

"What did he mean when he said 'I've already warned you to stay away?' I thought you'd never met my dad?"

Ryan rubbed over his jaw in thought and then gave me a hooded, guarded look. "I came here once, with Danny. Your dad took an instant dislike to me. Can't think why? After that, we decided to meet up at my place or anywhere away from here."

"Danny never mentioned anything."

"Why would he? Look… Em. Don't try and read something into this. It's nothing. Your dad didn't like his son being mates with a poor kid, that's all. I wasn't from the right side of town and he could tell. Probably wanted to keep me away from his beautiful daughter too. But that's never gonna happen. Not now."

He smirked and stroked my cheek as he moved closer towards me and my heart and stomach did that little flip thing again.

"If he thinks for one minute I'm going to stay away from you, after that kiss, he's got another thing coming." He bent down and planted a kiss on my forehead. "I'll see you soon, little Winters. Very, very soon."

TWENTY
Ryan

M y brother, Connor, he'd always told me, "Leave them wanting more," and usually I did. But not today. Today, I was the one who'd walked away feeling like I wanted, no, needed more. It was like I'd left a part of me behind when I left her. What fucking right did her father have to warn me off? It might've worked when I was younger, and he didn't like me knocking about with Danny, but that didn't wash anymore. Not where she was concerned. Daddy Winters needed to get used to the fact that his little girl wasn't little anymore. She was so fucking beautiful and so fucking mine.

Reluctantly, I made my way back to the garage to start my shift. Not that I'd be much use this afternoon after what'd happened with Emily. I had a feeling I was gonna be spending the rest of the day reliving the moment when I made her mine. That, and getting lost in thoughts about the other ways I was gonna show her what she meant to me. I was done playing games. I wanted her more than anything, and if I wanted to make that happen, I had to step it up, be the guy she needed me to be.

I pulled onto the forecourt and saw Brandon chatting to Connor over the hood of an old Aston Martin we were fixing up.

"Not working today, slacker?" I said as I shut the door of my van and walked over to join them.

"Got half the day off," Brandon shot back. "Although, God knows why I thought it'd be a good idea to spend it here with you fuckers."

Brandon worked at a local gym. It was shit money, but he got unlimited use of the equipment and he could stare at girls running on the treadmills all day, so it worked out great for him. He made a ton more from the fighting though. He could make in one night what he earned in a month at the gym by doing one fight. Those events were a lifeline for all of us. I had my cars, Zak was a whizz at computers and Finn worked in a call centre, but without the parties our asses would be broke as fuck. It gave us the revenue we all needed to pursue other things. Not to mention the thrill we got from doing it was off the charts. We were still scoping out the next venue. Finn had his heart set on an old pumping station just outside of town. He said it was the perfect setting to channel his creative flow. Thing was, the cathedral of sewage was overrun with rats and shit. As awesome as it looked on the outside, the inside smelt like death and would probably lead to it too. We had to have some standards.

The three of us headed into the office. I could stretch to making Brandon a coffee and then he'd either have to help out or fuck off. We had work to do. Dad and Kieron were sitting at the front desk, going through paperwork and other stuff.

"Nice to see you decided to drop by," Dad said, trying to sound sarcastic, but he knew I was the hardest worker here, and I knew he didn't mean it.

"Thought I'd better show my face at some point." I headed into the tiny room we called a kitchen and flicked the kettle on, setting the mugs out ready with everyone's order. I didn't need to ask what they all wanted, I made them hot drinks most days. As the kettle bubbled away, I stepped back out and froze when I saw Chase fucking Lockwood standing up at the desk, grinning like a loser. Brandon was flaring his nostrils and holding himself back for my dad's sake. Connor was frowning and looking between Brandon and Lockwood, trying to gauge what the problem was and probably deciding whether he needed to duck out the way or join in.

"What the fuck do you want?" I couldn't help myself. I didn't want this punk here at my garage, looking down his nose at us like he was doing us a fucking favour using Dad to service his car, or rather, penis extension.

"Ryan, watch your language." Dad turned round to give me a dirty look for dissing one of his customers, but when he saw the anger coming off me, he backed down. "Is there something going on here that I don't know about?" He turned back to look at Lockwood, who just shrugged like the pussy he was.

"I don't think your son likes me." He smirked and fished his car key out of his back pocket. "But then, you don't have to like me to valet my car and take my money, do you?"

This dude was begging for my fist to connect with his smug-ass face. And just to further his cause, he carried on…

"I need it ready for Friday. I have a hot date." He looked past my dad, towards me again and sneered. "With Emily Winters, so I need it sparkling. Gotta impress my girl."

I fucking lost it.

"Bullshit," Brandon spat as I lurched across the office space and flung the little gate dividing the front customer area from our desks open. Brandon came to stand next to me and Connor stayed by the door, grinning and rubbing his hands together. He loved a good fight. Dad stood up from his chair.

"I don't know what game you're playing coming in here, son, talking shit about our Emily, but I suggest you leave. Your business isn't welcome here." The fact that Dad had called her "*our Emily,*" made me bristle with something… Pride, maybe? I don't know. Dad had barely spoken to her, apart from when she collected her car that one time. But it felt good to know I had everyone behind me. Dad threw the keys back over to Lockwood and they fell on the floor. Guy couldn't even catch like a man.

"Whatever. I'll be sure to tell her you said hi when I see her." He stooped down to pick up his keys, but Brandon kicked them away.

"She wouldn't touch you with a ten foot pole, mate. I think you must be on something. Maybe it's best you don't drive? Wouldn't want you to get pulled over for being under the influence of whatever it is you're fucking smoking." Brandon leaned over and picked up the keys, tossing them in the air and catching them again. "And we'll say hi to Emily for you when we see her later. Good luck with that date on Friday, you know, the one with your right hand."

Connor laughed and Lockwood grinned and shook his head. I tensed, ready to shut his shit down once and for all.

"Whatever you want to tell yourself, man. I'm surprised Kian, your little lap dog, didn't tell you. He was there when I asked her. He saw the whole thing."

What the fuck?

"Maybe because he knew it was bullshit and never gonna happen," Brandon said getting right up into Lockwood's face and stopping me from pummelling him into our cheap linoleum floor.

"You need to do one, Lockwood," I said, gritting my teeth and clenching my fists. "Do you like hospital food or something? Because if you carry on the way you are, that's all you'll be eating for the next few months."

Lockwood took a few steps around Brandon, eye-balling him as he did. Mother fucker had more balls on him than I realised if he wanted to goad Brandon. Then he turned to face me.

"You're really tough when you've got your guard dogs on standby, aren't you?"

"I can go one-on-one with you any time, *mate*." I went to step into him, but the coward moved away.

"Young man, I think you need to leave. Because if my sons or their friend don't kick your ass out soon, I will." Trust Dad to get the final say.

Lockwood sneered again and then ripped his keys out of Brandon's hand and headed for the door, bumping Connor's shoulder as he did.

"Oh, I'm going, old man. Like I'd trust a bunch of hillbillies like you to do a good job on my car."

Me and Brandon followed him outside. He wasn't gonna get away with calling us names. Not when he was the biggest dickhead in this town. And as for disrespecting my dad and dissing this garage? He was a dead man walking.

"We'd do a good job on your car all right." I picked up the jet-wash hose that was lying on the ground close by. "We always do a really thorough job." I pressed the lever and the water shot out, drenching his ridiculously over-priced trainers and making him do a stupid dance to try and avoid the jets of water that were drowning his feet.

"And if you're not off our property in the next sixty seconds, it'll be the inside of your shitty car that gets the next wash down." I splashed the front of his car, then threw the hose back down, folding my arms over my chest and giving him a look of disgust.

"Run away like the little bitch you are, Lockwood," Brandon shouted, then in a quieter voice he said, "His time will come. Don't worry, mate."

I wasn't worried. Not about him getting what was coming to him, anyway. But I needed to make sure he didn't get his claws into her. He'd always been a sly asshole, but for some reason, no one ever saw through it. But they would now that I was on his case.

Lockwood's days were well and truly numbered.

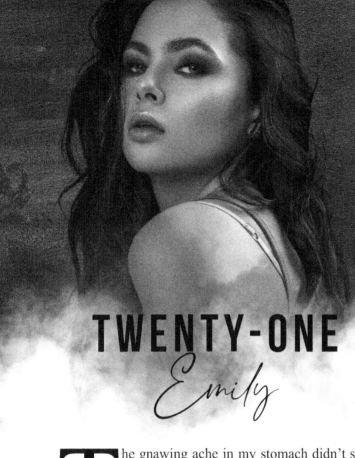

TWENTY-ONE

Emily

The gnawing ache in my stomach didn't seem to want to go away. In fact, it'd gotten worse as Friday loomed ahead like the unwelcome visitor it was. Now, it was Friday evening, and the gnawing was becoming a full-on, gut-wrenching nausea, only made worse by the fact that I hadn't heard from Ryan at all. I was starting to question myself over whether the kiss actually happened or was it a figment of my overactive imagination? Maybe it'd meant more to me than it did to him? Just another one of his twisted mind games.

I had felt guilty about the whole Chase thing and not telling

Ryan about it. I knew he hated Chase with a vengeance, and after the incident in the woods, I could kind of see his point. Trouble was, I still couldn't get through to Chase either. I had debated going to his house to call it off, but instead, I'd opted to go for the least confrontational route. Yes, I'd go along with the charade, but I wouldn't make an effort. I'd wear my ripped skinny jeans and grey tank top, with my hair scraped back into a ponytail and not a scrap of make-up on. If I acted like a douchebag, then maybe I'd be home for nine o'clock to get in an episode of *New Girl*. Every cloud and all that.

Liv had come round eventually and was apologetic for being such a dumbass and agreeing to the date in the first place. She even offered to go in my place and take one for the team, as she put it. I almost took her up on the offer, but I knew I had to shut this shit down myself. She'd owe me one though. She wasn't coping well with the whole 'Zak being a man-hoe' situation. Couldn't say I blamed her. Those Renaissance boys sure knew how to mess with a girl's head.

I heard the front doorbell and my stomach twisted into knots. I glanced at the clock on the fireplace; six o'clock. He was two hours early. Great. I huffed out my annoyance and stomped into the hallway to open the door. I did debate jumping behind the sofa and pretending no one was home, but I knew my mum would be flying down that staircase if I didn't open the door; letting Chase into the house to give out more of her cookies and fake parenting vibes. Not today, Satan. Not today.

I flung the door open, plastering a bored and disinterested expression on my face. When I saw Ryan standing on the other side my jaw dropped to the ground.

"Wow. You look *really* pleased to see me," Ryan said

sarcastically, looking at me from under his sexy curtain of hair.

I felt the knots turn to nervous butterflies and I took a deep breath, not sure what to say.

"I… Er… I thought…"

"You thought it was your hot date for the night. Lockwood?" The twinkle in his eye disappeared when he said that name, replaced with a look of distaste.

I gulped, trying to wet my dry mouth, but it didn't help. Sandpaper had nothing on my throat right now.

"How did you know about that?" My heart was beating ten to the dozen. I realised in that moment that I didn't want Chase to come between whatever it was me and Ryan were slowly building. Chase was a blot on my landscape and Ryan was a boulder that blocked everything out. He was my sun and Chase was a cheap forty-watt economy bulb that flickered to life and faded just as fast.

Ryan folded his arms before he spoke, giving me a pointed stare.

"Kian told me. Oh, and Lockwood, when he came by the garage the other day to gloat to my dad and everyone else that'd listen about how he wanted to impress *his* girl on their date." He frowned at me and took a step back. "I can leave if you want."

Was he angry with me? I hadn't done anything wrong here.

"No," I said defensively. "I mean… I don't know. He's supposed to be here at eight and I don't know what to do." It was official. I was an idiot.

"Do you *want* to go out with him?"

"No."

"Then don't. Come out with me instead."

I wanted to do a little happy dance at the thought of spending time with Ryan, but the polite part of me, the one my parents had instilled in me since I was born, felt a wave of guilt.

"I can't just stand him up."

"Why not? He's stood loads of girls up. Might do him some good to have a taste of some humble pie. Let's hope the fucker chokes on it."

Ryan was right. My guilt was wasted on someone like Chase. He hadn't responded to my calls. I could be lying at death's door in a hospital somewhere for all he knew. And he certainly wasn't thinking about my feelings when he came looking for me in the woods to get his dick wet all those weeks ago. The guy had brass balls, I'd give him that.

"He really came to the garage and bragged about it?"

"Yup." Ryan shook his head, and I knew then that something had gone down.

"Did he cause a scene?"

Ryan shrugged nonchalantly.

"He threw his weight around a bit, made himself look like a prize dick. But Dad threw him out, and Brandon and me gave him a little send-off he wouldn't forget."

Great, his dad had heard it all too. I didn't know Sean Hardy that well, but I didn't like being the reason he had shit to deal with at work. I was mortified.

"Did you hit him?" I winced waiting for the verdict.

"With my fists? No. But with the jet washer, right where it hurts? Yeah, I did." He laughed thinking about what he'd done. "Fucker can dance faster than Michael Flatley on speed when he needs to. So funny." He shook his head chuckling at the memory.

I stifled a giggle. "Oh my God. He's an idiot and an asshole. He's been ignoring my calls all week. I've texted him so many times to cancel and he never reads them. He's insane."

"Clearly. Now, are we gonna stand here and wait for him to show up and join in the conversation or are we getting out of here?" Ryan held his hand out to me and quirked his eyebrow.

"I'm out of here." I grinned back, then grabbed my bag and slammed the door behind me.

Chase Lockwood could go to hell.

***

Ryan held the driver's door of his van open and I smiled, climbing over the central console into the passenger seat. I wanted to ask him why he'd never fixed the damn thing. The guy had built his own cars from scratch, surely he could mend a broken door, but I didn't. In a way, I didn't want to admit that I knew about that part of him. It was a secret I liked keeping to myself.

"So, where are we going?" I asked, feeling excited about being in his van and so close to him again. I couldn't really give a damn if we went anywhere. I'd be happy to drive around or sit together in a car park and talk.

Ryan sighed. "Are you hungry?"

"Starving."

"Is a drive-through burger okay?" He didn't look convinced himself.

"Perfect."

"I bet Lockwood has a table booked at one of those fancy restaurants. You know, the kind that has bigger price tags than portions. You sure you don't want me to go back so you can sample his shitty food?"

I scoffed at his suggestion. He knew me better than that.

"Not in a million years. A burger is awesome. I'll need fries and a milkshake too, though. Oh, and maybe an apple pie?"

"What's the special occasion?"

He obviously hadn't seen how much fast food me, Liv and Effy could pack away once we got started.

"Dodging the Chase bullet."

"And being with me?" He smirked looking at me from out of the corner of his eyes. Damn that was sexy.

"Don't get ahead of yourself."

"Why not?" He licked his lips and focused back on the road ahead. My focus was all over the damn place. "This is a golden opportunity for me. Chance to show you I'm not the dickhead you always thought I was."

"I never thought you were." He gave me a cut the bullshit look, and I grinned into my lap. "Fine. But in my defence you've done some pretty dickish things to me over the years. And these last few months? You really upped the asshole stakes."

"I had to do something to protect myself."

I froze, feeling my heart stop in my chest.

"Protect yourself from what?"

He didn't answer, just took a deep breath and turned into the drive-through. And I sat there, wondering what exactly he thought he needed protecting from when it came to me.

He ordered us burgers, large fries and drinks, then pulled into the corner of the car park.

"It's my dad, isn't it?" I said, suddenly losing my appetite as I watched him dive into his burger like he hadn't eaten for a month.

"What... Huh?" he spluttered over his mouthful.

"You think you need protecting from my dad." I turned in my seat to face him. "What exactly is it you think he's done?

I think I deserve to know, seeing as you've got me spying for you."

Ryan finished his mouthful, dropped his burger into his lap and turned to look at me.

"I'm not scared of your dad, Emily."

"Then why did you need protecting?"

"I'm not... Oh, Jesus, for fuck's sake." He ran his hands over his face in exasperation.

"If you're not gonna tell me then-"

"Fine," he snapped. "It was you. I meant you. Fuck's sake. It was a joke. A throwaway comment. I don't want this to turn into a row. Jesus."

"Why would you need protecting from me?" I wasn't gonna let this one go.

"Because I like you, Emily. A lot. More than a lot." I noticed his cheeks going pink and he was staring straight ahead like he couldn't quite bring himself to look at me.

"I like you too. A lot." I smiled. "More than a lot."

"I'm not used to putting myself out there," he mumbled, picking his burger back up and taking a bite.

"I can tell."

"I'm not a pussy." He looked at me, but the walls he usually put in place weren't there.

"No one said you were."

"So, can we eat our burgers now without you thinking I'm some kind of loser?"

Typical guy. Always gotta think about the image.

"You're not a loser, Ryan."

"Yeah? I feel like one. If the others were here, I'd probably get kicked to the kerb for talking like a pussy." He gave me a lop-sided grin and I suddenly became hungry for something more than just a burger.

"Well, they're not here. I am. And I like the way you talk to me. I like your bubbles."

"My bubbles?" He chuckled and frowned at me. "Okay, is that some sort of chick code 'cos I have no idea what that means."

"It means I like being with you. Just you. You and me. Us." I sighed. "Now I feel like the loser."

I grabbed a handful of fries and shoved them in my mouth, hoping they'd help with the verbal diarrhoea I seemed to have developed tonight.

"Since Mum died it's been hard to open up to anyone," he said, glancing back down again. I could tell he found it hard to talk about his mum, like I found it hard to talk about Danny, but he was trying. With me, he was making the effort, putting himself out there. "I've spent years hanging with other guys," he added. "And I gotta admit, this… With you… It's all new to me. But I like it. I can be myself with you."

"Good. I feel the same."

He looked across at me, and we held our gaze, smiling a knowing smile. Like secrets were passing between us that we didn't need to say out loud. Our little bubble.

"I'm glad we're on the same page," he said, and I nodded, feeling the most relaxed I'd felt in days.

We finished eating our food in a comfortable silence, both of us grinning to ourselves. It felt nice to know I saw a part of Ryan no one else ever did. A part he hadn't been able to show the world since the tragedy of losing his mum. It made me feel special, considering how close he was to the Renaissance men.

I swallowed my last mouthful and asked the question that'd bugged me for years.

"Why do you call yourselves the Renaissance men? It's a really shitty name."

He threw his head back and laughed.

"It is. Wasn't my idea though. I think Brandon came up with that one and Finn thought it was cool. You know, arty. Me and Zak thought it was a load of bollocks."

"It is." I laughed, starting to realise that Ryan Hardy wasn't the opinionated asshole I'd thought he was.

"Why do you call yourselves the Renegade girls?"

I almost choked on my chocolate milkshake.

"Oh my God. We don't. None of us have ever used that nickname, ever."

"That's not what Liv told Zak at the bonfire."

I covered my face and shook my head with shame.

"No wonder he never called her back. What a dumb thing to say."

Ryan pulled my hands down away from my face as he laughed. "Listen, Zak's my mate. I've got his back, but I don't think he's the right fit for Liv."

"The right fit?" I felt my brow furrow, trying to think why on earth Liv wasn't a good fit for anyone. She was awesome. "Why?"

"Because he's a player. He changes girls faster than most people change their underwear."

Yeah, I'd already seen that side of him for myself, and those niggly little doubts crept into my brain again. "And you?" I couldn't stop myself from asking.

"I'm not Zak." He reached over and stroked down the side

of my face. "I never will be."

I froze, tense with anticipation. Was he going to kiss me again? He looked down at my lips, then licked his own and stroked his thumb across my cheek. I was putty in his hands.

"Can I show you something?" he asked, and my heart thudded in my chest, thinking what exactly it was he wanted to show me in this van, while he was holding my face and we were having a moment.

I nodded, unable to form words and he pulled away, starting the engine and leaving me feeling a little deflated.

Get a grip, Em. What did you think he was gonna do? Whip his dick out in the car park of a family fast food restaurant and say, "Get a load of this." I was seriously losing it.

He drove us across town, always sticking to the speed limit and glancing my way every so often to check I was okay. He didn't need to say why. Danny.

When he pulled up outside a rundown old building I frowned.

"Where are we?"

"Sandland Asylum," he said, staring out of the window at the grey monstrosity.

The pillars were worn and crumbling, the windows mostly broken, and the brickwork was flaking away. It was an eyesore, but it did have a gothic eeriness about it which kind of drew you in. Like the stone walls held years of silent screams and tortured tales. As haunting as it looked from the outside, I was intrigued to find out more.

"Another party venue?" I asked.

"Maybe, I don't know. Finn has his heart set on the old waterworks, but this place? There's something about it." He opened his door then held his hand out to take mine. "Come on. I want to show you something."

I took his hand as I scrambled across the seats to get out. Then he led me over the uneven ground and held the broken fencing open, so I could walk through.

"Your handiwork?" I asked, eyeing the vandalised metal fence.

"I'm not saying anything." He grinned back, and pulled my arm to lead me to the entrance.

The padlock keeping the front doors closed was hanging off, and he lifted it out of its holder and pushed the doors open. I heard the flap of birds' wings as we forced our way through the gap in the entrance. This place was so old even the doors had given up, only opening a few inches before the rusty hinges groaned and attempted to struggle back into place.

Ryan didn't let my hand go and we both stood in the massive foyer, looking around us at the crumbling walls and vast ceiling, that in its day must've looked stunning, but now the glass covering it was broken, discoloured and plastered in bird shit.

"It's just through here." Ryan pointed down the dark hallway that looked like something from an Alfred Hitchcock movie. Well, we did have the birds, I'd probably get vertigo if I stayed in here for any length of time, and I just prayed we didn't encounter any psychos in this asylum.

We picked our way through the rubble and down the murky corridor that had numerous doors leading off it, probably for the wards they used to use here. None of the doors were open though. Had Ryan done that? Closed them so I wouldn't have to see the metal frames of the beds or think about the horrors that could've happened here?

When we got to the end, we stepped down into a narrower walkway, where we both had to duck our heads to avoid the dust and low lying cobwebs. From Alfred Hitchcock to Indiana Jones in just a few short steps.

Once we got to the end, Ryan pushed open a little wooden door and we both walked inside. The setting sun was bathing this room in a glow that belied its harsh, sinister neighbouring rooms, and the stained glass windows that framed three of the four walls here made the dusty floor light up in a rainbow of colours. The glass in every window was still intact, unlike the exterior of the building, and a stone altar stood regally at the end of the room.

"This is the asylum chapel," Ryan said on a whisper as if he didn't want to disturb the serenity of the room and its sacred aura.

"It's beautiful," I replied, and it was. Sure, there was paint peeling off the walls, and in winter it'd be freezing cold. But today, with the sun's rays going down at just the right angle to bathe this place in a kaleidoscope of wonder, I'd have described it as beautifully distressed. Perfectly imperfect.

"I found this place a few days ago when I was scoping out venues. I thought it'd be a good fit for our next event. But when I saw this chapel, something stopped me. I didn't want to share this with anyone else. I definitely didn't want to use it for Brandon's fights or have Finn put his mark on it. I wanted to keep it for myself." He turned to me and smiled. "Do you like it?"

"I love it."

"Then maybe it can be our place?"

I stilled at his words. The idea of a place that was ours, just for us, made me feel special. Like we were special. He pulled me closer to him and wrapped his arms around my waist. I placed my hands on his chest, but not because I was going to push him away. I wanted to feel his heart beating. I wanted to know that I got to him just as much as he got to me. He leaned his head forward and brushed his lips against mine so gently I froze, scared to move in case I missed something.

"Is this okay?" he whispered as his breath mingled with mine.

I gave a slight nod, wanting to keep my lips as close to his as I could, and then he tilted his head and kissed me. Our second kiss, and this time there would be no dad to interrupt us. We had all the time in the world. He tasted like mint gum and every naughty, dirty thought I'd ever had. I wanted to drown in him and never come up for air.

I wrapped my arms around his neck and he bent down and then picked me up, deepening the kiss as I wrapped my legs around his waist. I felt wanton, free, and I didn't care. All that mattered was this moment, *being* in this moment, with him. I'd thought the room was bathed in colour, but he just doused my whole soul in a vibrance that no colour could match. He was the spark that set my heart, soul, body and mind on fire.

He walked us backward until I felt my ass bump against something solid and cold. The altar. I sat on it, but kept my legs clamped around him. I didn't want to let him go, ever. Our tongues explored, our lips entwined; this was a dance that I never wanted to end. The feel of his tongue sliding over mine made me hungry for more. The way it curled and teased me, tasting so fucking good. My heart ached for him, my body yearned for him, and in this moment, I wanted it all with him. He made time stand still and I loved it.

He ran his hands from my waist to my ass, squeezing and groaning into my mouth. Feeling desperate for more, I ran my fingers through the softness of his hair and then clung to him, like I'd die if he tried to break away. He was my air, my water, and everything I never knew I needed.

After today, I knew I'd never survive without this.

He pulled away first, but kept his forehead pressed against mine as he panted breathlessly. His eyes were closed, and I watched as he slowly opened them, showing me the depth of emotion that he felt and couldn't hide anymore. I didn't want him to. I'd fought against my feelings long enough. I couldn't do it anymore.

"Jesus," he said as he held my face in both of his hands. "I need to slow this down."

Instantly, my heart hit the floor so hard I felt the thump in my gut.

"No," he spluttered, seeing my solemn expression. "I didn't mean slow us down. I meant this. I don't want to scare you away."

I reached my hands up to hold his face, just like he was holding mine and I kissed him, a soft gentle kiss on the lips, then I pulled away.

"You aren't going to scare me away. You never have, and you never will. I want you, Ryan Hardy, rough edges and all. I. Want. You." I made sure to emphasise the last part. I needed him to know that I was in this one hundred percent.

He wrapped his arms around me to hold me close, and buried his face in my neck like he was breathing me in.

"There's no rush," he said. I could feel his heart beating

wildly in his chest and I squeezed him tightly to me.

"I know," I whispered back. "I'm not going anywhere."

We stayed like that for a while, me sat on the altar, and him stood in front of me, both of us holding the other like we'd found something so precious we were scared to let go in case the fragile moment shattered like paper thin glass.

Today, we'd given each other a part of ourselves that no one else had ever seen. He'd always be Ryan Hardy; tough guy, Renaissance man and one of the lads. But this boy, right here in my arms, he was my Ryan. Kind, gentle, loving, and all mine.

Reluctantly, after a time, Ryan pulled back and said, "There's one more thing I need to do tonight."

I smirked, having absolutely no clue what it was that he needed to get done. But I nodded, and he held my hand as I slid off the altar. Then he wrapped his arm around my shoulders and kissed the top of my head.

"It's a guy thing," he said with a hint of amusement in his voice.

Interesting.

***

Ten minutes later, we were pulling back up to the kerb opposite my house. I looked at my watch to see it was just before eight. Great. I was getting front row seats to watch Chase get stood up.

"Really?" I side-eyed Ryan. "You're gonna make me watch him get shot down?"

"You don't have to look if you don't want to, but I've waited all week for this." Ryan reached over and grabbed my hand, pulling it into his lap and threading his fingers with mine. Suddenly, I didn't care what we were here for. All that mattered was him. I leaned across and kissed his cheek and he turned to take my mouth in another toe-curling kiss. I loved the way we fit together so perfectly. His mouth over mine, our tongues laced together. The taste of him was hypnotic. I was well and truly under his spell.

We broke away when we heard a car engine roar to a stop next to us.

"Showtime," Ryan sang, settling further down in his seat and winding his window down. We watched as Chase checked himself in his mirror, patting his over-gelled hair and then grinning at his own reflection.

"What a knob." I shook my head and Ryan laughed.

"He loves himself way more than he could ever love anyone else. You probably did him a favour tonight, babe. The waiter only needs to put a mirror on the table. He can sweet talk himself all night."

I laughed, but the fact he'd called me babe, made the rest of his words sound like white noise. I liked being his babe.

Chase got out of the car and we saw him root around in his pockets and pull out what looked like a foil packet. Condoms.

"Motherfucker," Ryan spat, and I squeezed his hand as he tensed up beside me. Chase stuffed them back into his jeans and we both saw him smirk to himself. "I swear to God, I'm gonna kick the shit out of him one of these days."

"Not tonight, babe," I said, using Ryan's pet name and he turned to me and grinned, then lifted my hand up and kissed the back.

"I don't need to. I've got you. I don't need anything else."

I had to resist the urge to throw myself across the van and launch myself on him.

Yes, Ryan. You do have me.

Instead, we both went back to watching the farce that was my non-date with Chase unfold. He rang the doorbell, gave his hair one last pat and shape for good measure, and when my mum answered, he straightened up, no doubt giving her a full dose of the Lockwood charm. I could see mum frowning and then shrugging her shoulders.

Chase started to rub at his perfectly set hair, causing it to fall out of place as he tried to work out what the hell was going on. I wasn't there and being told no was something Chase Lockwood didn't like to hear, ever. Even when you actually said it to him, he didn't listen. It made me go cold thinking about other times I might've said no, and he'd just disregard my feelings. I'd had more than a lucky escape. Ryan had saved my ass tonight.

Mum and Chase stood for a minute longer, Mum looking uncomfortable and probably asking him if he'd like to come in and wait, and Chase shuffling on his feet hopefully feeling like a prize twat. Then he spun around and marched down the steps away from our porch. Mum bit her lip, scowled and then shut the door.

Just as Chase was about to open his car door, Ryan beeped his horn and Chase's head shot up. He narrowed his gaze like he was trying to make out who we were and then his face dropped. Ryan flipped him the bird, then he started the engine up and rolled the van forward a few feet to put us adjacent to Chase's parked car. Chase folded his arms and huffed a laugh, looking down the road and then back at us sat in Ryan's van.

"Fancy seeing you here, *mate*." Ryan leaned out of his window and gave Chase the once over. "Word of advice, next time you so much as look at my girl, you'll be drinking your food through a straw."

Chase laughed and went to speak, but Ryan cut him off.

"You're on thin ice, Lockwood. I mean it. Stay away from Emily and stay away from me. Understand?"

Ryan put his hand on my knee and rubbed it. Chase bent down, and his face turned to stone when he saw me sitting in the passenger seat.

"Enjoy slumming it, Em," he sneered. "When you want to try dating a real man, you know where to find me."

"That'll be a hard pass, Chase. I'd rather stick pins in my eyes," I replied sharply.

We didn't wait around for Chase to give us another word. We'd had our say. He'd been warned off and neither one of us wanted to look at the slimy toad for a minute longer than we had to. So we sped off and left him to eat our dust.

After a few minutes of driving around aimlessly, Ryan pulled over, cut the engine and turned to me.

"Let me take you out, on a real date, not one I've stolen off Lockwood."

"You didn't steal anything from him. That guy is delusional. But yes, a date sounds… Nice."

"Nice? It'll be more than nice."

He shuffled over to me and nuzzled my neck, making me collapse into a hopeless mess of giggles. I was way too ticklish.

"I'll look forward to our better-than-nice next date," I purred, finding his lips and losing myself in my Ryan.

TWENTY-TWO
Ryan

"**S**o?" Brandon sat forward expectantly, drumming his fingers together as they dangled in-between his knees. "What did you think of the asylum? Any good?"

"Nope. It's a no-go. Too many corridors and empty rooms. It lacked… Spirit."

He rolled his eyes at me and groaned. "We're not looking for a fucking wedding venue, Ry. Just four walls and some kind of roof to accommodate us for the night. Do you need me to take a look at it?"

Over my dead body. I wasn't letting him anywhere near the

place. This was not up for discussion. I knew he'd have loved it. He'd have used that chapel as his own private MGM Grand if he could. But it wasn't his to use. Not any more

"No point. I think we should check out the waterworks again. Or maybe the old foundry? We've had that place on our list for ages."

Brandon looked at me like he was scrutinising every word, but he didn't argue. Finn was the one who broke the stand-off.

"Did you get any further with Emily and all that shit with her dad?" He looked between Zak and me, but it was Brandon who replied.

"Fuck, haven't you heard? Did we forget to tell you? Ryan nailed Lockwood's ass to the cross last weekend over Emily. Dude got blown off faster than a groomsman with a Vegas stripper." He leaned over and slapped my knee to congratulate me. Shifting from suspicious, to pissed off, to proud all in the matter of a few seconds.

"Nice imagery, mate." Finn scowled and then laughed as Brandon filled everyone in on what'd happened on Friday night, like he'd actually been there watching the whole thing himself. He was like a proud parent with how he described it. I couldn't tell if he was more proud of me for stepping in or Emily for going along with it.

"So, its official now? With you and Emily? You're a thing?" Finn asked, and Zak smiled to himself.

"Yeah. She's mine." I shrugged, and I noticed Brandon grit his teeth. "You got a problem with that?" I asked, ready to go nuclear on his ass or anyone else's who wanted to call me out on it.

"Nope." Brandon shook his head, but he wouldn't look at

me.

"I'm taking her out again tomorrow. Any ideas on where's a good place for a date?" I was aiming that at Zak, and maybe Finn.

Brandon piped up. "What? Is the back of your van not good enough for her?" And then wiggled his eyebrows suggestively. Prick.

"Fuck you," I spat back, and he gave a fake laugh.

"Just remember which side you're on." Brandon sat back in his chair and tried to look like he wasn't pissed off with me.

"Speaking of sides," Zak stood up and wandered across his living room to gather some papers he had on his table, and then he came back to join us. "I've had a bit of a break through with this account. It seems Daddy Winters likes to keep things clean, if you know what I'm saying."

We nodded, but Zak carried on like we didn't.

"Looks like he's laundering a hell of a lot of money through this account. A few of the names I've followed up have led me to some pretty shady places." He turned to look right at me. "Let's just say, if that was my girl living in his house, I'd get her the hell out of there."

I don't know what power he thought I had over Emily, but I'd need more than a hunch and Zak's hacking skills to convince her. I needed solid proof that spelt it out for all of us. Alec Winters was a no-good, self-serving thief, and if my suspicions were right, he had more than money laundering on his hands. His were soaked in blood.

"There was one name that sprung out at me though. Troy Barker. Ever heard of him?" We all shook our heads. "A pretty hefty sum of money was transferred two days after

Danny's accident into an account in his name. It might just be a coincidence, but I'm looking into it. Maybe see if Emily knows who he is? And if you could get eyes on that toxicology report or anything, it'd really help," Zak said, addressing me.

"I need more time. Danny is a sore subject for her. I can't ask outright. I need to build up to it."

"Jesus, Ryan. Can you hear yourself? Did you gift wrap those balls before you handed them to her for safe keeping?" Brandon snapped.

"She can do whatever she wants with my balls." I grinned back, and he tutted, standing up to head into Zak's kitchen and escape my smugness. I don't think his sarcastic comment had got the reaction he'd wanted.

"I'm serious." Zak pulled me back in again, giving me a look that told me I needed to stay focused. "I tried hacking into the official records, seeing if I could bring the toxicology report up or anything from the inquest, but there's nothing. It's like the accident never happened. Online anyway. Every trace of it has disappeared. Apart from his shitty interviews and the whole 'our younger generation are doomed' bullshit he spouts. We could really use a leg-up here."

I agreed. I needed to man up and remember that I was doing this for Danny too. If anything had happened to me, I know for a fact he'd have stopped at nothing until he found out the truth.

I needed to bite the bullet and talk to Emily.

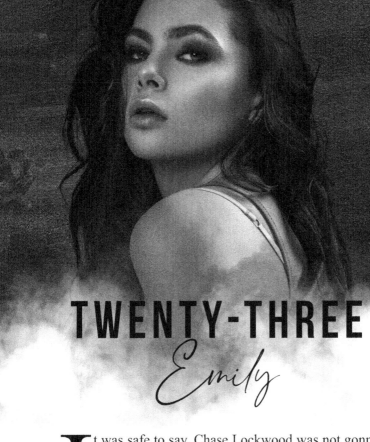

TWENTY-THREE
Emily

It was safe to say, Chase Lockwood was not gonna be welcome at our home any time soon. Apparently, he'd been beyond rude to my mum on Friday; who was home alone after Dad had had to make an emergency dash back to London on urgent business. She made it very clear that I was not to invite him back here again, despite the fact that his dad did business with us, otherwise he'd get an earful of her well-rehearsed lecture on bad manners and etiquette.

Sometimes my mum was awesome. Not often. But sometimes.

Tonight was my first official date with Ryan. He was picking me up at seven, but I had no idea where we were going and no idea what to wear. The guy ran illegal parties as his side-line, I doubted it'd be some upmarket club or bar and truthfully, I was okay with that. More than okay.

Ryan was the most real person in my life right now, aside from my girls. But I didn't want to wear jeans again like every other time he'd seen me. Oh, apart from the white old lady dress I'd worn to the warehouse a few months ago. So, I went for a cute black skater dress. It was fun and flirty with just the right amount of sexy. Plus, the flared skirt meant I'd be able to scale a fence if needed without being restricted by the material. As long as he didn't look up, that is. I'd have my ass on full display with the lacy thong I had on underneath.

I slipped on my heels and then popped a pair of flats into my handbag for emergencies, like uneven woodland floors or picking through rubble. I had to cover all bases, right?

When seven o'clock came, I heard the doorbell and rushed to open it before my mum made an appearance. Ryan stood there looking like a tall glass of water in a desert. He was wearing a tight black T-shirt with tight jeans and a leather jacket. He oozed that sexy bad boy vibe and I knew I had to get him out of here before my mum copped a load of him and fucked up my plans for the night.

"Damn, Em. You look…" He looked me up and down like he was having the same thoughts that I was, but I jumped forward, slamming the door shut and cutting him off.

"Yeah, you too. Let's get out of here."

He raised his eyebrows, then must've remembered what my parents were like 'cos he turned around and marched right after me, down my driveway, without giving the house a second glance. He made a grab for my hand to slow my steps and when I looked at him, he smiled and said, "Slow down. I want this to be special."

We reached his van and I went to walk around the back, aiming for the driver's door.

"Ah, no need. I got it fixed." He opened the passenger side for me as I stood there gawping at him.

"You fixed it?" *Nothing like stating the obvious, Em.* Maybe I was a little more nervous than I realised?

"Yeah. I didn't need to before. No one ever used it. But I had to fix it." He shrugged. "It's your door now."

Most guys melted a girl's heart with flowers, chocolates or jewellery. My Ryan had melted my heart into a pool of goo with a new door for his van. I honestly felt like dry-humping him in the driveway to show him how grateful I was. He was so perfect without even knowing it.

"No more climbing over the gear stick." I put my hand over my heart to pretend I was flattered by the gesture. I shouldn't have pretended. I was flattered. "I feel so special."

"Em. That door had been broken for nearly two years. I wouldn't fix it for just anybody."

"You say the sweetest things." I fake batted my eyelids.

"I'm just getting started, baby."

We drove in relative silence. I surreptitiously studied his profile as he concentrated on the road. His strong jaw and slight stubble made me lose focus and start fantasising about what it felt like to kiss him. To stroke his rough cheek and feel those soft plump lips on mine. I watched as he turned the wheel, flexing the muscles in his arms and gripping tightly with his long tanned fingers. I wondered what else he could do with those fingers and

I blushed, snapping my head back to look out of the window.

"You okay?" he said, reaching over to squeeze my knee.

"Yeah. Where are we going?"

He sighed and went back to glaring at the road ahead. "I thought about taking you to the chapel again, maybe cleaning the place up and having our first date there, but I wanted to do something a bit different. So, I'm taking you to one of my other favourite places."

We pulled into a car park and I couldn't stop myself, "A park?"

"Not just any park. This has a forty-acre woodland garden. Plus, it's a royal park. If it's good enough for Liz, it's good enough for me." He gave me a cocky smile and I narrowed my eyes at him.

"I never had you down as a conservationist."

"I know a lot of hidden gems around these parts."

Yeah, like disused buildings for illegal purposes. I narrowed my eyes at him.

"This is different though," he said as if he'd read my mind and he gestured to the greenery outside his window. "My mum used to bring us here when we were kids. I think the overdose of testosterone in our house got to her sometimes, so she brought us here to feed the ducks and connect with nature. Probably to regain some of her sanity too after a day of refereeing our fights."

We got out of the van and Ryan grabbed a large backpack from the back and hauled it onto his back. It looked like he'd packed enough for a weekend stay.

"Are we hiking?" I asked, thinking I'd probably need those flats now, instead of the heels I'd got on. I rooted through my bag and dropped the ballet pumps onto the floor and then kicked my heels off, storing them in the footwell, and slipping into the much more comfortable and foot-friendly sparkly slippers.

Ryan laughed at me as I changed my footwear. "I guess I should've told you to wear shoes for walking. I didn't think. I'm not used to all this girls' stuff," he said, pointing to my feet.

"Don't worry about it. I'm always prepared. Like a boy scout." I didn't want him to feel bad about bringing me here. He'd obviously put thought into the date.

"You mean a girl scout?" he corrected.

"Yeah, that's what I said."

He chuckled and held his hand out for me to take. "Come on, Dora. Let's go and explore. Then we can find a good spot to eat this picnic my brother, Connor, packed for us."

I raised my eyebrow at him. The Hardy boys were full of surprises. "Your brother, Connor, made a picnic? For us?"

"He can be an asshole sometimes, but what he doesn't know about baking isn't worth knowing. He could give Mary Berry a run for her money."

I was shocked he even knew who Mary Berry was. "Is this the same Connor who works with you at the garage?"

"Yep. He'd always wanted to go to catering college, but then Mum died, and he dropped out. Guess we all made sacrifices for the good of the family back then."

Damn, this boy was continually throwing me off my game.

"Your dad must be really proud of you all."

I gave his hand a squeeze as he led me along a path, through trees decorated with blossom and bushes of flowers with the most vibrant fuchsia pinks, lilacs, and splashes of yellow that I'd ever seen. I was clueless on the names. Unless it was a rose or a lily, I didn't stand a chance at guessing.

All I knew was this place was beautiful. Nature at its best. And Ryan was sharing it with me.

"He's the best. He's had to put up with a lot over the years," Ryan said, starting to open up to me. "When Mum died, he pulled us all together. Then it all went off with Liam and Connor-"

"He doesn't live round here, does he? Your oldest brother, I mean." I wanted to ask what'd happened, but I didn't want it to look like I was gossiping. Word around town was Liam left after a fight with the family.

"No. I see him every few weeks. He still won't speak to Connor, though. I guess walking in and finding your fiancée in your little brother's bed will do that to you."

"Oh my God! That's awful! Did he still marry her?"

"No. And in Connor's eyes, he did Liam a favour showing him what she was really like."

I was starting to get a clearer picture of the Hardy family and why Sean was so wary of Connor when I met him. "I think he could've found a better way to out her as the bitch she obviously was."

Ryan laughed. "I didn't much care for her. Couldn't understand what Liam saw in her to be honest. She was a spoilt brat."

"Well, they do say love is blind."

"It must be, 'cos when she left she took the contents of his bank account with her and he didn't even try to get it back."

I winced. "Ouch! That's brutal."

"Yep. He definitely dodged a bullet there."

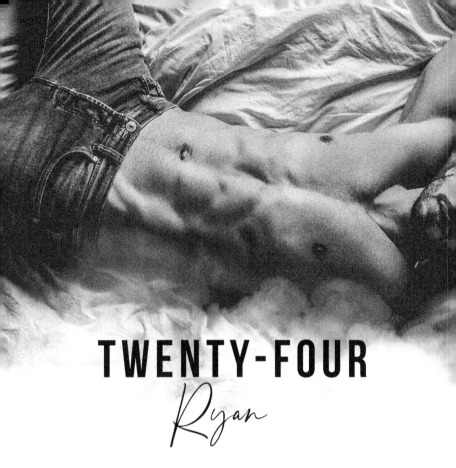

TWENTY-FOUR
Ryan

I knew this park would be a winner. I'd asked Connor for his advice on the best place to take a girl to get her to open up and he'd nailed it. Even baked a shit load of scones and fucking fairy cakes to help me 'seal the deal' as he put it. I wasn't lying when I said Mum loved this park, she did. We usually tore through the gardens at high speed though, back in the day. Racing to get to the open space so we could kick the football around. Mum would've loved a daughter like Emily. Someone to share all her lighter moments with. They were mostly lost on us.

I could tell Emily was interested in what I had to say. She

hung on my every word and asked questions about my brothers, genuinely interested in my response. I'd never really told anyone about the Liam-Britney-Connor shit-show, because I was a guy. We never talked about feelings and shit. My mates heard what happened, thought, 'fucking hell,' the same as I did, and we all moved on. Well, all of us except Liam, but that was another story.

I held Emily's hand as we strolled amongst the flowers and tried to keep a clear head and not pull her into the undergrowth and show her what I really wanted to do. The place was more or less deserted, save for a few dog walkers and the odd elderly couple. When we came to the little decked pond area, she lit up like a Christmas tree and we stopped to watch the ducks. I would've offered to feed the fuckers, but I didn't want to attract them over to us. I hated the snappy beaked little shits.

"So, I know a little more about you. But I know nothing about how the whole Renaissance thing started. What happened there?" she asked, no doubt fishing for some gossip.

"What, you mean that period of discovery, also known as the rebirth, from the middle ages? Or my three asshole friends from high school?" I replied, stalling for time.

She gave me a playful slap on the arm. "Your friends, dummy. Unless you have a burning desire to give me a history lesson."

"My knowledge of the real Renaissance ends there I'm afraid." I gave her my best cheeky smile and then nudged her arm. "What do you want to know?"

"I guess I want to know how you all got to where you are. What made you friends? You were always the popular guys at school, but sometimes, I watch you with Brandon or Finn, and you're just… different." She shrugged and went back to watching the ducks.

"Popular? I think you went to a different school than us."

"Oh, shut up. You guys had the whole school wrapped around your little fingers and you know it. You said jump, and everyone asked how high."

She wasn't wrong there.

"Apart from you."

"Apart from me. But I noticed you." She leaned against the wooden fencing, watching a family of ducks swim past us.

"I noticed you too." I moved closer and rubbed my nose against hers. She gave a low laugh and pulled away shyly.

"Are you trying to distract me?"

"Is it working?" I smirked.

"Maybe."

I thought about guiding her to somewhere quieter, and I put my arm around her waist to pull her closer to me. Then I remembered that this date wasn't all about me. It was also a chance to get her to tell me about Danny and the accident. To open up about her dad too. To do that, I needed to open up as well.

"We weren't always the popular kids." I sighed. I didn't like trips down memory lane at the best of times, but today, I had to learn to suck it up. "I guess we were the misfits of middle school who just happened to find each other at the right time in our lives. I was the kid whose mum died, and Zak was the first one to talk to me like I wasn't a leper. He had a PlayStation and we couldn't even afford an Atari, so I started going to his house most days after school to play Street Fighter and stuff like that. His mum and dad are pretty cool. His little sister is a pain in the ass, but then every family's got one, right?"

"Like me, you mean." She gave a sad smile and it was on the tip of my tongue to ask her about Danny. "What about Brandon?" she said, interrupting my thoughts.

"Brandon was always the angry kid. Can't say I blamed him. He was left on his own when he was three for five fucking days while his mum got high at some crack den in London. Social services picked him up after a neighbour gave them the tip-off. They found him scrabbling through the bins for food, caked in his own shit. Don't tell him I told you that, by the way. He'd kick my ass if he knew I'd talked about it."

"That's heart-breaking."

"Yep. Good job his Nan stepped up to take care of him. Otherwise, he'd have been chewed up into the system and spit out at eighteen. He has issues, but he hasn't turned out too bad considering."

I watched the ducks as they waddled back onto land. The parents fussing over their ducklings and fluffing up their feathers. Even animals took better care of their young than Brandon's mum had. The woman truly was a piece of work.

"Does he still see his mum?"

"I don't think she'd even recognise him if he walked up to her in the street, wearing a T-shirt that said 'I'm your son.' I don't think she even cares." Emily scoffed and shook her head. I guess her mum wasn't looking quite so bad now compared to Brandon's egg donor.

"That's so sad."

"He's fine." That was a fucking understatement, but I wasn't about to wade into the murky waters of the Mathers' family history and bring us both down. So, I moved onto the last of our crew. "Finn didn't speak for the first seven years of his life. Not to adults, anyway. His parents palmed him off on so many different counsellors, we all lost count. He's always loved art though. It helped him to communicate, and then, once he joined our little gang, it didn't matter if he stayed silent for weeks on end or chatted complete shit about abstract-expressionism or neo-classical whatever. We just let him do his thing. Turns out overpriced psycho-babble is no match for a decent set of friends and someone taking the time out to really get to know you."

"Wow."

"Like I said, we were the misfits."

"And the parties? How did they come about?" She really wanted to get to the nitty-gritty.

"We all wanted to make something of ourselves. When we sat down and put our heads together, the party thing kinda made sense. I do numbers. It's my thing. So the money side was mine."

"And the gambling," she added with a hint of sarcasm.

"It's all numbers. Who else is gonna manage those odds and get the money rolling in? Zak has the computer know-how. He worked all the technology; messaging people, getting word out there and setting us up on social media. He bagged that D.J. gig from the start too. If we left it to Brandon, we'd all be listening to hard-core rap, gothic rock or dark metal. Finn wanted to do his thing. We were never gonna argue with that. And Brandon? He has three main skills; fighting, drinking and women. He had the last two already covered, so we went with the fighting. It channels his negative energy and we all make a lot of money."

"You've got it all covered," she said, using our chosen saying with her response.

"Exactly." I grinned. I was proud of what we'd built. We

were four working-class lads with nothing, but now, we were on our way to better things.

"And Danny? Where did he come into all this?" And here it was. My golden opportunity to manoeuvre the conversation round to where I needed it to go.

"He came to a few parties, helped us with some of the legal stuff."

"Legal?" She scoffed, giving me the side-eye. "What would Danny know about that?"

"He helped me check out venues. Made sure the floor wouldn't collapse on us all. You know, logistics and shit."

"He never talked about it. Not to me." I could tell she didn't quite believe me. Or maybe she didn't want to think about her brother being the fifth Renaissance man.

"He didn't want you involved. None of us did."

She bit her lip in thought, then turned to me. My stomach flipped over at what she was gonna say, because judging from the look on her face, it wasn't good.

"Kian said something the other day, when we saw him at the café in town."

"Kian talks a lot of shit," I spat back, knowing exactly what she was going to say. Kian had already given me the heads-up. "The guy was born with no filter."

"I know, but he said that it was you that warned people away from me. Not Danny. I didn't believe him. In fact, I don't even know why I'm bringing this up. It's crazy."

"It's not crazy," I said, hoping a dose of reality might work in my favour. "It's true. Danny didn't want you involved in the parties…" I took a deep breath and jumped off that tall as fuck cliff into the abyss. "But I didn't want anyone else near you."

She frowned, not getting what I was saying at all. "I don't-"

"I didn't want some other douche-bag dating you. I noticed you, Em. I wanted you. So, I put the word out that you were untouchable."

She sucked in a breath. "What? I don't get it? I didn't think I even registered on your radar. I was Danny's gawky little sister."

"You were mine. Even back then, I knew you were mine." I tried to look her in the eye. I wanted her to see that I meant what I said, but she stared straight ahead to avoid me.

"Ryan, that's crazy, and weird, definitely insane and I should be kicking your ass for totally destroying my high school experience. I went to the end of year eleven dance with Effy as my date. It was mortifying."

I shook my head, trying to look regretful, but I wasn't. I couldn't give a fuck. I did what I did and I still stood by it. The girl was mine. She was too young to be with me back then, but I sure as hell wasn't going to stand by and watch some goofy kid muscle in and take her away from me.

"Seriously, I thought there was something wrong with me. I thought I wasn't good enough, Ryan. That's a really shitty thing to do." She looked at me now, and the pain in her eyes made me doubt myself a little. I pushed that weak motherfucker to the back of my mind right away.

"You were too good, Em. I'm not gonna apologise."

Shit, this was going downhill fast. I needed to put the brakes on this.

"Well, it's lucky for me I had good friends and an awesome brother. It didn't destroy my self-confidence... Much."

"I'm an asshole, Em. I've never claimed to be anything else."

"You are an asshole."

"But I'm your asshole." She tried to keep the stern look on her face, but I was winning her back round, I could tell.

"I could make things very difficult for you, you know." She narrowed her eyes at me in a threat.

I loved that fire in her. She probably could make things very difficult for me. I already had the worst case of blue-balls I'd ever known. My girl could do untold damage. I'd take it though, because it was her. "And I'll love every minute of it," I said, egging her on.

"Ugh. You frustrate the hell out of me sometimes."

"But you love me." Shit that fell out of my mouth before my brain could engage. "You love it," I said, hoping to claw back some self-respect.

The wide eyes she'd given me at my first statement softened slightly and she grinned. "I'll tolerate you. For now."

"In my defence, Danny didn't try to stop me. He was all for me warning them off. I think he liked that we all protected you."

Nice swerve, Hardy. Let's get off that four letter L word and back on track.

"I miss him." She sighed, so I pulled her closer into me and kissed her cheek.

"I was with him, you know. That last night."

She gasped and turned to face me. Her eyes back to saucers again.

"What happened?"

I took her hand and led her to a clearing where we could sit on the grass. I plonked my rucksack down and took out the blanket Dad had insisted I pack. Apparently, women don't like sitting directly on the grass. Who knew?

Emily sat down, and I sat next to her, taking her hand in mine. I wanted to offer her some kind of comfort as I explained to her all about what'd happened. That, and I just couldn't seem to keep my hands off her. I needed to keep touching her whenever she was near.

I told her about Danny only drinking Diet Coke. That he hadn't touched a drop of alcohol and didn't do drugs, ever. I also told her that someone else had picked Danny up. Danny wasn't driving that night. Or at least, he wasn't when he got into the car.

"That makes no sense." She furrowed her brow as if the answers would come to her here in this park. "Danny was found in the driver's seat. There wasn't anybody else there. And the reports-"

"Did you see the reports?"

Bingo. We have a winner.

"No. But Dad said the coroner found all this… Stuff in his system."

And I call bullshit.

"Your dad told you? You never saw any evidence yourself?"

"Why would my dad lie?"

Because he's a self-serving asshole.

"I don't know, Em. And I don't want to upset you, but you need to see if you can find that coroner's report, or a toxicology exam or something. I have a bad feeling about this."

"You think this wasn't an accident, don't you?" The fragile look in her eyes almost broke me.

"I don't know what I think. Listen, Danny was a good guy. But what came out afterwards? It was all horseshit." I took a deep breath before I hit her with the next bombshell. "Does the name Troy Barker mean anything to you?"

"Troy is Dad's mechanic. He maintains all his classic cars. He does other stuff too. I think he's a jack-of-all-trades. Dad's known him for years."

That made sense. If he maintained the cars, then he'd take a pretty nice sum home for his efforts. But something deep in my gut told me something still wasn't right. "And you? Do you know him?" I asked her.

"Not really. He barely speaks when he does come to the house, which isn't often. They do most of their business in Westminster. Dad drives the cars to him. To be honest, he kind of creeps me out. He's scary looking." She grimaced, and I felt myself tense up. I didn't like her being scared of some fucker like this Troy Barker, whoever he was.

"Why does he scare you, babe?" I asked, shifting closer towards her.

She smiled slightly, probably because I'd called her babe. I could tell she liked that. It always made her blush.

"He's got this aura about him. Like he'd take you out without breaking a sweat and probably smoke a cigarette over your dying body afterwards and use you as his ashtray. It's probably the scars. He has some nasty scarring on his face. Dad said they were from the army, but I don't think you get jagged knife scars from the military." She shrugged. "I guess I just don't trust him."

I was glad to hear it. Whoever this guy was, I didn't like to think of him being around her. Not until we'd found out everything we could.

"If he scares you, stay away. Call me if you ever need me."

She chuckled at me. "My knight in shining armour."

"I wouldn't need armour. I'd kick his ass if he even so

much as looked at you the wrong way." I grinned then drew the conversation back round to Danny. "I think your dad would rather use Danny as a soundbite for his campaign than find out the real truth." I didn't want to tell her I thought her dad had Danny's blood on his hands. So, I went with the political angle. It worked.

"That's exactly what he wants." She took a deep breath and a little hiccup escaped. I didn't want her to get upset. I wasn't the best at dating, but I knew crying wasn't ideal on a first date.

"Babe," I said, twisting to face her and taking both of her hands in mine. "Whatever happened, we'll get to the bottom of it, you and me. But let's not spoil today. Danny wouldn't want you getting upset, and if he was sat here with us now, he'd call me out for being a jerk and making you cry."

She laughed through a little tear that'd escaped and rolled down her cheek. "I know."

"Please, don't cry." I brushed her tear away and leaned forward to give her a little kiss. Anything to take her mind off the heartbreak she was facing.

I couldn't help but groan as she kissed me back. She tasted of strawberries, cotton candy, and every fantasy I'd ever had about her.

I could get lost in this girl for days if she'd let me.

She shuffled closer to me and her mouth opened up to let me in. I slid my tongue over hers and her hand went to the back of my head, pulling me in further. Suddenly, it was like the whole damn world fell away, and all I could focus on was her. Her mouth, and the way she felt in my arms, all soft and willing. I pushed her down onto the blanket and she let me. Then I put my leg in-between hers, lying over her and kissing her, desperate to take this further, but wanting to slow it down and capture every second of this in my memory.

I'd waited a long time for her.

I wanted to enjoy every moment with my Emily.

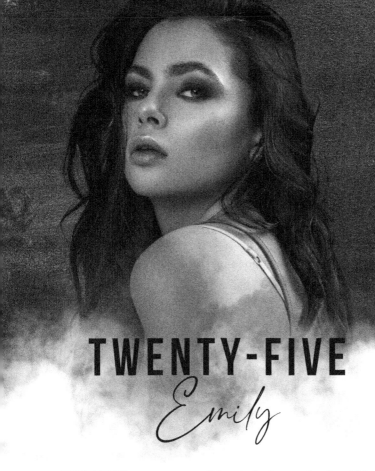

TWENTY-FIVE

Emily

There was something truly hypnotic about kissing Ryan. Even in a wonderland such as this, where the heady scent of flowers invaded your senses and the sound of the breeze blowing and rustling through the trees made you feel at peace, all that faded to nothing. He could make me forget where we were. The pain that I felt losing my brother wasn't gone, but he did a damn good job at overshadowing it. When I was with him, he eclipsed everything.

He lay over me as we kissed on the blanket in the middle of the park, not caring who was walking by. He set my body on fire. Made me desperate and wanton for him. The way his lips moved over mine just felt... right. Like we were meant to fit together like this. I'd kissed guys before, but no one had ever kissed me like Ryan did. He kissed me like I was always his, with urgency and a hint at the promises it could lead to. My body melted into his and I ran my fingers through his hair then scraped my nails along his scalp and down to the nape of his neck. I wanted to pull him further into me, drown in him if I could. I couldn't get enough. The way his tongue teased mine had me squirming and moaning softly underneath him.

Ryan was the first to pull away. I didn't want him to, but he did. He stroked my face as he looked at me like I was the most precious thing he'd ever seen. He held his face millimetres from mine as he caught his breath.

"Damn. What are you doing to me, Em? I've turned into a sixteen-year-old, making out in the park."

I laughed. I guess when you're caught up in a moment it doesn't matter where you are, you've got to go with it.

"I've never made out with anyone in a park before, so I wouldn't know." His face dropped as soon as I said that, and I realised why. He thought I was calling him out on it.

"I didn't do stuff like that... I was just... I..."

"Relax," I said, lifting my head up slightly to plant a quick peck on his lips. "I didn't mean it like that. I like making out like sixteen-year-olds in public."

He let me kiss him, but he soon frowned and pulled away again. "I don't think I like the public bit. I don't like sharing you."

"That's something you'll never have to worry about with me," I replied, making sure he understood from my expression that I was as far removed from his brother's ex-fiancée, Britney, as they came.

"Me too." He stared straight into my eyes and made my heart swell that little bit more for him. "We should really eat some of this food Connor packed for us." He didn't make any effort to move off me, just stared at my lips like he had other plans for them on his mind.

"I don't think I'm hungry." I bit my lip and I noticed a fire ignite in his eyes as I did. "Not for a picnic, anyway."

He gave a low, sexy chuckle and then bent his head down to nibble and kiss my ear and then moved down to my neck. That was a weakness of mine.

I groaned and tilted my head to the side, and Ryan moved further over me, grinding his hips into me as he did. I think kissing my neck and hearing my moans were a weakness for him too, judging from the bulge I could feel in his jeans.

I didn't have that much experience with guys, and I always thought I'd feel awkward and embarrassed about doing stuff, but with Ryan it felt natural. I wanted to experience everything with him. I wasn't so naive to think he'd been saving himself for me, but I'd never seen him with another girl. And the stories I heard were always about Zak and Brandon. Ryan had always been more mysterious, like Finn.

Ryan went from nuzzling my neck to kissing along my jaw and then back to my mouth. His hands had started to move up my body and he was squeezing my hips, then they were moving round to my ass, through my dress. I'd never hated a piece of clothing as much as I hated this one. I wanted to feel his hands on me. I wanted to feel him.

I pushed him up off me gently and whispered, "I don't think

we should be doing this here."

He hung his head in shame and said, "I know. I'm sorry. I couldn't help myself." I didn't like seeing the guilt that swam in his eyes.

"No. I meant we need to go somewhere else."

A sly smile crept onto those plump lips of his and the twinkle in his eyes came back. "I think I know just the place."

He climbed off me and held his hand out to help me stand up. I took it and then stood, brushing down the skirt of my dress and trying to hide the blush that was staining my cheeks at seeing another older couple a few feet away, who probably witnessed everything we'd been doing.

"You're cute when you blush," he whispered into my ear and then brushed past me to pick up the blanket and put it into the back pack. "I'm gonna enjoy finding other ways to make your cheeks go red."

That comment had me blushing even more.

We walked back to the van hand-in-hand. I didn't even notice the stunning surroundings, with its wild flowers and rugged beauty. But I did notice we were gripping each other's hands tightly and were so focused on getting out of here that we were both panting as we walked. My heart was threatening to crowbar its way out of my chest and drop onto the dusty path at Ryan's feet. And as for my body, every nerve-ending was sparking to life in anticipation.

Ryan Hardy was fast becoming an addiction for me.

An addiction I didn't want to come back from.

I'd never seen this side of him before in all the time I'd known him, well… known of him. He'd always been the aloof, guarded, quiet one. Not as quiet as Finn, but he didn't speak unless he really had to. I wondered if he'd been like this with anyone else. I hoped not. I liked to think that this softer, sexy side was all mine.

"You're frowning. What's up?" he said, pulling me from my thoughts. We'd reached his van and he opened the door for me, but when I got in, he stayed where he was and crouched down in front of me. "I don't like those kinds of frowns. Talk to me. Do you want me to take you home?"

"No," I shot back. Home was the last place I wanted to go. "I just… I was thinking…"

"Oh, God. This is gonna be bad, isn't it?" He hung his head then looked back up at me and I reached forward to brush his hair out of his eyes. It made him smile and I felt a little less anxious about what I was gonna say next.

"I was thinking about you… Us… And other girls."

He choked, and his eyes went wide. "Okay. Wasn't expecting that. I'm not Zak. I don't… What?" He looked at me like I'd spoken a foreign language. The weird, hopeless expression on his face made me give a nervous laugh.

"I think I worded that wrong."

"Yeah. And I think I need to sit down to have this conversation."

He lifted himself up and wandered round to the driver's side. I closed my door and turned to him as he blew out a few deep breaths.

"So, you're either asking me about ex-girlfriends or I totally read you wrong and you've got some fetishes that I never saw coming."

"You're different… I mean, with me. You've always been this closed off jerk-"

"Gee, thanks," he cut in.

"You know what I mean. You're a jerk, most of the time. Sorry, but it's true. I'm not saying *I* think you're a jerk, I just-"

"Get to the point, babe." I stopped talking and took a few seconds to gather my thoughts.

"I want to know if you've been like this with other girls. The way you are with me, I mean."

"Em. If you're asking me if I'm a virgin, it's a no." He stared at his lap like he'd just heard it was the end of the world. "I'm sorry. I wish I could tell you otherwise."

"I know that. I'd kind of guessed that already."

He looked across at me and after a few breaths he spoke. "But if you're asking me if I've ever been in love with anyone else, then the answer is no. And no, I've never felt like this before."

He closed his eyes and sighed. When he opened them, I could see honesty and truth there.

"I like being with you, Em. I like what we're building here. I do feel different when I'm with you. I feel like I can be myself. I might still act like a prick when we're in public. I'll definitely act like one around the lads, but that doesn't mean that I'm not aching inside, desperate to get you alone again. There are no girls you have to worry about. Trust me."

"I'm sorry. I shouldn't have asked."

"Yes, you should've. I don't want to put you on the spot about this stuff. But trust me. I'll take all of this at your pace. You control everything."

***

We pulled onto the forecourt of Ryan's family garage, but he drove the van down the side and then stopped when he was adjacent to the workshop. His workshop. I hadn't told a soul about Sean, his dad, showing me around here. It wasn't my story to tell and I kind of liked having a little secret glimpse into Ryan's world. We both got out of the van at the same time and Ryan took my hand.

"I wanted to show you something else. I don't let a lot of people see this," he said as he opened up and stepped back to let me through first, into his space. "This is my workshop. I make cars here." He spoke quietly behind me.

"Wow. It's amazing," I said, thinking I was doing a really good job of appearing startled and in awe. Turns out, I was a crap actress.

"You've seen it already?" He smirked and shook his head.

"What? No! This is all new to me. This is-"

"My dad showed you, didn't he?"

I couldn't hide my smile. "Yes. But before you go off on him, he just wanted to share with me how proud he was of you. Don't get mad."

"Unbelievable." He chuckled. He wasn't mad. I wasn't quite sure what he was, but mad wasn't it. "I told him this part of the lot wasn't open to anyone."

"Well, your dad didn't think I was just anyone."

He must've thought I was hurt because he came over and put his arms around me to hug me.

"I didn't mean that. I meant he needed to go through me first. I don't mind you seeing it. You could never be described as just anyone."

I hugged him back and then the corkboard on the wall caught my eye.

"What is this?"

It was the polaroid picture of me at the warehouse in my white dress, the one I'd seen hiding under the paperwork, back when Sean had given me the grand tour. Only this time it was pinned up on display.

I walked over to it and flicked my finger underneath the picture. I'd hated that night, but then again, if I hadn't gone, would I be standing here right now? On second thoughts, maybe I hadn't hated that night as much as I said I did.

"You think I'm a creeper, don't you?" He tried to look guilty. It just made him look cuter.

"What?" I said sarcastically, rolling my eyes. "You've chased me, freaked me out, scared every guy I've ever met away and now you have polaroids of me pinned to the wall. Why would I think you're a creeper?"

He laughed and picked up the camera that sat on his workbench. "When you put it like that, I sound like more than a creeper." He lifted the polaroid camera and took another photograph of me smirking at him. When the photo shot out, he pulled it free and fanned it, then stuck it next to the white dress one. "I'll own it. When it comes to you, I am a creeper. Maybe stalker sounds better? Or hunter?" He cocked an eyebrow.

"Or guy who takes pictures and isn't freaky or weird at all. I think I'd go with that. You have enough douchebag labels, *Mr Renaissance*."

He threw his head back and laughed, and I swear my whole body went into meltdown. I'd always loved it when he laughed like that, but here in this confined space, standing right in front of me, I couldn't contain myself. I wanted to jump up and climb him, like a monkey climbing up a tree.

"So, what are you working on?" I asked, glancing at the

silver car that sat in the middle of his workshop. It'd transformed even more since I was last here. I'd say it was ready to fly. It looked spectacular.

"Working on? I'm working on trying not to come across as a douchebag to this really hot, really beautiful girl. Even though she's probably thinking up a million excuses to get out of here and escape."

His gaze went from comical to lustful in seconds and he reached over and ran his fingers down my arm. Such a small gesture, and yet I felt goose-bumps break out all over me.

"I think you're doing just fine," I managed to say as I struggled to catch my breath.

He leaned forward to look at me with his hair falling over his eyes. I put my hands on his chest and I could feel his heart beat thumping, racing almost as fast as mine. He swallowed and then with a gravelly voice he said, "If at any time I'm not doing… fine, just tell me. No pressure."

I nodded.

There was a sofa against the back wall and he took my hand and led me across to it. I kicked my ballet pumps off and sat down, curling my feet underneath me. Ryan edged closer towards me, then brushed my hair behind my ear and stroked my cheek.

"Just kiss me," I said, not wanting to wait a second longer, and he did. He crashed his lips to mine in a desperate hungry kiss, taking what he needed. This wasn't sweet and slow like our other kisses. This was raw and passionate. He was holding my head in place and gripping my hair. I did the same, threading my fingers through his hair and pulling him into me. He moved his hands down to my thighs, pushing underneath my skirt and sliding them up until he was cupping my ass, my bare ass.

"Fuck-" he said, pulling his lips away from mine, lifting my skirt and looking down. I guess he liked black lacy thongs, because when he saw what I had on underneath he went full-on animal on me.

He pushed me back, so I was lying down and covered me with his whole body, pressing me into the sofa. Then his lips were back on mine; his tongue tasting and teasing me, his hands massaging my ass and his hips grinding into me. I kissed him back, lacing my tongue with his, loving how warm and sexy he felt. I ran my hands from his hair to his neck then I did some exploring of my own, dipping underneath his T-shirt to feel the rock-hard abs he had hidden under there.

He broke away, both of us panting like we'd run a marathon, and he reached behind to pull his T-shirt off over his head, all the time keeping eye contact with me. He was perfection. Tanned, toned and looking good enough to eat. He threw the T-shirt onto the floor and started to kiss me again. I couldn't keep my hands off him. He felt so smooth, so sexy and so mine. I hated that my dress was stopping me from getting the full Ryan Hardy experience. I wanted his skin against me without any barriers.

He started to kiss down my neck and I gasped, closing my eyes. His fingers toyed with the straps of my dress and then I felt him pulling, sliding them down my arms.

"Is this okay?" he asked in a husky voice. I couldn't stop this even if I wanted to. Scratch that. I didn't want to stop it. Boy, I couldn't even form coherent thoughts right now.

"Yes," I replied in a breathy voice. He lifted up onto his elbows slightly and I managed to pull my arms free of the straps of my dress. I lay there in my black lacy bra with my dress bunched around my waist. Ryan's breathing was deep, and he touched my chest delicately with his fingers, tracing over the lace. Then he bent down and put his mouth over my breast, sucking through the lace. I gave a little cry and pushed myself up into him. It felt good feeling his hot wet mouth on me, even through the material.

He bit down gently, taking my puckered nipple into his mouth and rubbing it with his tongue. Then he let go and moved to my other breast, giving it the same treatment. I writhed underneath him. I knew breasts could be sensitive, but they'd never felt like this. Having him kiss them was making me wet, and I could feel pulsing in-between my legs. I hooked one of my legs over his hip and angled myself, rubbing against him to get some kind of friction.

Ryan's hand went around my back, feeling for the hook of my bra, and then he snapped it, pulling it right off and dropping it next to his T-shirt. I didn't feel shy or embarrassed lying under him like this. I'd always thought I would, but I didn't. He made me feel safe, protected, desired. The heat in his eyes made me feel powerful. A power I liked having. I wanted more.

"You're so beautiful, Em," he whispered as he looked from my eyes to my breasts and then his mouth was on them again; sucking, biting, driving me absolutely crazy. I couldn't stop panting. I was breathless with need. He massaged them with his hands as he went to work with his talented tongue and I held his head, grabbing fistfuls of his hair in desperation.

I could feel the hardness in his jeans and I ground my hips into him, trying to get some relief. He moved his hand down my body and back onto my thigh, lifting my skirt. He kneaded my ass then he moved to inside my thigh, his fingers stroking so so close to where I needed them, but not quite getting there.

"Please," I begged quietly into the air and he moaned, rubbing his fingers over my pussy through my underwear. So fucking good and still not enough.

"You're so wet," he groaned into my ear. Rubbing me over and over. I lifted my hips, wanting, no, needing more. "Can I touch you?" he asked. I nodded then gave a low, guttural groan as he ran his finger underneath the thin strip of lace and pushed it aside. Then his finger was on me, sliding through my lips and over my clit, making me roll my hips in time with him.

He rubbed in circles and then slowly he moved lower, pushing his finger inside me and making me moan louder. I could feel the palm of his hand against me as he stroked inside, curling forward and making me sweat and pant for more. It felt so good. Too good. He was fucking me with his fingers and I loved it.

"I want to taste you," he gasped into my ear and I nodded again. I wasn't capable of speaking. I was too lost in the sensations he was creating. All I could focus on was what he was doing to me and grinding my hips to make it feel even better.

He kissed down my stomach, flicking his tongue into my belly button and I watched him, my eyes heavy and my body like liquid. I stroked over his hair as he ventured lower and he looked up at me, full of lust and desire. I knew right then I'd do anything for him.

He pulled his finger out and I moaned at the loss of him. But he just smiled and then pulled my thong down my legs and clean off. Then he opened my legs wider and sighed. "So fucking beautiful and so fucking mine."

He bent down, using his thumbs to part my lips and then

he ran his tongue over my clit. My hips bucked forward involuntarily, and I cried out. Holy shit, I'd never felt anything this good in my whole life. He licked over and around my clit and then sucked it into his mouth, rubbing his tongue over and over before letting it pop out again.

Fuck, this was gonna send me over the edge.

He carried on licking, swirling, sucking, teasing me with his tongue and I rocked my hips onto his mouth being more brazen than I'd ever been. I didn't even recognise this Emily. She was wild. He made me wild.

I could feel myself tighten up down there and I clung to the edge of the sofa.

"Oh... Ryan, I'm..."

He pushed his finger inside me as he fucked me with his mouth and I lost all ability to speak. I couldn't even finish my sentence. I felt a build up inside me and then my whole body started to shake. My pussy clamped down tightly onto his fingers, like the muscles were going into spasm. My clit was pulsing fast like a drum and my legs were quivering like jelly. Holy fucking shit. So, that was what an orgasm felt like.

He lapped gently in-between my legs as little sparks and aftershocks went off. I lay there with my eyes closed feeling like I'd just gone through something biblical. Life changing. Truth be told, I had. Was it always like this? This all-consuming, heart-stopping, mind-blowingly amazing? From what Liv had told me, it wasn't. Maybe I'd hit the jackpot. First time lucky.

Ryan rested back over me, he still had his jeans on, and when I kissed him I could taste myself on his lips. It was such a turn-on. And as sated as I felt, I still wanted to feel him. Do for him what he'd done for me. I ran my hand over the front of his jeans and I could feel how impossibly hard he was. He broke our kiss, but kept his forehead pressed against mine.

"I don't expect you to do anything. Tonight has been perfect," he said. I bit my lip and nodded, then popped the button on his jeans. I could feel his dick already poking out of the top. Even his boxers couldn't hold him in. "Are you sure?" he asked.

"Yes. I want to see you. Touch you." I smiled, and he helped me to push his jeans and boxers off. He kicked them off onto the floor and lay next to me on the sofa, completely naked. "You're beautiful," I said, mirroring his words from earlier and he laughed.

"That's the first time I've ever been called beautiful." He pecked my nose and then rubbed it down the side of mine, giving me a slow seductive kiss. I loved Ryan's kisses. I loved tasting him. But right now, he was distracting me. I moved my head to look down at his dick which was hard, long and thick. It was resting on my stomach and I went to touch him, but hesitated.

"Touch me, baby," he said, taking my hand and wrapping it around his length. It felt soft like velvet even though it was hard. I wasn't expecting that. He kept his hand over mine to show me how he liked to be stroked. I was glad. I didn't have the first clue how to do this, but he didn't seem to mind. When I found my rhythm, he moved his hand away and started kissing me again, squeezing my breasts and thrusting his hips into my hand. I wasn't done exploring though, and when I took my hand away from his shaft and started to stroke over his balls, he moaned.

"Oh, baby. Just like that." I knew I had to go gentler here and so I stroked and tickled, dragging my nails oh-so-delicately across his skin before cupping them. "So good." He moaned and when I moved back to rubbing his shaft, he started to thrust faster into my hand. "Harder, baby. Hold me a little tighter." I did, and he settled his head into the crook of my neck and started to grunt, pistoning his hips into me.

Suddenly, he pulled away and kneeled in-between my legs.

"I'm gonna come," he said, moving my hand away and pumping his dick fast in his hand. I watched fascinated as he lifted my skirt back up with one hand and then beads of white cum spurted out of his dick onto my stomach. Hearing him groan made me start pulsing all over again. It was the hottest thing I'd ever seen, watching Ryan come on me… because of me.

"Holy fuck," he said, resting back on his haunches and throwing his head back. "Fuck."

He opened his eyes and looked at me, panting. I reached forward and ran my thumb over the tip of his dick, saving the last drop, and then I sucked my thumb into my mouth. His eyes bugged out of his head.

"Fucking hell, Em. That's so fucking sexy. I really want to kiss the fuck out of you."

"That's a lot of f-bombs, babe."

"All very necessary right now," he said, leaning over to grab a box of tissues from the work bench behind him. He wiped himself off my stomach and then lay back over me, pulling me into him and kissing me. "Why have I waited so long? I should've locked you down ages ago." He gave me a cheeky smile and I wrapped my arms around him to hold him close.

"Because all good things come to those who wait. Or is it save the best till last?"

"First, last, I don't care. You, Em are everything."

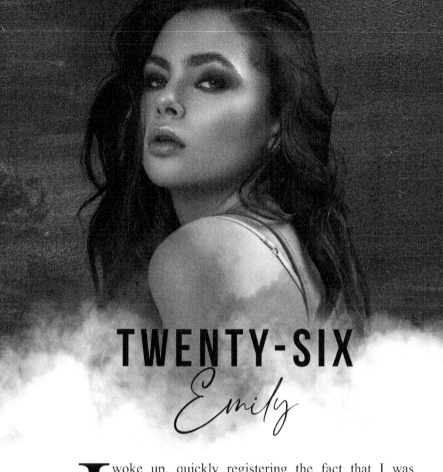

TWENTY-SIX
Emily

I woke up, quickly registering the fact that I was resting my head on a very warm, very solid chest and shamelessly drooling all over it. I reached my hand up slowly to wipe the evidence away and hoped he wasn't awake to notice. As I moved, he stirred too, stretching his arms and then he planted a kiss on the top of my head. We were still tangled together on the tiny sofa in his workshop. I had no idea what time it was, but I was hoping it wasn't too late.

Ryan reached down to the side of him and picked up his mobile phone from the pocket of his jeans. The screen flashed to life and he jolted, sitting upright, but making sure not to throw me off him as he did.

"Shit. Babe, it's five-thirty."

My mouth went dry. How the hell had we managed to sleep through the night? I wracked my brains, trying to remember if my dad would be home or still in London. I didn't have a curfew as such since turning eighteen and I was technically an adult. But I knew if I got caught by him, sneaking in this morning, my life wouldn't be worth living for the foreseeable future. Especially if he put two and two together and worked out where I'd been. Luckily, by my calculations, he wasn't due back until tomorrow.

"I really need to go home."

I still had my dress on, albeit gathered around my waist. I smoothed the skirt to cover my modesty and looked past Ryan to the floor to see where my underwear was. He was gloriously naked without a care in the world. I was covering my chest with my arms and trying not to blush. In the harsh light of day my confidence was starting to ebb away.

"Don't hide yourself from me." He sighed, pulling my arms down and giving me a gentle kiss. "You're beautiful. Own it."

"I'm not as body confident as you," I said, trying but failing to not stare at the impressive erection he had going on.

"It's morning. It always does that." He laughed and then he reached round and picked up our clothes from the floor, passing my bra over and then shifting around to put his boxers on. He stood up and got himself dressed in record time while I sweated with embarrassment and wrestled with my bra clasp. My first morning after the night before and I got it now. I understood why Liv had called it the walk of shame. I didn't feel shame as such. I didn't regret anything I'd done with Ryan last night. But I felt the burn of awkwardness and self-consciousness this morning as it singed my skin. I was sure I was the colour of a beetroot right about now.

Ryan turned to face me, and he must've noticed my unease. He was getting quite good at reading me.

"Are you okay?" he asked, concern washing over him. He sat back down on the sofa next to me and took my hand in his. "Please tell me I haven't scared you away. I know we got caught up with everything last night, but I can honestly say, hand on heart, that was the best night ever." The little boy smirk he gave me melted any tension I felt in an instant.

"Enough already. I told you, I don't scare easily. Not when it comes to you, anyway. I had a good time last night."

"I didn't even feed you. I should stop off to pick us up some breakfast on the way back to yours. We need coffee too," he said on a big yawn.

"I think I need to get back before my mum gets up. I'd prefer to avoid the twenty questions."

"Tell her you stayed at your friend's house."

"I would, but I'm a crap liar. She'd see right through me in a second. No. Best to get home and face the music."

"Can I see you tonight?" he ventured as if he expected me to say no.

"I'd like that."

We held hands as he led us out into the dusky morning. The sun had barely come up and the breeze had that dewy crisp morning feel to it. I felt alive and I took a deep breath, smiling over at Ryan as I did. He went to open the van, but a deep voice stopped him.

"Morning, Emily, son. Good night was it?"

We both turned to see Sean standing a few feet away with

a steaming mug in his hands. He was dressed in his overalls, ready for his working day. I had no idea they started so early.

"Hi, Mr. Hardy. Sorry. I would stay to chat, but I'm late home." I waved awkwardly and cringed at how ridiculous I sounded. Ryan must've agreed as I heard him give a low chuckle.

"It's Sean, I told you." He glanced at his watch then looked back up at me. "And I'd say you're about seven hours too late, young lady. I hope your dad doesn't get the shotgun out. He might look fit, but my son can't run for toffee."

It was my turn to scoff under my breath.

"Son, run in a zig-zag. It'll make it harder for him to get a decent shot in," Sean said laughing.

As if the morning wasn't mortifying enough, Connor, Ryan's brother, chose that exact moment to come out and join us. He wasn't work-ready though. He had a towel wrapped around his hips and rivulets of water still trickled down his chest from the shower he'd just taken. I tried not to look, but it was hard not to.

"Jesus. Really, Con?" Ryan said, and he grabbed the door handle to the van with a bit too much aggression, yanking it open and huffing as he did.

"Did you like my scones?" Connor asked, looking at me with a twinkle in his eyes. "They're pretty good, aren't they?"

"Best scones I had last night," I answered, and Ryan smirked.

"I'm taking Em home, then I'll be back to clean up and get to work," Ryan said addressing his dad. "And next time you talk to my girl, put some fucking clothes on," he snapped at Connor.

Connor threw his head back and laughed, then he sauntered off towards the house they all lived in that adjoined their thriving little garage. That must be a Hardy family trait, I guessed. No wonder all the ladies they dated were losing their shit. That laugh did things to a girl.

"I'm sorry about my asshole brother," Ryan said, starting the van up and grinding his teeth in irritation. "I swear to God he does that shit on purpose, just to fuck with me."

I reached over to squeeze his thigh as we pulled out onto the road. "I have no idea what you're talking about. I only had eyes for you back there."

He chuckled and glanced at me before focusing back on his driving. "Good answer, babe. Good answer."

As it turned out, the Gods were on my side that morning and I managed to sneak back home just before six without waking anyone. Mum's empty bottle of chardonnay still sat on the island in the kitchen. She probably crawled off to her vacant bed in a wine-induced haze and wouldn't be up until around midday. She tended to drink more when Dad was away. I guessed she was lonely. I'd tried to fill the gap, create movie nights and give her the attention I knew she craved, but I was a poor substitute. Most days, when Dad worked, Mum was on the wine by mid-afternoon.

***

"That's what a great orgasm will do to you." Liv cackled as I filled her and Effy in on everything that'd happened since the Chase Lockwood debacle. I wasn't sure how they'd take the news about me and Ryan being... Well, I wasn't sure what we were. Was he my boyfriend? We were definitely dating.

"It's a scientific fact," she carried on, talking way too loudly in the café we were in and drawing unwanted attention our way. "Some hormone or chemical that it creates. You orgasm and then you have the best sleep ever. I tell you, a hot guy is the cure for all insomniacs."

"I don't think insomnia is cured that easily," I whispered shaking my head, but I couldn't help smiling at her enthusiasm.

"Maybe not. It helps me though." Liv winked and then continued to grill me on every sordid detail she could get out of me, which wasn't a lot. I was happy to share the basics, but the rest was private, between Ryan and me. I liked it that way.

"Any news on the Zak front?" I asked, steering the conversation away from the size of Ryan's dick.

"Don't say that name to me." Liv clammed up and Effy took over.

"He was in Walkabout last night with Kelly Hopton. They looked pretty close."

Walkabout was a local bar in town and I raised my eyebrow in surprise at what they'd seen. If Zak was gonna settle down and date, Kelly Hopton would've been the last girl I'd have expected him do that with. Even Kelly didn't do relationships. Hell, maybe that was the point. They were the perfect fit.

"And he said he didn't do dating. Fucking piece of crap. I hate him." Liv took a gulp of her coffee and then hissed when she scorched her mouth.

"He doesn't deserve you, Liv." I patted her knee, then gave her a side hug.

"He doesn't." She nodded, sniffing back a sob. "I hope for your sake Ryan is different. Those boys are assholes."

I saw Effy's eyes go wide and she opened her mouth to speak, then thought better of it and closed it again.

"He is," I answered, because truthfully, I believed he was. "Ryan and Finn are good guys." Effy nodded in agreement. And I reminded myself to ask her about Finn later when we were alone. There was a story there, I could tell.

TWENTY-SEVEN
Ryan

The gym where Brandon worked could've done with a Finn-style overhaul. The walls were stark white with inspirational quotes painted onto them in a black uninspiring font. There was nothing motivating about them at all other than the fact they told you to do better, reach your goals, push yourself to your limits. We did that every day. We didn't need some shitty quote to tell us. I figured a bit of self-reflective art from Finn's warped and sometimes depraved mind would've worked better. But what did I know? I dealt with cars and numbers for a living.

The buzz and whir of the equipment in the main workout

area drowned Kanye out beautifully from the speakers around the room. I walked through and headed towards the back where the lads were waiting in the room with the boxing ring. I think Brandon would've preferred to have the ring in the middle of the gym. Give him a chance to showcase what he could do to all the girls working out. Instead, he had to come back to a private room to punch the shit out of the punch bag, or any fucker that was stupid enough to get into the ring with him. We weren't complaining. It made for a better, more private meeting place.

I opened the door to find Zak and Kian already there, leaning against the wall and gritting their teeth. When I glanced at the ring I could see why. Brandon was in there with Finn, giving him another boxing lesson. I could already tell Finn was over it, but Brandon wouldn't give up. Finn wasn't a fighter. He wasn't weak, but he didn't lose his shit like the rest of us. Brandon saw him as his pet project though. In Brandon's mind, he was going to train Finn, so he could defend himself from any motherfucker that didn't look at him the right way. Thing was, I don't think Finn even noticed the way people looked at him. The problem seemed to weigh heavier on Brandon than it did on Finn. I guess that's the sign of a good friend. They've got your back even when you don't think you need it.

"We need to work on your upper cut." Brandon raised his pads up, but Finn shook his head and lowered his arms, letting them fall limply at his sides. "Come on, man. Give me five more jabs. Only five. You can do it."

"Screw this," Finn said, wandering over to the edge of the ring and motioning for Zak to help him get his gloves off.

"You'll never get better if you don't practise." Brandon rolled his neck and did a few jumps like he was limbering up for his next fight.

Finn held his bare hands up in front of him. "I appreciate the sentiment, but these are my tools. They create my art. I don't want to damage them."

"It'll be your face that gets damaged if you don't learn how to protect yourself," Brandon shot back. "How will you make art then, if you can't see through two swollen black eyes?"

"Why does he need to protect himself? He has us," I piped in, earning myself a scowl from Brandon for my troubles.

"We might not always be around," Brandon said in a low voice, giving me a pointed stare that told me to back the fuck off. Then he threw his pads down and sat in the middle of the ring, staring at each of us like he was picking his next opponent.

"Is there something I'm missing here?" I asked, turning to Zak.

Kian was grinning like an idiot. He wasn't usually in on our meetings. It must've gone to his head. Fucker looked like a ball-boy at Wimbledon, he was so desperate to do something useful. It was on the tip of my tongue to tell him to get the coffees, but Zak caught me off guard.

"I think we're good to go."

"What do you mean, we're good to go?" I looked between the guys to see if they knew more than me. I didn't like being left out of the loop.

"I mean, we have all the evidence we need to bury that fucker, Winters. He's gonna go down for a long time with the shit we've got on him and don't get me started on Morgan fucking Rotherham." He grinned, rubbing his hands together. "I broke through, Ry. I got names, addresses, account details, everything. He's been scamming for years. Made millions. He'll be paying it all back at *Her Majesty's Pleasure* once we've set our plans in motion."

"Shit. This is gonna be fucking epic, man," Brandon said smirking.

"What have you got?" Kian asked with a puzzled look on his face.

"Nothing for you to worry about, mate," Zak replied and then gave me a look that told me the less Kian knew the better. He wasn't the best at keeping his mouth shut.

I patted Kian on the back and decided the coffee idea was the way to go. "We could do with some drinks in here, Ki. You know our orders, don't you?" I ushered him towards the door and stuffed the cash to pay into his hand.

"I... Er... Okay, Ry. Whatever you say, man." He kept the grin on his face, but I could tell he was disappointed at being side-lined. It wouldn't be for long. I just needed to hear the full story and then we'd pull him back in, like we always did.

Once he was gone I turned to face the others. "Hit me with it."

Zak took a deep breath and sat on the edge of the ring. "Winters is in bed with some pretty nasty dudes. He's using businesses he's taken over, local businesses, to clean their dirty money. Drug money. He's giving them a legitimate source to run their funds through. I have it all in black and white. He tends to float around the companies, using different ones to avoid detection. He made a massive mistake using the Rotherham account though. He gave us a link. I tell you, this guy is going down for life once we hand this over."

I grabbed the back of my neck and took a deep breath. I knew my dad had been approached by Winters a few years ago.

Promised him a cash injection to support his business, all in the name of Sandland. Supporting his local area like the hero he wanted everyone to think he was. Luckily, Dad told him where to stick his cash. Good job too. This guy had fucked half the town in the ass without lube and none more so than his own family. What the hell was I supposed to tell Emily?

"That guy, Troy Barker, he's a mechanic. Works for Winters," I said absent-mindedly. All I could focus on was what I was gonna say to Em. Her whole life was about to be blown wide open, and even though I knew this was gonna happen when we started all this, I hadn't really thought what the impact of the fallout would be. She'd lose everything. Her house, her family, her goddamn mind. After what'd happened to Danny, I wasn't sure how much more she could take.

"He's no mechanic." Zak looked over at Brandon then back to me. "He's a fixer."

"Fixing what?" I was losing patience fast. I had to think of a plan for after. A plan for her. I couldn't lose her. Not now.

"That's where my online breaking and entering falls short. I was kinda hoping that Brandon might be able to help me with another way," Zak said cryptically.

"What? To pay this guy a visit?" I asked

"Sort of. But not really." Zak looked guilty as hell. He might've been a whizz at computers, but he couldn't make a poker face to save his life.

"Do you think he'll talk to you?" Finn added.

"We won't give him a fucking choice," Brandon said clenching his jaw in irritation.

"What you gonna do, beat the truth out of him?" I knew Brandon had a mean right hook, but we had no idea who this guy was. And from what Emily had told me, he could turn out to be a big fucking problem for us.

"Ask me no questions and I'll tell you no lies." Sometimes Brandon's bravado packed more of a punch than his actual fists. He was a loose cannon. Which might've served us well in the fights we staged for money, but in real life, I was worried it could all blow up in our faces.

"I don't need to ask any fucking questions, I can already guess what you're gonna do. Just make sure you don't leave any evidence behind. You don't want to get stuck sharing a cell with Winters for the next five to ten years." Brandon rolled his eyes at me.

"I've got a question." Finn spoke and we all stopped in our tracks. "How do we shop him without incriminating ourselves? 'Cos I'm pretty sure there's a law against the hacking we've been doing. Not to mention the parties and-"

"You let us worry about that," Brandon said sharply. "Tom might help us. Anyway, I'm pretty sure they'd overlook our scams if it meant they could catch some bigger fish like Winters. That's the gift that keeps on giving. All those links to the cartel? Nobody's gonna turn that shit away for the sake of a few dudes throwing illegal parties like we do."

"I hope you're right." Finn nodded, but the way he bit his lip, I could tell he had more on his mind.

"Spit it out, Finn," I said, folding my arms over my chest.

"Do you think we can pull this off? The plan, I mean?"

We all looked at one another.

"We've been planning this for years. This is going to be fucking epic, my man," Brandon said, jumping up from his seated position in the ring. "I've been living for this moment."

He laughed and started to jab his fists into the air like he was fighting an invisible opponent.

"It'll be fine. Don't worry so much." Zak patted Finn on the back and smiled as Kian walked back through the door with four Starbucks coffee cups in a holder.

"This is gonna break her," Finn said in a low voice so only I could hear. "Are you really ready for that?"

I closed my eyes and let my head fall forward.

"I'll have to be."

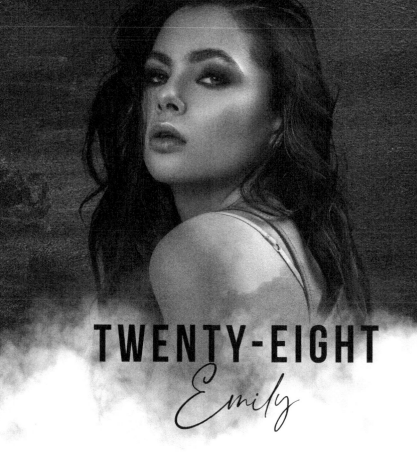

TWENTY-EIGHT
Emily

My phone buzzed for the hundredth time that afternoon. I glanced down at the screen and smiled when I saw Ryan's message staring back at me.

Can I see you later?

I thought about making him wait, letting the message stew for a little longer on my phone, but I was never the most patient person, so I fired off my response.

You can see me whenever you want. x

I hadn't even put my phone down again when it buzzed with an answer.

That'll be a lot then.

I couldn't believe how things had changed. Months ago, Ryan Hardy was the bad boy in town that I couldn't even look at directly. He was too intimidating. Now, he was all I thought about. He consumed me in every way possible.

I heard the doorbell go, and knowing my mum was out for the day, I reluctantly stood up and dragged myself to answer it. I laughed when I saw Ryan standing there with a beautiful bunch of pink peonies.

"I thought you wanted to see me later?" I laughed, taking the flowers. They smelt heavenly, as did he.

"This is later." He shrugged and stepped past me into the hallway, giving me a peck on the cheek as he did.

I closed the door, struggling to keep the grin off my face. "I need to put these in some water. Do you want something to drink?"

He smirked and started walking down the hallway, not waiting for me to lead him.

"Are your parents here?" he asked, craning his neck to look through each doorway he passed. I'm pretty sure he already knew the answer to that question, seeing as I'd let him in. After his last encounter with my dad, I'd figured it was best to keep those two parts of my world separate if I wanted an easy life.

"No. Dad's working and Mum's getting her Botox topped up. Is Coke okay? Or do you want something else?"

"I'll take the Coke for now," he said in a raspy voice. "And then the something else… As long as it isn't a plate of fucking cookies."

Fireworks. That's what I felt. Pure fireworks going off inside me at the way he was looking at me. I had an overwhelming urge to drop the peonies on the floor and jump on him. Ryan Hardy was in my house and he wanted *something else*. Knowing that did something to me. I was a little nervous, maybe scared, but definitely turned on. I shuffled around in the doorway, not knowing what to do with myself.

"There's a card in the flowers." He nodded to the bouquet in my hands as he sat down on the sofa and grabbed the remote to turn on the T.V.

I balanced them in the crook of my arm and took the little white envelope out from the top. My hands were shaking so much, I must've looked like such loser. Inside was a little card with an address on and a smiley face. I frowned, having absolutely no clue what this was about. I'd expected poetry or at least a cheeky comment, not a random address with an emoji drawn at the bottom.

"It's the next party," he said as he flicked through the channels. "I didn't want you getting some generic message this time. You get the V.I.P. treatment."

"Wow. I'm honoured. This isn't the chapel though. Where is it this time?" I'd have died a little inside if they'd have gone ahead and used that stunning little sanctuary to get crapped all over by half the town.

"Old furniture factory. Finn's there now making a start on his latest masterpiece. It's gonna be a bitch to clean it up and get it ready, but we'll do it. We always do." He settled back into the sofa as the theme tune for Top Gear played out.

"I can't wait to see it." I sighed and went to head to the kitchen but stopped and turned back round. I was all over the damn place today.

"What's up?" he asked, muting the T.V.

"I tried to find a toxicology report, but there's nothing. Mum said Dad shredded everything linked to the accident after the inquest. She said he was too heartbroken, he needed it all gone. I'm sorry." I felt the shift in atmosphere. Ryan had pinned his hopes on me and I'd come up short. Would he change his mind about us if he didn't think I was useful anymore? Was that what this was? A way to get to my father? I felt a sharp pain in my chest and I winced. I didn't want to be the pawn in any of his games.

He stood from the sofa, but I held my hand up. "I'm okay. Really."

He didn't look convinced and came to stand in front of me, putting both of his hands either side of my face so I'd have no choice but to look him in the eyes.

"You don't have to be strong with me, Em. I'm here for you."

I sighed, feeling myself get lost in those sympathetic green eyes of his. The depth of emotion I could see there made me soften and I felt myself leaning into him.

"Honestly, it's fine. Bringing up Danny, asking about the accident, it helped. Me and Mum spoke about him, I mean really talked about him for the first time in months. I think it helped us both. We argued, got mad, cried. Everything we should've done months ago. I'm not saying we're running for mother and daughter of the year, there's still a long way to go, but last night was a start." He smiled and placed a soft, gentle kiss on my forehead. "Bet you didn't know your snooping around would bring me and my mum closer together."

"Nice to know I'm good for something." The look he gave me made my stomach twist with expectation at what else he was good at. This boy was turning me into a hormonal mess. If I didn't move soon I'd be a pool of desire melted at his feet.

"I'm sure you're good for other things too." I tried to sound sexy in a nonchalant way, but my breathy voice gave me away.

"Yeah? Like what?" He leaned closer to me now and the tension that was building up inside me reached fever pitch.

"I don't know. But when I find out, I'll let you know." I really needed to up my seduction game. The words coming out of my mouth sounded more like a brush-off than a come-on. My heart screamed at me to get on my damn tiptoes and kiss the hell out of him, while my head told me to play it cool, be more guarded. I chose me, right? Jesus, that felt like a lifetime ago, when Nurse Constance played cupid on acid. And I'd thought I was so strong, making it all about me. But now, standing in front of Ryan, I realised that strong was taking a chance on something that scared you half to death. Taking the leap into the unknown to see where it could lead. I might be heading for a whole lot of heartbreak where Ryan was concerned, but on the other hand, it could be the best thing to ever happen to me. *He* could be the best thing to happen to me. If I didn't take a chance I'd never know.

I remembered my mum once telling me, all those years ago before things turned sour, that it's the little things in life we should treasure. "Don't sweat the big stuff," she'd said. "It's the little things in life that count. Those moments in time that are as fleeting as a butterfly. Beautiful, but gone so soon." I knew what she meant now.

A memory was worth more than any possession and I wanted to create memories with Ryan. No matter how long this lasted. I wanted to be strong and let myself see where this could go.

I backed away slowly, holding up the flowers to indicate that I was taking them to put them in some water. Ryan didn't move, just pierced me with his seductive stare, making it harder for me to turn away from him, but I did, and I floated down the hallway, ready to dump the flowers into the first vase of water I could lay my hands on, grab the drinks and get back to him.

When I walked back into the living room a minute later, Ryan was gone. My heart dropped, thinking he'd given up on me and bailed, then I tried to recall hearing the door shut. I hadn't. Where the hell was he?

"Ryan?" I called out, leaving the cans of Coke on the coffee table and wandering back out into the hallway, feeling all kinds of mixed up.

"Yeah?" I heard him answer from upstairs.

What the hell was he up to?

I climbed the stairs expecting to find him in Danny's room, but he wasn't there, and my bedroom door was wide open. When I reached the doorway I saw Ryan, lying on my bed with his trainers kicked off and his hands behind his head. He'd turned on my T.V. and looked pretty comfy settling down to watch something. He was so cocky and self-assured, all traits that I would've called him out on a few months ago, but not now. Now it was sexy as hell.

"The T.V. in the living room is bigger than this one." I folded my arms and leaned against the doorframe trying to appear unaffected, but seeing Ryan lying on my bed was hot and very distracting.

"Maybe I didn't come up here for the T.V." He pointed the remote forward and switched the T.V. off. "Maybe I came here to find out a little bit more about you. Be in your bubble. You did say you liked bubbles." He gave me a playful smirk and I laughed.

He patted the space next to him, so I stepped in and closed the door behind me. Then I went over and sat on the edge of the bed. He quirked his eyebrow at me and pushed himself up on his elbows.

"You're not gonna make this easy for me, are you?" he said, reaching over and stroking my arm, leaving a trail of goose-bumps behind.

"All good things are worth fighting for," I managed to say, even though my heart was about to burst wide open. Being on a bed with him was like every birthday and Christmas rolled into one.

"I think we've done enough fighting."

He leaned over and put his hand behind my head, pulling me down to kiss him. I gave in. I always did when it came to him. I fell onto the bed, lying half over him as he wrapped his arms around me. I loved the way his lips moulded with mine. The way our tongues laced together; tasting, teasing, opening up to one another. My hands were itching to touch him everywhere. I ran my fingers through his hair and he groaned as my nails raked over his scalp and then down to his neck. I moved lower, running my hands down his firm chest and reaching underneath his T-shirt to touch the velvet, rock-hard abs he kept hidden under there.

"I love the way you touch me," he whispered as his kisses moved along my jawline then down to my neck. He rolled me backwards and crawled over me, pressing me into the mattress as he kissed my neck then my shoulder. His hands skimmed down my sides, grasping my hips and then his fingers traced circles on my thighs, dancing up and under the skirt of my dress. He went back to kissing my lips, but I lost all focus as his fingers worked their way up higher, reaching my ass and squeezing hard.

"Don't be scared to touch me there too," he said, leaning away slightly and looking down at where my fingers hovered over the buttons of his jeans. He lifted his T-shirt over his head and threw it to the floor, then looked at me and smirked. "I'll let you do the rest."

A surge of confidence swept over me and I pulled on the buttons to loosen his jeans. Then I sat up on my knees and he lifted his hips to help me take his jeans and boxers off. His dick was long, hard and… Would you call a dick beautiful? He certainly was stunning lying here on my bed, totally naked. I couldn't take my eyes off him. He was perfect.

He sat up and pulled me to him, kissing me and running his hands through my hair. I let my fingers glide over his taut thighs and then in-between his legs, and he moved slightly, opening himself up so I could explore, touch and stroke him better. He broke our kiss so that he could watch me, panting slowly as I feathered delicate touches over him. I could tell he was as affected by this as I was.

He took the skirt of my dress in his hands and lifted it up and over my head. Then when he saw me, sat there in my pink lacy bra and knickers, he groaned.

"I swear to God, Em. You're the most beautiful girl I've ever seen. I can't believe your mine." I loved that. That he said I was his.

"So are you." I blushed as I spoke, and I could tell by the look in his eyes he needed more. "And you're mine." The heat that was smouldering between us turned into a blazing inferno and I couldn't hold back anymore. Neither one of us could.

He pushed me down onto the bed and kissed me hard, his body covered mine and I could feel him pressing against my stomach; hard, warm and ready for me. He reached round to open the clasp of my bra and pulled it off slowly. Then he was on my chest, taking a nipple into his mouth; sucking and biting then rubbing his tongue over to ease the sting.

The way he kissed and nibbled over me made me pulse with longing. I felt myself rubbing up against him and his hands squeezed my ass. Then he grabbed behind my thigh, nudging my legs open. His fingers were on me, circling my clit and through my wetness. I moaned quietly as he circled and stroked, spreading my wetness and making everything throb with need. When he pushed his finger inside me, I gasped, and he covered my mouth with his again, stroking his tongue in time with his finger. I rocked my hips into him, desperate for more. The way he curled his fingers inside me sent me spiralling into an ecstasy I remembered from the other night.

I reached down to take his dick in my hand and I stroked him, matching the rhythm he'd set. He pushed his hips forward, using my hand to bring him to his own release.

"Oh, baby. This feels so good." Ryan grunted, as he buried his head into my neck and fucked me with his fingers. The way his thumb and palm brushed over my clit sent sparks straight through me.

He started to piston his hips faster into my hand as he teased me between my legs. The burning tension turned to a pulse and then I could feel myself falling, heading towards something mind-blowing.

"I'm coming, Ryan," I managed to say just as my legs gave way and my whole body started shaking. The pulse and the sparks were insane. It was out of this world crazy shit, and I couldn't get enough. I cried out as he carried on rubbing me, prolonging my orgasm, and then he gave a low moan, and whisper-shouted, "Fuck," before I felt him thicken and come on my hand and the bed.

He rode out his orgasm and then slumped over me, his head buried deep in-between my neck and my pillow. We lay together for a few minutes to catch our breath. Then Ryan lifted up slightly, kissed my nose and reached over to grab some tissues from the side of my bed to wipe away the evidence of what we'd done. I watched him, waiting to see if he'd make another move, maybe try to take it further. As much as I'd enjoyed it, I knew he wouldn't be satisfied with just my hand for long.

As he cleaned us both up I started to stutter over my words. "I… That was… I don't know… I've never…"

Real smooth, Em. Come on, girl. Get your shit together.

He grinned and pulled me into him, pulling the corner of the duvet so it rested over us. "Like I said before, we have all the time in the world. No rush. No pressure. I like that we're taking this slow."

I wanted to laugh. This was his version of slow? In the last two weeks I'd done more sexually than I had ever done in my whole life. His slow was pretty fast in my books, but then I started to get what he meant. He wanted me to set the pace. I had full control. Our first time together, of properly being together, was my call and he was willing to wait for as long as it took. He was the opposite of a guy like Chase, and that was a pretty rare find these days.

"I love this… Being with you like this," I said, breathing him in and feeling like I wanted to open myself up to him in more ways. Let him know what he meant to me.

"I love it too." He pulled me even closer and nuzzled into my neck. There wasn't much space between us before, but now it was as if we were one person.

"Why me?" I said. It wasn't that I was doubting myself, but I wanted to know what it was he saw all those years ago. Why he'd chosen me.

"It was always you, Em." He settled me, so that I lay with my head on his chest and he drew slow gentle circles on my back as he spoke. "I guess the first time I really noticed you was at school, at lunchtime. Elliot Small, rotten name by the way considering his size, but that's… Whatever. Anyway, Brandon was being a real asshole, trying to show everyone what a dude he was. He watched Elliot walking across the canteen with his lunch tray and he stuck his foot out, made the kid fall flat on his ass; spaghetti and meatballs everywhere. The kid was a fucking mess and not just from the tomato sauce. Everyone was laughing. He looked ready to burst into tears and I was just about to head over there and tell Brandon to stop being a jerk when you appeared. A five-foot-nothing firecracker, ready to tear Brandon a new one."

I remembered that day. That was the first time I spoke to Elliot and we became good friends after that.

"You were fucking awesome that day. You told Brandon he was a piece of shit. Well, without the swearing, but you made him feel like a prized twat. Not many people have done that. Then you helped Elliot stand up, getting spaghetti sauce all over you as you did, and you helped him to a table, even shared your lunch with him."

"He ate more than I did." I laughed at the memory. I'd had no idea Ryan had seen that.

"You blew me away, Em. You were half Brandon's size, but I reckon you'd have tried to knock him out if you could've. Watching you that day did something to me. Sure, there were other things, but that stands out to me. I knew then that you were the girl for me."

"Ryan Hardy." I slapped his chest playfully. "You fell for the geeky, nerdy kid that no one liked." I said it as a joke, but he didn't take it that way. He put his hand under my chin to lift my face to his.

"You were not geeky, nerdy or disliked. I put a bloody block on you for Christ's sake. No one dared to go near you. But they liked you. Why wouldn't they? They just did a really good job of hiding it. They knew I'd kick their asses if they tried anything."

"You're an asshole… And thank you… I think. I really don't know what to say." I frowned and smiled at the same time. Confusion was becoming a good friend of mine.

"Em, you're the girl who flipped my whole world upside down. You might've been an afterthought in your parent's lives, but not in mine. I love the way you've never let their negativity get to you. You've never let it change who you are."

"And who am I?" I pushed, wanting to bleed him dry of every beautiful word he had to give.

"You're the girl who always puts everyone else first. Family, friends, strange guys spilling their meatballs all over the place. You fight for what's right. God knows you've called me and the guys out enough times over the years. You are the girl who makes people feel better just by being in a room. You have this power to make everyone feel good. It's like a light or, I don't know, a super power. You're the girl who everyone wants to be with. The girl who stole my heart."

I was gone. I didn't think it was possible to feel any more for this boy lying with me on my bed, but right then he stole the heart right out of my chest and claimed it as his own.

It was official, I was falling in love with Ryan Hardy, and not knowing what to say back to him in that moment, I kissed him. I had no words. Actions would have to suffice.

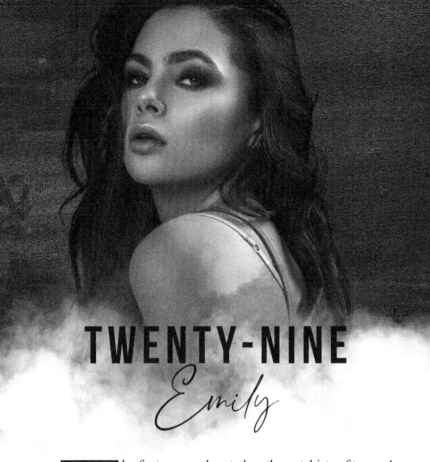

TWENTY-NINE
Emily

The factory was located on the outskirts of town. A prime position for the boys' and far enough away that any noise wouldn't disturb local residents. I was fast learning that was a win for them. No irate residents, no police presence, more time to party and make money.

Since my first experience at the warehouse, I'd come to respect them for their work ethic and tenacity; albeit for illegal events, drinking, gambling and whatever else they could turn their hand to, but they had a real knack for it. They were driven and focused. All traits that my father had drummed into us from an early age, but he wouldn't see it like that. If he knew I was standing in the middle of a derelict factory with hundreds of others, he'd have gone completely mental.

"Looks like he's moved on from Kelly." Liv was glaring daggers at Zak as he moved through the crowd towards his D.J. set with Eloise Campbell hanging off his arm. That boy sure was spreading the love around like it was confetti.

"You are way too good for him." I moved so I was standing in her line of vision. Hopefully blocking out Zak's free-loving ass. "Just don't look. There're loads of guys here tonight. Get with one of them and to hell with Zak."

"Em, I'm happy for you. You found a good one... We hope. But I'm gonna take a break from guys. A man-hoe-liday." She stood tall as she spoke, proud of her efforts already. I didn't believe her for a second.

"Okay, Liv. You do you, girl."

"Oh, I will. I have multiple BOBs to keep me happy." I stared at her, not having the first clue who Bob was. "You know, Bob. Battery-operated-boyfriend. You have those too, right, Em?"

I nodded then shook my head, feeling like I'd entered another dimension.

"Why would she need one? She's got Ryan for that," Effy said then blushed profusely. "I mean... I don't... You probably... Oh shit."

"It's fine, Eff. Like I said, you do you. And no, Liv. I don't have a Bob, as you put it. But if shit hits the fan, I'll definitely look into it."

"I'll even buy you one myself." Liv grinned from ear to ear. I'd no doubt she'd give me tips and pointers on how to use it effectively too.

An hour later and Effy was nowhere to be seen. Probably off in a dark corner discussing brush strokes with Finn, Liv had commented and I'd had to agree. Anytime we were with the guys lately, Effy and Finn were drawn to each other. I was glad. Effy deserved some fun. Only problem was, I was stuck playing third wheel to Liv and some guy called Pete who looked like a classic stoner. So much for her man-hoe-liday. Liv was lapping up the attention like the cat that got the cream.

I tapped her on the elbow to let her know I was going to find Ryan. I knew the guys were always busy at the beginning of these nights, but I couldn't stay away any longer. I forced my way through the crowds and into another corridor where a partially dilapidated staircase led to the next floor.

"Stairs are outta use. The floor's collapsed up there," some guy said, looking up at the flaking ceiling. I turned and headed in the opposite direction. "If you're looking for Mathers and the fight, it's in the basement. It was dark as fuck down there earlier, but we used the generators and the floodlights are pretty good."

I had no idea who this guy was, but I gave him a thumbs up and a, "Thanks," and moved on. I made my way through the groups of people standing around smoking, drinking and dancing to the bass from the main factory floor. I soon managed to find the small set of stairs that led to the basement area. The guy was right when he'd said they'd put lights up, but it did nothing to combat the eerie, dark feeling that crept over you when you came down here. It smelt musty and metallic, like this wasn't the first fight that'd happened down here. I shivered, but as soon as my foot hit the bottom step I felt a pair of strong arms wrap around me and pull me close. A warm chest erased the chill in my bones.

"I was about to come back up and find you." Ryan nuzzled into my neck and kissed me. I spun in his hold and wrapped my arms around him. I felt dizzy. This boy certainly had me under his spell.

"I got bored waiting." I didn't care who was watching. I didn't care if it got back to my dad that I'd been here with Ryan. I buried my face in his T-shirt and inhaled him. Filling my lungs with everything that calmed me and blocking out the outside world.

"I saw you with Liv and Effy." He bent down and kissed the top of my head. "Then with Liv and Pete, but I didn't want to interrupt you. I don't want to be the asshole boyfriend who takes you away from your friends."

Boyfriend. I liked that. It made my heart swell and my stomach flip.

"You can interrupt any time. I want you to get to know my friends. Their jury is still out on you. You need to change that."

He nodded and then pulled me to one side, away from the stairs and the crowds of people drifting into the basement.

"Fuck. What the hell are *they* doing here?" I turned to see where he was looking and saw Chase with his older brother, Jensen, and his friend, Brodie Yates. Jensen and Brodie had gone to the same high school as us, but they were in the year above Danny and Ryan. Jensen didn't live in Sandland anymore. Since graduating university he'd moved to London and joined some accountancy firm that my dad had dealings with. God knows what he was doing here. I wouldn't trust him though. He might play the part of the successful honest businessman by day, but I'd heard he was a bit of a thug after hours.

We watched them strut around like they owned the place, heads held high and chests puffed out like a trio of half-witted peacocks. Then Kian sidled up to us all flustered and flapping.

"Ry. Jensen wants in on the fight tonight. He wants to fight Brandon." Kian was out of breath, his eyes darting around like he expected Brandon to jump out of the shadows and tackle him to the ground.

"Does Brandon know?" Ryan didn't flinch. He wasn't fazed at all by what Kian said.

"He's all for it. Said he's gonna kill him. I don't think it's a good idea, Ry." Kian was twitchy, wringing his hands together and fidgeting on the spot. Anyone would've thought he'd been asked to fight Brandon himself.

"I think it's a great idea. Brandon needs this. He deserves it."

Kian snapped his jaw shut, nodded like a lunatic and then spun on his heels and walked away. I always thought he was a tad weird. That'd just proved my point. The guy was a fruit loop.

"What's going on? Why doesn't Kian think it'd be a good idea for Brandon to fight Jensen? Is Jensen that good?"

Ryan huffed and gripped me a little tighter as he glanced their way. "Jensen thinks he's good, and five or six years ago he might've been better than Brandon, but not anymore. Brandon will annihilate him."

"So, what's the big deal? Are you worried he'll sue or something?"

Ryan shook his head and then sighed, pulling me further into the corner of the basement. He looked tired, his eyes telling me that tonight was about more than a show of physical strength.

"Do you remember when I told you about Brandon's mum and how shitty his family life was? Well, the whole 'social services taking him away covered in his own shit' kind of made it to school somehow. Brandon was bullied for years by Jensen, Brodie and the rest of those assholes. They made his life hell. Some of the fucked-up shit they did to him in middle school was… Well, it was tough for *us* to come to terms with, let alone Brandon. I don't know how he survived it. We helped him where we could, but we weren't as strong back then."

Ryan nodded over to where Chase and his brother stood. "That guy over there is the reason Brandon worked so hard to build himself up. They're the reason he fights like he does. When he's psyching himself up, it's his face he pictures in his mind. And I know for a fact that it's Jensen he's punching every damn time. If Jensen wants to go against Brandon, I say let him. The fucker's owed some payback and Brandon deserves to be the one to give it to him."

I'd had no idea Brandon had been bullied at school. I always thought he was the bully. He'd been awful to Elliot Small and some of the other guys in the lower years. But I guess everyone has a story to tell and Brandon was carrying more baggage than I'd realised. He had a score to settle. Seems tonight was going to be the night for payback.

"Is that why you hate Chase?" I asked. Chase had been in our year, but he'd always been close to Jensen when he was living at home.

"Chase is a piece of shit. He stood by and watched his brother do what he did. He could've stopped it, but he didn't. He liked seeing someone else suffer. The whole Lockwood family are twisted motherfuckers. They've all got it coming to them, but tonight, its Jensen's time."

I had a bad feeling in my gut. I didn't like how this was playing out. I'd seen what Brandon was capable of and putting those kind of feelings into the mix would only lead to disaster. Disaster for the four boys, and even though Brandon wasn't my favourite guy, I didn't want to see him behind bars for something I could've stopped.

"I don't think he should, Ryan. I think you need to stop this. What if Brandon goes too far?"

"He won't. He might look like an animal, but he knows when to stop. That fear and anger, he'll use that as a form of energy, a way to channel his victory. He needs this, Em. It's not just about the money or the glory. He needs it for his own peace of mind. He's spent too long being haunted by his past and feeling ashamed. He has something to prove tonight and this is the best arena for him to do that."

Ryan pulled away but held my face in his hands. "Trust me. If it gets out of hand, I'll step in, but I won't need to. The ref will stop it if it gets too much. It might look barbaric, but there is an honour in all of this." Then he kissed me, and the feel of his lips on mine made the burning tension inside ease up slightly.

What did I know about fighting? Not enough to form a decent argument against it and I trusted Ryan completely. If anyone had Brandon's back, it was Ryan.

When Brandon walked into the basement to a round of catcalls and chanting, he grinned that psychotic moronic grin that I was slowly becoming to realise was his signature look. He saw Ryan and me stood in the corner and he put two fingers up to his lips and then kissed them, throwing them back over to us in greeting. He really did believe his own hype. Trouble was, no one else was willing to step up and prove him wrong. Until tonight that is. He turned to where Jensen stood with Chase, Brodie and some other men I didn't recognise. Brandon flared his nostrils and I could see the way his chest was moving with the panting breaths he took. He flexed his muscles and jumped on the spot. Kian handed him a water bottle, but he brushed him off. He was going the extra mile to psych himself up this time. He didn't want any distractions.

"This is gonna get fucked-up," some guy next to us said to his mates.

"I would not want to go against Lockwood. He's a fucking animal. A machine that renders men unconscious," another said laughing.

"So is Brandon," I jumped in and the group of guys standing by us all turned to look at me, probably to call bullshit, but when they saw Ryan standing behind me with his arms wrapped around my waist they soon changed their minds. "Yeah, that's right. Shut the fuck up and just watch, assholes." I didn't know what had come over me, but I was suddenly rooting for the little guy.

"God, I love you," Ryan said, chuckling and kissing the top of my head.

I froze.

Did he just use the L word? In a basement, when we were about to watch two men kick the shit out of each other? Was I supposed to say something back?

I felt him go tense behind me. He'd obviously just realised what he'd said, and he wasn't sure how to react.

"I'll always have your back. All of you," I answered, hoping to cut the tension. I didn't want him to clam up on me or think that I took it any other way than how he meant. He loved that I stood in his corner. That I defended his friends too. I had to remember not to read too much into things. I was, after all, the worst for over-analysing.

The guy who I assumed was the referee for the fight said a few words to Brandon and Jensen. Both men stood facing each other, shirtless, with their fists held up ready. The familiar hay bales kept the rest of the people out of the ring and they leaned over them shouting their encouragement. When the referee stood back, and the fight started, I felt my stomach twist into excruciating knots. Ryan's arms around me went solid and he started to shout over to Brandon.

Jensen threw the first punch, landing a nasty smack on Brandon's jaw, but Brandon stood his ground, waggling his jaw and running his taped-up fist over his mouth, before holding his hands back up in front of his face. He wasn't rushing into this fight. He was doing what he did best, studying his opponent, waiting to see where their weakness lay. I just hoped Jensen didn't use Brandon's previous eye injury against him. The stitches were long gone, but the area would still be tender.

"What if he gets his eye?" I shouted into Ryan's ear over the noise of the crowd. "Brandon will bleed out like before."

"He'd rather have twenty hits in the head than one in the body, trust me. The bones in the head are stronger than the ones in your hand. If Lockwood keeps hitting him like that, he'll do more damage to himself than Brandon. It's the body punches that hurt the most."

I wasn't convinced and when Jensen started hammering blows down on Brandon's head I had to turn away. I couldn't take it. The sound of the smack as his fist hit the skin and the hissing sound they made as they punched each other, it all made me nauseous. Brandon got in a few good punches, but from where I was standing, Jensen looked like the better fighter.

"How long till this round is over?" I said into Ryan's ear as I avoided watching the blood bath playing out.

Ryan laughed. "There's no rounds, babe. No bells, no rounds, no judges. You fight until you win, that's the beauty of it. There's no draws and no chicken-shits either. Just boom and goodnight. This is the purest form of combat." He hugged me and looked down at me. He didn't look shit scared like I did. "Relax. He won't lose. Losing isn't an option for Brandon. It isn't in his mind-set."

The crowd around us suddenly let out an almighty roar and we both turned our focus back to the fight, to see Brandon reining blow after blow to Jensen's body and face. Jensen was grabbing his head, trying to shield himself from the hits, but Brandon was relentless. He'd found his focus and he was primed and ruthless.

"See. He thrives under pressure. He needed Lockwood to have the upper-hand, so he could rise up and fight back harder." Ryan joined in the shouts of the room, spurring Brandon on. As gritty and primal as this whole scene was, I couldn't look away either. I wanted Brandon to win.

Suddenly, Jensen dropped to the floor. A knockout. The ref jumped in front of Brandon to stop the fight. He probably knew Brandon liked to taunt his opponents and an all-out fight with Jensen's crew wasn't the best finish to the night. Brandon spat his mouth guard onto the floor and took the bottle of water Kian was holding out to him. Then he took a huge gulp, spat it out and doused himself in the rest as the crowd cheered.

My adrenaline was through the roof, so Brandon's must've been in orbit. I never thought I'd have felt something so visceral whilst watching two men fight in such a brutal way, but I did. I felt pride and I was grateful that Brandon had got the retribution he'd deserved. I didn't doubt for a minute that it'd all end here, but this was a good start. Brandon had had his day. Wasn't that what every victim wanted?

The referee cleared the ring and two other men stepped up, ready for the next fight. We didn't stay to watch though. Ryan led me back out to the corridor and down to a side room. Zak was there with Finn, both of them grinning like lunatics.

"That was fucking awesome," Zak said, and we all nodded.

Brandon and Kian were the next to fall through the door. Brandon's face was cut and bruised. His eye would probably be so swollen tomorrow he'd struggle to see out of it, but he didn't care. He looked like he'd won the lottery. He jumped onto Ryan and the others followed suit, hugging him in congratulations.

"Un-fucking-defeated. Every. Fucking. Time," Brandon shouted, fist-pumping the air.

I stood back, letting them have their moment.

"Get in here, Winters. I think I deserve a hug from you too." Brandon waved me over, but I stood still. I was proud of what he'd done. I felt happy for him, but I wasn't patting him on the back. That was never gonna happen.

"Back off, mate," Ryan said, coming to stand next to me and pulling me into him.

Brandon didn't like that and flipped faster than a fish out of water. "She needs to leave. We have business to discuss."

He was so high off the endorphins it must've made him punch drunk. What 'business' did he have to discuss now, with a face that was throbbing and swelling right before our eyes?

"She's going nowhere," Ryan bit back. "Whatever you wanna say, you can say it in front of her."

I noticed Zak grimace. They wanted to talk about me, or my father. It didn't take a genius to figure out they were digging dirt. But to be honest, I didn't care what they had to say.

"Okay, I'll keep it brief." Zak folded his arms over his chest, took a deep breath in and then looked around the room at each of the boys. "We have it all set up. We have everything we need. We go live next Friday. How you want to play this is entirely your call, Ry. Finn, you know what you need to do. Brandon and me will sort out the security. Kian, I'll speak to you separately. Is everyone cool?" They all nodded in agreement and I just bit my lip. Talk about cryptic.

I had no idea what they were on about, but I'd find out.

Whatever was going live on Friday, I wanted to know about it.

THIRTY

Ryan

"What's going on, Ryan? What's going live on Friday?"

I couldn't get Emily out of there fast enough. I was buzzing that we were finally shutting this shit down, but at the same time I felt like a lead weight had hit my stomach. The thought of hurting her, which we would, felt like the biggest tug to my gut. I didn't want to lose her. Not now. I couldn't. I'd only just found what I'd dreamed of for so many years. There was no one like my Em. No one that sparked a fire in me like she did, and I wasn't going to let that go, not for anybody.

"It's nothing for you to worry about, babe." I knew she liked me calling her that. Her face was an open book to me, but she didn't flinch or soften her look.

"Don't bullshit me. Something is going on and you don't want me to know about it."

What was I supposed to say? Your dad is about to go down for a stretch? You'll probably lose your house, your reputation and your dignity?

I knew Zak had found something out from Troy Barker, the mechanic, or rather the fixer for her father. I didn't know what exactly, but whatever it was wasn't going to be good for Emily, that much was certain. I had to protect her first. And if that meant keeping this from her until I'd done what I had to do with the guys, I would. Then I could focus my full attention on her. Make sure I was there to pick up the pieces. If she'd let me.

If I told her before Friday what I knew, I doubted I'd be able to go through with it. It was a fucked-up logic, but it was the only logic I had. Out the fucker first, deal with the fallout later. Show my girl I was there for her one-hundred-percent and pray she didn't hold me responsible for how shit went down.

"It's just business. Call it another revenge plan, a bit like Brandon's fight tonight. Once it's done, I'll tell you everything."

"Please tell me you aren't going into bare-knuckle boxing? I don't think I could survive that." I watched as she swallowed back, looking like she was about to either pass out or go ape shit on my ass.

"No. I promise you, I'm not going to fight. Not with my fists, anyway." I kissed her, and she wrapped her arms around me, finally softening and moulding herself into me. I had to remember that. Contact and holding her close was the key to cutting off an argument or distracting her as best I could from stuff I needed to protect her from.

"I trust you," she said all breathy, in a voice that went straight to my dick. Jesus, if I didn't have inside of her soon, I was going to explode. I wanted to give her time and I stood by my rule, no pressure. But damn, I don't think I'd jerked off as much as I had lately at any other time in my life. This woman was all I thought about, and knowing how soft and tight she felt on my fingers had me imagining all kinds of fucked-up shit I wanted to do to her. I was losing my goddamn mind.

"I need you to do something for me," I whispered into her ear, running my hands down to her ass and giving it a good squeeze.

"Anything." She gasped, burying her head into the crook of my neck and making me want to pick her up, leave this shithole and never come back.

"Stay with Effy or Liv on Friday night. Do whatever you girls do, have a girl's night in or whatever, but stay with them. I don't want you at home on your own on Friday."

She pulled away, looking at me with a million questions burning in her eyes, but a deep set frown on her face.

"Why? Can't I stay with you?" I had three answers to that question. The one my heart gave, which went along the lines of, 'Baby, you're always with me. On Friday, I'd love nothing more than to hold you all night long in my arms.' Then there was the one my head gave, that went something like, 'Em, I need you safe. After I've dealt with my shit, I will be by your side twenty-four-seven, but please, let me do this.' Then lastly it was my dick, which always had a say whenever it came to her. That answer involved my bed, my empty house at the weekend courtesy of my dad's overnight stay at a trade show, and a whole lot of time spent making her forget whatever it was we were about to put her family through. The jury was still out on which one would win, but eventually I went with the head on my shoulders as opposed to the one in my pants and repeated myself. She needed to be with her friends. I needed her away from it all.

"Fine. I can do that." She wasn't happy, and if I was being completely honest with myself, I didn't fully believe that she would stay with them, but I didn't want to argue. I was done talking about this.

She sighed, obviously done with this conversation too, and lifted herself on her tiptoes to kiss me. Like a red rag to a bull, I felt the need for her surge inside me, and I pushed her up against the wall of the corridor where we stood. The bass from Zak's set vibrated the walls and people knocked past us as they moved from the basement to the main area, but I didn't care. I kissed the ever-loving-fuck out of her and grabbed her ass again, pulling her closer so she knew what she was doing to me. She hooked her leg up over my hip and I held it in place, using my hand behind her knee so I could grind my dick into her, letting her know where I wanted to be; buried right between her thighs.

Pure fucking heaven.

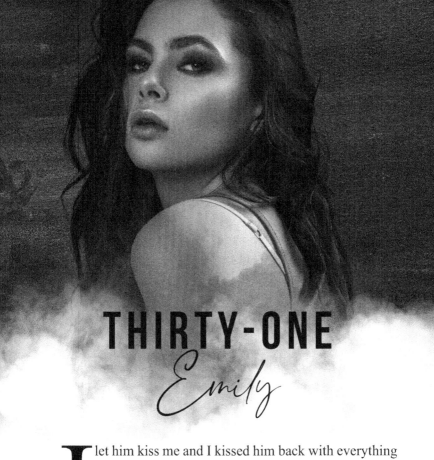

THIRTY-ONE
Emily

I let him kiss me and I kissed him back with everything I had, but this wasn't over. I wasn't going to bow down like the little woman. If something was going to happen on Friday, I wanted to be at the front and centre of it. I wasn't going to be beaten down by anyone, no matter how good a kisser they were, or how much they made me yearn for more.

I knew the boys were as thick as thieves when it came to their little crew, but they had a weakness, every organisation does. Lucky for me, when Friday came, that little weakness was sitting in the corner of a local café nursing a hangover and an espresso with extra shots.

"Hey, Kian." I sat down opposite him, blowing on the latte I'd bought as he shuffled uncomfortably in his chair. "You all ready for tonight?" I wasn't sure how much Kian knew about me, but he knew a lot more about the boys' plans than I did, and I was going to use that to my advantage.

"Uh, yeah, sure. I'm on the doors." He shrugged, not looking happy with that job, so I pressed further.

"Where did you want to be?"

He took a sip of his molten coffee and winced. Probably because it tasted like liquid shit, then he banged his hand down on the table in frustration.

"I wanted in on the whole show. I wanted to be on the stage or sorting the tech out with Zak. I'm good at that. I know as much stuff as he does. I guess they don't trust me enough yet." He darted his eyes around the coffee shop and then settled them back on me. "I might not have a head for numbers like Ryan, and I'm not fucking Picasso like Finn, but I can hack into anything that Zak can. I have skills."

Strike one. Kian had given me the first little nugget of a very large rock that I was chipping away at. So Zak had hacked into something. My dad's accounts no doubt. He'd found shit to pin on him and that was something I was entitled to be a part of. I wanted in now more than ever.

"Kian, I know you have skills. Ryan knows that too. He's always talking about how much he trusts you. It's why you're on the doors tonight. Do you think they'd trust anyone else with that? If the wrong people get in, they're fucked." He nodded along, and I could see his shoulders relax, the tension and anger were starting to ebb away. I had him right where I needed him.

"Ki, you might not be in the main part tonight, but you are the keystone to all this. If you're not there it all goes to shit."

"You're right." He gripped his coffee cup with both hands, cradling it like it was his lifeline. "Brandon's sorted the security. It helped that Zak could hack into your dad's emails and cancel the company he'd already booked. Brandon's using guys from the gym tonight. But I'm the gate-keeper, aren't I?"

Strike two. Another little nugget. They were planning some kind of attack on my dad that involved wiping out his security. It didn't take a genius to guess that Brandon's guys were there as fake guards. They'd protect the guys before they'd ever protect my father. It didn't bother me like it should've. My dad was big enough to look after himself and I had a feeling he deserved whatever was heading his way.

"Are you heading down there now to do any checks?" I held my breath, willing Kian to spill the tea. I needed in on whatever it was that was happening tonight.

"I might do, yeah. I haven't seen what Finn's done and I probably won't see it if I'm stuck watching the fucking doors. Zak's there now, setting up his gear. I could give him a hand. The community centre had a new projector fitted, so he'll need to link into that and do a sound check."

Bingo. Strike three and you're out.

My dad kept his diary of events on lockdown. No one saw that shit other than his secretary and maybe my mum. I never knew where he was from one day to the next. But I did know the local community centre had recently undergone a refurbishment. The main hall to be exact. So, that's where I needed to be tonight, and wild horses wouldn't keep me away.

"Well, good luck, Kian. Maybe I'll see you there later." I

stood up and left him grinning to himself. He had absolutely no idea what he'd just done.

***

I had my hair up in a messy bun and chose a pair of black ripped skinny jeans and a grey hoodie, in the hope that I'd blend in with the crowd. Then a few streets away from the community centre I went into panic mode. What was I thinking? This was a political event orchestrated by my father. I'd probably stick out like a sore thumb in amongst the power suits and over-priced designer dresses. Nevertheless my feet kept moving, despite my brain screaming at me to turn and run the other way. When I got to the corner though, I let out a nervous sigh. Groups of people my age were wandering into the venue and jeans and hoodies looked like the uniform of choice. At first, I thought it strange that they would choose to spend their Friday night at the local community centre, but then I realised, they weren't here to see my dad, not like that, anyway. This was the work of the Renaissance men. They'd probably sent invites out to this thing.

I crossed the road and tagged onto a group of girls who were chattering away and queuing to get in. Kian was on the door as planned and he looked pleased as punch to be there. I was glad. My pep-talk had done him some good and he was loving his job right now. He started talking to a red-head who was just in front of me, putting the moves on her. A plus for both of us, because I managed to get through the door without him paying me any attention and he managed to get her phone number for later.

Once inside, I broke away from the cackling group of girls who were fast giving me a headache and pushed my way through into the main hall. I tended to shy away from events like this, that my dad attended, but I knew they usually kept numbers to a minimum and put chairs and refreshments out for the attending press and dignitaries. Here, there was nothing. We were packed in like sardines, standing shoulder to shoulder. I saw a few men walking around the outside of the hall with security emblazoned across their shirts, but I laughed to myself. They might've appeared tough, but they didn't look like they were here to stop the fighting. They looked like they were here to oversee it.

I glanced behind me and saw a ton of computer equipment set up, but no Zak. Not yet. At the front of the hall there were chairs set out on the stage and the red curtains were closed. All very dramatic. The perfect setting for the tragedy that was about to unfold. I spotted my mum and dad, and the general noise and hubbub around me settled down as they climbed the steps to take their seats to the left of the stage. I looked around feeling totally confused at what the hell was going on. Apart from Kian on the door and the fake security, it didn't look like anything was going down. The boys were nowhere to be seen.

My phone buzzed in my pocket for the hundredth time that evening and when I pulled it out I saw a message from Effy.

Where are you?

I fired a response back, relieved it wasn't another call or text from Ryan. I was actively avoiding him for the next few hours. I didn't want to lie to him, but he wanted to know where I was. So, I figured I'd delay my response until I could tell him the truth.

I'm at an event for my dad. Same old boring shit. Why?

Those three dots started dancing around to tell me Effy was replying.

Because Ryan's got a hold of my number and he's asking if you're here with me. He said you're avoiding his calls. What's going on, chick?

Fuck. That was all I needed, for Effy to tell Ryan I was here. *Don't tell him anything yet. I'll call him. Text you later, hun. Don't worry. Nothing is going on. I'll explain when I see you.*

I stuffed my phone back into the pocket of my jeans and watched as the Mayor took to the stage to start his spiel about the community centre being the heart of Sandland, and how proud he was that my dad had agreed to do the official reopening. The usual brown-nosing crap. I zoned out. His words were just a soundbite. They meant nothing. When he turned to my dad to welcome him up to the mic, there was a loud bang and the lights in the hall went out, leaving us all standing there in darkness and confusion, wondering what the hell was going on.

Suddenly, strobe lights cut across the crowd and the booming bass from *The Prodigy's, "Omen"* started playing through speakers all around us. I stood there, wide-eyed and frozen in place, mesmerised by the music. A few people around me began to dance like they were at one of the boys' parties. Up on the stage, the Mayor was fumbling around, not quite sure if what was happening was part of the show. My dad looked totally confused, but he stayed seated and grabbed my mum's hand.

Two figures dressed all in black, wearing hoodies that were pulled down low on their heads and bandanas to hide their faces, took to the stage and stood next to my parents. Judging from their expressions, I could tell the black figures had said something. My dad went to stand up, but the figure closest to him put a hand on his shoulder to keep him in place. Dad was rattled. Well and truly pissed off.

Then a spotlight shone onto the stage and everyone turned

to focus on that, ready to see what would happen next. The curtains drew back, opening to reveal massive graffiti artwork with the words *The Writings on the Wall* written in stark red and black paint. Huge words that were as tall as the wall they were written on, like a slap in the face to anyone who saw it. A reminder that something bad was about to go down and they had been warned. The crowd started hollering and cheering as the song reiterated the words painted up there; reminding us that it won't go away, we need to stop and listen.

The boys wanted to make a statement and they were doing a kick-ass job of it. The whole room was buzzing, waiting on the show they'd started.

On the stage, a screen slowly came down from the ceiling, momentarily covering Finn's artwork. Then it flickered to life and there in front of us was someone wearing a Guy Fawkes mask. The mask that had come to symbolise defiance towards a corrupt system and social injustice. When the person on the video spoke it was with a voice changer. I had no idea if that was Ryan, Brandon, or the queen speaking on that video, but from what they were saying, I knew it was all the work of the Renaissance men.

"By now you will know that this is no ordinary event. What I am about to tell you tonight is the work of many years of struggle to have our voice heard. They have tried to shut us down. They don't want us to be heard. We will be silent no more. This is our time. We will have a voice."

The crowd whooped and cheered as the screen flickered again for effect and a line of 'security' men stood shoulder to shoulder protecting the stage. From who I wasn't sure. I think they were there to keep my parents and the mayor on the stage, and not the rest of us off.

"As I am speaking to you now, copies of every document, video and tape recording you are about to see is on its way to the chief of police, the prime minister and every tabloid newspaper editor in this country. We will not be silenced."

I watched my dad try to move out of his chair again and he was pushed back down by the hoodie. My mum spoke to him, but it didn't help. He looked ashen-faced, like he was at the gallows about to meet his maker.

"There will be three truths you hear tonight. Listen and listen carefully. Those in power want us gone. They want us weak. They use us. We won't be used anymore. We will make a stand."

People dressed in black hoodies like the ones on stage started to mingle in amongst the crowd, handing out papers to anyone who'd take them. I took one and when I looked down I saw the Morgan Rotherham account my dad had flipped out over, with every transaction listed, some highlighted too.

"The papers you're looking at are account documents. Evidence of the dirty money that one man has cleaned using our town and the people in it. That man is Mr Alec Winters."

My dad started to protest, trying to flee this character assassination that he was being forced to witness, but he wasn't going anywhere. His hooded guardian made sure of that.

"He's taken companies run by hard-working, honest people, and made them trust in his good name. Convinced them that he'd do what was right for them, for the town we've all grown up in. But that never happened. Our upstanding Member of Parliament, Mr Alec Winters, has used each and every one of those businesses to wash his money. To bleed this town dry. You were nothing but a means to an end. A legitimate way he could launder millions.

"And whose money was he cleaning? The scum of the earth. Drug lords. Criminals who run this town and the cities of our country with their filth and corruption. It was easy to point the finger at the delinquent youths of society. To use them as a soundbite for his fucked-up political campaigns. Create a smokescreen that covered the real fire that he's started. A fire that threatened to destroy this town. Alec Winters is a thief, a liar, a criminal with no remorse. He will try to talk his way out of this, but Mr Winters, the writings on the wall. The accounts with every name in your little black book are out there. We will not be silenced."

The tension running around the room was palpable. No more whooping and hollering. No more dancing like it was party hour. Everyone was stood staring at the screen like we were all trapped in a horror movie and no one knew what the next move was.

"Shortly, there will be police here to take Mr Winters to his rightful home. A jail cell. Forty-eight square feet with his name written all over it. But we aren't finished yet. We will be heard. And there are two more truths that you must hear.

"On December sixteenth last year, Danny Winters was tragically killed in a car accident."

I went cold. Hearing that date and my brother's name being spoken made my whole body tremble in fear. I felt sick. But I couldn't leave. I had to know what they were going to say.

"His father told us all it was a case of drunk driving. Even hinted that Danny may have had worse in his system. But this was not the case. Tonight we stand for justice for Danny.

Tonight the lies end. If you look at your handouts, you will see that a large sum of money was transferred to a Troy Barker just twenty-four hours after Danny died. We will now play you an audio tape of why that transaction needed to be made. This is our truth."

The screen went black and then a hissing sound of a phone conversation started to play. The screen in front of us provided the script so we were in no uncertainty about what was being said. I listened and read the transcript with my stomach in knots.

Troy Barker: "Talk."

Alec Winters: "Oh God. Oh God. I don't know what to do. Shit. It's fucking... Oh God, please. Troy. I don't know what to do."

Troy Barker: "Calm the fuck down and tell me. What's happened?"

Alec Winters: "It's bad, Troy. It's fucking bad."

Troy Barker: "Just spit it out, Winters. I haven't got all night. Tell me where you need me, and I'll be there."

Alec Winters: "Curborough Lane, just past the bend. You need to come quickly, Troy. I think he's dead."

Troy Barker: "Who's dead? Give me details. I need to know what I'm walking into here."

Alec Winters: "My son. Danny. I think he's dead."

Troy Barker: "I need more than that. Is it a hit?"

Alec Winters: "No. I... Shit. I picked him up... I'd been drinking. Fuck, Troy. I've been drinking. This is gonna ruin me. I can't lose my position."

My heart ripped open and my legs almost gave way underneath me. I watched as my mum pulled her hand away from my dad's, wrapping her arms around herself and rocking back and forth. She was crying, and I felt the urge to go to her. But I couldn't. I had to hear this out. I needed to know it all.

Troy Barker: "So let me get this straight. You picked up your son."

Alec Winters: "Yes."

Troy Barker: "In a car."

Alec Winters: "I used Danny's car. It was the last one on the drive and I just took it. All the others were boxed in."

Troy Barker: "And you drove when you were drunk."

Alec Winters: "I didn't know this would happen. I didn't mean for any of this."

Troy Barker: "You think your son is dead?"

Alec Winters: "He took his seatbelt off to get something from the back seat. I saw something on the road and I swerved. There's blood everywhere, Troy. I need you here now."

Troy Barker: "I'm on my way. Do not call anyone else. Do not move or touch anything until I get there. If anyone else stops, keep them there, stall them, but do not call the police or an ambulance. I will deal with this."

The phone call cut off and the masked man appeared on the screen again.

"What you heard was a transcript of a phone call recorded on the night of Danny's death between Mr Alec Winters, Danny's father, and Mr Troy Barker, the fixer. Lucky for us, Mr Barker kept records of every phone call and interaction he had with Mr Winters. Even his fixer didn't trust him. You will find no police records on Danny's case, because they were all destroyed. You will find no toxicology reports, because they were all destroyed. The tests done on the car, the blood spatters… All faked, and all on the say so of our elected Member of Parliament, Mr Alec

Winters.

"So what happened when the fixer got there? Mr Barker and Mr Winters moved Danny from the passenger seat where he'd died, to the driver's seat. They destroyed evidence that would've cleared Danny's name. And when they were confident that every single trace of Mr Winters having been there, having driven that car, had been erased, they left. They got into Mr Barker's car and they left Danny's dead body behind to be found by a factory worker driving past at five o'clock the next morning. They left the scene to save Mr Winters' career. Then they used his son's death to make a saint out of Mr Winters. A symbol of all that's good, fighting against the poisoned youth. He used us like he used his own son, to further his political career. To make money from the death of the innocent."

I wasn't sure how much more I could take. My mum was sobbing into her hands. My dad was curling himself forward, trying to look sorry for what he'd done. And I felt numb. Numb because I no longer had a father. I would never forgive him for what he'd done.

The room was silent and eerily dark, save for the lights from the screen in front of us. I swallowed, struggling to breathe, feeling like I was drowning. And then the voice changer started to speak again.

"Three truths we are delivering tonight. And three truths you will hear. One, Alec Winters is a corrupt thief, laundering money through Sandland like it's his own private fucked-up bank. Two, Alec Winters has blood on his hands. He was responsible for his son's death. He was driving. He left his son's dead body to rot in a mangled car while he fled the scene like the rat he is. But Alec Winters' deceit doesn't stop there. He lost a son that night, but he still had two daughters."

I hadn't heard that right. I mustn't have heard that right. Two daughters?

"We did a little digging into the Morgan Rotherham account that Winters used for his dirty money. Why that name? We asked ourselves. What or who is Morgan Rotherham? Morgan Rotherham is the child Alec Winters had with his long-term mistress, born three months after the birth of his other daughter, Emily."

I couldn't stop a sob coming from the depths of my soul. Everything I'd ever believed in was being ripped apart in front of all these people. Everything I knew was a lie. My whole world was shattering at my feet and it was all being used for entertainment here tonight.

I felt broken.

Another spotlight shone from the stage onto the crowd and I turned in a daze to see what they were about to unveil next.

"Ladies and gentleman, let me introduce you to Miss Katherine Rotherham and her daughter, Morgan."

Standing a few feet away from me was a girl, her face as pale as mine, and looking like she was about to pass out or bolt, just like I was. The older woman next to her, her mother I guessed, went to take her hand, but she pulled away sharply and mouthed something that looked like 'what the fuck'. This girl looked more like Danny than me, but she had the same dark hair as I did, only hers was poker-straight. I had a sister. A sister who was the same age as me. Why did I have to find out about this with the rest of the town? This was beyond fucked-up.

"I don't want any part of this," she suddenly shouted into the hall. "Whatever this fucked-up show is, I don't want to know."

She looked over to where my father sat on the stage, with his head in his hands. "And you are not my father. You never will be. I hate you." She pushed past her mother and ran out of the hall. I took one look at my parents sat on that stage and I realised then how alone I was. I couldn't trust anyone, not even Ryan. He'd known all about this and he hadn't told me. He'd put this show on, letting the whole town into my family's disgusting secrets before he'd told me. I was devastated.

So, I turned and ran too, pushing my way through the crowds that didn't part for me as easily as they had for Morgan. When I reached the doors I saw Kian and Finn standing there and Finn's eyes shot out of his head when he saw me.

"Oh, fucking hell. Emily, you weren't supposed to see that. Ryan's gonna go ape shit-" I cut him off, barrelling my way through the doors, hoping the fresh night air might ease the tightness around my chest.

"I had a right to be here tonight," I said with more strength than I felt. "And now, I'm done."

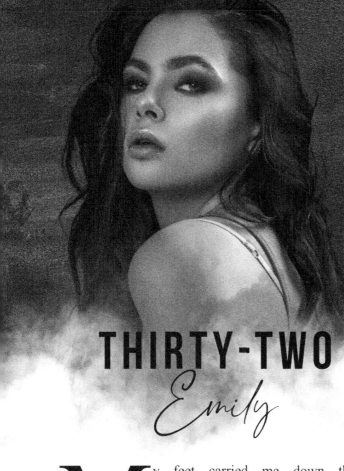

THIRTY-TWO

Emily

My feet carried me down the road subconsciously, but my brain was a million miles away, detaching itself from the carnival of crazy I'd just witnessed, refusing point blank to make sense of it all.

What was going to happen now? Do I even care anymore?

I saw a fleet of police cars with their sirens blaring shoot past me, off to take my loving father into custody I guessed. The flash of their lights and the wail that penetrated through the air made it feel like I was in a disaster movie. Only this wasn't pretend, this was my life burning to the ground as I walked through the flames. The heat of the fire prickling my skin, making me want to claw my nails across it and draw blood; do anything to dull the pain in my heart. The smoke clogging my lungs, making it difficult to breathe and stinging my eyes with tears I didn't want to shed. But like any good disaster movie, I was determined I wouldn't go down without a fight. My world might've caved to rubble, but I wasn't a quitter. I was a warrior. I had to be.

I heard footsteps behind me and felt someone grab at my arm.

"Wait, Emily. Please." It was Finn and I spun round, my face set like stone as I stared blankly at him.

"What?" I was seconds away from turning back and walking away from him; from all of them.

He ran his hand over his face and I watched as his eyebrows pinched together. I don't think he knew what to say to me now he'd got me in front of him. I didn't have time for this. I was done with the bullshit and lies. As I went to walk away, he reached out to me again.

"Em, he doesn't know you're here. If he did, he'd be tearing this whole town down to get to you."

I huffed out a laugh and shook my head. I highly doubted that. He had bigger fish to fry. I didn't register on his radar tonight.

"You know what, Finn? I don't care anymore. He made his choice tonight when he decided to go against me. He put you and everyone else in this town above me. I should've known what was going on before anyone." I thumped my chest as I spoke, feeling hurt and betrayed. I'd trusted Ryan. I thought he had my back. It hurt to find out I was so wrong.

"It wasn't like that." Finn took hold of both my arms,

keeping me in place as he spoke. He obviously thought I was a flight risk and I had to admit he wasn't wrong. "When we had that meeting at the factory the other night, he didn't know half of what was going on. Sure, he knew about the money laundering, but he didn't know about Morgan or Danny."

I felt another piercing sting in my chest when he said my brother's name. A million knives thrust into my back wouldn't feel as painful as the one slicing through my heart at this very moment.

"It doesn't matter. He knew tonight. He chose to hang me out to dry. Do you think I'll ever be able to show my face around here ever again? After what you've all done?"

"No one is going to blame you, Emily. You aren't your father." He hung his head in shame then took a deep breath before breaking open my fragile heart some more. "He didn't want to do it. When we told him everything, he wanted to come straight to you, but we stopped him."

"If he wanted to tell me, he could've. Since when has Ryan done anything he doesn't want to do?"

"We told him he needed to stay focused. We'd been on this for years, Em. We couldn't take a chance on anything fucking it up. Not tonight. Ryan wanted to tell you, but we convinced him it'd be better if he waited until after the opening. Get the truth out there, then find you. Tell you in his own way. We knew if he told you first, he wouldn't go through with what he did tonight. It needed to be done. If you'd known all that stuff before we outed your dad, would you have stopped us? I think you would've. We couldn't take that chance."

I wasn't sure what I'd have done. It would've been kinder to hear it in private. To have Ryan tell me himself, but then he did try to keep me away. My stubborn ass had just pushed and pushed to get to the truth. But sometimes the truth is the hardest thing to face. My truth was I was alone, and I didn't know who to trust anymore.

"Was it him? In the video with the mask?" The whole world went on pause while I waited for his response.

"No. That was Zak. Ryan was on the stage though, with Brandon."

That fact made me feel somewhat better, not much, but it was something. "Where is he now?"

"He's still back there," Finn said, gesturing to the community centre we'd both fled. "When Kian tells him we saw you, he's gonna lose it, Em."

"He's broken my heart." My voice cracked as I spoke. My heart was breaking for so many reasons tonight, and knowing that Ryan had been the cause of it made the pain that much sharper.

"He never wanted to break your heart, Em. He wanted to own it. He loves you. Has done for years. This is gonna break him too, you know."

Hearing Finn say that Ryan loves me should've made me feel something. Hope, maybe? But it didn't. All it did was make the hurt so much more unbearable. "I guess he should've thought about that before he did what he did."

"He did it for you." Finn started to tug on his hair. He wasn't getting the results he wanted from our little chat and it was starting to get to him. "When we told him about Danny, shit, I've never seen Ry so cut up. He cried, Em. And not because he'd lost a friend like that, but because he wanted to shield you from it all. The stuff with your sister, that really pushed him over the edge." I winced when he said that. I wasn't ready to acknowledge that girl as anything other than my father's other daughter.

"He wanted to go to your house and confront him right there," Finn said, ploughing on with his justice for Ryan speech. "He wanted to take you away from it all and look after you. We knew if that happened, your dad would find a way to bury it. He'd make it all go away. Probably make us go away too."

That knife wedged into my heart twisted at the thought of something happening to Ryan. I started to gasp for air, but every breath just didn't feel like enough. That's when I realised, despite all the heartache and pain I felt now, a life without Ryan would be so much worse. He had brought sunshine when everything had turned grey after losing Danny. He brought clarity, security, a reason to smile through the day. He gave me life. He was my life. I loved him.

Tonight, he'd done a really shitty thing, and it was going to take me a long time to get over it, but Ryan hadn't done it to hurt me. He wanted the maximum impact to hurt my father. I'd thought I was collateral damage, but if I stopped for a second and really thought about it, I wasn't.

Listening to Finn, I realised I was duped and conned just as much as the rest of the town, maybe even more. Even though I knew he was driven by his job, deep down, I'd trusted my father to always do the right thing. To put our family first no matter what. But he hadn't. He'd put his own selfish, self-centred greed first. The money, the power, the status; he'd had his cake and eaten it, keeping my mum and some other woman on the side. I couldn't bring myself to analyse the Danny situation yet. That was still too raw, and my brain couldn't comprehend how he could be so evil. But Finn was right. My dad would've buried it. These truths would've never seen the light of day if Ryan had shown his hand too soon.

And me? I was never a very good poker player. I wore my heart on my sleeve and my emotions on my face. If I'd known this before tonight, I'd have broken down completely.

"Em?" Finn broke through my reverie, rubbing my arm and trying to get my attention back to the here and now. "Do you want to come back with me? See Ryan? I think you need to talk, and I'm worried about you."

"I need time." I pulled away, but I looked Finn dead in the eyes, so he knew that something had shifted in me. Some of his reasoning had penetrated through, into my psyche, and I was starting to see the wood for the trees. Not all of it, but it was a start.

"Do you want me to pass a message on to him?"

I bit my lip. I wasn't sure what to say. I could barely string a coherent thought together, let alone a sentence.

"Tell him… I think I get it, but I need space. There's too much going on in my head right now. I need to process." I shrugged and Finn smiled.

"I get that. Don't push him away though. He's waited a long time for you. He won't let you go and I think you both deserve a bit of happiness once all this dies down. Be angry at your dad. Give us hell for hacking and digging like we did. But remember everything Ryan did was to try and protect you. You come first with him, always."

***

I didn't want to go back to my house. I knew no one would be there, but there were ghosts there that I wasn't ready to face.

My father would be holed up in some police station tonight, with my mum waiting on him, desperate for any scraps she could salvage from her life. That was a life I wanted no part of any more.

I thought about going to see Effy or Liv, but I didn't feel right unloading all of this hurt onto them. The burden of grief and hatred was a heavy one. So, I opted to go to the one place I knew I wouldn't find any judgement. A place I'd actively avoided for months because denial was easier to bear than acceptance.

"Hey, bro." I tugged at the tufts of grass that the mower in the cemetery hadn't reached when cutting around his marble headstone and then brushed my fingers over the carving of his name. Even now, seeing his name written there, it didn't feel real.

"I'm sorry I haven't been here in… Well, forever. I just find it so hard. There isn't a minute of the day that I don't think about you. I carry you with me, always. But here…" I looked around the eerily quiet graveyard where the sentiment of my words were only felt by the birds and the breeze. "Here it's too much. Too final. Sometimes, when I wake up, I forget about what happened and just for a split second I don't remember anything. It's like you're still here with us. Everything is as it should be. But then my brain kicks in and it all goes downhill from there."

I felt a tear trickle down my face, the first of many to follow.

"Dan, I found out what happened today when you had the accident. I'm so sorry that I didn't do more to clear your name. Thinking about what Dad did, how he used your death to promote himself, it makes me sick. I thought we had shit parents. Guess that was the understatement of the century. But I can't shake the feeling that we all let you down; Dad, Mum and me. I knew in my gut… I knew you hadn't taken anything. I knew you didn't drink. Why did I let them pull the wool over my eyes like that? I should've fought harder."

I lay down on the ground next to his grave and stroked my fingers through the soft grass that covered my brother.

"Not everyone gave up on you though, Danny. Ryan fought for you. I know you're probably looking down on us and cursing him, maybe me too, for how close we've become. You always were over-protective, but he's a good guy. He did a really shitty thing today, not telling me about the stuff with Dad, but the more I think about it, the more I can see why he didn't. I think Finn was right. I would've stopped him, and your truth needed to be told. Everyone knows now. They know you're innocent. You weren't driving. I think Dad's gonna go to prison. Not just because of you, Dan, but he was laundering money too. Looks like Mum and me are going to be moving to new digs soon. I don't care though. I hate him. I never want to see our father again. He doesn't deserve to be called that." I sighed. The emotions of today were like a boulder in my stomach and it crippled me.

"God, I miss you."

I hiccupped as an image of Danny doing his ridiculous diving into the pool during our last summer holidays flickered into my mind. He'd always do anything to make me smile. He pissed me off every day too, usually by hogging the T.V. remote or being an arse, but isn't that what all brothers do? Mine was the best. He'd belch in my face then smother me with hugs, making me go from fuming to giggling in a nanosecond. I'd give anything to have that again.

"Dad had another family," I said with zero emotion behind

the words. When it came to that truth, I felt like a robot going through the motions, but refusing to open up to the reality of what it meant. "He has a daughter, Dan. She's the same age as me. Did you know? What am I saying, of course you didn't. You'd have told me if you did. You'd have kicked his ass too for doing that to Mum."

I lifted myself up and sat cross-legged at the side of his grave and picked a few daisies out of the ground, giving my trembling hands something to do.

"I heard three truths today. They say bad luck comes in threes. Mine came hurtling towards me like giant bowling balls. Each one was fired by them, Dan. Ryan was a part of that and I want to be angry at him, fuck, I am angry at him, but I... I love him, Dan, and I don't know what to do. Do I walk away? Turn my back on something that could be the best thing to ever happen to me? Or do I stand firm? Show them they can't knock me down like that. Do I fight for him? For us? I'm so confused. Everything's gone to shit, and I feel like I'm losing everything; you, Mum, Dad, and now Ryan. It's too much."

I took a deep breath to try and calm my raging thoughts.

"What would you say if you were here? What would you tell me to do?"

I closed my eyes and imagined Danny was standing right in front of me. I knew him as well as anybody and I wanted to tap into his mind. Pull out the wisdom he'd give me if he were here.

I felt the wetness on my cheeks seep into the collar of my hoodie, but I let them flow. I needed to. Tonight, all the hurt from when Danny died had been reopened. My pain was as real now as it had been on the morning that we'd got that life changing call.

"Em, what have I always told you? Our parents are basket cases, but we are not our parents. What Dad did was fucked-up, and let's not kid ourselves, Mum will forgive him. She always does. No matter what shit he puts her through, she takes it. She's blind when it comes to him. We are not.

"When I was there I always tried to play all the roles for you. The annoying older brother, the father figure who actually stuck around and gave you some ground rules, and the mother's ear you never got from her. I hate that I'm not there to do that anymore. But I haven't left you, Em. I'll never leave you. I see you when you need me. I hear the words you say and the ones you don't. When you feel so broken that you can't carry on, I'm there, Em, putting my arms around you to hold you up. But you know what? I haven't had to do that as much lately. Not since Ryan took that role from me. I'm not gonna lie, he wouldn't have been my first choice for you. I knew he had a thing for you. He'd ask about you constantly and he couldn't take his eyes off you whenever you were around. I ignored it. I had to. He was my best mate and as much as I'd wanted to knock him out, I knew he was a good guy. If you chose him, then that was between the both of you. As long as he'd make you happy, that was all that mattered to me.

"Ems, what he did wasn't against you. It was against our dad. It was a smack in the face to the injustice that shouldn't go unnoticed. Dad doesn't deserve to get away with what he did, and Ryan was strong enough to stand up for that. Em, you need to thank him, not bury the guy. If I know Ryan, and I think I do, he'll be feeling a million times worse than you could ever imagine. That dude acts like he's a tough-nut, but he's a softie at heart. Ask him to tell you about Battlefield, I think it might surprise you.

"So, little sis, I guess what I'm trying to tell you in my rambling incoherent way is, you need to go easier on yourself, and Ryan too. He loves you. I know you love him. Life's short. Take the happiness where you can. Hold onto it so tightly you feel dizzy from that shit. I want my sister to enjoy her life. And if he fucks up, dump his ass, but he won't. Let him be the strength you need when you're too tired from holding it all together. I know you'll do the same for him when the time comes, and it will. Lose the guilt. Let it go. Imagine me dressed as Elsa singing that to you and when you've finished laughing, listen again and do it. I love you, Em. I'm only ever a heartbeat away."

I fell onto the ground sobbing. I had no idea where all that had come from. That whole conversation I'd just made up in my head had exhausted and reawakened me at the same time.

I sucked in a breath, realising I needed to see Ryan. I wanted to be with him. I was in love with him and I had to make it work. My family lay in tatters at my feet, my name was mud and my feelings shredded to nothing. But the positives in my life had to win. My friends, my courage to survive, and my love for a man who, in the short space of time that we'd been together, had done nothing but stand up for me, with Chase, with my family. Whenever I'd needed him, he'd been there. I wouldn't get over what had happened overnight. I'd still harbour some anger towards him for not telling me first, but I understood his reasons. Now, I wanted to move forward with him by my side.

I looked down at my lap and saw the little daisy chain I'd made. I smiled and hung it off the corner of Danny's gravestone.

"Next time I'll bring some proper flowers. For now, you can have my daisy chain. I know how much you loved having those planted in your hair when we were kids." I stood up and smoothed my hands down my jeans. "See you later, bro. I love you."

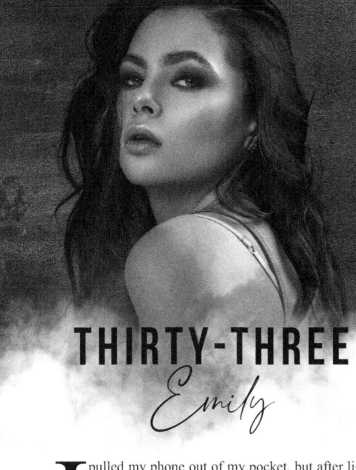

THIRTY-THREE

Emily

I pulled my phone out of my pocket, but after lighting up it showed me I had one percent charge, and powered off. So, I went back to the community centre, thinking maybe I'd find Ryan there. The police were taking statements and the crowds from earlier had died down, but the boys were nowhere to be seen. I turned to leave and that's when I noticed Kian in the corner of the room, trying not to draw attention to himself. When he saw me he flinched and then reluctantly he made his way over.

"I'm so sorry, Em." He held both of his hands up as he walked towards me, then stopped and in a low voice he asked me, "Are you okay?"

I wasn't ready to go another round with anyone else about what had gone down tonight, so I cut right to the chase. "Where's Ryan?"

"He's not here. Finn told him you saw everything, and he bolted. The rest of them left soon after. It's been a shit-show, Em. They've arrested your dad."

I didn't give a shit about him. I wanted to know where Ryan was. I was exhausted enough without having to drain the truth out of Kian yet again.

"Where, Kian? Where are they?"

"I don't know, but if I had to guess-"

"Please do. I don't have time for this," I snapped, ready to bolt myself.

"The gym. Brandon's gym, where he works. That's where they usually meet. Of course, there is Zak's place, but..."

I didn't let him finish. I headed out the door and turned left. Every minute that I was away from him felt like an extra pound of misery weighing in my chest. I couldn't deal with any more. He held the valve to provide some release. If I didn't find him soon, I felt sure I was going to implode.

***

The lights inside the gym were still on, but the sign on the door said closed. I pushed through regardless and found a young guy on the front desk.

"Evening." The guy gave me a cocky smile, but it soon faded when he saw how fraught I was. "Are you okay? Can I help you with anything?"

"Where's Ryan?" I didn't bother with second names. I assumed if Brandon worked here and they used this place as their meeting point, he'd know who I meant.

"Probably out the back with Brandon." He gestured across the gym to a set of doors. "The boxing ring is through there. Tell Brandon I'm locking up now…" He went to say something else, but I just threw my hand up to show that I'd heard. I didn't stick around. I had my focus elsewhere.

When I opened the doors I didn't find the boys, only Brandon sitting on the edge of the boxing ring, hunched forward and looking like he'd just suffered the worst defeat of his career. When he heard the door slamming behind me, he looked up, then straightened his back and jumped to his feet. I'd always found it difficult to read Brandon and tonight was no different. Was that remorse? Or defiance? Did *he* even know how he felt?

"Is he here?" I asked, looking around all the shady corners of the room. There were a few punch bags suspended from the ceiling and the ring that dominated the centre looked like it'd seen better days.

"No. He's out looking for you. Are you okay?" He stepped closer towards me like I was a wounded animal and he wasn't sure how best to approach me. I hadn't actually seen Brandon look nervous or vulnerable, but that's how he seemed now. He was being cautious.

"No, Brandon. I'm not okay." He stopped when our feet were almost touching, and I felt uncomfortable being this close to him, but I didn't step back. Brandon lived off the fear of others and I didn't want to show any weakness. Tonight, I had to have the upper-hand.

"You weren't supposed to see that. We didn't do that to hurt you, Em." I sighed. I'd heard enough of the excuses. I wasn't here to get Brandon's version of events. I just needed to see

Ryan.

"Where is he?" I repeated, ignoring his sympathetic stare and dodging the second round of justification.

"When Kian told us you'd heard it all, I felt sick. I never meant to hurt you, Emily. Thinking that you were out there, heartbroken, crying. It did something to me."

I felt like giving him a round of applause for his Oscar winning performance. Who was he trying to kid? Brandon Mathers didn't care about anyone else's feelings, only his own. "This isn't about you, Brandon. I need to speak to Ryan."

"I care too, Emily. I care more than you know."

I didn't know what his game was, but I wasn't about to open myself up to him, no matter how contrite he attempted to make himself appear.

"I'm sure you do. Danny was a friend to all of you. Can you text Ryan and ask him to come here?"

He shook his head. "I need to make it right between us. I can't bear the hurt I feel." He grabbed the front of his T-shirt, grimacing. He wasn't making any sense. "I'm dying inside, Em."

"I'm sorry you feel guilty about shitting all over my life. I'll buy you a gift basket if it'll make you feel better." He didn't crack a smile, just pushed himself further into my personal space.

"You know that's not what I mean. I can't go on like this anymore. After what happened tonight, I realised I needed to put it right. I should've fought harder for you. For us."

"What are you on about?" I frowned, trying to sift through his garbled words to come up with something that made sense.

"I love you, Emily." Before I could get my next breath, his

hand was holding the back of my head and he was kissing me, not slow and gentle like Ryan, but rough and desperate.

I used both of my hands on his chest to push him away. When he realised I wasn't reciprocating whatever fucked-up admission this was, he took a step back and wiped over his mouth with the back of his hand.

"Why the fuck did you do that?" I gasped, covering my mouth and fighting down the bile that was rising up.

"I know Ryan loves you, but I do too. I always have."

I went cold hearing those words. Their sentiment only made me uncomfortable and confused. I'd done nothing to encourage him. Where the hell was all this coming from?

"What?" I managed to splutter out. "You've been a shitty human being to me for ninety-nine percent of the time I've known you, Brandon. That's not love. What kind of sick game are you playing?"

"I'm not playing a fucking game. All I'm asking for is a chance. I want a chance to make you happy. Ryan had his turn, now it's mine."

He sounded like a spoilt kid fighting over a toy. He was un-fucking-believable.

"Oh my God! I'm not some prize you can pass around." Did he really think that's how adult relationships worked? You wanted your *turn,* so you threw your toys out of the pram to get it?

"I didn't mean it like that. I'm just letting you know you have other options."

"Options? What the fuck, Brandon? This is messed up. I don't love you. I don't even like you. I wouldn't be with you even if you were the last man on earth. That's never going to change. Trust me."

He closed his eyes and when he opened them again, I could see the old Brandon was back in play. The one who used hate as a weapon to protect himself.

"You think Ryan's so special, don't you? You think he's all that. Do you know he only went out with you for revenge? He took one for the team. He dated you so we could get what we needed out of you. It was all about your father, never about you. You meant nothing to him. That day, when you broke down in your car and Ryan saved you, he set that up. Everything he's done was to get to the truth. He doesn't love you, Emily. He never has. It was all lies."

I knew he was lashing out. Seconds ago he'd told me Ryan loved me. Now he was trying to turn me against him. It wouldn't work.

"Save your breath. I know everything," I said, praying to God he wouldn't come out with anything else to challenge that theory. "I know he used me at the start and I know it was you guys who chased me, hounded me until I caved in. You wanted to break my father and you didn't care whether I broke too. But none of that matters now. I don't need to justify myself to you or anyone else. Ryan loves me. I know that. I love him too. But you? You're nothing. You live your life to make others feel worthless. You're like a leech, feeding off of other people's happiness. I won't let you do that to me or Ryan. Nothing you say will change the way I feel about him. What we have is stronger than that."

Something deep within him snapped and he lurched forward again, trying to grab me.

"What the fuck is going on?"

Brandon's eyes widened at the bellowing voice and he swung his head round to face Zak and Finn who stood in the doorway. I stayed rooted to the spot. I didn't think I needed words to defend myself. My actions had said enough.

"I'm giving her a few home truths." Brandon smiled that evil smile he usually saved for his opponents in the ring. "She needs to know where she stands. I told her Ryan used her." He took another step back and shrugged like it was nothing. Zak and Finn looked like they'd been slapped in the face.

"You know he's going to kill you when he finds out?" Zak said to Brandon, then he turned to address me. "It's not true, Em. He didn't use you."

"I know the truth." I walked over to the door, feeling safer next to Zak and Finn than I did with Brandon. "And it's okay. He wanted to use me, but it's more than that now." I looked back at Brandon. "It doesn't matter what anyone says or does, it won't change how I feel."

"Did he hurt you?" Zak said in a low voice.

"If a kiss can hurt, then yes, he hurt me." I wanted to get that last twist of the knife in. Brandon didn't deserve to be defended. He was good enough at deflecting the blows that came his way, so I happily threw in one of my own.

"The fuck?" Zak's nostril's flared and he marched into the room. "You kissed Emily? Are you fucking insane? Do you want to shit over everything we've built?"

Brandon narrowed his eyes at me as he spoke to Zak. "She knows why I did it. She needed to know. I won't apologise for it. I was letting her know there are other roads in life. She doesn't need to settle."

I almost choked on thin air. "Fuck you, Brandon. If I settled for you I'd be letting myself in for a lifetime of misery. I think I deserve better than that. Don't you?"

I didn't want to stay around for the encore. I'd had enough confrontation for one night and I hoped I'd made my stance pretty clear where Brandon Mathers was concerned. The devil himself would've been a more appealing life partner than him. At least with that fucker you knew what you were getting in to.

THIRTY-FOUR

Ryan

The moment Finn told me she'd seen it all was the moment my whole world came crashing down around me. I should've known she'd find a way to get to the truth. She'd always been headstrong, but I'd hoped I'd covered my tracks well enough to buy me a bit more time. Assuming she'd gone to Effy's for the night, I'd blanked out the pain of betrayal and focused on what I had to do. But looking back now, she'd never actually told me outright that she was there. She didn't tell me anything and now I was trying to piece together the shattered parts from the fall-out.

I'd resigned myself to the fact that she'd blame me. I hadn't told her, and I knew deep down I should've. She had every right to know, but I'd been blindsided by years of plotting a revenge plan. When the others told me about Danny, I was shocked, but if I was completely honest with myself, it didn't surprise me. It tore my fucking heart out, but it was no surprise. Emily's dad was ruthless. He didn't care who he hurt in his scramble to the top. He was the guy who'd step over anyone and everyone to get there. Emily didn't deserve to have such a shitty father, neither did Danny, or the secret kid he'd kept hidden from the world.

My only goal now was to find Emily. She needed me. Finding out that her whole life was built on a web of seedy, tacky lies would be killing her. I knew my girl and she'd be going through a whole maelstrom of emotions; anger, guilt, hurt, betrayal. Thinking of her facing that alone broke my heart. I had to be there for her, even if she wanted to use me as her punching bag, I'd take it. As long as she kept talking to me, that was the main thing. Talking so she could heal.

I couldn't lose her. Not now. I'd waited years to get the chance to win her heart. I think I was doing a pretty good job too after a lukewarm start a few months ago. Having her in my life made everything brighter. She brought light when everything had always felt dull and grey. She made me bounce out of bed most mornings, and that was no mean feat. I was one miserable bastard first thing. But that's what she did to me. She healed me in ways I didn't even know were broken; my hope, my faith, my dreams for the future. Now it was my turn to be the strength she needed. All I had to do was find her.

I tried ringing her mobile, but every time I did it went straight to voicemail. Ringing Liv and Effy didn't help either. They had no idea where she was, and they couldn't reach her. I glossed over what'd happened, filling them in on the basic facts. They hadn't heard about it, so I guessed Emily's shame ran deeper than even I imagined. She couldn't even bring herself to open up to her two best friends.

I left the others to wrap up the stuff at the community centre. The police had come to arrest Alec Winters and they were taking statements, but I managed to bypass them and get outside. When I finally pulled up outside her house a few minutes later, the whole building was shrouded in darkness. I cupped my hands to peer through the windows, but I couldn't see anything. Not wanting to leave any stone unturned, I decided to try the back. The gate was locked, but that wasn't going to keep me out. I managed to climb over easily. I tried all the doors, not expecting to find any open, but surprisingly the patio hadn't been locked properly and I was able to get into the house.

"Em? Babe? Are you here?"

I raced through the kitchen, looking into the empty living rooms as I sped past. Then I bolted upstairs, but she wasn't here. No one was. Her room was quiet, untouched. I'd hit my first dead end of the night.

Grabbing the back of my neck in frustration, I racked my brains to try and think where else she might be. A lightbulb went off in my brain. It might be a long shot, but it was worth checking out.

I pulled up in front of the old Asylum and cut the engine. It was eerily dark out here and there was no sign of life, but I figured, if she wanted somewhere to hide, here was as good a place as any.

I squeezed through the broken fencing and picked my way over the rubble. I couldn't see shit, so I used the torch on my phone to help light my way. As I pushed into the building, the sound of the birds flapping around at my disturbance made me jump.

"Em? It's me. Are you here?" I called out into the darkness, but the only response was my echo reverberating off the walls and shattering my already shredded nerves. It wasn't looking good.

I ignored the thumping pain in my heart and made my way down to the chapel. I'd been planning on bringing her here this week. I'd got it all worked out. A date with that special Ryan and Emily touch. But now, those plans were falling away faster than the rotting bricks and peeling paint on the asylum walls.

When I got to the chapel, with the rainbow lights from the stained glass windows dancing around the dark and dusty interior, I stopped. She wasn't here. Where the fuck was she? I'd run out of options.

My phone vibrated an incoming call, and when I saw Zak's name, I answered.

"Ryan, mate. Where are you?" Zak sounded frantic. I felt a spike of adrenaline hearing him like that. I knew I wouldn't like what he was about to tell me.

"I'm looking for Emily. Is she with you?" I grit my teeth waiting on his response. My stomach was in knots. I knew Finn had spoken to her and pleaded my case, and I was grateful to him for that. It wasn't ideal. I'd have rather spoken to her myself but thinking about her hearing everything from the others before me, getting comfort from them, that pissed me off the most.

"She was."

My mouth went dry. What the fuck kind of answer was that?

"What do you mean, she was? Where the fuck is she now?"

I was losing my shit fast.

"I think you need to come to the gym. I don't want to do this over the phone."

I didn't have time for his bullshit. I cut the call and ran out of the chapel. Once I was back in the van, I tried calling Zak again on speaker as I drove, but he didn't pick up. None of them did. What the hell was I going to find out when I got there?

***

I barged my way through the doors into the back room, where Finn, Zak and Brandon stood in some kind of weird stand-off.

"Tell me what the fuck is going on?" I glared at each one of them, but they all looked as guilty as fuck and stared down at their feet like a bunch of morons. "What happened? Where is she?"

"She took off about a half hour ago. I've no idea where she's gone. I'm sorry, mate." Finn was a good guy. He liked to keep the peace. But I didn't need his apologetic neutral shit right now. I needed answers. It was obvious something had gone down.

"Why? What the fuck happened?"

Brandon stood up and crossed his arms over his chest. I could tell right away from the defensive stance that whatever it was had Brandon-fucking-Mathers written all over it.

"Did you upset her? I swear to God, Brandon, if you've done something to her I'll fucking kill you."

It wasn't Brandon who spoke next, it was Zak, and what he said had the blood rushing to my ears and my brain drowning in a mixture of white noise and rage.

"Brandon made a pass at her. He kissed Emily and when she pushed him away he told her you didn't love her, that it was all one big fucking joke. He said you were only dating her to get revenge on her father." Zak glared at Brandon as he spoke. Me? I couldn't even see straight. If he wanted to see what revenge looked like, he was about to get a big fucking lesson.

"Well, it was. Wasn't it?" Brandon had the nerve to shrug, like what Zak had said didn't mean a damn thing. "I put the girl out of her misery. I couldn't stand to see her pining around you for a minute longer." He turned to face me and grinned. "Guess I did you a favour. No need for the long drawn out break-up."

I lost it.

I really fucking lost it.

I barrelled over to Brandon, throwing my whole body into his and wrestling him to the floor. He didn't put up a fight and when I reared back and punched him in the face, he laughed. The fucker actually laughed.

"She didn't believe him," Finn shouted as I took another swing at my ex-best friend's ugly smirking face. "She told Brandon she loved you. She loves you, Ry. Mate, she knows about you using her at the start and she doesn't care. She said nothing he could say would change the way she felt."

I knew what Finn was doing. He hated confrontation. But this wasn't about Emily's feelings for me, whether what she'd said was true or not. This was about Brandon doing what he always does; treating people like pawns in his fucked-up games and avoiding all the consequences. He'd put his hands on my girl tonight. He'd said things that I'd never ever forgive him for. He was a dead man walking as far as I was concerned.

I carried on raining down blow after blow on Brandon's face, but he kept laughing like a maniac. Then I felt the force of being tugged backwards. Zak and Finn were dragging me off of him, telling me he wasn't worth it and to let it go.

"Let it go? Let it fucking go? He kissed my girlfriend."

"Your fake girlfriend." Brandon spat blood out onto the floor and sat up, glaring over at me.

"Nothing about our relationship was fake. You know fuck all."

"I know she's still a virgin. If you'd let me take care of her like I'd suggested at the start, I'd have tapped that ass within days. Probably wrapped the shit up with her father sooner too. You're a fucking pussy, Ry."

I launched myself towards him again, but Zak and Finn were faster this time and held me back.

"You kissed her. Why did you do that? You knew how I felt about her. It wasn't about her father. It hasn't been about him for a long time. Why the fuck would you do that to me?"

The smirk on his face disappeared and he leaned forward, rubbing his hands over his face. He'd shelved the bravado and he was trying to look sincere.

Too little too late, you back-stabbing bastard.

"I love her too," he said quietly as he dropped his head down in shame.

I couldn't believe what I was hearing. Was he for real?

"What the fuck did you just say?"

"You heard me. I love her too. I figured I'd take my chances." He shrugged, then I watched as his expression changed, falling right back into the old Brandon. The one who didn't give a fuck about anyone but himself. "Maybe she'd only been dating you to try to get to me all along." I laughed. The man was delusional.

"She fucking hates you, dude. She can't even stand to be in the same room as you." Zak and Finn held onto me as I tensed against them, trying to break free. The fact he'd told my girlfriend he loved her made me want to cave his face in. I wanted to beat him until they'd have to use dental records to identify his shitty carcass. The thought of him near her made me crazy. The idea of her in his arms made me murderous. The fact that he'd probably spent every moment in her presence thinking of her in that way made me unhinged and homicidal. She wasn't his. She was my girl. She always had been, and she always would be.

"I should be laughing at you." I eased up in Zak and Finn's hold and smiled, knowing I had the power to hurt Brandon way more than any punch could. "Did you really think she'd tell you she loved you back? Why would she love a screw-up like you? What would you have to offer to a girl like Emily? You're nothing. Even your own mother didn't want you."

It was a low blow, but I was already in the gutter. It was all I had left to fight with.

"Fuck you, Ryan. Don't think you'll be taking home any boyfriend of the year trophies just yet. She knows you used her. I might have a shitty family, but at least I own it. I know who I am. You? You don't know who you are from one day to the next."

"Oh, I know exactly who I am. I'm the guy who's gonna be by her side every damn day. I'm not the one that's lying to himself, getting lost in nameless, faceless one-night-stands to try and drown out the rejection he's felt every day since he was born. Using fists to dull the pain of being such a loser and a fuck-up." I had more I wanted to say, but Finn butted in.

"That's enough, Ry."

I turned to face Zak and Finn, but they couldn't even look me in the eye.

"Enough? He put his hands on my girl then broke her heart. He stabbed me in the back with that big fucking grin on his face. Enough? It'll never be enough. Not for me."

I walked over to where Brandon sat hunched on the floor. He glared back at me with defiance in his eyes and I searched inside of myself to try and find an ounce of pity for the guy, but I had none. I hated him. No, I loathed him.

"I'm done," I said with zero emotion. "I'm done with you, with this gym, the lies, the little digs. I'm done with all of you. The Renaissance bullshit, the parties, the money. I am done."

Zak stepped forward and grabbed my arm, trying to force me to turn around and look at him. "You don't mean that, mate. Come on. Brandon fucked up like he always does, but let's sleep on it. Talk about it in the morning."

"You're not listening to me." I wrenched my arm away from Zak but kept my eyes on Brandon. "I don't want to talk to any of you. She's the one I want to talk to and I can't fucking find her 'cos you've driven her away. She is all that matters. She comes before any of you. So count me out. It's over for me. Emily comes first. I've got no time for the rest of you. You can all go to hell."

I didn't want to be there anymore. Brandon had pissed all over my life. I couldn't even stand to breathe the same air as him. I turned and headed for the door.

"Please, Ry. Don't say that. Everything's heated right now. Don't say things you'll regret tomorrow." Finn was delusional if he thought we could sort this out over a coffee and a few games of Call of Duty. Brandon had severed any hope of a friendship with me tonight. What he'd done was unforgiveable. I didn't want to be anywhere that he was.

"The only thing I'll regret is ever listening to you and not telling Emily about her dad. Everything else means nothing."

Brandon jumped up from his pity spot on the floor. "You want out, then fuck off. We don't need you anyway. Me, Zak, and Finn, we'll manage just fine. And when she finally dumps your ass, don't come running back to us."

I glanced over my shoulder and gave Brandon my parting shot. "I don't want to see you ever again. Stay out of my way if you know what's good for you. Our friendship is over."

I shoulder slammed Finn as I stalked out of the gym without looking back. I was so over all of their shit. The only place I wanted to be was with Emily; holding her in my arms and making sure that this God awful night hadn't destroyed us for good.

I felt broken inside, like the splinters of my heart were penetrating my lungs, making it impossible to breathe.

She was the only one who could make that better.

She was my everything.

THIRTY-FIVE
Ryan

I'd run out of ideas. I had no clue where to head to next. It was getting late, but I wasn't about to give up. I drove round to Effy's house, thinking maybe she'd headed there after leaving the gym. One look at Effy's face told me she had no news. She was as worried as I was. She rang Liv as I stood in the doorway pacing back and forth, but we had no joy there either. Emily's phone still wasn't connecting, and I was starting to panic.

I decided to head back home and grab my phone charger. It was running on five percent and I needed to keep it going for the rest of the night. I was determined to drive through every damn street until I found her. I didn't care how long it'd take. I wasn't giving up. I drove by her house again on the off chance she might've gone home, but the place was still in darkness.

When I eventually pulled up outside my house, I noticed Connor's car was gone and I pulled into his space.

The house was silent. Dad was off at the trade fair and Connor was God knows where for the night. I took the stairs two at a time, desperate to get my charger and get the hell out of there. When I opened the door to my bedroom, I stopped dead in my tracks. There, in a little bundle under the duvet, was my Emily. I thought she was asleep, tucked safely under the bed covers, and I held my breath for a second, thankful that she was here. All this time I'd been running around town like a madman and she'd been with me all along. I was who she'd come running to.

She turned slowly to face me. The room was dark, save for the glow of the streetlamps outside, and it took a few seconds for my eyes to adjust, but I could tell she'd been crying. Her whole body looked defeated as she lay there, looking over at me.

"Connor let me in," she said quietly into the room. "I hope that was okay."

"Of course it's okay." I closed the door behind me and went straight to her, sitting down on the bed and reaching over to stroke her hair. "I've been worried about you. I've driven everywhere tonight looking for you. Why didn't you answer my calls?"

"My phone had no charge. I'm sorry," she said, but she had nothing to be sorry for. I was the one who needed to be apologising. I should've been on my fucking knees right now, begging her to forgive me.

"Em, I'm sorry. I didn't…"

She sat up and wrapped her arms around me.

"I know, Ryan. I can't talk anymore about what happened with Dad tonight. I can't deal with it yet. I will, I promise, but not now. I don't blame you. I understand why you did what you did. But tonight, I just can't dissect another second of it. I just need you."

She pulled back and took my hand in hers. That's when she noticed the grazes on my knuckles.

"What happened?"

"Mathers. That's what happened. He told me what he'd said to you tonight… And what he'd done. I punched him and told him to go to hell. I'm done with it, Em. I've had enough."

"You know I didn't believe him, right? I know we didn't have the most conventional start, but I know what we have now isn't fake. It's real. For me, anyway." She traced her thumb softly over my knuckles but looked down as if she expected me to contradict her.

"It's real for me too. I love you, Emily. I always have, and I always will."

She looked back up at me, her eyes wide and her mouth open like she couldn't quite believe what she was hearing. Did she really doubt me? I thought I'd made me feelings pretty fucking clear. But maybe not? I would from this moment on though, that was for sure.

"You're it for me, Em. From now on, you will always come first, before all of them. You are what matters the most to me."

"I love you too." She held my cheek in her hand and I leaned into it, loving being this close to her. "I came here because I needed to be with you. I figured you'd come home eventually, and I couldn't stop myself from getting in your bed. It smells like you. It's my favourite smell." She blushed, and seeing her all embarrassed, cute and warm, wrapped up in my bed sheets did something to me. I knew then and there that I'd die for this girl.

"Can I get in with you? If I don't have you in my arms in the next few seconds, I think I'm gonna go insane." She laughed and shuffled backwards to give me space to get into the bed. She was fully dressed, but I stood up and took my hoodie off, then I unbuttoned my jeans and pulled them down. Her eyes grew wide as she watched me.

"I don't want any barriers between us tonight," I said, leaning over to grab her hoodie and pull it up and over her head. She lifted her hips and unbuttoned her jeans under the covers and I watched as she shimmied out of them and dropped them on to the floor.

"Is this okay?" I asked, climbing under the covers and grabbing her around the waist to pull her into me.

"More than okay." She sighed. She was warm and smelt of vanilla and me. I buried my head into her neck, so I could fill my lungs full of her. Being with her like this felt so right, like coming home. I'd never felt this before, like all I needed was to be with her and everything would be okay.

I didn't want to put any pressure on her. I wasn't here for anything other than to comfort her. But when she lifted her lips to mine and we started to kiss, I couldn't stop my body from reacting. I wanted her badly. The ache I felt was painful. She ran her fingers through my hair and scraped her nails over the back of my scalp. I loved it when she did that, it gave me goose-bumps. I kept my arms wrapped around her waist, but my hips had a mind of their own, and right now they were grinding into her, letting her know exactly how much I liked her being in my bed.

Our kiss turned more frantic and I rolled her, so she was lying on her back. My tongue slid over hers, tasting and teasing both of us until we were gasping and writhing under the covers. I used both of my arms to hold me up over her. I didn't want to make her feel uncomfortable. Slowly, I pulled away from our kiss, and with one hand I stroked her face and looked in her eyes. Her lips were swollen, and her cheeks were flushed. She was the most beautiful girl I'd ever seen, and she was all mine.

"I love you so much, Em." I placed my forehead gently onto hers and breathed her in like she was my air.

"I love you too." She bit her lip and then pulled me down to hug her. Then in the quietest most breathless voice I'd ever heard her use, she sighed, "Make love to me, Ryan. Please."

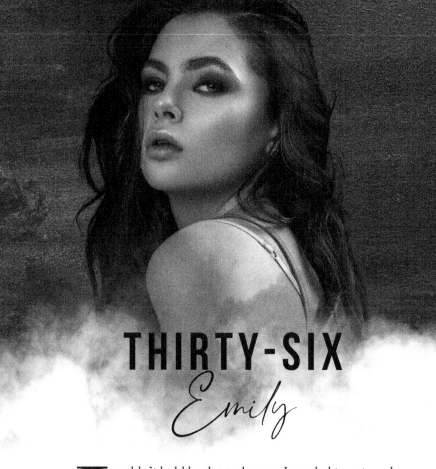

THIRTY-SIX
Emily

I couldn't hold back any longer. I needed to get as close to him as I possibly could. I wanted that connection. I wanted him to be my first, my last, my only. He lay still for a second, taking deep breaths before he finally answered.

"Are you sure, baby? There's no pressure. We can just cuddle."

I loved Ryan's cuddles, but tonight I needed more.

"I want you to take the pain away." As soon as I said it, I knew I'd worded it wrong.

"Em, don't do this to block out what's happened tonight.

You might wake up tomorrow and regret it. I don't want you to regret anything about us."

"I don't. I didn't mean it like that." I turned my head to look at him, so he could see exactly how strong my feelings were. "I want you, Ryan. I want to love you as deep and as hard as I can. I need this. This connection that we have, it's so strong. I can't hold myself back any more. I want this with you. I want you to love me in every way you can."

"I do love you in every way."

"Then shut up and kiss me."

His body was half over mine and I could already feel how hard he was from the way his hips ground into me. When he kissed me again, it was tender and loving. His tongue stroked mine and he moaned as we pulled ourselves closer together, but it still wasn't close enough.

I ran my nails down his back and then grabbed his ass as he rocked against me. I loved his ass. It was round, muscular and it felt so sexy flexing as he circled his hips. I ran my fingers under the waistband of his boxers and slid them down. He pulled away, breaking the kiss and panting heavily as he kicked them off. His dick was thick, hard and it slapped against my thigh as it sprang free. I held him and rubbed slowly, running my thumb over the tip that had a little bead of wetness there. Then I cupped his balls and the groan he gave as he sank into the pillow and nuzzled my neck spurred me on further.

He opened his legs to give me better access and then his mouth was exploring too. Kissing from my ear to my neck and down towards my breasts. He reached around the back of my bra and unhooked it. Then he pulled it off and threw it onto the floor. He grabbed one breast in his hands, kneading and stroking over my nipple while he licked and sucked the other into his hot mouth.

I pushed forward into him and closed my eyes, getting lost in the sensations. The way he used his hands and mouth on me made me throb between my legs. I was so wet, so turned on I could barely breathe.

I started to circle my hips into him, desperate for any kind of friction. Ryan could read my body better than I could and he moved his hand down to my underwear, pushing his fingers underneath my panties as his tongue carried on licking and sucking my nipple, driving me crazy. He ran his fingers along my wetness and I opened my legs, needing him to go further. His finger circled my clit and my hips bucked at the contact. Then he pushed a finger inside me and I arched my back off the bed, moaning when he curled it inside and made me see stars in the darkness of his room. His fingers slid in and out of me, and he used his thumb, then the palm of his hand to rub over my clit. I moaned louder, and he moved his mouth from my nipple to my lips, capturing every sound that I made, feeding off them. His tongue moved in the same rhythm as his fingers and I gasped, feeling my nerves sparking to life.

"I'm gonna come," I said, rocking onto his hand and pumping his dick at the same time.

Then I felt it.

That explosion of ecstasy right from my core, radiating everywhere and making my whole body shake.

He gently worked me back down from heaven and then pulled his hand out of my knickers and lifted himself up, pulling them down my legs and exposing me to him completely. I felt swollen and oversensitive, but I didn't want our night to end there.

"If you want to stop at any time just tell me, okay?" He looked me right in the eyes as he spoke. He still hadn't come, and I was desperate to feel him inside me. I nodded, and he leaned over to his bedside cabinet, opened the top drawer and pulled out a condom.

"Any time," he repeated as he ripped the foil with his teeth. "You can stop this at any time." I nodded again as he rolled the condom on. Then he settled in-between my legs and pulled my knees up high. "I don't want to hurt you, baby. I'll go as slow as I can."

He rubbed himself up and down my pussy, then he put his cock over my entrance and I tried to relax and open myself up to him as best I could. He put both of his arms next to my head and stared right into my eyes as he nudged slowly into me. I felt a sharp pain as he pushed against what felt like an impossible barrier and I couldn't stop myself from grimacing. Instantly he froze.

"Are you okay?"

I nodded and grabbed him around the neck to pull him into me.

"Don't stop," I whispered into his ear and he put his hand under my left knee to lift my leg higher. As he did, he thrust forward and I cried out, feeling an unforgiveable stretch as he filled me completely.

His hips were pressed against mine, but he didn't move. He took deep breaths as he let me get used to him being inside me like this. I was sweating and shaking with what I now realised were nerves, but soon the sting became a dull ache.

"You okay?" he asked again, sounding like he was anything

but.

I wrapped my arms around him and kissed his neck. "I love you," I said. I wanted to cry, but I held it in. The intensity of this moment was drowning me.

"I love you too." He kissed me softly on the lips as I felt a gentle pulse in-between my legs. Was that him or me? I had no idea, but when he said, "I'm gonna need to move now, baby. This is killing me." I smiled and wiggled my hips.

He groaned and then I felt him pull out of me before sliding back in slowly. He started to circle his hips and thrust, and each time he did felt better than the last.

I held him close as he rocked into me and I angled my hips, so I could mirror his movements.

"That's it, baby." He moaned as I tilted my hips to take him in deeper. "Holy fuck."

The swell of love I felt for him in that moment as he thrust inside me was so overwhelming, I couldn't get enough. Our bodies worked together; grinding, rubbing, and sending us both to the edge to eventually fall off that cliff. We were panting, gasping for breath as we clung to each other. I wrapped my legs tightly around him and he held my thigh as he pounded into me more forcefully than before. He was coming undone.

"Harder, Ry. Please," I begged, and he moved his hand from my thigh to reach between us and rub over my clit. In seconds I was coming hard, clamping down on his cock and crying out with the intensity of the pleasure. This was stronger than the other orgasms. It was powerful and as I rode wave after wave of ecstasy I shuddered, clinging to him as he continued to rock into me.

"Jesus. Fuck," he cried out and then groaned. I felt him

thicken and from the erratic way he moved I guessed he was coming too.

I never expected my first time to be as special as it had been. I was fully prepared for some kind of horror story or let down, judging from what Liv and all the other girls at school had talked about. But with Ryan, it was perfect. He was perfect. I was so glad I'd waited to find him.

My person.

My soul mate.

My whole world.

We lay together, catching our breath. Ryan's body pinned me to the mattress, but I didn't care. I liked feeling the weight of him on me. I loved hearing him breathless because of me. Once we'd steadied our breathing, he whispered, "We're gonna be doing that a lot from now on."

I laughed.

"I'll be holding you to that."

When he pulled out of me, I sighed. I didn't like feeling empty again. He sat up and pulled the condom off then strolled off to his bathroom giving me a superb view of his gorgeous ass. When he came back he had a wash cloth in his hand and he knelt down and started to clean me.

"What are you doing?" I wriggled slightly. I felt sore, but his warm cloth was helping.

"I made you all dirty so I'm cleaning you up. I would take you into the shower, but I think you need a rest." He winked up at me and I shook my head, smiling.

"I should shower…" I raised my hands up and yawned. "But I'll do it later."

He leaned down and placed a kiss over my most sensitive

spot and said, "I'm sorry I hurt you, but for the record, I really enjoyed it."

"Are you talking to my vagina?" I laughed looking down at him.

"Yes. Your pussy is my new best friend."

"Oh my God. I just can't. You're unbelievable." I covered my face with the shame.

"I know. You love me though."

"I do. So much."

He threw the cloth to the floor and crawled back up the bed, pulling me into him, and before I knew it we were both fast asleep.

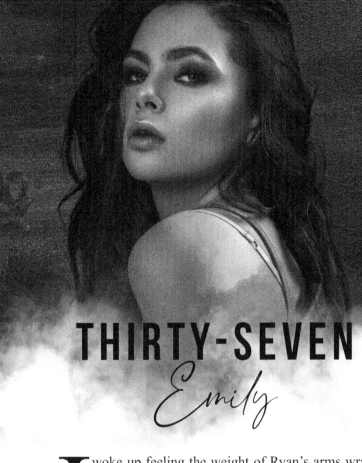

THIRTY-SEVEN
Emily

I woke up feeling the weight of Ryan's arms wrapped tightly around my waist and the heat from his body as it cocooned mine. I didn't want to move and wake him up. I wanted to lie here for as long as I could and savour this moment. Staying as still as I could, I listened to his steady breaths, feeling them dance across the back of my neck. I felt the rise and fall of his chest against my back and despite everything that'd happened, I felt safe.

I knew today was going to bring a whole new set of challenges and headaches my way, but this was how I wanted to wake up every day; in the arms of the man I loved, feeling cherished and adored.

He began to stir behind me and when he kissed my neck and started to stroke my hair, I reached my hand up to cup his face.

"Good morning, beautiful," he said, nuzzling into my hair, pulling me further into him. I wriggled my ass and he groaned. "I could get used to this every morning."

"Me too," I replied, pushing my ass into him and feeling how hard he was.

His hands started roaming, stroking over my thighs in a lazy massage and then he pulled my leg up and back, so that I was more open for him. His breath was becoming ragged and when he ran his fingers along my pussy, he moaned. I was wet, and even though I still felt sore from last night, I wanted him more than anything.

He circled my clit and rubbed me with his expert fingers. My hips began gently rocking in time with him, and when he pushed a finger inside me, I gasped.

"I need you."

"You want some lazy morning sex, baby?" He didn't need to ask. My body had already answered for me.

"Not sure about the lazy, but yeah, I do."

His dick was pressed against my ass and he was grinding up on me as he fucked me with his fingers. His other arm was still under my waist, holding me tightly to him. Of all the bubbles he'd created for us, this was my favourite one.

He leaned over to the bedside drawer and pulled out another condom. Then he moved back slightly and pulled the duvet down off us. He wanted to watch what he was doing; see himself slide inside of me.

He rubbed his cock along my folds, spreading my wetness

and making me grind right back onto him. Then he was there, pushing inside of me and pulling my leg up as he did, so he could get the angle he wanted. I was expecting a sting, but this time it was different. The way he stretched me wasn't painful, it was fucking awesome and I arched my back into him, wanting more.

The lazy sex he'd talked about turned into something else. He pulled out of me and slammed back harder, each thrust slapping against my ass and making me groan. I held onto the metal bed post as he grabbed my hips and drove into me harder and harder. I ground back onto him, my hips rotating and moving in time with his. As he increased the pace, so did I. We worked together to bring us both to the edge. Each thrust made me hungry for more and I reached my arm around to grab his ass as I used the bed post to steady myself. We were fucking so hard and fast I felt like I'd fall off the bed if I let go.

I buried my face into the pillow. My cries were so loud they could probably hear me down the road, but I didn't care. I was so close. I moved my hand up to grab him around the neck. We were both panting, breathless, lost in each other.

Ryan held my stomach with one hand and reached down to rub over my clit with the other, and before I could even cry out, I came hard, contracting and squeezing around him. He grunted, and I felt him pulsing inside me. He was coming too. I let him ride it out, bringing us both down from the orbit we'd just circled. Our hard thrusts turned to steady rocking and then he slumped his head onto my pillow and kissed my shoulders and neck gently, all the time whispering that he loved me. I didn't think it was possible to feel this fierce kind of love. The kind of love where you need that person more than air and water, but I felt it, in that moment. A love that was raw, achingly beautiful and uniquely ours. A love that felt so powerful we only needed each other to survive. The rest of the world seemed pointless, inconsequential to what we had created together.

Our world.

Our bubble.

I took his hand in mine and threaded our fingers together. He was still inside me and I felt like I never wanted him to leave.

"You're so good at that," I blurted out in my orgasmic brain-dead state.

He chuckled. "We're good at that. We were made for each other, Em. Not everyone gets this you know?"

I turned my head to look at him. Did he mean people wouldn't get us? As in, understand why we were a couple? Or was he saying the way we felt, the closeness and the sex wasn't always like this?

"What don't they get?"

"To feel like they've found the other half to their whole. To know what it's like to love someone so much you'd do anything for them. That their happiness comes before your own. We're lucky, Em. Not everyone finds that, but we have." He placed a gentle peck on my nose and I sighed.

He was right. My life wasn't perfect. Far from it. I had no idea where I was going to be living after today. My dad would probably go to prison. My mum would lose her shit, and everything I thought I knew in my world was burning to the ground. But I still had love in my life. I was healthy, and I had my friends. But most of all, I had Ryan. When I was with him, nothing else mattered. Thinking about that made me realise I could rise from the ashes stronger than before, because I had him by my side. I could make something better than what I'd had. Build a life that I could be proud of.

"What are you thinking?" he whispered into my ear.

"I'm thinking that I couldn't possibly love you any more than I do." Then I remembered something from the night before. Something I'd conjured up in my head when I'd been at the cemetery and spoken to Danny. It probably meant nothing, and I was delusional, making things up in my weakened grief-stricken state, but I had to ask. "What's battlefield?"

Ryan's eyes widened slightly, and he gave a low gasp.

"Danny told you about that?"

I swallowed, not wanting to admit that I'd heard it in a lucid dream-like fantasy. "I want to hear you tell me."

He smiled and rested his head on my shoulder as he spoke. "You were about fifteen or sixteen. It was Danny's birthday and you'd ordered Battlefield1 for the Xbox to give to him. Only it hadn't arrived, and Danny heard you crying to your mum, asking her if she'd take you into town to buy another copy. Your mum said it was a waste of money to buy it twice and you'd have to give him his present a few days late. Danny said you were inconsolable when he overheard you."

I went cold. I hadn't expected this. I didn't think it'd mean anything, but now I was starting to realise that maybe my mind hadn't played tricks on me. How else would I have known to ask about this? Danny really did speak to me last night. He'd been there when I needed him.

"I remember that day," I managed to say, even though my throat was so tight I could barely swallow. "But the parcel arrived a few hours later. I don't get it?"

"I couldn't stand the thought of you being so upset on your

brother's birthday. Your mum was a waste of fucking space and Danny was held up with some event your dad had dragged him to that morning. So, I went into town and bought another copy. I boxed it up and then I posted it through your door. I had to tell Danny what I'd done because I knew the original parcel was due for delivery any day and I didn't want you to find out that my one was from me. I wanted you to have something to give him."

I couldn't speak. I had no idea that had happened. All those years ago, when I didn't even know he knew I existed, Ryan had done that for me. He'd gone out of his way to fake deliver my brother's birthday present just so I wouldn't feel down on his birthday. What had I done to deserve such an amazing boyfriend?

I squeezed him so close to me as my tears fell. Tears for a lost brother who meant the world to me, and tears for a boy who was my everything, my future, my Ryan.

"Don't cry," he said, wiping my sadness away and kissing my damp cheeks. "I did it so you wouldn't cry."

I laughed and hugged him even harder.

"Thank you. That's probably the nicest thing anyone has ever done for me… And for Danny too. You, Ryan Hardy, are one in a million and I'm never gonna let you go."

"I'll hold you to that."

***

Once we'd showered and dressed, we made our way downstairs into the kitchen. I froze when I heard the sizzling of a frying pan and smelt the bacon and eggs cooking.

"Morning, lovebirds." Connor was standing at the oven, rustling up a breakfast feast, grinning like an idiot and wearing an apron that said, 'Wanna see my sausage?' "Figured you two would need the energy from a good hearty breakfast after your bedroom Olympics last night… And this morning."

I felt the heat burning up my face and I glanced over at Ryan, but he was glaring daggers at his brother.

"Put some headphones on next time," he spat back, then under his breath he muttered, "fucking perv." He walked over to me and gave me a hug then turned back to his brother. "You've embarrassed my girlfriend. I know you're shit at talking to women, but show some fucking respect next time, okay?"

"It's fine," I said, trying to calm him down.

Connor just huffed out a laugh and looked back at me as he shuffled the frying pan. "You're not shy around me are you, Em? Don't be. I'm a pussy cat."

Ryan went to say something, but the banging of the front door made us all jump.

"Who the fuck is calling round this early?" Connor took the pan off the gas, turned the oven off, and stalked away to answer the door.

When Zak and Finn came charging into the kitchen seconds later, looking like they hadn't slept a wink, I knew our day was about to get a hell of a lot worse.

"What the fuck is going on?" Ryan asked, looking between the two of them. From the tone of his voice I don't think he really wanted to know.

"We've been trying to ring you both all night," Zak said and then looked to Finn for back-up.

"Our phones died. Why? What's going on?" Ryan took my hand and we both sat down at the table in the middle of the kitchen. Zak and Finn stayed standing and Connor busied himself plating up the eggs and bacon.

"Want to stay for breakfast?" Connor asked, not reading his audience very well.

"We're not hungry." Zak grimaced and Finn nodded.

"Jesus, guys. Talk about dragging out the suspense. You're worse than old women. Spit it out, Atwood," Connor said as he put the food onto the table and sat down next to me, helping himself to a large portion of scrambled eggs.

"It's Brandon."

"Isn't it always?" Ryan interrupted.

"It's worse this time. It's so much worse. He's gone. Last night… It all went to shit. The police are after him. We have no idea where he went, but it's… Fuck, it's bad."

Zak wasn't making any sense and Ryan pushed the chair next to him out to tell him to sit down.

"You need to slow down and start from the beginning, mate. What happened?"

Zak slumped into the chair and Finn pulled out another one to join him. They both looked beaten, and when they started talking, we realised exactly why.

THIRTY-EIGHT
Brandon

I'd put everything on the line tonight. I'd stuck my fucking neck out for that girl, to tell her how I felt, and what did she do? She ripped my fucking heart out and threw it away like it meant nothing. I thought she was different. That she got me. But she was just like the rest. All she saw was a fucked-up mess, a fighter, a street rat. I wasn't good enough for her. I wasn't good enough for anybody.

When she'd pulled away, scowling at the fact that I'd kissed her, that hurt. But when she laughed in my face and told me she'd rather die than be with a man like me, I felt my insides crush with the weight of rejection. I'd never felt that pointless and fucking worthless before. Well, not for a long time, anyway. Emily Winters had managed to achieve what every opponent had failed to do to me over the years. She'd brought me to my knees and made me weak. It wouldn't happen again.

I should've known Zak and Finn would stab me in the back the first chance they got. They couldn't wait to tell Ryan what'd happened, making it sound like I was some fucking predator out to hunt his girl. I know I'd lashed out when I told Emily about the plan, but she had a right to know what'd happened. He wasn't blameless in all this. He'd used her. He'd played a big fucking part in taking her down along with her father.

As far as I was concerned, they deserved each other. Ryan had the nerve to say he was done. Well, so was I. Some fucking best friend he was, putting pussy before his mates. I guess you never really know someone. I certainly didn't recognise my friends tonight. Each and every one of them had turned their back on me. They'd chosen their sides and it wasn't mine. The battle lines were drawn, and I was on my own.

When I'd left the gym earlier, Zak and Finn had made a feeble attempt to call me back to try and talk to me, but I knew it was all fake. They didn't want to make it right. They didn't care. If they did, they wouldn't have stood by and let it all play out like that. No. I was back to square one, alone, with only myself to rely on. It was the best way to be. People only disappointed you and let you down. I was done with letting myself be used. I had to be smarter. I needed to show them they couldn't push me around.

I was Brandon fucking Mathers.

I was shaking with anger when I scrolled through my phone and found Pat Murphy's number. He was the king of bare-knuckle boxing in our area and I knew he had fights fixed up for most nights of the week. Right now, I needed to let off steam and a punch bag just wasn't gonna cut it. I needed to fight.

He answered on the second ring and told me he could fit me in tonight. He was using a barn on the outskirts of town and he gave me the directions. I didn't know who I'd be fighting, and I didn't care. I felt sorry for the guy who went up against me. I was feral, unhinged and shutting down every last emotion like a machine. I'd rather feel a punch or a kick than the pain I felt now. In fact, I needed that physical pain to ease the mental scars that never seemed to close up. The scars that chipped away at my soul like a nagging, angry, open wound. The everyday reminder that I was nothing and I would always be nothing.

I got to the barn just before midnight, but the fights weren't over, they were in full swing. I could hear the shouts and chants of the men inside, and that buzz from the crowds sparked my adrenaline. Pushing the door open, I made my way through the crowds and when I found Pat he called over to a mate of his to take over, so he could talk to me.

"Son, you don't look right. Are you sure you're up for this?" I knew I looked like shit. I also knew Pat didn't fuck around. If he thought I couldn't fight, he wouldn't let me.

"I'm fine. Just a bad night. I'll be right. I need this."

He took a second or two to study me then nodded and patted me on the back.

"I had quite the response when I told my men you were heading down here. You need to start fighting for me, Brandon. We could make far more money than that shitty little ring you've got going on with your boys."

I'd always turned Pat down when he'd offered to manage me

before, but times were changing. Maybe I did need a different route?

"Maybe. Let's see how tonight goes," I said, to keep the lines open, but in truth, I couldn't see past this next fight.

"I think you're gonna like this." Pat grinned as we walked back towards the hay bales that separated the fighters from the crowds. "You might know your opponent. I think he went to the same school as you. Brodie Yates?"

That anger that I was channelling from tonight, ready to unleash on my fighting partner, turned into a fucking tsunami.

Brodie fucking Yates.

That motherfucker deserved everything that was coming to him. Yates and Lockwood had made my life hell back in middle school, and although I'd got in a few digs and lucky punches over the years, I'd never really had the chance to give him a proper pasting. Looks like tonight was my lucky night. Brodie Yates was about to experience the full force of hurricane Mathers.

"Are you fucking on something?" One of Pat's guys asked, looking at me like he couldn't work out if I was crazy, insane or just off the wall.

"I'm high on life, mate." I gave him my signature grin and he laughed.

"Looks like you've already been a few rounds too. Is that a cut lip?"

"You should see the other guy." I shrugged not giving a fuck.

"Your eyes... Look at the state of them. You look like a fucking demon. I'm glad I'm too old to fight if that's how they're training you these days."

I took it as a compliment. If I could psych out Brodie Yates just by looking at the fucker, then he'd be dead meat in seconds. Fear and violence, that's what fed me right now. His fear and the sheer level of violence I wanted to offload onto him. The most dangerous man you can ever go up against is one that has nothing to lose. I was that man.

I heard someone behind me call my name and I turned to see Chase, Jensen, Brodie and some of their friends walking towards me.

"No friends tonight, Mathers? They finally seen you for the loser you are?" Jensen said, giving me the once over.

"That's funny. I seem to remember beating your ass just a few days ago, Lockwood. I'd wait for the bruises to fade before you come at me again. You might sound more convincing."

"You wanna know what I see?" Jensen didn't care what I said. He was the big man with his crew around him. Get him on his own and the guy would've pissed his pants at the thought of going up against me again.

"I couldn't really give a rat's ass, but I'm sure you're gonna tell me. You just can't seem to shut your mouth, can you?"

His grin turned to a snarl. He didn't like that I wasn't threatened by him. If anything, he spurred me on even more. I liked being the underdog. Shit, I'd take them all on if Pat would let me.

"What I see is a lonely, washed up nobody. A wannabe Tyson Fury without the charisma. You're less gypsy king and more shitty king. You know, like the shit they found you in when your mum left you to bone every drug dealer she could get her hands on."

I snapped and threw myself at Lockwood, but Pat and his

men held me back.

"Woah! Save that shit for the ring, son. You're up next," Pat said, shaking me and giving me another look that told me he wasn't taking any shit tonight. He wanted a clean fight.

I nodded in silent agreement. My fighting was going to be as clean as I could get away with. Pat was all about the honour of bare-knuckle boxing, it's what he stood for. But tonight, it was my honour at stake. I wasn't fighting to win. I was fighting to destroy.

I pulled my T-shirt over my head and threw it to the side as I stepped into the fight zone. Brodie smiled at me, but I just glared back at him, using those precious seconds to focus my energy.

I thought about Emily and how she'd looked at me like I was dog shit on her shoe.

I saw Ryan as he straddled me, punching me like I was the scum of the earth and he needed me gone.

Then I remembered being beaten by Brodie and Jensen. I heard the names they called me. Then I saw an image of Jensen in my mind, holding me down in the boys' bathroom while Brodie smacked his fist into my face until my nose bled. I swear if the teacher hadn't disturbed them that day they'd have killed me. I was seven years old. They were nine, maybe ten, and the only punishment they'd received was a slap on the wrist and a warning not to do it again.

That's what happens when you're poor and your family aren't worth shit in this town. You have to wait until you're older to get the revenge you're owed.

In the distance, I could hear the referee reciting the rules. No head butting, no biting, no elbow smashing. I nodded, but I wasn't listening. All emotion was drained from my body. All I had left was fire, anger, fury.

The ref stepped back, and it was on. Brodie held his fists up in defence.

"Come on then, you pussy. Show me what you got. Or did Jensen wear you out the other night? You've always been a disappointment. All these people here tonight to watch you fight and look at you, nothing but a weak-ass pussy with a chip on your shoulder."

I didn't hear him. He thought his words would get to me, but I already had fourteen years of hatred stored up inside me. There wasn't room for any more.

He jabbed his fist out and I saw it, but I didn't duck like I usually would've. I wanted him to get a few hits in. Those knocks would help to numb the pain. The crowd booed, probably thinking I wasn't trying. They needed to shut the fuck up. I was in control here. I knew what I was doing.

Brodie got another punch in, hitting my side. The pain that radiated through my body helped to release some of the pressure in my head, as if it gave my brain somewhere else to focus. It was exactly what I needed. I tensed my core, letting him get a few more hits in. The crowd were screaming now. They thought this was done and dusted, but I hadn't even started. In this ring I wasn't a man, I was a machine, and that machine had just flipped it's switch and shifted to attack.

I grunted as I threw a punch into his face, putting the whole weight of my body behind it. Brodie jerked back and seemed to grow unsteady on his feet. One hit and I was already gaining the upper-hand. He wiped over his face and shook his head to try to steady himself. Blood was pouring from his nose and I grinned. A broken nose was my first gift of the night.

I charged into him, pushing him up against the bales and pounding my fists into his stomach. I wanted to add a few broken ribs to the list, but when Brodie dropped to the floor, the ref intervened and I had to back away. Fucker didn't stay down for long though. He was buying time. I had him right where I wanted him, and he knew it. He was about to get his ass handed to him on a plate in front of all these people, and it was fourteen years in the making.

I stood firm with my fists held up ready. Brodie wobbled on his feet, but he wasn't about to give up just yet. It was a good job too. I wasn't done with him by a long shot. I had a lot more fight left in me.

I swung my fist back and smacked him at the side of the head, catching his jaw and sending him flying backwards. He stumbled and tried to regain his footing, but he took a tumble and that's when I heard it, the crack of his skull as he landed on the cobbled barn floor. He'd caught his foot on a loose flagstone and judging from the amount of blood pouring from the back of his head, he wasn't getting back up any time soon.

My ears were ringing with the buzz of the adrenaline and I could just about make out the screams around me. Then people started to push and jostle around the edge of the ring. I stood over Brodie as he lay there, bleeding out, his eyes closed and his body twitching, and I was about to spit on him when I saw a flash of blonde hair. A girl knelt down and started to cradle his head. She checked his pulse and then screamed up at me, "I think he's dead! You killed him! You fucking killed him!"

Harper.

Harper bloody Yates, Brodie's twin sister.

I had no idea she was even here. What the fuck had I done?

I'd just beaten her brother to death in front of her. There was gonna be a new place in hell reserved specially for me after tonight, and if truth be told, I didn't fucking care.

Pat and a few of his men shoved me out of the way and started giving Brodie first aid. I just stood there, my life balancing on a knife's edge. I didn't want to stick around for the aftermath. I'd done what I'd come here to do. I'd shown everyone what'd happen if they ever crossed me. I hadn't factored in the guilt from seeing Harper wailing over her brother. I didn't need to add more weight to the shame that was my life. I felt worthless enough already, but now I had even more reason to hate myself. I was a fucking liability. I couldn't even do revenge right.

Shutting down the emotions that were surfacing and threatening to drown me in self-loathing, I turned and pushed my way through the crowd. A few people shoved me, shouting in my face, but I didn't listen.

"Call an ambulance," I heard Pat shout out. I knew the police would follow and I wasn't about to stick around to be hung out to dry. I left the barn, got into my car and drove away. I threw my mobile out of the window and kept going. I was gonna drive until my fuel ran out and then I was gonna keep going. I had nowhere to go. I had no one to care.

From this moment on, Brandon Mathers was no more.

A ghost.

A forgotten man.

I doubted anyone would mourn me. I wouldn't even mourn myself.

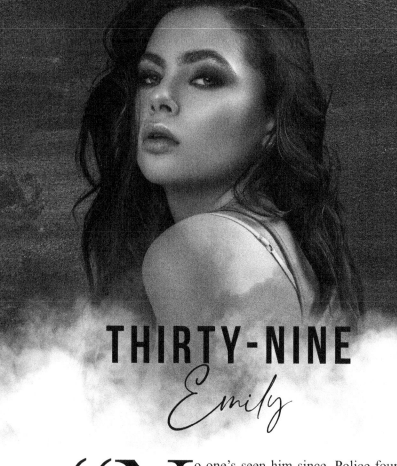

THIRTY-NINE
Emily

"No one's seen him since. Police found his phone discarded on the path outside the barn. His car was left abandoned about thirty miles away. We don't know what to do. There's a warrant out for his arrest, but we've got no idea where he might be. What do we do, Ry?" Zak was frantic, and Ryan looked as shell-shocked as I felt. I thought we'd had our full quota of bad luck last night, but it seems fate wasn't done with us yet.

"Any news on Brodie?" I asked as Ryan sat there stunned.

"He was in surgery most of the night. We don't know much,

the police aren't giving anything away, but it sounds like he had internal bleeding and swelling to the brain. They were trying to ease the pressure or something, but he went into cardiac arrest when he was under and they couldn't save him. He fucking died, Em."

I couldn't speak. I put my arm around Ryan as he fell forward and ran his hands over his head in pure exasperation at how shitty this whole situation was. I'd woken up to a nightmare that just kept getting darker and more hopeless.

"Shit. He's gonna go down for this." Ryan looked up at Zak and Finn, and then hung his head again. "He's gonna go down for life and it's all my fucking fault."

"This is not your fault." I shook him, so he'd look at me, but he couldn't.

"It is. If I hadn't gone in on him like that last night, he wouldn't have had that fight."

I looked over at Zak and Finn, willing them to help me out. I couldn't risk letting Ryan spiral down a dark tunnel into a pit of despair. I might never get him out again.

"She's right, mate. Brandon was gonna do whatever Brandon wanted to do. The beef with Lockwood and Yates had been brewing for years. Something like this was always gonna happen," Zak said, and Finn nodded in agreement.

"And if we're pointing the blame at anyone, I'm as much to blame as you," I added, holding his hand with both of mine. "I said some pretty shitty things to him myself, remember?" I wasn't about to let Ryan take the fall for this. I didn't want him blaming himself. We needed to work together to get through this awful mess. Blame wouldn't help anyone now. Not Brandon and certainly not Brodie or his family.

"Have you spoken to the police yet?" Ryan snapped his head up, going from dazed to alert in a split second.

"We've both given them a statement," Zak said. "They'll probably be round here soon to take yours. We told them the truth. We saw him earlier in the evening, but we left him around ten o'clock. We weren't anywhere near the Murphy's barn. We saw nothing."

"Let's go to the station now and get it over with." I didn't feel like waiting around for the police to come to us and I wanted to find out what'd happened to my dad after last night's arrest. Why not kill two birds with one stone? Ryan agreed and the four of us headed out, leaving Connor to the now stone-cold breakfast.

***

We both gave separate statements, telling the police exactly what we knew, which was nothing. They questioned us about where Brandon could be, but we had no clue on that either. When we left a few hours later, I headed back to the main desk to ask about my father, telling Ryan to wait for me in the car park. I needed to do this alone.

The last person I expected to find sitting in the reception when I got there was my mother and the woman who my dad had kept as his dirty little secret for so long. The two of them sat in awkward silence, and when mum saw me she jumped up and grabbed me into a hug.

"Em, thank God you came. I've been trying to call you all night."

I highly doubted that. I think I was a long way down on her list of priorities today.

"They're keeping your dad in. The solicitor is with him

now, but he doesn't think he'll make bail."

I couldn't believe what I was hearing. Did she really want him out? Was she delusional? Obviously she was, seeing as she was sitting with his mistress like nothing had happened.

"I couldn't give a fuck, Mum."

"Language, Emily," she scolded, and my eyebrows shot up.

"Really, Mum? After everything that's happened you're gonna pull me up on saying the word fuck. That's fucking rich."

She tutted and rolled her eyes. "I know he's made some mistakes…"

"Mistakes? He killed my brother, *your* son. Or did you conveniently forget that part?"

Her eyes misted over, and I felt a twinge of sadness for her. "I know what he did. And no, I'll never forgive him for that. There's not a day goes by that I don't miss Daniel. I cry every single day. But maybe, with counselling, your dad-"

I cut her off. "My dad doesn't deserve to walk out of here. He deserves to rot in hell for what he did. He left Danny there. He knew Dan needed help and he did nothing. He didn't even call an ambulance, Mum. He scurried away like a rat to save his own skin. I hate him. He's dead to me." My mother seemed intent on seeing the good in everything when it came to my dad and I didn't have the energy to argue with her anymore.

I moved past my mum to stand in front of the woman my dad had kept hidden from us. His dirty mistress. "Did you know?"

"I did what I had to do to protect my daughter," she said holding her nose in the air with fake airs and graces. She needed to cut the bullshit and stop pretending to be a lady and own who she was; my father's whore.

"A daughter he never acknowledged, and we knew nothing

about." She glanced past me to look at my mum, and that's when I snapped. I spun round to face her again. "You knew? What the fuck, Mum?"

"I had a feeling."

"And you stayed with him? Do you enjoy being a doormat? This is messed up, even for you." I couldn't believe my own mother had suspected my dad of having an affair, fathering a child, and she had turned a blind eye. No wonder she'd taken to the bottle and become a shell of a woman. I would've shook some sense into her, but I think she was beyond help.

"So, what now? Are you two gonna become best buddies? Get your nails done and compare notes on my dad? Or better yet, why don't they come and live with us, Mum? Then we can all be one happy fucking family."

"Don't be ridiculous, Emily. Once your dad is home we'll work something out."

I shook my head at her. My mother was certifiably crazy.

"He isn't coming home, Mum. Even I know the jail sentence for money laundering is pretty steep. Add the manslaughter charge and he won't see the outside of a prison cell for a very long time. I'd get used to living on your own, Mum, because Dad isn't coming home, and neither am I."

She gasped and tried to stop me as I headed for the door.

"Don't be ridiculous. Emily, stop and come back here. We need to talk about this. You can't just leave. Where will you go?"

I stopped, ready to give her one more minute. It was all she was going to get from me for a long time.

"I don't know, Mum. I'll stay with Liv, Effy, or maybe Ryan's dad will let me crash at theirs."

She frowned. "Ryan? Daniel's friend, Ryan?"

"Yes, Mum. My boyfriend, Ryan. Not that that's any of your business. I think you forfeited the right to have a say in my life the minute you chose Dad over us."

"It was never about choosing sides. I wanted, no, I needed to keep my family together." And a fucking stellar job she'd done at that.

"I don't think Dad got the memo. He was too busy making another family without you." I could see the hurt on her face as I said that, but she needed to hear the harsh truths. Her life was no rose garden and she was trying to preserve something which was irrevocably broken. Paper over cracks that were huge gaping holes. No amount of damage control could save us. As a family, we were finished.

"The house is in my name, Emily. Whatever happens to Dad, they can't take that away from us. I have money. We'll be okay."

I knew what she was saying. The police would freeze Dad's assets. But I think she was fooling herself. It wouldn't be that easy. Every part of her life would be scrutinised too. Suddenly, a pang of regret and remorse hit me.

"Mum, if you need me, you've got my mobile number. Whatever it is, I'll be there."

I heard a car door open and I turned to see Ryan standing next to his van, giving me a look that asked if I was all right. Mum sighed behind me and then said, "Make sure that boy takes good care of you. I only ever wanted the best for you. For both of you." She started to cry, so I put my arms around her.

"It'll take time, but we'll get through this, Mum. You have to be strong."

She pulled away first, dabbing at her eyes to stop her make-up from running. Then she painted on her smile and said, "I'll let you know if there's any news. The solicitor should be out shortly."

She wouldn't change. It didn't matter what I said. She was stuck in her little world that revolved around my dad. I felt sorry for her.

"Okay." I sighed. All my fight was gone. I had to concentrate on me now. She was a grown woman. I couldn't live her life for her and I didn't want the kind of life she led for myself. I had to get away. Distance myself from the Winters' circus.

I had a future and it was standing in the car park waiting for me.

EPILOGUE

Ryan

Three months later

The last few weeks had been some of the toughest I'd known since Mum died. Emily had moved most of her stuff out of her family home and was living with Effy, although technically that wasn't true. She spent every night with me, and Dad loved having her around, we all did. It wasn't always easy to find time to be alone, and that was part of the reason I was taking her out tonight. I had a proposition that I hoped, no, prayed she'd take me up on.

We'd tried to look towards the future and plan a life together.

Dwelling on the past didn't help either of us, but it was hard to switch off sometimes. Emily's dad's trial date was set for next month, but it wasn't looking good for him. The maximum sentence for money laundering in the U.K. was fourteen years. Add the manslaughter charge for Danny's death and he was looking at maybe twenty years, probably life. The fact he'd left Danny in the driver's seat, and the drink driving, meant the odds were stacked against him. In my opinion, he deserved everything that was heading his way. Em didn't want to talk about it, but I had to prepare her as best I could. The press and media intrusion that'd follow the case was gonna be a shit-storm to get through, but we'd weather it out together.

I'd always be there for her.

After everything that'd happened, Emily had decided she wanted to pursue a career in journalism. I guess she liked finding justice and truth where she could. I'd given her the bug for it. It was while we were looking at prospectuses for courses she was interested in that we started to talk about my kit car business and how I could expand and make a good living from it. I didn't want to work for my dad forever and the demand for work was there. I just needed help knowing what to do next, where to take it.

We managed to find a part-time business and accountancy course at one of the colleges she was looking at, so we both applied for our separate ventures and we both got accepted. I never thought I'd see the day when I'd be going back to school, but the look on her face when she saw those acceptance letters made it worthwhile. I'd do anything to keep her smiling and give her the happiness she deserved.

As for Brandon, no one had heard from him since the fight

night. It was as if he'd been wiped off the face of the earth. We checked in on his Nan every week, and even though she'd insisted she didn't know where he was, we noticed a few new things dotted around her room. A new T.V. that she had no idea how to use, an iPad that was never switched on and various other things that an elderly lady would never use. We didn't ask her where she got the money from and we didn't want to know. Whatever was going on was her business. We were just there to make sure she had a fully stocked kitchen and to lend a hand with any heavy lifting or chores she couldn't manage. It was our brotherly duty. Brandon would've done the same for us.

Zak, Finn and I had decided to start the events up again too. At first, it felt wrong doing it without Brandon, but it was what we were all good at. We missed the brotherhood, and even though there'd be no fighting we still had the music, the art, the bonding it brought to a community that'd been shattered by the events of the last few months. Our generation needed the release it offered, and we needed to feel useful again.

I sat on the sofa, pretending to watch the T.V., but really, I was waiting on Emily. She was getting ready for our date in our bedroom. Connor had stepped in to help me set everything up earlier and he'd just text to let me know where he'd left the food and what to do once we got there. Like I needed fucking instructions on how to plate up his pasta.

When she finally came out to let me know she was ready, I did a double take. My girl was stunning in a light blue dress covered in glitter and sparkly shit that just about skimmed her ass. I'd look forward to taking that off of her later.

"Is this okay?" she asked, spinning around to give me the full effect. It was more than okay, and my dick was straining in my jeans with how much I liked it, but I didn't think that was the best answer to give her.

"You look beautiful," I said, standing up and wrapping my arms around her. "You always look beautiful, but this is just… Wow."

She beamed back at me and when Connor walked through the door seconds later and gave her a wolf-whistle I knew it was time to leave. I loved my brother, but he never knew when to stop.

***

We pulled up outside the front of the asylum and she sighed gently beside me. I had damn butterflies and felt like a complete pussy, but I plastered on my smile and kept that shit to myself.

"Good job I brought my flats." She laughed and fished her little ballet pump things out of the glove compartment. She always kept them there. She knew me well. I wasn't the best at planning out the logistics from a woman's perspective, but I was learning.

"Sorry. I should've said, but I didn't want to spoil the surprise." I leaned over and gave her a peck. Not satisfied with that, she slid her arm around my neck and pulled me back in for a proper kiss.

"You don't ever have to apologise," she said as she broke away. "Now, come on. Let's go and explore."

We held hands and picked our way over the rubble. This place still hadn't been knocked down or ear-marked for regeneration, but I was glad. I liked the beauty it held amongst all the decay. It was ours. We'd been here a few times recently, and Emily had talked Finn into using the main building to create some pretty amazing art work. He hadn't touched the chapel though. That place was off limits.

Once we were inside, I led her down the hallway that Finn had painted to resemble an underground tunnel, like some kind of burrow with creatures hidden in amongst the tree roots. I swear that guy could paint anything if he put his mind to it. This corridor kind of freaked me out though. Like some twisted Alice in Wonderland shit without the whimsically magical part. Stay in one spot too long and those roots might just wind their way around your legs and drag you under. I guessed that was the vibe he was going for. A hidden twist of horror. A warning to never get too comfortable with your surroundings, you never knew what was lurking in the shadows.

When we reached the doorway to the chapel, I stopped and told her to wait outside for a moment. I needed to make sure everything was perfect, and it was. Connor had followed my instructions to the letter. There were fairy lights strung up all around, giving it that magical touch, with candles around the edge of the floor that I lit, ready for the big reveal. The table and chairs were perfect, with the pink table cloth and silverware and a pink flower arrangement in the centre. Connor knew his shit.

I flicked the switch of the machine on and then headed back to the door. She spun around, and when she walked through the doorway and saw our chapel, she covered her mouth and turned to me with tears welling up in her eyes.

"Oh my God, Ryan. This is beautiful. Did you do all this?" She went over to the bubble machine and laughed, holding her hands out to catch the bubbles that fell and popped as they touched her skin.

"Connor helped. He set most of it up for me, but it was all my idea."

I came to stand behind her and wrapped my arms around her waist, pulling her back into me. The bubbles were coming out faster than I'd realised, and before long, we were surrounded by them, dancing on the air and reflecting the rainbow of the stained glass windows like a kaleidoscope. The twinkling of the fairy lights made it feel extra magical, like we were standing in our very own snow globe. Only, it wasn't snow, it was bubbles.

Our bubble.

"You create the best bubbles. I love your bubbles." She rubbed her nose against mine and I picked her up, kissing her and holding her as tightly as I could.

"Our bubbles are the best," I whispered into her ear as I peppered kisses down along her neck. "Only the best for my girl."

"I could stay in your bubbles forever. I don't need anything else," she said, giving me the perfect in for my next surprise.

"I'm glad you said that, because I've brought you here to ask you something. It's not the big question," I said when I noticed her eyes go wide and a little shocked. "That'll come, trust me, but not today. Today, I wanted to ask you if you'd take the next step with me? I know we haven't been official for long, but I think we both know this is right. We were meant to be together, nobody can deny that. You're it for me, Em. So, with that in mind, would you move in with me? I mean, into a place of our own. Somewhere with no dad or Connor cramping our style. Just me, you, and maybe a pet or two if that's what you want. A place that's ours."

I had verbal diarrhoea, I was so nervous. I shouldn't have been though, because she jumped up into my arms and squealed, "Yes!" before I had a chance to second guess myself.

"The money from my cars will help with a deposit and I'll still work for Dad when I can in-between the college course. The parties bring in a bit too. Not as much as when Brandon was fighting, but it's something…" The words just kept flying out of my mouth, justifying why I thought it'd work. I think I'd spent so long overthinking this I had an argument for every angle.

"We'll both work. It won't all be on you. I can help too." She bit her lip and I could see all the emotions pass across her face. She was excited and probably already planning what colour cushions to buy for the living room. The woman was obsessed with cushions. They were all over our bedroom, back at Dad's. I didn't get it. They all ended up on the floor every night. What was the point?

I had planned to save the last surprise until the end of the night, but we were in each other's arms and the bubbles and lights had made my head dizzy. So, I reached into my pocket to pull out the box.

"Now, I know I said this wasn't the big question, but I have bought something for you. Something that I hope you'll wear for me." I put the little velvet box in the palm of my hands and her face went from playful to serious. "It's not an engagement ring, not yet, baby. I'm saving up for that. This… This is a promise ring. It's my promise to you that I'll love you forever. That I promise to always put you first in everything I do. A promise that one day you'll be Mrs Hardy, if you'll have me. I want you to wear this so everyone knows you're mine."

I watched as a tear fell down her cheek and she reached out to take the box and open it. As soon as she saw it she smiled and took the ring out of the box, putting it straight onto her left hand.

"It's beautiful, Ryan. I'm speechless."

"I had both our names engraved on the inside and Effy helped me to get it sized right. Is it okay?"

I don't know why I asked that, she hadn't taken her eyes off the delicate diamond encrusted heart since she'd put it on.

"But I want you to wear one too." She looked up at me frowning. "I wish I'd known. I'd have bought one ready to give to you."

"If I'd told you, it would've spoilt the surprise, and I like surprising you." I gathered her back into my arms feeling like I wanted to bypass the food Connor had made us and go straight to dessert. Her. "If it makes you feel better, we can go and buy one tomorrow."

She nodded and then leaned back to look me in the eyes.

"You've earned some serious brownie points, Hardy, and we haven't even started the date properly yet. You're so gonna get laid tonight."

"That goes without saying. Did you really think I'd be able to keep my hands off you when you're wearing a dress like this? We'll be lucky to make it through dinner."

"Why do you think I wore a dress? Easy access." She leaned closer and whispered in my ear. "And I'm not wearing any panties tonight."

I don't think there are any sweeter words a guy can hear than those.

"I'm hungry," I growled into her neck as I lifted her up. She wrapped her legs around my waist and I walked us both to the altar. "And I don't mean for Connor's pasta bake either." I winked as I set her down and then my bloody phone vibrated in my back pocket to let me know of an incoming text. After what'd happened recently, I couldn't let it go. As desperate as

I was to devour her on the stone she was perched on, I held my finger up and said, "One second. Don't move. Let me just check this isn't a life-altering text message and our house isn't burning down."

She smiled, licking those plump pink lips of hers and I felt my dick stir, thinking about how I was going to put those lips to good use. I glanced down at my phone and like a wave of cold fucking water had just smothered me, I froze.

We know what you've done.
It's payback time.
We are coming for you.

EPILOGUE PART 2

Brandon

I don't know why I expected anything would change.

They'd carried on with their lives like I never existed. Blanked me out like a stain on their history that they needed to scrub away. But I see them. I watch them all the fucking time.

I'm the shadow in the darkness that follows them around.

I'm the problem they want to forget but never will.

I'm the demon they thought they were finally rid of, but no one can drown me out. I have a voice and it's about to get fucking loud.

Soon… I'll be their every waking nightmare.

Tick, tock, motherfuckers. Time is running out.

Brandon Mathers is coming for you and he wants his revenge.

The End.

FOR NOW…

Thank you so much for reading. If you enjoyed Ryan and Emily's story, then please spread the word and leave a review.

Copyright @ Nikki J Summers 2020

ACKNOWLEDGEMENTS

First and foremost, I need to thank my husband and children for putting up with me when I constantly zone out and for supporting me when I become consumed by my stories. I'm always lost in my head, but you guys keep me grounded. You are the best and I love you.

To my book besties and total queens, Lindsey Powell and Ashlee Rose. I am forever grateful for meeting you both, and for the amazing support and friendship you've given me. I don't know what I'd do without you. Thanks for beta reading Renegade and loving my boys as much as I do. If you haven't already, go and check out their books. They are fantastic.

An extra big shout-out to Robyn for being totally awesome and making the best teasers. She is an absolute diamond. Thanks for beta reading Ryan and Emily. I don't know what I'd do without you. If you aren't following her, then get to it. You'll find her at @books4days_with_robyn

To Lindsey, Tammy, and Lou for being so utterly awesome and polishing this story for me. I'm so glad I found you. You've helped to make my little book shine brighter. Thank you, ladies.

A big thank you to Michelle Lancaster for taking the cover photo, Tommy 'Rev' for being the best Ryan, and Lori Jackson, for bringing this cover to life.

I will always be indebted to the hard work and support of all the bloggers and bookstagrammers on social media. Your posts and graphics are amazing. Thank you for every single post, share and comment. It means the world. Special thanks to Natalie @ allireadislove, Suny @bookslover09 and Natalie @fromreader.

withlove for the amazing teaser graphics. You guys are always the first to share anything. Thank you! You are awesome! I wish I could list everyone. You all do such a fabulous job.

To the indie author community, I love how encouraging, supportive, and utterly brilliant you are. I feel proud to be a part of such an amazing community. #indiepower

Last but not least, to all the readers out there who've taken the time to download, read, and review my book. Thank you for taking a chance on me. I'm always immensely grateful for every read and review. Reviews are the lifeline of every author, especially us smaller indies. You guys make my day and make it all worthwhile.

Thank you for reading Ryan and Emily's story.

Lots of Love
Nikki x

For updates on my new releases and other news, follow me on the following platforms.

INSTAGRAM
FACEBOOK
READER GROUP
TWITTER
TIKTOK
BOOKBUB

Printed in Great Britain
by Amazon